# A STORM OF SHADOWS

FATES & FABLES 3

WILLOW QUINN

*A Storm of Shadows*

*Fates & Fables Book 3*

*By Willow Quinn*

Cover art by Amanda Santos @ehmandinha on Instagram

Proofread by Kaitlin Slowik



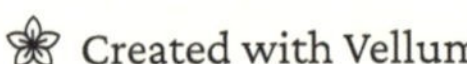
Created with Vellum

# CONTENT WARNINGS

A glossary and pronunciation guide is provided in the back of the book. It is also available on my website, as is the map.

**Content warning:** Sibling and parental death. Violence and gore. Survivor's guilt. Sexual assault (off page, mentioned vaguely). Physical abuse, verbal abuse.

Iltain
Realm of Earth
Aeria
Medeis
Realm of Fire
Realm of Water
Hydrost
Lesern
Realm of Wind
The Drowned City
Port Arro
Undien Sea
Treben Ocean
Pertus
Icia
Elf Glen
Nemus
Selevein
Orc Haven
Thon
Yeolent
Nixvem Isles
N
W
E
S

*For my readers. I hope these pages are a portal to magic, love, and hope for you.*

# PROLOGUE: ONORA

*The Human Realm, Nemus*

The last time Onora cried she was eight. A pyre blazed in front of her, casting flickering shadows as the heat dried her tears. The flames devoured her parents' bodies and the tiny one wrapped between them. In a moment, she had learned how fragile life was, how easily her entire world could shatter.

And how easily controlled humans were by the more powerful and magical beings of the world.

A shadow approached her. His wings spread out behind him, black as the night, horns spiking back from his head. He knelt as a slow smile formed on his face.

She should feel fear. She should be trembling, screaming, running away. But she couldn't find it in herself to care. Only a numbing coldness wrapped around her.

"What should we do with her?" another demon asked from somewhere in the dark.

"Keep her alive," the male in front of her said. "This one has something I need."

He took the shackles and carefully placed them around her neck, tightening it just enough that the iron bit coolly into her skin if she moved. The chain tugged heavily as it fell to the ground, snaking into the hands of her parents' killer.

The Cruel Lord of Shadows.

~

She sat in the blazing hot firelight of the great hall, staring as the flames licked at the air, dancing with the shadows they created—similar, yet so different from that night five years ago. The iron choker still bit into her neck, the chain falling around her feet. She had a new master named Varek, no less vile than the current demon lord. Varek was the male that the ruler of the demons had set in charge of the human lands of Nemus.

The demons sat in the great hall that had once held the human ruler of these lands, drinking the mead the humans made, eating the food they cultivated and raised. The chain went taut, her head swaying to the side, and she looked up to see Varek's drunken eyes taking her in. He tugged again, and she scrambled to her feet, coming to his side. His wings were gray, tucked behind the custom chairs they'd made shortly after occupying the village. His horns were thick and curled like a ram, his blond hair falling messily around them.

"Yes?" she asked.

He frowned, giving a sharp tug on the chain that made her stumble forward, bracing against the large armrest of his chair. "Watch your attitude, girl."

A million retorts rested on the tip of her tongue. A million words she'd like to lob at him and the other demons. But she'd seen where that had gotten her friend Amberly. Lifeless eyes and cold veins in the ground. So she held her tongue, pursing her lips, unable to stop the hatred in her eyes. She had to watch her steps. She had plans to execute and impatience would ruin them.

He ran a finger along her cheek and she involuntarily jerked back, internally cursing herself because she knew, even before she felt the hit, what he would do. Her face swung to the side as the back of his hand hit her face, and then she fell forward when he tugged again on the chain, this time chafing against her neck.

"I would have killed you ages ago if you weren't the Lord's special pet. He's saving you for something big, and when your destruction comes, I'll be front and center to watch, girl," Varek spat.

She stared up at him, trying desperately to be demure and failing. Her eyes darted beyond him to her friend Jackson, who sat next to his master. He gave her a pleading look.

How many times had he urged her to apologize, to grovel, to kneel? He'd begged her one night, sobbing because she was all he had left, and it was the only thing that kept her from defying them to her death. It was the only thing that made her scheme and plot and plan.

Her own life was forfeited. She hadn't thought of her future since she'd been taken captive. But each day she woke and saw the indignity with which they treated Jackson lit that spark of life light in her chest again.

Onora had only two things left: her honor, and her unyielding need to save Jackson. Sometimes both of those contradicted each other. Sometimes she begged them to stop her beatings because if she didn't, they would kill her. Sometimes she took his beatings so they wouldn't kill him.

The night wore on and the drinks kept flowing. There was always one demon who stayed sober, watching, lurking. She'd learned early on that as much as the demons viewed humans as weak, worthless, and stupid, they knew that hatred could make a powerful enemy of anyone. So they partied with abandon, but someone always kept their wits to make sure that no one tried anything.

That was fine. Onora didn't need them all drunk, only Varek. He kept her close by lately. The Cruel Lord was set to return soon, and he'd specifically told them no harm was to come to Onora. She didn't know why, but it couldn't be good. She had to act soon.

Tonight.

Varek laughed and joked with the demons next to him while others played music and danced in the middle of the hall. No one looked at her or noticed anything she did.

She'd been practicing this for a year now. It had started with her and Jackson. Then she'd moved on to some of the lesser demons, slipping her hand into their pockets and stealing inconsequential things.

None had caught her, though a few had looked at her as if they thought she'd bumped into them. She had practiced and practiced until it was done without error. Still, sweat dripped down the small of her back.

If she messed up now, they wouldn't beat or kill her. Instead, they would target Jackson to punish her. Taking a steadying breath, she reached into Varek's pocket and carefully grabbed the keys to her and Jackson's locks. She'd been so careful to never give him the impression she'd ever try this. Others had, and so the keys went solely to Varek. Because his *pet* only had a smart mouth. They'd told her many times she was weak and stupid, and she played into it. She talked back because she was a brat, not because she would ever actually do anything.

Fools, the lot of them.

She stuck the keys in her trousers, securing them so they wouldn't clank, and settled back, leaning against the wall, watching as the demons drank themselves into oblivion. As Varek had the last drinks of his life, the last laughs with his friends, as he imbibed and lived joyously, completely unaware that tomorrow would not come for him.

~

Onora lay on the ground next to Varek's bed, the chain laying slack on the floor. She moved, letting them clank, and looked up to see if he would wake. His mouth hung ajar, his arm off the side of the bed, hand brushing the floor as he snored. She clanged them again.

Nothing.

It felt impossible, unreal, that she was moments away from having this iron away from her neck, a moment away from grabbing the dagger Varek so carelessly left strapped to his thigh. She breathed in, then out, and carefully grabbed the keys. Unlocking the choker, she set it down. Her neck felt oddly light, the sensation disorienting. She rubbed the chafed and calloused skin, something expanding inside of her that she hadn't felt since they'd put the iron on. Something that grew and unfurled, stretching like a cat, reaching up and up.

It was cold as the dead of winter, vast as the stars, and distinctly alive.

*Hello.* It seemed to whisper, and she slammed it down, her breath coming out hard and fast.

She stood carefully and put her hand on the dagger, ever watching him. The blade fit perfectly under his chin, against the apple in his throat. She could kill him here and now, do it quietly and be done.

But she didn't want that. It was too easy. He deserved to die full of fear. Just like her parents and brother had. Just as she had felt for the last five years. Taking the iron shackle, she clasped it around his neck. He stirred, flopping on his back and blinking awake. He took her in, frowning.

"What are you doing, girl?" he rasped out, reaching for his dagger, then sitting up hastily when it wasn't there.

She yanked hard on the chain, and he yelped, bending forward, his eyes going wide with realization.

"This is for my family," she said, driving the dagger into his heart. He let out a muted cry, and she pulled it out, slamming it in over and over again. Warm blood sprayed her face, her clothes. Time ceased to exist and her being along with it. When she came to, he lay cold and dead, covered in blood.

Her hands shook, and she stumbled back. It was a nasty sight and not nearly as satisfying as she thought it would be. She turned and vomited on the floor, wiping her mouth with the back of her hand. She shouldn't have done that. What if someone heard? She needed to get Jackson out.

Padding into the hall, dagger in one hand and the keys in the other, she made her way to Jackson's room two floors down. Not a soul stirred, and she breathed in relief as she carefully opened his door and roused him.

He rubbed his eyes, then shot to his feet. "You're covered in blood."

"Varek is dead," she replied flatly.

Jackson swallowed, nodding. "Good."

She unlocked his chains, grabbed his hand, and they snuck out, looking around corners, leaving the estate as carefully as they could. On the first floor were guards—demons that weren't allowed to take part in the celebrations. They stood at all the doors, front and back, so that would be a no-go. Looking down at the keys, she realized the key to Varek's study was there. They snuck to the room, looking around before unlocking it. When they got inside, she locked it again and ran to the window. She didn't see any guards on patrol, but she did see the stable.

A horse would be best for traveling. They could make good distance before anyone realized they were gone, and they rarely kept much of an eye on the horses. The demons could fly to destinations faster than a horse could gallop, so they only kept them as beasts of burden or for the humans.

She hauled the window open and looked out to make sure they were clear. When she felt confident, she climbed out, feet landing softly on the grass, then beckoned for Jackson to follow suit. They darted to the stables, afraid each moment that her feet hit the ground that they would be found out. But some goddess seemed to be watching over her because they came to the stable without incident. They saddled two horses and opened the doors.

"If one of them shoots me, Jack," she said, "you have to keep going."

Jackson nodded. "Likewise, Onora."

She nodded but knew she wouldn't. If Jackson was shot, she'd do whatever she could to save him. With a deep breath, they opened the barn doors, mounted their horses, and fled into the night. No one followed. Not a sound stirred as they crossed the plains. Hours passed, and her fear slipped away like the midnight hours.

"Where are we going?" Jackson asked, the first words either had dared to speak since leaving.

"Venatu," Onora said. Venatu was the last human stronghold against the demons. It was the only place safe from their rule. "To the Hunter's Guild."

Because after her mind had cleared, Onora realized that killing one demon wasn't enough. She needed to train with the Hunters, the people specially equipped with magical weapons from the elves, to fight against demon kind.

Because some day, the Lord of Shadows would be felled by her own hand.

# CHAPTER 1
# DRYSTON

*15 years later*
*Orc Haven, Orc Realm, Nemus*

A bloodcurdling scream rent the air, seeping through the wooden floors and halting the music in the tavern. Dryston shot to his feet, wings spreading out defensively, and his sister, Enid, grabbed him by the wrist, tugging him to the chair again.

"It's not your baby," she said in the same tone used for toddlers. "Sit down."

Dryston shot her a glare, crossing his arms, tapping his foot and looking at the stairwell of The Tipsy Tavern. Aife had already kicked him out of Melina's room for "meddling," as she called it. Then he'd been banished from going above the second floor because he'd kept poking his head in to make sure it was going just fine.

"The last time I heard a noise like that, a man was dying on a battlefield," he said, chewing the inside of his cheek.

Melina was human, birthing a half-demon baby. He wasn't certain how easy the delivery would go, and he'd been more nervous than even Kaemon was—the father and his brother. Dryston had retrieved the best healers from Elf Glen and had them waiting around for the last two weeks to help with the delivery.

But what if it wasn't enough?

Images flashed in his mind of the day his parents died over ten years ago. Whispers haunted him, taunting that if he'd been quicker, a little more prepared, paid attention better, then perhaps things would have been different. Kaemon wouldn't have been captured and their parents wouldn't have died.

"You haven't been around many pregnancies, have you?" Avenay, Enid's mate, asked, raising her brows.

"Is that normal?" Dryston asked incredulously.

Enid and Avenay nodded.

"Delivering a baby is no joke, Dryston," Enid said.

He rolled his eyes. "I'm aware of that. I just didn't think it would sound like she was dying the entire time."

Mandel, his second-in-command for the royal guard, chuckled as he stood from the table. "I'll get you more to drink, since you're as wound up as if it were your own baby and mate."

Dryston stood, deciding that moving would clear his head and help the buzz of energy that skittered through his veins. "I'll come with you."

They walked to the counter next to another demon, Kalen, and Dryston leaned against it, rubbing his forehead. The elven healers had insisted that death during birth had become uncommon with the techniques and spells they'd developed, but Dryston didn't know of any half-human, half-demon babies born in recent memory.

Melina was part of his family and colony now. He couldn't imagine the devastation that would occur if anything happened to her.

The doors opened, letting in the chill, the bite clawing up Dryston's bare arms. He turned to see a group of orcs, nymphs, and goblins entering, arms laden with gifts for Melina and the baby. Quilted blankets and small clothes, baskets of preserved food that would help heal her after the birth, and a variety of what looked like salves and other odds and ends.

The goblin behind the counter climbed up on it and shouted loud enough to split through the noisy room, "Gifts over in the corner!"

He pointed to a table off to the side that was already overflowing. Melina had been in Orc Haven for a little over a year, but she and Kaemon had quickly become an integral part of the community. Melina had started her own tailoring business that took off with surprising speed, and he'd seen how she would take the scraps to fashion clothes for the people who couldn't afford her services. They were fine pieces, and she knew how to make them so they could be adjusted if someone grew or shrank.

Lily, another demon in his command, slid into the bar seat next to him, leaning forward. "You look stressed," she said, voice sultry as she looked up at him through her lashes.

"Melina is making sounds akin to being flayed alive. I don't understand how everyone isn't stressed," he grumbled.

Lily gave a breathy laugh, leaning forward more, her hand coming to his forearm and tracing lazy circles there. Her advances had become more pronounced in the last year, reaching a fever pitch since they were in Orc Haven—since he returned from his trip to Evolis three months prior. With both of his younger siblings mated already, it wasn't uncommon for him to become the target of interest. It now felt inevitable that he would find his mate as well. And he was the current Lord of Shadows, a prestigious title that anyone would be happy to latch on to.

Which made his chest tighten in irritation. He was the youngest lord in recent memory. Usually, the Lord of Shadows was chosen well after they had found their mate and settled down. He had taken over after his father died. When he returned home, his magic was the strongest, and the realm was still unstable since the Cruel Lord's reign, and everyone wanted the son of Kian and Emilia to take over. So he'd spent the last eleven years trying to be worthy of the title.

And dodging people who saw only his power.

Lily stood and leaned on his arm, looking up at him, portraying her gentleness and weakness. It was common mating behavior. With demons, it was always a dance of submission and dominance, and as the lord of the realm, he was seen as dominant. And he *was* dominant. But something about their feigned helplessness saddled him with anxiety, made his gut coil and his desire diminish ruthlessly.

He'd tried to reason it out many times. He should enjoy the dominance and control. But what he was being offered now was not something he wanted.

"Lily," he barked, and she stepped back, going rigid as a soldier. "I'm listening to Melina scream her guts out, trying to have my brother's child. Let me be."

Her pale cheeks flushed, and she nodded her head, walking away.

Mandel's gaze slid to him. "You know, I always wondered why you didn't bother finding a mate, but maybe it's better for everyone that you haven't. When you treat people like that."

Dryston glowered at him, and Mandel raised his brow in challenge as he took a sip of his beer. Mandel was Enid's oldest friend and like a little brother to him—but that meant the demon was far too comfortable with Dryston, sometimes overstepping by giving him advice he didn't care to hear.

"You have your pick of any male or female of The Darkened City as your mate, and you refuse all of them," Kalen said, judgment clear in his voice.

Dryston exchanged a quick glance with Mandel. Kalen had always been a bit of a stick in the mud. He had a keen idea of how things should be and how they should go, and if they didn't, then he was frustrated. Even if it didn't concern him. He'd harassed Dryston for years about settling down with someone. He was the Lord of Shadows, so the mate bond was likely to fall into place easily with any pick of a submissive partner, if he'd just let it.

But it hadn't yet. It never had.

"You have people throwing themselves at you. Can't you take a chance on one and see if a mate bond forms?" Kalen asked.

Dryston rolled his eyes and looked at Mandel for support.

Mandel shrugged, then nodded his head toward Enid and Avenay. "Both of your siblings have found their mates."

"And neither of them found them in the Shadow Realm. So what's the point in trying to force something?" Dryston was still trying to figure that out. It wasn't completely unheard of, maybe it was coincidence or the right combination of situation and finally being open to it, but it made him wonder if that was why he'd never found his mate.

Mandel looked like he was about to speak again when they were interrupted by Jorah's booming voice saying, "The baby is here!"

The tavern erupted in shouts of joy. The orcs present began to sing an old song, their voices low and rumbling, reverent and steady, as they bestowed the blessing of Yeolah.

Not a soul who met Melina didn't love her, and it was evident by the sheer number of people who had stuck around in the tavern when they heard her labor had started. Her water had broken while she was serving, and she'd gone quickly into labor.

Twelve hours ago.

Still, the people had stayed; the goblin taking over serving, many others taking over the cooking so Aife and Jorah could assist the birth.

Dryston battled through the crowd, meeting Enid and Avenay at the stairs. They followed Jorah up, and Kaemon poked his head out of the room, beaming from ear to ear.

"Is Melina okay?" Dryston asked.

Kaemon laughed, nodding his head. "She is. And so is the baby."

"Let them come in," Melina said softly.

Kaemon looked back into the room. "You need to rest."

"I don't think Dryston will rest until he sees with his own eyes we're fine."

Enid tipped back her head and laughed, and he just drew in a weary breath, following them upstairs to the loft.

Melina lay on the bed, her hair plastered in sweat against her face, eyes tired. In her arms was a small babe with a mass of black fuzz on its head and the tiniest little wings, dusted brown.

The sight hit Dryston like a hammer. So this was what a miracle was. He didn't care if the others thought it was commonplace and he was overreacting. Twelve hours of labor and they were fine and here was a little baby. A brand-new life. He swallowed the sudden and mysterious lump in his throat.

"It's a girl," Kaemon said, pride in his voice, on his face, practically flowing off him.

"What's her name?" Avenay asked.

"We haven't decided," Kaemon replied, chuckling.

"I was convinced it was a boy because of how I carried her," Melina said, looking at her mate as he gazed back with love. "But I think we should name her Emilia."

"Oh," Enid said softly, her eyes lining with tears, and Dryston had to choke back the emotion rising in his throat again.

Their mother's name.

"It's perfect," Kaemon replied.

DRYSTON STOOD ON THE PORCH, smoking his pipe while everyone was still celebrating. Kaemon had come down briefly to share his good news and had been patted on the back and given drinks until he was able to sneak back to Melina. Enid came out and leaned against the railing with him.

"I still can't believe it," she whispered.

Kaemon being alive. Kaemon having a mate and now a child. Ten years of thinking he was dead and only recently discovering he'd been living in Nemus this whole time. Dryston had known it for five months now and every day with his brother felt like a dream.

"I can't, either."

The full moon crested high above them, and he looked up at it, giving thanks to the twin moon goddesses for the birth. For all of it.

"They can't stay here," he said, looking in at the people celebrating.

Enid pursed her lips but nodded. “The baby looks more like a demon than a human.”

Dryston drew in a drag of smoke, then blew it out. “The Hunters won’t just try to take the baby.”

He’d heard rumors of half-human, half-demon babies that were born without wings and horns, taken, and “cleansed.” He didn’t know what that involved, but he assumed nothing good. But one with wings and surely horns to follow? They would kill it.

“Give her a few months, then we can take her back to The Darkened City,” Enid said.

She’d come back for the birth, leaving their city in the hands of their next-in-command and bringing gryphons back for Melina to ride. They had only briefly mentioned it to Kaemon, since he and Melina both had a life here, with friends and work, but seeing the wings on the child meant that they would have to act quicker than he’d anticipated.

“You’re coming back with us, right?” Enid asked.

He shook his head. “I need you to be interim lord for a few more months. I’m so close to gaining an audience with the orc lord, but the birth has offset my timing.”

He had secured an alliance with the elven ruler, King Leeth, and the orcs in general didn’t tolerate foreigners being attacked in their realm, but he wanted to secure a solid trade deal here. The demons had a terrible reputation the world over because of what the Cruel Lord had done, and Dryston had put so much energy into trying to change that. Gaining these two alliances could be the tipping point. And increasing exports and trade would only help his people more.

“You’re keeping the royal guard, though?” Enid slid her gaze to him. “You have to be careful here, too.”

Dryston sighed, rubbing the spot between his eyes. “I know. Kalen and Maria will stay, but the others need to escort all of you safely back. I also don’t want too strong of a demon presence here. The elves gave us guards and I don’t want to set the humans too on edge.”

Even if he hoped he had an ally there now.

Onora.

She'd traveled with them and saved his life in Evolis. He'd be a fool to think there was any warm regard between them, but a Hunter saving a demon was unheard of. He hoped that she'd gone home and told the others that he wasn't like the Cruel Lord, that they could have alliances in the future. Maybe there was hope of humans and demons living in peace with one another, and maybe that had started with Melina, and would continue with Onora.

## CHAPTER 2
# ONORA

*Venatu, Human Realm, Nemus*

Dryston lay under Onora, his verdant eyes gazing up at her with that signature intensity, his broad chest rising and falling heavily with each harried breath. She leaned forward to whisper in his ear, her body coming flat against his, her curves meeting his hard planes.

"Beg," she commanded.

He swallowed hard, throat bobbing. "Make it quick, please."

His words descended into a sobbing plea. She could grant his request, but she never did. No, this recurring dream was never for mercy.

It was only for vengeance.

She slit his throat, watching red burst and spill from the clean line, making streams in the cobbled floor below.

Heart racing, her eyes flung open to a darkness so pure that time and space lost all meaning. She felt suspended in the air, floating as if in water, stomach dipping and whirling as nausea clawed at her throat. The air tasted bitter like ash, and she gripped the bedsheets in an attempt to gain some sense of grounding.

She clamped her eyes shut, gritting her teeth and breathing out in heavy bursts through her nose. Magic poured out of her like a dam bursting. A buzz and a snap made her eyes open to arcs of light that splintered the absolute darkness.

*Hello.*

She shut that voice down and steadied her breath. One slow and deep one in, one long and ragged one out. Her room was a myriad of darks and lights, the shadows swirling around her in a funnel, her hair lifting up, the sheets rippling. She breathed in again, steadying the flow of magic in her, trying desperately to control it.

Since the well of magic opened in Evolis seven months ago, many humans had encountered similar problems. Random bursts of power and magic flowing through them, sometimes building up because they didn't know how to release it fully, some catching their homes on fire or destroying the woodlands nearby. She'd been called back from her normal ranger duties in the west to help with the damage caused by the flare-ups.

The dream about Lord Dryston visited her almost every night, and afterward she always woke to a pitch-black room of shadows lit by arcs of lightning. As much as she hated waking up with vertigo, it was far better than the other dream that often frequented her instead.

*"Are you okay?"*

She shook her head, trying to erase that memory. Those words haunted her every step, a taunting phantom of night that she couldn't cut loose in the daytime. If she could erase Dryston from her memory entirely, she would, but unfortunately, these shadows and the tattoos on her body were a constant reminder that the demons had done something to her. Something she couldn't explain and could barely control.

As she pulled the shadows back, one brushed up against her face in a caress that made her snarl before it tucked behind her ear. She pulled the nightdress sleeves back to look at her arms. From wrist to shoulder on each side, spanning down her back and snaking around her hip, were swirls of black tattoos.

They were in the fashion and style she'd only ever seen on demons. It had happened right after Enid opened the well of magic. They had burst into her arms, searing her, making her skin sore and puckered red for weeks after.

She'd told no one. Being a Hunter and being marked by a demon was a bad combination. Best-case scenario, they would send her to the temples of the Holy Mother and cleanse her.

But they didn't exist anymore.

No, Evoleen, the Holy Mother, was found to be a murdering psychopath and while some still clung to the ideas they'd had, refusing to believe the evidence in front of them, the Hunters had promptly stopped sending their demon-enthralled people to them.

There was no way to tell what others would do if they saw her new power—the very evidently demonic powers. In Evolis, she'd woken every morning with this. She'd chalked it up to her being a sink, someone who could draw and use power from other sources, and her being around three demons who cast shadows naturally.

But the demons were nowhere near her now, and she still woke in a sweat from her nightmares and a room full of darkness.

She swung her feet over the side of the bed.

The world tilted, and she ran to the restroom and vomited. Trembling, she stood and cleaned herself. Pulling on tactical leathers, she carefully placed daggers in the different holsters on her body, then attached her sword and bow before grabbing the small, packed bag and slinging it over her shoulder.

The chief had told them to dress as mercenaries or rangers for this mission—to leave the clearly identifiable marks of being a Hunter at home. They were to go to Orc Haven to observe only. Not to cause a turf war with the orcs and elves and demons in one blow.

The moon hung low in the sky, bright and taunting in the early morning hours. She'd always loved it growing up. Before her parents' deaths, they had taught her the phases and ways of the moon and its power. They used it to predict weather and help with the growing season.

Now shadows popped out from behind her ears, running like a finger along her shoulders, and she had to yank them back in. Demonic powers came from the twin moon goddesses. She'd always thought it a folktale. But these shadows seemed desperate to dance in that light.

She had an apartment in the Hunter's Guild, a small one room on the first floor, granting her more privacy than the newer recruits had in their rooms shared with three others. The buildings were all connected, and in the middle were training grounds and a garden that mostly housed vegetables and fruits, medicinal plants, and poisons. Onora enjoyed the flowers the gardener insisted kept bugs away. Ones that vined up the white fence greeted her, their flowers opening in the moonlight and closing up in the day. She ran a finger along its soft blue petal.

"Enjoying the garden?"

She turned at the voice and grinned. Jackson returned the smile and walked up to her, looking down at the flower.

"Moon Bloom," he mumbled. "Your mother always had these outside your house."

"Yeah," she breathed, the vision clear as if it were that day. Jackson and her playing in the woods, getting lost until late at night, their parents and the rest of the villagers searching for them and sobbing thankfully when they were found. They went back to Onora's small house and were fed stew, having gone hungry all day, and her mother took a flower bloom and placed it in her hair, calling her moon child.

Jackson knocked his elbow against hers. "I hope you're ready to actually talk and spend time with the rest of us on this mission." She gaped, and he threw his hands up. "You've been avoiding all of us since you returned, Ornery. It will be nice to actually spend some time with you."

Concern peeked through his words, unable to hide behind his

playful nickname for her, Ornery, and she drew in a deep breath and nodded. She'd been isolating—she was good at doing that when dealing with any internal turmoil. Jackson always saw and pulled her out, even when she wanted to curl up in it further. But she'd do anything for Jackson. He was her family. As were the other Hunters. Many of them had all come from some background of experiencing the Cruel Lord's terror firsthand.

She walked beside Jackson to the stables, where the others were waiting for them already. Andrea stood from lacing her boots, her long black braids falling over her shoulder as she grinned, coming up and engulfing Onora in a hug. Onora washed down the wave of emotion that the simple display of care brought her. Andrea never expected Onora to talk about things she didn't want to, or to get over things quickly—yet things never changed between them. Jackson and Andrea were like guiding stars in the night, never wavering, always bright.

Avery, an older Hunter, clapped her good-naturedly on the shoulder as he passed by, going to his horse and putting his pack on the saddle. "It's been ages since we've had a mission together, Ornery."

She rolled her eyes. Jackson used to be the only one to call her that. Over the years, others learned of it, and though she protested, it only stuck more.

"It will be good to have your expertise on this endeavor," she said.

He raised a brow, smirking. "Did you rehearse that? I think this trip will do you good. You've spent too much time in the wilderness."

An arm snaked around her shoulders, tugging her against a tall, slender body. "Well, I like my women a little wild, so I don't mind. Don't let Avery get you down." She looked up to see Jin, the youngest of the group, standing next to her, shirtless.

She groaned and pushed him away, only to stop abruptly, her blood going cold. His skin was pink and angry, swirls of black lining his arms and chest, stopping at the base of his neck and wrists. Her heart hammered loud as a gong in her ears as he flexed to show off to the others.

"You finally did it," Avery said, pulling back the sleeve of his shirt to show similar tattoos snaking up his arm.

Bile burned up Onora's throat as she instinctively tugged her shirt down lower.

The tattoos mimicked the ones on the Lord of Shadows that came from an enchantment and made a specific set of swirls and patterns. It was a sign of great power and authority.

Hunters had started adopting the tattoos themselves, claiming it showed their own power and authority over the strongest demon of their race, the Lord of Shadows. It had always felt childish to Onora.

Now it terrified her.

In the past she'd seen the tattoos the artists did as similar to the ones that the demon lords had, but now that she herself had magically sealed demon tattoos, she could see the glaring difference. And if anyone saw hers, they would know. They would know that the demons had put their mark on her.

And then what?

There was no chance of cleansing at a temple now.

Only death.

Jin came back next to Onora, thrusting his arm in front of her face. "What do you think?"

She raised her brows. "Cute."

Jin groaned. "Come on, Ornery, tell me they look nice or I won't sleep well. I have to know the ladies think they make me look strong and capable."

Onora made a humming sound, unconvinced, grinning. "I don't think a few tattoos will help with that."

Jin rolled his eyes, slumping and laying his head on her shoulder. "You wound me."

She patted his head. "There, there."

She smiled, missing this. It had been too long, and the way she slid so easily back into these dynamics was a comfort. She looked up and saw Andrea looking at her with relief, that edge of concern gone in light of Onora's smiling face. And she smiled brighter at her friend, squashing down the rising emotion of love that threatened to overwhelm her at the concern.

This was her family, her people.

"I think they look—" Andrea stopped, head whipping to the door as it creaked open.

In walked Vincent and Vera, and behind them was Brayden, their commander.

And the one person Onora had been avoiding the most. She sighed, a smart remark on her tongue when Amherst, the commander of all the Hunters and her adoptive father, walked in, too. They all immediately stood at attention, and a slithering feeling of anxiety wound its way around her stomach. Amherst's gaze landed on her with a soft smile that couldn't abate her fear.

"Brayden and the twins will be accompanying you on the mission," he said softly. Too softly. Too sympathetic. As if he knew the blow would hit and he wanted it to do less damage.

Which only made it worse.

She swallowed. "Sir, I don't believe that's necessary."

Brayden walked to her, his hand brushing her elbow in a familiar and intimate way. Once upon a time, she'd welcomed that touch, thrilled at it, desperately wanted it more than anything. Now it took everything in her not to slap it away.

He pursed his lips. "This will give Vincent and Vera more experience. They have a lot they can learn from you."

"Okay, they can come then. We hardly need two lieutenants to go."

Brayden cast a glance at Amherst, both of them exchanging a knowing look that made her blood boil. Amherst jerked his head to the side, and she followed him outside the stable. He placed heavy hands on her shoulders, giving her the fatherly look that she'd become accustomed to.

"I know you and Brayden have a history—"

"It's not that," she hissed, and Amherst's expression changed to the stern fatherly look that made her swallow the next words on her tongue.

It *was* partially that. Amherst didn't know what she'd gone through with Brayden. She and Brayden had always been in competition with each other for the top spot at the Hunter's Guild. If she complained about him coming along, then Brayden would say it was favoritism. She would never be able to earn her place here on her own merit if she told Amherst about their history.

"You're going to observe Lord Dryston and find out why he hasn't left Nemus yet. You and Lord Dryston traveled together for a while, and I just think it would be good to have someone with you who can remind you of what human love feels like."

She clenched her jaw, holding her tongue.

This again. Amherst had sent her to help King Leeth of the elves on his mission to find the lost city of Evolis. On that mission were Lord Dryston and his siblings. She'd been cordial and professional, not fighting any of them and even working with them.

Upon her return, Amherst and Brayden had interrogated her about what she'd seen and experienced with the demons, expecting some terrible tales of their evil.

All she'd been able to say was that Dryston was arrogant and controlling and annoying. Kaemon and Enid had been easy to work with—people she would trust to have her back in a fight. They chalked that up to her being put under his thrall—a magical spell done by demons, usually on humans, to make them do as they commanded, claiming love and desire against their own wishes.

*"Are you okay?"*

She shoved that memory far, far away and swallowed. "I'm not under a thrall, commander."

He rubbed her shoulders soothingly, a pitying look in his eyes that made her feel rage and shame in the same measure. "I know you aren't. We all know you aren't." A lie. "I just think he may try to pull you under one, and I don't think it's bad to have an old paramour nearby to remember. You and Brayden were always so good together."

Amherst had no idea. He—and many others—had blamed Onora for the breakup.

"Fine," she said. "He's not needed, but I can be professional. If it's what you command, sir."

He nodded. "It is."

## CHAPTER 3

# DRYSTON

"How long will you wait for the orc lord to respond?" Kalen asked as they wove through the busy streets of Orc Haven's merchant district.

"A few more weeks," Dryston responded.

He'd been away from The Darkened City too long, and he was anxious to return. How long could he stay in Nemus before the humans saw it as a problem? He didn't want to know.

"We can't wait forever, Drys," Kalen said, lips tight.

Dryston's gaze slipped to his companion as they sidestepped a group chatting in the square. "You seem awfully eager to get out of here."

Kalen opened his mouth to say something when his eyes narrowed ahead of him, mouth slamming shut in a frown, nostrils flared. Dryston followed his gaze to see Silenus trotting up to them.

The satyr had come to live at The Tipsy Tavern when Melina was pregnant to help and hadn't left yet, claiming he enjoyed the lively atmosphere. He and Kalen had butted heads multiple times, but Dryston hadn't been able to get to the bottom of it yet.

Silenus came near, his wavy blond locks falling over his shoulders and bare chest. "Good morning, Dryston dear," he said with a bright smile, producing a letter.

Dryston grabbed the letter, losing all sense of propriety when he saw the seal, and ripped it open. It was from the orc lord, accepting his request for an audience in two days' time. Lord Killgan was difficult to pin down—he couldn't bother to tarry.

"Silenus, I could kiss you," he said, grinning from ear to ear.

Silenus smiled back, eyes twinkling. "Don't make promises you don't intend to keep, Lord Dryston."

Dryston laughed, shaking his head, then stopping when a flash of blond hair in the crowd caught his attention. In a moment it was gone, his blood thrumming. As if in a trance, pulled along by some invisible string, he stepped around the satyr and wove through the crowd. He couldn't see who it was, but he knew, anyway. Somehow, he knew.

The square was thick with bodies, loud with yelling and bartering, the smell of cooking meat and iron in the forges. Still, he followed that line, growing tauter until, suddenly, there was something sharp poking his ribs in the one small area of his leather armor that was exposed. Looking down, a slow smile spread across his face.

"Are you following me, Lord Dryston?" Onora asked.

A braid fell over her shoulder, loose strands framing her high cheekbones, as those sharp blue eyes narrowed on him.

"You're the one in my town," Dryston said. "Seems like you may be following me. I'm surprised it's taken you so long—after all we shared on our travels."

Her brow furrowed deeper, her eyes turning stormy, and he chuckled. Her glare faltered momentarily before coming back stronger. He leaned down so he could whisper in her ear, "Careful how you let that mask of hate slip, Onora. Someone might think you actually do like me."

Her breath caught momentarily, and she turned to look at him, their faces inches apart. Dryston could admit that he'd woken a few too many times from dreams of his lips exploring hers. His hands fisted in her hair, her harried breath hitting his skin.

Even if he knew she hated him. Even if he knew it was only her own integrity and honor that had made her save him that day. The dagger in his side pressed in a little farther and the pain met him, sharp and wonderful.

Someone cleared their throat and Dryston looked up to see another Hunter, a man tall as Onora, broad shouldered and staring at Dryston as if he were plotting exactly how he'd like to skin him. It took all his willpower to keep his wings from spreading out and intimidating the man, and he was barely aware that he took a step closer to Onora, his hand gripping her arm protectively. The man's eyes dipped to where his hand rested, and Onora stepped away from Dryston, ripping her arm back violently.

"Keep your hands away from me, bat," she spat.

Dryston grinned. A million responses rested on his tongue, but he didn't need to aggravate either of them more. "What brings Hunters to Orc Haven?"

"We're conducting an investigation," the man said, his suspicious eyes darting from Dryston to Onora and back.

"Ahh. Well, let me know if I can be of any help," Dryston responded.

Onora met his gaze, a myriad of emotions swimming there that he wanted to dive into, drenching himself in the depths of them.

He took a step back. The demonic thrall may have been a myth, but whatever enchantment this woman had put on him left him scrambling for some semblance of control around her.

Kalen was suddenly next to him, a low growl rumbling from deep in his chest, and both humans tensed. Dryston's arm shot out in front of Kalen, and he gave him a warning look. Kalen's brown wings tucked in.

Kalen was the last remaining member of their family's original colony, his family having been slaughtered by Hunters the same day all those years ago. He was tightly wound but fiercely loyal, and someone that Dryston would trust with his life.

But right now, he needed him to not unravel at the sight of the

Hunters. If he'd known any would be coming to Orc Haven, he would have sent Kalen away with the others and kept Mandel.

"There seems to be an infestation of demons here," the man said with a smirk.

Dryston clenched his jaw and Kalen started to take a step forward when Onora barked, "Shut up, the lot of you. We're going, Brayden."

She cut a glare to her companion, and he pursed his lips. Dryston's pulse hummed at her command. He watched her turn and walk away, his eyes dipping to the cut of her ass in her tight leathers.

"I don't like that Hunters are here," Kalen said.

"It's odd," Dryston replied.

He debated for only a second before trotting up to Onora, ignoring the withering look from Brayden. "How long are you here for?"

Onora didn't spare him a glance as she weaved through the crowds. "However long it takes."

"See, I find your story a bit odd." He was poking a bear, he knew it, but he couldn't stop himself, never had been able to.

"How's that?"

"Aife and Jorah know all the news, and they tell me. They haven't mentioned anything of late that would need investigating."

She scoffed, and he had to tamp down the anger that leapt into his throat.

"I wouldn't expect a demon to tell me the truth of a situation, anyway." Her gaze finally slid to him, derision clear on her face as her eyes traveled the length of him, disapproving.

He bristled, his tail twitching at the challenge in her eyes, the hate in her words. "I meant it when I offered my help, Onora. We worked together on King Leeth's mission, and quite well, I might remind you."

She stiffened at his words, and Dryston didn't miss the look of scrutiny Brayden gave her.

Interesting.

"I was commanded to aid you, Lord Dryston," she said, each word sharp as a knife. "Don't misconstrue my dedication to orders as anything more than that."

They stared at each other a moment, her eyes boring into him, and it took all his concentration to keep his wings from fanning out in a show of dominance, matching the energy she lobbed at him.

She could say what she wanted, but he remembered what had happened that final night in Evolis. How he was lying on the ballroom floor, his magic seeping out of him, putting him at the mercy of the witch Hevena. He was about to die. He would have died too, if Onora hadn't come in and saved him. And perhaps that was only honor, but there was a piece of a Hunter's cloak in his room at the tavern that spoke differently. She hadn't just saved him from the witch, she'd ensured he lived.

"How could I ever think it was anything different?" he asked, letting a knowing smirk loose.

She turned on her heel, waving a hand of dismissal as she did. He followed her through the crowds, her and Brayden throwing looks at him over their shoulders as he did.

Brayden finally stopped and turned, facing Dryston down. He was a large man, but still stood well enough below Dryston that he could see Brayden swallow as Dryston hovered over him in response.

"Why are you following us?" Brayden demanded.

Dryston waved behind them dully at the sign of The Tipsy Tavern. "It's the only inn in town. I currently live here, and I assume you will be getting rooms here tonight?"

Brayden drew in an exasperated breath and turned, stalking into the tavern with Onora following, shaking her head.

Dryston could go up to his room or sit in a booth far away from them. He knew he probably should. But instead, he followed them to the counter and sat down, getting a glass of water from Aife as he did. He wanted to hear what they would say or if they would give away any reason for their investigation. Something wasn't quite adding up.

Onora came to Jorah, and the orc smiled. "How can I help ya?"

Onora returned the smile, and Dryston's hand stilled as it brought the drink to his mouth. He hadn't ever seen her smile—the closest had been a neutral expression that was only vaguely threatening. The way her features softened made his heart thump painfully against his ribs and he knocked the water back quickly, looking away to ignore a new, yet somehow familiar ache in his chest.

"We'll need four rooms," she responded, her tone so different from how she addressed Dryston that the taste turned bitter in his mouth. "For me and my companions."

"All of you are Hunters?" Jorah asked, voice neutral, calm.

Onora nodded.

"What business brings the guild out this way?" Jorah's gaze flickered to Dryston briefly.

"Just investigating the woods and trade routes. Been hearing tales of bandits and thieves attacking innocents."

That was a lie; he could hear it in her voice—how she said it too smoothly, too rehearsed. He could also hear it in the slightly elevated thumping of her heart.

They took their keys and went to their rooms, and when they were safely up the stairs, Jorah came near him.

"Do you believe what they said?" the orc asked.

Dryston shook his head. "I don't know. Felt like a lie, but Onora doesn't strike me as a liar . . ."

Jorah nodded. "My thoughts exactly. Watch your back. They could have been sent here to shadow you and see what you're up to."

Dryston nodded. He could see that being the case. If he stepped onto human-owned lands, he had no doubt he'd be immediately captured and imprisoned. It was maybe a foolish hope, but by setting up enough alliances in Nemus, he wanted to build up his reputation with the humans and come to some understanding with them.

The Cruel Lord's occupation had been terrible. He'd heard enough about what he and his soldiers did to the humans and what all they had been through.

It wasn't long before Onora came back down the stairs and found a table in the corner, alone. Aife brought her food, and she sat back, casually observing the room. Her eyes landed on his more often than not and then quickly looked away.

Silenus played his flute with a band in the corner, flirting with everyone who came by, carefully avoiding the nymph, Naida, now sitting at the bar. Dryston didn't like gossip, but he couldn't turn his brain off from noticing things, and there had been a shift. Silenus and Naida had been friends for a moment, and now there was a tension that Dryston couldn't name.

His eyes drifted across the room and landed on Onora. She was staring at him again, but her eyes flicked away. Dryston was not fool enough to think that it was a casual interest that had the Hunter's gaze constantly on him, and he narrowed his attention on her.

He stood, and in a few moments he was at her table, pulling out a chair, making her startle from the scrape it made on the wooden floor, and slipping in next to her.

"Tell me more about these bandits," Dryston said, his gaze meeting hers in a challenge.

Onora leaned forward, setting her dagger heavily on the table in front of her, elbows down, her own gaze narrowed. "How about you tell me what could be so interesting to a demon in the orc lands that he stays here for the better part of a year?"

"I was here for my brother and his mate," Dryston replied coolly.

"They aren't here anymore, haven't been for a couple of months. Yet you remain."

Dryston felt the hair on his arm stick up. "I didn't realize you were keeping track of me so ardently. Feels a bit obsessive, but I can't say you'd be the first to fall prey to my charms."

Her lips flattened into a thin line, fury dancing like a thunderstorm in her glorious eyes. "I've heard a great deal about a demon's charm, yet I've never once witnessed it."

"Yet you can't take your eyes off of me." Dryston leaned forward, meeting that steely gaze with his own fire, letting his eyes drop to her mouth and back up. "You never have been able to, have you?"

She drew in a sharp breath, her own eyes dipping for a second to his mouth and back up, making his blood warm. "Does a rabbit ignore the fox? Neither should a human ignore her biggest threat."

"I'm no threat to you, darling, unless you want me to be," he purred.

In a swift motion, the dagger disappeared, and she brought it down on the wood of the table, nicking his finger and drawing blood. "Don't flirt with me, bat. You wouldn't survive it." Her voice held a cool command, a tone that brooked no disagreement, and his mind scrambled to not dip into that unholy place of imagining what hate fucking her would be like.

Glorious.

Ruinous.

Worth every ounce of the potential fallout.

He stood swiftly. That was a crazy thought and one that would get him in deep waters if he let it run amok. "Good night, Onora. I look forward to seeing more of you."

# CHAPTER 4
# ONORA

Onora slept like shit that night. She told herself it was from traveling, from being in a new place, maybe even because Dryston was somewhere in the building, and only because he was a threat to her.

Obviously.

But the horrifying dream she woke from was more likely the cause. Dryston's lips on hers, his hands exploring her body—and worst of all, her enjoying it. She woke with a start, her shadows dancing around her playfully, but not engulfing the room, and she stumbled out of bed.

It was early, but she could still hear the faint murmuring of patrons in the dining hall below, and the smell of cooked bacon hit her nose and made her stomach rumble. She hastily got ready for the day, running through her head what she needed to do.

The others were on duty following Dryston today and she would be seeing what she could get from the locals about him, while familiarizing herself better with Orc Haven. She'd been here a few other times, usually years apart, and she had stayed at this inn each time, coming in late and leaving early.

Outside of her official business, she had another personal one.

She'd heard that the elf that had traveled with them to Evolis, Vasu, was in town.

She grabbed her daggers, placing them on the different parts of her body, only a couple in plain view, then stepped out of her room, going to the dining hall, signaling to the female orc, Aife, for food. In a moment she brought coffee and sausages with potatoes to the table and she thanked her generously, as Jackson and the rest of her squad came down and joined her.

"It's good to be all back together and on a mission," Avery commented, smiling and thanking Jorah as he brought a pitcher of water and glasses for them.

His eyes scanned them, friendly but observant, keeping as much watch as she was on Dryston. She understood it, though. A group of Hunters posting up in Orc Haven wouldn't be suspicious if it weren't for the continued and persistent demonic presence of the last year in the town.

The Hunters' presence no doubt felt pointed.

Onora supposed it was.

They'd been told to not come in as aggressive, but they didn't have to hide the fact completely that they were here for the demons. Though they would deny it if asked, of course.

She hated the politics of it, even if she understood how tenuous the alliances were and how easily lines could be drawn, causing a major conflict. One that would most likely end poorly for humans, worst of all. They were weaker not only in magic but in physical size and strength, and the humans of Nemus had never fully recovered from the losses caused by the Cruel Lord.

"I'm just glad to see Onora outside her room for once," Jin commented, receiving a glare from Andrea. He shrugged, giving Onora a sheepish look.

"I'm glad to be out and about again. With my squad, especially," she said.

Jackson squeezed her hand affectionately, and she ducked her head and kept eating, never certain how to respond to their care. An arm wrapped around her shoulders and she involuntarily shivered in disgust, even before she saw who it was. Brayden sat in the seat next to her, also waving Aife down, but something in his manner made her teeth grit. The way it felt like a demand, as if he were so far above the orc.

"I'm also glad you're out and about, Onora," he said. "I'm actually shocked you insisted on coming on this trip at all. Everyone would have understood if you decided to stay home."

Jackson gave them a keen look over his steaming hot coffee, never quite missing the intricacies of any interactions. She and Brayden had been in an on-again, off-again relationship since she started at the academy. He was four years older than her, and he'd treated her as an equal, sparring with her and not holding back like others did. She'd fallen for him, but that was ages ago. Before he broke up with her over and over again, always, suspiciously, after she received accolades that cemented her once again as a real contender to take over guild leadership when the chief retired.

She'd caught on to the pattern quick enough, recognizing the oozing, aching blood of an always wounded ego. Still, she'd taken him back every time. Why? Well . . . she took a gulp of coffee to dislodge the tightness that was now in her throat from annoyance.

Sometimes life was lonely, and a body in the bed was better than nothing.

She could never decide if she'd volunteered to be a ranger in the elven lands to avoid him, or because the mountains had always called to her with an eerie beckoning that made her soul ache. Looking at maps had always filled her with a nostalgic longing for them, long before she'd ever seen them. Either way, it felt the same. That hollowness only ever abated by momentary bliss. As if there was something in her always searching and never quite finding it.

"I needed the fresh air," Onora replied.

Onora knew something in her had broken all those years ago. Looking around the table, she knew it was the same for the others there, too. Except Jackson.

Onora had held on to her honor and integrity. Jackson had clung to love and goodness and never let it go. There was a light and joy in his eyes that, when he laughed, made her feel whole again.

*"Don't cry," Amherst had said the night he found her. "When you cry, they win."*

Amherst had taken her and Jackson in when they rode to the guild in Venatu, practically falling off their horses in exhaustion. He'd raised her and trained her, honing her fear and hatred into a blade sharper than any made of steel.

"Leave her be," Andrea said. "Onora has more important things to do than deal with your bullshit, Brayden."

"Like what? Write love letters to the demon lord?" He snickered.

Onora stiffened as a look of disgust washed over Andrea's face. "Onora would never be brought under a demon's thrall."

Andrea had a similar background to Onora, but from another village. She was a bit older and had experienced horrors Onora had narrowly escaped. The demons had always talked of the thrall, how they used their magic to seduce others into believing they were in love and doing as they pleased. Andrea had seen others come under it, but she'd only ever pretended to be caught in it as well. She believed certain people couldn't be swayed, no matter how strong the enchantment was.

Brayden laughed. "I'm teasing. I know Onora wouldn't be. She wouldn't even be caught in love with a human."

"Just you," Onora retorted, taking a bite of bread as Andrea and Jackson chuckled.

"Stop bickering," Avery said.

If there was one thing about the Hunters, it was that they understood each other. Mostly, that is.

Brayden had been raised in Venatu by a wealthy family. He had a younger brother who was sensitive and kind, but Brayden had been trained early to be a knight, and when the demon occupation happened, he quickly switched to being a Hunter. And he was an excellent one, matched only by Onora in skill. He hated demons as much as any other Hunter, but he never could quite understand what the rest of them had been through.

Jackson lowered his voice, leaning into the table as the others followed suit. As humans, their hearing wasn't nearly as good as the other magical beings of the world, so they'd learned to keep quieter around others. "Avery, did you find anything about the demons?"

Avery and Jin had been sent into town the night before to ask around about Dryston and any other demons in the area.

Avery shook his head. "Not much. People clammed up fast when we started asking about them. But it seems many of the demons have vacated. The one with the human . . . What's his name?"

"Kaemon," Onora replied quickly. Everyone gave her a sharp look, and she had to stop herself from rolling her eyes.

She'd isolated herself because of the abilities she had now, but also because she didn't know what to do with her experiences with the demons. Kaemon wasn't someone she had ever felt threatened by. As a matter of fact, if she were in danger and had to run to Brayden or Kaemon for help . . .

"Kaemon Erebus," Avery said, clearing his throat and moving on. "Well, it seems the woman had the baby, and they took them and most of the demon warriors back home."

"That's still good news. I've only seen the three, so that may be all that's left," Jackson responded. "Curious that there aren't more."

They continued talking, quietly and in more coded language. It was still early, but many of the patrons were filling into the tavern. A small goblin woman in stylish clothes came to the front and gave baked goods to Aife, orc mercenaries sat at another table, eating in silence, geared up for their next mission. Dryston came down, hair damp and face fresh—that godsdamned jawline cut like marble by a divine hand. She didn't realize she was staring until he turned her way, giving her a slow perusal up and down, then flashing her a smile, making her heart do this infuriatingly silly flip-flopping thing. She turned back to her group, all of them looking hastily away from her, clearly having seen the interaction.

Great.

Wonderful.

Exactly what she needed.

She stood, placing coins for the food and a tip on the table. "I'm going to explore the town and ask around in a way that won't make the residents clam up."

She gave a pointed look at Avery, who threw his hands up. "How was I to know people would be loyal to demons here?"

How? Perhaps because she'd told them all that the Erebus family was well respected in the orc and elf lands. She shook her head, and walked out, only getting outside the tavern before Jackson jogged up alongside her.

"Avery is old school," he said, shrugging.

"Is it that, or is it that they don't listen to my experience with the demons because they think I've been enchanted to be in love with Lord Dryston?" She spat the last words like they were poison.

"It's hard for them to not be concerned about you, but that's all it is." He gave her a pleading look and she acquiesced. She hoped that's all it was.

"I have a rapport with Lord Dryston, even if it's slightly hostile," she said. "I want to leverage that so I can trail him, but it's hard when everyone looks at me like I'm committing a crime."

"I know. I'll have a talk with them."

"What good is a talk? I need them to believe that I wouldn't compromise my integrity for this."

Jackson nodded, squeezing her shoulder. "I know. And I think everyone knows it more than you think they do. Give it a bit of time. And trail Lord Dryston as much as you need. I won't let the others get in the way."

THE DAY WORE ON, with her spending most of it just getting to know some of the key players in Orc Haven. Onora had never been known for her charm, but she knew how to make people feel comfortable around her, and that's all she needed. She spent most of her time asking about Vasu, his role in Orc Haven, and where to find him. Many didn't recognize the name, but finally she found out that he'd set up an apothecary shop at the end of town, offering lessons on magic control for the locals.

She wandered through the streets, finally coming to the small building that was tucked between a stationery shop and a specialty items store, and ducked in.

Vasu sat behind a desk, head buried in a book, his topknot coming loose but still looking stylish as a few jet-black strands fell against his ochre-brown forehead. "Welcome in! I'll be with you in a moment!" he called out, not looking up as an enchanted quill furiously scribbled down notes on parchment next to him, his right hand twisting and flicking here and there to control it.

She came up, leaning against the desk and peeking over to see what he was reading. It was in a language she couldn't understand. He glanced up for a second, then back, then to her again, halting his writing and reading, a grin bursting across his face as he exclaimed, "Onora!"

"Hi, Vasu. What are you working on?" She dipped her head at the scroll.

He held up his notes, all in the common tongue. "I'm translating a fascinating scroll I found in Evolis. I'll be sending it to Avenay to match up with what she's found as well."

On the scroll it said: SPELL OF REANIMATION.

"Umm . . . is that . . . ?"

They had seen many strange things in Evolis and the surrounding woods. The dead turned to creatures of violence and desperation. An entire city frozen in time, never aging, but bound inside the city walls. The magic had been powerful and terrible.

Vasu sighed. "We think it may be. We're following a trail Avenay uncovered a few months ago with the history of witches in Evolis."

"I'm shocked you left the city. I thought you and Avenay would be there for the next twenty years—at least—uncovering all the history."

Vasu chuckled. "Well, I felt that way too, but at some point, you have to get back into the world. And I've heard of the humans and other races having difficulty with controlling magic, so after helping with Melina's birth, I decided to stay here and offer my knowledge. Orc Haven is central in Nemus and safe for all to get here."

Vasu gave her a curious look, a question there. Was she here on official guild business? Or something more personal?

She cleared her throat. "Well then, I came to the right place. I've been having issues with magic myself."

"Interesting. Describe it to me."

She told him about waking up in total darkness, of shadows dancing out of her even though she was nowhere near a demon or anyone with those abilities, and how sometimes lightning arced and splintered the darkness.

"How long has this been happening? Did it start while we traveled with the demons?" he asked.

She nodded. "Yes, but it's become more intense since the well was opened. Can you keep a secret for me, Vasu? Don't tell anyone, not even Avenay?"

Vasu nodded, suddenly serious as concern crinkled around his eyes.

Onora swallowed, then pulled back her sleeve, showing him the tattoos. His brows lifted as he leaned forward to examine it better. "These were burned on my skin the moment the well opened. I don't know why or how."

Vasu ran a finger along the black swirls. "It's magical, that's for certain, and very detailed. It looks demonic."

Onora drew in a shaky breath. "That's what I thought as well."

"You were with Enid when it happened? Right?"

"Yes. She was performing the demonic rite by herself. Her power left her, and when it returned, the well was opened and these tattoos were on my arms and torso."

Vasu chewed his lip. "I *will* keep this a secret, Onora. But I'm sure Dryston could help you make better sense of it than I can. The demonic rites are sacred and mysterious rituals. Few outside of demons know about them and rarely are they talked about in detail. So much so that I only know it's a miracle Enid was able to survive doing it herself."

She groaned. "I was afraid you'd say that."

Vasu chuckled. "I see neither of you are friendlier now than when I last left you? Well, in the meantime, I can teach you a few tricks to control your powers, if you want."

She nodded. "That would be amazing."

# CHAPTER 5
# DRYSTON

Dryston sat in his room, squinting against the dim candlelight as he composed the letter to Lord Killgan. It didn't matter how many times he had written missives to other rulers, he could never stop himself from overthinking it.

Probably because his requests for even an audience had about a seventy percent fail rate. And of the ones he did receive an audience for, those rarely panned out to be anything considered an alliance. He rubbed his forehead, trying to stave off the headache slowly throbbing in his temples.

He never should have been chosen to be the Lord of Shadows. Was he the most powerful demon? Yes. Did that matter when he lacked the political skills needed to rule? He doubted it. In the last eleven years since he'd taken over, it had been a series of defeats to remind him of exactly how much of a failure he was. Any time there was a border conflict or a battle, he did amazing. He'd been built for war. Not politics.

A cool breeze drifted through the window, darkness following, the candle suddenly bright against it. He turned to see shadows twining up and through the window.

Curious.

He leaned out the window and looked down at the gardens behind the tavern. Standing amongst the hedges was Onora, shadows around her, shifting and twirling up at her command. She looked like the moon goddess in that light, smokey tendrils dancing around her hair and up to the sky.

But then they shuddered, dancing, flicking her hair and teasing. She let out a low growl, trying to command them, only for them to become more rambunctious.

Dryston chuckled, and she looked up, scowling at him. He swung a leg over the windowsill, and jumped down, landing in front of her with a thud. She let out an alarmed gasp and stepped back.

"Why are you still awake at this hour?" she asked.

"I could ask you the same thing."

"I think it's quite obvious what I was doing." She looked around nervously. For fear of being alone with him? He took one step back, making his wings come in tighter, less imposing.

"It seems your shadows have a life of their own." Some demons reported their shadows acting in that way, but it wasn't common, and since shadows weren't innate to her, it went against what he expected. They should just be a manifestation of his and the other demons residual energy from nearness to them.

"They're unpleasant things," she replied.

"Do you need help?"

She raised a brow, and he held out his hand. "Give me yours."

She stared at it with mild disgust.

"I'm not going to infect you, Onora."

"Are you going to put me under your thrall?"

Did she think a thrall was real? He knew some humans did, but he'd thought it was the mystics or people with less exposure to the world. Not her.

"Trust me, I wouldn't, even if I thought I could bring you under one."

"How do I know you haven't already?"

His lips tugged at a smile. "Have you been experiencing a thrall with me, Lieutenant?"

Her cheeks turned rosy, and she swallowed hard.

Oh.

Now that was an interesting response.

"Not at all," she said, her voice cool and unaffected.

"Then you have nothing to worry about."

He gestured again for her to give him her hand. She hesitated, but finally did. He cupped it, palm up, tracing the center. Her hands were rougher than his, wrought, no doubt, from a life in the woods and wilds. She drew in a sharp breath as he continued his swirling, and her eyes darkened, darting away when he looked at her.

Well, fuck.

This woman might very well be the death of him, the way those simple sounds and manners made heat rush straight to his groin.

He needed to focus. Keep his mind on helping her and building a bridge of trust for a future alliance.

He didn't need to think about fucking her until she screamed his name. And he especially didn't need to wonder what that would sound like.

He shifted on his feet, swallowing as he concentrated, swirling his fingers until he felt it, that connection of his shadows to hers. They met, the magic so similar yet somehow distinct from his. With humans, their magic acted as a conduit, taking the energy from other beings or around them as it flowed and then learned to manipulate it.

This felt like nothing he'd ever encountered before.

"Your magic is strange," he said.

She pursed her lips, cheeks fully red now as she met his gaze, and he clenched his jaw, shoving away the fluttering feeling the sight sent to his stomach.

"Gee, thanks," she said. "That cleared things up."

He rolled his eyes. "My magic is different from yours, so I can only help a little. I thought I could with this, but it seems there's something odd about yours . . ."

She pulled her hand away, frowning and taking a step back. That seemed to strike a nerve, but he couldn't parse out why. She rubbed her hands, looking down at them in confusion, glancing up at him and opening her mouth, then slamming it shut again before speaking.

He crossed his arms and raised a brow. "What is it?"

"What is what?" she asked.

"You want to ask me something."

She hesitated, and he could see it in her eyes. The distrust. It hit him like a blow. Maybe he shouldn't care what she thought of him. Maybe he shouldn't care what anyone did. But as the ruler of his realm, he didn't have that luxury. What others thought of him was what they thought of all demons. The Cruel Lord had seen to that. He'd spun lies and woven sparse truths in order to make them believable. He'd only cared about bringing people under his rule, conquering, and making the world fear demons.

He hadn't thought of how long lasting that effect would be.

Dryston didn't want to admit that he hated even more that Onora didn't trust him—still. A human from Nemus not trusting him was one thing. But he and Onora had spent several months together to find Evolis. They'd worked together and fought together. He thought he'd shown her his integrity.

Even if he wasn't the easiest to get along with. Enid reminded him of that often. Controlling and angry is what she called him. A hothead is what the gossip pages back home painted him as.

Maybe he was.

But he'd argue that there was only so much disrespect a person could take before they had to stand their ground.

"Why are you still here, in Orc Haven?" she finally asked.

That wasn't a question he'd been expecting. He wondered how much to share with her. His ego hated to admit that the Shadow Realm was low on allies, and he'd been waiting months for Lord Killgan to respond.

He sighed. "There are rulers here that are willing to have an audience with me."

"Why not focus on your own continent? Why come here where the Cruel Lord oppressed us? Many people don't welcome demons here."

"I want to continue the work of my father and try to make right the wrongs that the Cruel Lord did."

Her eyes narrowed, lips curling into the beginnings of a snarl, and she let out a mirthless laugh. "Sounds about right."

She brushed past him, leaving him in the garden, wondering what in the darkest pit he'd done to warrant that response.

# CHAPTER 6
# ONORA

Onora kept to the shadows of the trees, her feet soft and light, silent as any creature of the wood. Dryston was far enough ahead that he wouldn't hear her. His bow was in one hand, a quiver of arrows on his back. He didn't look alert, but having it drawn made her question what he was doing out in the woods. Hunting? Or something more sinister?

Dryston had left early, and she'd only noticed because of her own fairly sleepless night and the fact that he was down the hall from her. He'd grabbed a bit of sweetbread from Aife and then headed into the woods outside the city. He'd been hiking for hours now, following an old, worn path with intent.

She'd wondered a few times if trailing him this long and deep into the woods was worth it, but considering how far he was going, and remembering his words from the night before, she was on edge.

*"I want to continue the work of my father . . ."*

Shadows burst from her hands as anger thrashed through her anew. His father. The one who had ambushed Venatu when he'd come, claiming it was a peacekeeping mission. His father, the one whose violence had gotten her old mentor killed defending the human stronghold. His father, a male no better than the Cruel Lord he'd deposed.

She remembered that day clearly. She'd been seventeen, not quite old enough to go on missions, younger than all the first-year recruits. Her mentor, Hadley, a woman who had taken her under her wing since Amherst took her in, told her that the new demon lord was coming, along with his wife and their extended family of adults they called a colony, on a peacekeeping mission. Everyone had been on edge, but Lord Kian had come a few times before and convinced the King that he truly wanted peace. He had to bring his colony to perform a secret and sacred ritual in the woods to untie the magical ley lines under a temple and allow the elves to use it again.

Onora had woken each night leading up to it, screaming in terror and Hadley had started sleeping in her room as a comfort. She was like an older sister, as dear to her as Jackson.

After a few days of negotiations, the horns of the citadel sounded, and the best Hunters were sent to the forest to defend against the attack from the demons. The demons had all been killed, but so were so many Hunters. Hadley included.

Finally, a clearing appeared and in it was a small cabin next to a stream. She hung by a tree, hiding behind it as he approached, taking in the entire area. He had a solemn expression on his face as he walked around, running his hand along the wood of the cabin before opening the door and entering. She darted around the trees until she could sneak up to the building and sneak around, looking in the window. It was small but cozy, with a bed and a homemade quilt on it, a small bookshelf that was empty, some pots and pans and a small stove and washbasin. Dryston sat on the bed, looking around, stricken.

She was lost in the scene, the image, the expressions crossing over his face. There was something like regret and longing there, an emotion so deep that it felt . . . human. She swallowed and tried to ignore that pang of empathy that reared its ugly head too often around him.

*"Demons will mimic human behavior and emotions to pull you under*

*their thrall," Amherst had taught them early on. "They will try to ingratiate you to their good graces and pull you into their tangled web of lies because they know our emotions are a great threat to ourselves. Never trust a demon's sadness or kindness or happiness—and especially not what they call love."*

But Dryston had no audience. He wasn't trying to fool her or put on a show.

"He's quite handsome when he's lost in thought, isn't he?"

Onora whipped her head around at the loud, but flutey, voice that came from behind her. It was a satyr she'd seen in town. He played the lyre at the tavern at night. His long blond hair tangled with antlers, where gems and shining chains swooped between.

Her heart crashed against her ribs.

Shit.

*Shit.*

She was going to be found out by Dryston.

Dryston stood, and Onora ducked down below the window, receiving a chuckle from the satyr as he walked forward to the door where Dryston met him.

"You have an admirer," he said, and Onora wanted to die.

She looked around for an easy exit, any way that she could flee, and hoped that the description the satyr gave him was bad enough to give her plausible deniability.

She stood and was about to run when a strong hand clamped down on her shoulder and a shiver ran through her body.

"Onora . . ." Suspicion dripped from Dryston's voice, and she turned to see it reflected in his eyes. Cold and calculating.

She drew in a deep breath. "Fancy meeting you here."

He cocked his head to the side. "I was about to say the same thing."

"Who's your friend?" the satyr asked, popping his head around Dryston's wings.

"I'm Lieutenant Onora," she responded, not taking her eyes off Dryston.

"A Hunter?" The satyr gave a low whistle. "What did you do to piss her off, Drys?"

Dryston gave him a dull look. "Why don't you go inside and start packing up, Silenus? I'll handle her."

"Oh, I bet you will," Silenus said, innuendo dripping like honey from his tone, eliciting a sharp look from Dryston, which he ignored. He gave a broad smile to Onora and stepped forward, taking her hand and bowing to kiss the back of it. She raised her brows, too startled by the gentlemanly conduct that she didn't know how to react. That was not a move often used on her by males of any race. Usually they approached her in fear and trembling, or with such inflated egos that the slightest prick of her tongue and they deflated into a blubbering mess. "It's a pleasure to meet you, Lieutenant. I'm Silenus."

"Likewise," Onora croaked out, and Dryston huffed a laugh.

Silenus sauntered off, going into the house, and started placing items in the backpack he carried.

"What are you doing here?" she asked.

"How about you answer that question first?"

"I'm not the one raiding a cabin in the woods."

"Neither am I. And I wouldn't say Silenus is, even if it would get him riled up, and I greatly enjoy doing that."

He smirked, and the tension in her gut eased while her chest tightened in an entirely different and more discomforting way.

She swallowed. "I was scouting the woods and saw you, so I decided to see what you were up to."

He squinted his eyes, and she didn't believe for one second that he believed her. "This is my brother's old cabin. I'm gathering the last of his valuables to take back to The Darkened City."

She peered into the cabin again. She'd heard a lot about Kaemon and his human bride. He'd been living in the woods for close to ten years, keeping mostly to himself and running under the radar of the Hunter's Guild. Then a man came to the guild, claiming that a demon had kidnapped his niece and had her under his thrall.

They'd been captured but escaped, killing many of the Hunters. Before any retaliation could happen, an alliance was secured with King Leeth of the elves, providing them with protection.

Onora had been sent to be a ranger for their group on the trip to find Evolis and told by Amherst to keep an eye out for any damning evidence. She'd spent so much time with Dryston, Kaemon, and Enid, waiting for their facade to slip.

She'd found no evidence.

"Find anything interesting in the woods?" he asked her, crossing his arms and cocking his head to the side.

She shook her head. "Nothing out of the norm."

Except demons roaming freely. It was startling to behold. She hadn't seen that since the occupation, when people cowered in fear at the presence of demons. Now, the people of Orc Haven seemed to have forgotten all of that.

"Well, good luck out there, Lieutenant. Call if you need anyone to protect you in the big bad woods." The corner of his mouth twitched at a smile and her eye twitched in anger.

He had once knocked her out of the way and saved her. Probably. She wouldn't let him know that he did. She still insisted that she could have saved herself. But he knew it riled her up, and he liked to bring it up.

"I don't need your help, now or ever." She turned and stalked into the woods, debating whether to leave and head into town or stay. She decided to stay. Dryston could be up to anything, and she wasn't about to leave him now.

Hours passed of her hanging in the woods, waiting for them to be done. They left with very little, but she'd heard them laughing and joking, and she assumed they'd been wasting time. Her time, at least. Quietly she followed them back into town, where Dryston left the items with another demon, the one who had been with him the first day, and then he took out a letter and left the inn.

She weaved through the people, using whatever she could to cover her as she trailed him through the bustling city and to the post office, where he dropped the letter off. She needed to know what was in it. Correspondence to his home?

He left, and she followed him, noting the looks others gave him. He was big and foreboding, but no more so than the average orc. Still, his wings and horns and tail stood out, and his cocky grin that he flashed at females and males alike made them stammer and blush, and she rolled her eyes.

Then he dipped between buildings, and she let out a curse, rushing forward to find an empty alleyway.

Fuck.

How had she lost him so quickly? There was no apparent exit, and she was certain she would have seen if he had flown. She jogged to the back, finding only a wall, despite her attempts to find an exit or place to scale it.

She turned, halting and letting out a gasp as she came face to face with him.

He flashed her a smile, but it wasn't the dazzling and flirty one he'd given the others. No, this one was harsh—a mask all its own.

"If I didn't know better, Lieutenant, I'd say you were stalking me." He turned, taking one heavy step toward her.

She took a careful one back. She had somehow managed to get herself blocked into the corner of an alleyway with her greatest threat. "I'm merely curious."

"Oh? I can think of two reasons you'd be following me. One, my roguish charm has your knickers in a twist"—he chuckled at her angry expression—"or two, you're plotting my murder."

"Maybe I'm trying to be your friend?" The words sounded ridiculous to her own ears and his following laughter made her clench her jaw.

He took two more steps forward, and she took another back, his proximity making her alarmingly aware of how much larger he was than her.

"Or maybe it's reconnaissance for the guild. Keeping watch on the Lord of Shadows."

He was close now, too close, and she took another step back, hitting the wall. She said nothing, afraid the sound of her hammering heart would give any lie away.

He stepped in closer now, one hand bracing the wall, encasing her as he leaned down so their faces were close.

"I don't mind. I certainly could have a much worse Hunter than you following me. And I can't say I don't understand the orders to do it."

"Then why are you cornering me in the alleyway?" She breathed, unsure if her racing heart was fear or something else far more embarrassing.

"Because I'd like your assurance that you'll leave my family and colony alone."

She raised her brows. "You're on orc land, Dryston. You'll be fine. But you know the laws. If any of you step into the human realm, you'll be dead before your next breath."

He leaned closer, his body so near that it blocked out the sun above, the halo around his horns lighting up like a fire. His wings spread out, long and strong. It was meant to intimidate, and her thundering pulse was a testament to its effectiveness.

"You harm anyone in my family, Onora, and I won't hesitate to snap that pretty little neck of yours."

He was serious, very serious. The hard lines of his face screamed resolve. But the way his eyes trailed to her lips, lingering as he drew in a deep and labored breath in, told her enough of his other feelings on the matter.

How much they mirrored her own conflicting emotions toward him.

Hate and lust. Passion in equal measure.

She smirked, making him frown. "Ohhhh," she crooned, "you think I'm pretty?"

Then she took her dagger, and, in one swift motion, lodged it in his shoulder.

He let out a curse, and she snaked around him, taking several quick steps backward toward the exit.

"You little heathen," he seethed.

"You'll heal in five minutes. Don't be a baby."

"You stabbed me," he growled.

"Threaten me again and I won't miss your heart next time."

"It's not a threat, it's a promise."

She rolled her eyes. "Cute."

She turned and sprinted into the busy streets again, clenching her trembling fists. Images flashed in her mind, memories she'd long buried, reaching their hand beyond the grave.

Suddenly, she felt like that little girl again. The feel of Varek's bruising hands on her arms, yanking her about. She could feel the iron shackle around her throat, digging in. She could hear the screams of other girls, unlucky enough to be older than her and more appealing than her. Her stomach roiled, and she darted into an empty alley to empty her stomach.

She needed to get a grip. Usually, she could separate her memories and emotions from the rest of her. Locked away in a glass case where she could peer in, but they could never reach her. She was objective, cool and collected, unflappable.

But Dryston had a way of unsettling her in every way. His threats felt empty, but they were too close to ones she'd heard ages ago.

She came to The Tipsy Tavern, where Brayden, Andrea, and Jackson were sitting at a table, talking. They stopped when they saw her and Andrea stood, concerned as she came to her and wrapped an arm around her shoulders.

"You're white as a ghost," Brayden said.

Well, fuck.

"I ate something that upset my stomach," she lied.

Part of her thought she should tell them what Dryston said to her, the threat to snap her neck.

Another part of her stalled. It was no more serious a threat than she'd made to him.

She cleared her throat. "Dryston sent a letter off to someone today. It had his official seal on it."

"Did you see who it was addressed to?" Jackson asked.

She shook her head. "No, but—"

She halted as the doors opened and Dryston walked in. Her heart thrashed against her ribs, and she had to remind herself to breathe. The sun hit his wings, lighting up orange around him, the clawed tips rising almost to the ceiling. His eyes landed on her, verdant and intense. He smirked, pulling a dagger up—her dagger—and placing it in his boot.

She gritted her teeth. Yeah, she probably shouldn't have left that on him. Was he going to accuse her of attacking him unprovoked? She *was* following him. This could spell trouble for them if he did.

Instead, he went to the bar instead, asked Aife for something, showing her the wound in his shoulder and she brought him out an ointment. He thanked her, heading for the stairs and giving Onora one last glance before heading up the stairs.

"How does he have your dagger?" Brayden asked, a bite in his tone that made Onora whip her head to him.

"I must have dropped it," she said.

No one looked like they believed her.

Brayden gave a chagrined smile, leaning back and observing her with an unnerving intensity. "I heard tale that the two of you were seen in the garden together last night, late and all alone."

Who the fuck would have seen them and told Brayden?

"I was getting fresh air, and he followed me out."

Brayden raised a brow. "Someone said he was awfully close to you."

"He's a flirt. I can't seem to get him to stop. It was nothing, though."

"It makes me uncomfortable how much his attention is fixed on you."

"Me, too. But it's to our benefit. We need to keep an eye on him, and I have previous experience with him. So maybe instead of interrogating me, we can keep doing our jobs."

Brayden's jaw flexed. "Take the day off tomorrow. I'll trail him." She opened her mouth to protest, but he held his hand up. "I'll take Avery. You need a break. Get some rest." He said the last part with concerned care, how he used to talk to her before his ego made him hate her. She didn't want to take a rest and a break. But she also knew arguing wouldn't help her convince anyone she wasn't under his thrall.

"Fine," she said.

## CHAPTER 7
# DRYSTON

Morning barely peeked over the edge of the horizon as Dryston woke the next morning. He'd told Lord Killgan he'd be in Yeolent in two days to meet with him. He knew better than to delay and be late to any meeting with the hard to pin down orc lord.

As he exited his room, Onora exited hers and both stopped in surprise, staring for a too long moment.

Far too long. Her eyes took in his raiment, snagging on his chest, her eyes dipping up to the tips of his wings, the slow perusal making him want to preen.

Oh no.

That was too dangerous.

His shoulder still ached from the stab wound she'd given him the day before, and he could still hear her words ringing in his ears—she wouldn't hesitate to kill his family if they were found in the human lands. Usually a wound like that would heal in a day, but it must have been dipped in a poison that affected his magic because it was taking forever to fully heal.

He slung his pack over his shoulder and brushed past her, telling himself to avoid her gaze and failing. Like a beacon in a storm, his attention always drifted to her.

"Are you leaving?" she asked.

"Do I detect a hint of sadness in your voice?"

She scoffed, those blue eyes narrowing in that way that made him feel crazy. With anger or lust, he couldn't decide. "Hardly. I can't wait for the day that I don't have to see your face every day."

He grinned. "I don't believe that at all."

She opened her mouth, then shut it angrily. Her nostrils flared, but he couldn't think about how angry she was. All he could think about was how the shape of her lips were maybe the most kissable ones he'd ever seen. "Where are you going? More work in the woods?"

He debated telling her for a moment. No doubt she would run away and tell the other Hunters, but maybe, just maybe, it would show the humans that others were coming around to trusting them. "I have a meeting with Lord Killgan. I'm hoping to secure an alliance."

Her brows shot up, her scowl melting away in surprise and curiosity, but she said nothing. He could see the wheels turning and bitterness coated his tongue.

"What? Did you think I was hanging around here just to wreak more havoc in Nemus?"

Her expression softened even more. The world felt tilted, upside down, the vulnerable expression on her face something he wasn't used to.

She shook her head. "I didn't know why. What do you want to gain from alliances in Nemus?"

Her tone had an edge of defensiveness—worry. He knew the Cruel Lord had done a great deal of damage to the continent, and especially to the humans. He carried the duality of hating what the Hunters had done to his family in the same breath as understanding why Hunters had come into existence. They were the only thing that had kept any humans safe from the Cruel Lord's tyranny.

"We don't have a lot of allies," he said, hating to admit it. "We need more for trade. I'm still trying to rebuild the Shadow Realm. But it's slow work and slower without trade partners."

She stared at him, calculating, curious, and he didn't want to move, didn't even want to breathe. It felt like he was making some semblance of progress with a feral cat, and the slightest wrong action would send her scratching and biting.

But he had places to be. He stepped down a few more steps. "At the very least, you'll get a reprieve from seeing my face for a few days."

She rolled her eyes, and he chuckled as he made his way down the stairs.

It took the better part of the day traveling to Yeolent, with stopping and resting along the way. The walls of the fortress loomed ahead, flags of green waving in the breeze. Warriors in leather armor, holding axes and shields greeted them at the gate. They were escorted to the main hall where orcs dined loudly.

One orc, older, with a long salt-and-pepper beard and long braids to match, sat at the front. He wore the leather armor common to orcs, with metal pauldrons and a helmet with intricately woven designs sitting on the table in front of them. Lord Killgan.

Kalen and Maria knelt in honor before him, bowing their heads and crossing a fist over their heart, while Dryston bowed as Killgan stood and came forward, shaking Dryston's hand.

"Come, take your seat next to me, Lord of Shadows," Killgan said, gesturing to the seat on his left.

Dryston obliged and the music in the hall began, a rustic and jaunty tune with an eight-stringed instrument that chimed through the hall as servants brought in platters overflowing with an assortment of berries, breads, and beer.

"Thank you for meeting with me," Dryston said, taking the beer handed to him and clanking his mug against Killgan's.

"It's an honor to host you," Killgan said. "I'll admit, I was wary at first. But anyone I questioned about you and your family assured me that you take after your father. I remember Kian. He was a good and fair male."

Dryston took another drink to swallow down the lump in his throat from those words. "My father always spoke highly of you, Lord Killgan."

The orc chuckled. "Your father could drink any orc under the table —which is quite the feat."

Dryston tucked that bit of information away like a treasure. He'd had so few years with his father, and he'd never seen him in a situation like that. Loose and having fun with peers. A keen pain stabbed at his ribs, and he took another drink to wash it away.

"That would explain why he never delayed coming to visit you," Dryston said with a chuckle.

A smoked ham was brought out with roasted potatoes, a variety of cheeses, and vegetables. They talked for hours about Dryston's parents, then shifting the conversation into the happenings in the orc realm and what kind of beneficial trades could be made between the Shadow Realm and the Orc Realm of Nemus.

"Strange happenings are underfoot," Killgan said as the minstrel began singing a slow and low ballad.

"Have you been having issues with magic flare-ups here?" Dryston asked. He'd heard of homes being destroyed and people dying because they didn't know how to handle their newfound abilities.

Killgan shook his head. "No. Any orc having an issue has been able to manage it. A strong community is one of our pillars, so information spreads quickly and people are well taken care of. I was referring to the odd sightings in the woodlands and burnt-out rings in fields. Have you heard anything about this?"

Dryston frowned. "No, I haven't. What kind of sightings?"

Killgan's face grew dark, shadows dancing in his eyes, matching the ones that candles cast on his face. "I haven't seen any of it, personally. I've only heard reports. But there are creatures—ones from old fables, creatures said to be birthed from dark magic, skulking in the cover of the trees and darkness."

Dryston shuddered from Killgan's tone alone. He'd seen plenty of horrors on his trip to find Evolis that he couldn't write this entirely off as merely folktales coming to life from too much drink or imagination. "I'll ask around and see what I can find."

Killgan clamped him on the shoulder. "Stay safe, Lord Dryston. There are many who would like to hold any demon accountable for the actions of a few. You're safe in the orc lands by my decree. But still, be careful."

Dryston nodded, thankful for the warning. If strange things were afoot, maybe the Hunters' presence in Orc Haven had more to do with that than with him. And he had every intention of getting that information from Onora, one way or another.

## CHAPTER 8
# ONORA

Dryston was back.

Onora whipped her head to the door of her room, trying to shake off the odd feeling.

The odd *knowing.*

Because the knowledge slipped into her mind and nestled next to her heart with a surety that she couldn't reckon with. Her shadows slipped out, twining around, playing with loose strands of her hair, and she batted them away. Standing, she was out the door and down the hall, with her hand poised to knock before she even knew what she was doing.

Before she even knew *why* she was doing it. It was as if some string pulled her to him and trying to fight it felt like madness.

She wasn't going to knock. It was late, and that was insane. Besides, she didn't know that he was back—it was just her shadows playing tricks on her. Her mind playing tricks on her. She should go back to bed. Get some sleep.

Still, her hand stayed poised to knock.

She was being ridiculous. Why was she even here?

Maybe because he was always at the periphery of her awareness, lurking in her mind's eye, waiting to snatch her attention.

Which is exactly why she should leave.

She shook her head, pulling her hand away when the door opened, and she stared in shock as Dryston halted in surprise, standing in the doorway with his head cocked to the side.

Shirtless.

Wrapped only in a towel.

Water dripped down his muscular torso, over his strong pecs, and down his chiseled abs. He crossed his arms, and her eyes snagged on the bulge of his biceps. Great goddess, he was huge.

"To what do I owe the pleasure?" he purred, a smirk hinting at the corners of his mouth.

She scowled, sifting through her mind for any reasonable excuse for why she now stood before him. She fixed him with a steely gaze, crossed her arms and said, "I want my dagger back."

His brows raised. "I'm afraid you relinquished ownership of it when you left it *lodged* in my *shoulder*."

"You had me cornered. I was afraid. You can hardly blame me."

He clicked his tongue. "The great and mighty Onora? I have a hard time believing that."

"Are you going to argue with me about everything?"

He nodded. "Isn't that our 'thing'?"

She drew in a deep breath and he chuckled, shifting to the side so half the doorway was open.

"It's on the nightstand, go ahead and take it."

There it was, beside his bed. But to get to it, she would have to squeeze past him and his bare, glistening abs. Her eyes dipped to them again, and she heard a breathy chuckle come from him. She shot him a glare, and he grinned with a smugness that infuriated her.

Very well, then.

She squared her shoulders and squeezed past, but not before she took her fingertips and softly grazed his lower abdomen. The feeling of his skin on hers sent a jolt up her arm and she fought to keep her face cool and unaffected, the heat from it dipping to her navel and sending her stomach fluttering. Well, fuck, that was supposed to unnerve him, not her.

His cocky smirk gave way immediately to a desperate look of shock. She grabbed the knife and came by again, running the flat end of the blade over his lower belly this time—as a warning. A strangled moan sounded in his throat before he swallowed, and it was her turn to smirk.

"Careful, Lord Dryston, you may just—"

She was stopped as his large hand gripped the back of her head, tangling with her hair and pulling her against him. Their faces were inches apart, and her breath caught in her throat as she blinked up at him, his eyes darkening with a hunger that threatened to consume her.

She feared she may beg him to.

His thumb traced over her mouth, and she shuddered, closing her eyes to recover her senses. The trace of his finger, rough and calloused, against her lips made her mind play out fantasies she would be better off locking away.

He shifted, his breath hitting her ear, and she placed her free hand against his chest, hating how good it felt to be pressed against him, how good it felt to have her skin on his.

"Two can play at this game, Lieutenant," he whispered, voice like gravel.

She drew in a deep breath, her head tingling and dizzy. If he kissed her, she would let him. If he wanted to strip her down, she would beg him to. She felt unanchored, her very being bending and tilting like a willow toward him, aching for more, more, more.

"There you are, Onora," a familiar voice said.

It took a moment for it to register in her mind—the fear in Andrea's voice, the way Dryston was holding her.

But when it did, she shoved him away with a fierceness that shocked even her, and she stumbled back. The emotion flickered across his face so fast she almost missed it—hurt—before it was replaced with that damnable cocky smirk again. Impenetrable, impassable, unbothered. Maybe she'd imagined the other look. Because it had only been a game. Cat and mouse. The lord of demons and the demon hunter.

Nothing more.

She drew in a breath and turned to Andrea, who stood at the landing of the stairs, looking back and forth between them, her dark eyes narrowed and calculating. Finally, they landed on Onora.

"We received a letter from Amherst," Andrea said, holding up a piece of parchment. Onora walked over and scanned it as Andrea continued. "There's an emergency at the border, and he's calling all available Hunters to answer immediately."

"What kind of emergency?" she asked, finding nothing in the letter, hoping there was a second part with more information. Andrea only shook her head.

"We don't know the details, but Brayden sent another letter to Jackson. Some kind of disaster at the farmlands on the border."

"Is there any way I can help?" Dryston asked, and Onora looked back to see his brow furrowed in concern. Genuine concern. Her stomach did that fluttering thing again, and she swallowed hard.

"No," she said. "It wouldn't be good if you showed up in the human lands."

He nodded, pursing his lips. "I can send resources, or other help if need be. Once you know more, don't hesitate to ask. And, Onora? Be careful."

His eyes scanned her with a worry that made her feel lightheaded again.

She nodded, then headed down the stairs, throwing on her gear then meeting the other Hunters in the stable to saddle up their horses. Andrea was next to her, finishing up saddling her horse.

"You and Lord Dryston . . ." she whispered, confusion riddling her features.

"He's very forward." Onora dipped her head to adjust the tack, hiding her expression.

"Was he assaulting you?"

Onora shook her head, horrified. "No. He's just like that. It wasn't anything that . . ." Her voice trailed off at the look of concern on Andrea's face. How was she supposed to explain that she'd started it as a taunt? How could she explain it and not make it look like a thrall? "It's nothing."

"He seemed genuine when he was offering his help," Andrea said. "He seemed genuinely concerned about you."

Andrea said the words with disbelief, the same feeling Onora often had with Dryston.

*"Are you okay?"*

She chased the phantom voice away. She had to focus now. There were more pressing matters at hand.

It was well past midnight when they reached the farmlands, going full speed. Onora's horse, Thunder, was the fastest, and she rode at the helm of the group, Jackson and the others just barely behind her. As they approached, the landscape slowly changed, going from wild, lush plains of golden grass dying at the hint of winter, to blackened earth. Every aching beat of her heart seemed to make it lodge higher and higher in her throat.

"Demons," Avery said, the grit and horror in his voice piercing straight through her.

A demonic attack.

Her inertia seemed to tilt, and nausea almost knocked her off Thunder.

For all she'd claimed that her report of Dryston was from honor and honesty, she had also trusted them to an extent. As much as she could. They hadn't attacked her, they'd even . . . her mind drifted back to that haunting voice that followed her every waking thought.

*"Are you okay?"*

She shook it off, anger mixing with disbelief like bile, sour and burning. Dryston had met with Lord Killgan. It couldn't be him.

Sprawling hills rose before them, dipping and looping back up before disappearing into thick, dark woods. Small homes and barns dotted the landscape, hedgerows keeping the sheep in.

The sheep that now lay dead. She spared only a glance at their bodies, drained and distorted, queasiness roiling anew in her as she pressed on. The grass to the east gave way to blackened earth, a burning, decaying stench hitting her nose with a ferocity that made her gag.

A woman was screaming, sitting in the middle of the field, holding someone in her arms, rocking back and forth.

Onora trotted up, slowing her horse down enough to jump off and land nearby, sprinting to the woman. Her face was covered in soot and dirt, tears streaking down her face. A man lay in her arms, mouth agape, eyes staring up, lifeless, his skin pulling taut against his skull as if he'd been drained of blood.

Onora knelt next to her. "Are you hurt?"

The woman still screamed, the agony raking across Onora's spirit like a knife. She gently placed a hand on her shoulder and the woman's wild eyes finally took her in.

"They came . . . t-they came. And. And." The woman's breaths came in great gulping gasps.

Jackson moved close, followed by the others. The woman's eyes darted to them and their Hunter's clothing, a sob escaping her again.

"Too late. You're too late. They already came. They already killed everyone."

Dread snaked through Onora's stomach. "Who?"

She shook her head, trembling in shock. "I don't . . . I can't remember well . . ."

"It's okay," Jackson said as Avery gently removed the man's body. Jackson took her by the face and made her look at him. "It's okay, we just want to get you somewhere safe and taken care of."

"It's hazy," she said, swallowing hard. "I just remember horns and the sound of wings."

A heavy pit formed in her stomach, pulling endlessly until she thought she might vomit.

She looked around at the soot-blackened earth and the dead animals. If demons caused this, it was not only a sign of war, but it was also a strategic way of cutting off their supplies before a war started.

If this was caused by the demons, then the House of Shadows was coming to destroy the humans again.

THE CANVAS FLAP gave a thud as Onora ducked into the muggy tent. It was lit by a lantern where Amherst stood, looking over a map with his second in command, Terrance. They both looked up as she entered, taking in her soot and bloodstained clothes. It had taken all night; the dawn rising up over the hills and exposing how terrible the destruction was. She'd stayed on the fringes, helping the first few farms bury their loved ones. The life had been drained out of them as if every drop had been pulled out.

Amherst pulled her into a hug as she came close and she leaned into it, too weak and tired to try and hold up a brave front. He would never endure her weakness, but he would comfort her. She breathed in his scent, a cologne he always wore and the leather oil he used to care for his light armor.

She pulled back, and he looked her over, sorrow in his eyes. "How is the cleanup going?"

"Good. We're almost done. I want to investigate the forest and surrounding areas. Whatever magic happened here is like nothing I've ever seen."

"I have Hunters doing that now. I need you for something else."

The tent flap opened again, and Brayden walked in, his face streaked and stained as much as hers. His eyes raked over her in a hungry way that made her skin crawl. There was something about her distress that made him always want her more.

"Perfect timing, Brayden. I have a mission for both of you," Amherst said. "Lord Dryston is clearly behind these attacks, and my sources tell me he's still in Orc Haven. I need you to retrieve him and bring him back to Venatu so we can render justice."

Onora shifted. "Are we certain it's him?"

She couldn't fathom it. He'd seemed so genuinely concerned, confused by the emergency. Not to mention he'd traveled in the opposite direction to meet with Lord Killgan. She'd had plenty of time in the long hours to stew over it, and the pieces weren't adding up.

"If you would rather not arrest Lord Dryston, I understand. You spent a great deal of time with him . . . I've heard whispers that perhaps you're more amenable to him than you've let on," Amherst said, clearing his throat.

She opened her mouth like a fish, too startled to speak at first. "I don't know what you're implying, but my logistical concerns have nothing to do with my dedication to justice. We can't just bring in the Lord of Shadows, retrieving him from lands he is protected in without causing war with the demons and the orcs and elves. I'll arrest Dryston if we can do it without starting an all-out war with the orc clans."

"Lord Dryston." Amherst fixed his gaze on her with scrutiny.

"Yes . . ." She frowned.

"You called him Dryston, as if he were a friend."

She clenched her fist at her side. "Perhaps I think his title gives him a greater honor than he deserves. Now, can we stop focusing on every little word I say and please listen to my very legitimate concerns?"

"He did it, Onora," Brayden said, his tone accusing, cutting. "Do you not believe me?"

She drew in a deep breath to calm herself and pull in the scathing words that begged to burst free from her. "Lord Dryston said he and the other demons were meeting with Lord Killgan. That's the opposite direction from here. I don't understand how he could have done this."

She braced herself for the looks, the accusing.

"He didn't meet with Lord Killgan," Brayden said. "He lied to you."

She frowned, wanting to ask a million questions—but she was too afraid to.

"He headed north, this direction. I followed him and I lost him in the woods, but he wasn't heading to Lord Killgan."

Onora blinked. The moment with him in the hall turned sour, the concern he'd given her suddenly manipulative and calculated. She looked at Amherst who nodded solemnly.

"Others have described a being that looks like Lord Dryston. He will have his trial, Onora, we can guarantee you that justice, but the evidence is damning."

She stood there, every emotion in her rising up like a wave and crashing with violence against her spirit. Could she have been so wrong about him? Was she truly under his thrall?

Amherst placed his hands on her shoulders and gave her a sympathetic look. "I'm sorry. You know I'm only worried. I don't want to put you in a position that would leave you vulnerable to a demon. And one you've spent so much time with already. But you and Brayden are my best, and he is one of the most powerful demons."

She let out a heavy breath, trying to steady the rage building in her. If she wasn't careful, those shadows would come out, showing Amherst that perhaps he did have something to worry about with her, just not what he thought. "I can do it. But we have to be careful. We will have to take him stealthily. We can't go in with force and not expect the orcs to fight back."

Amherst squeezed her shoulder. "Very well, I trust you and Brayden to handle it."

Onora nodded. She would. After seeing what she had that night, after realizing she'd started to believe that Dryston wasn't as terrible as the Cruel Lord . . . she would have her vengeance, and it would be delivered by her own hands.

## CHAPTER 9
# DRYSTON

"We shouldn't tarry here," Kalen said as they walked through the streets of Orc Haven's merchant district.

He was right. They'd secured an alliance with Lord Killgan and now he needed to head home and keep his end of the bargain, sending exports to the clans. There was nothing else keeping him here.

Nothing except a pair of stormy blue eyes that seemed to reach out and twine around him, tethering him in place. He shook his head. That was foolishness. Even if he hadn't been able to get the feeling of her hand on his chest out of his mind. Even if the sharp intake of breath when he pulled her close replayed like a siren's song every minute since he'd heard it. Even if he'd had to fight off fantasies of burying himself deep between her thighs.

Kalen slid him a suspicious glance. "Why haven't we left yet?"

"Because you and Silenus are the best of friends," he said, flashing a grin.

Kalen screwed up his face. The animosity between the two had only ramped up as time went on, and for the life of him, Dryston couldn't figure out why the two males hated one another. It didn't matter, though. It worked to divert Kalen's attention away from why Dryston was actually dragging his feet to leave.

A few more days, that's all he wanted.

Because some part of him needed to at least hear that Onora was safe. That the emergency that had called her away hadn't harmed her. He'd almost taken flight several times, ready to head in the direction she'd left and just see what was happening, but she was more than capable of handling it, and she was right. It wouldn't be good to traipse into the human lands.

They came to the tavern and breathed in the warmth of the fire, taking a seat at the bar and eating the dinner Aife laid out for them. It wasn't long before the doors opened and, like a needlepoint on his senses, Dryston felt the presence.

Her presence.

He turned, expecting to see nothing, when he took in the sight of Onora in her full Hunter's raiment. He stood without thinking, taking two steps toward her before her gaze pinned him in place, full of ire. It hit him like a punch to the gut, and he halted. She kept her steely gaze on him as she walked past, Brayden following behind like a pup, and went up the stairs.

"Damn, Drys, what did you do to her?" Kalen asked.

"I have no clue," he muttered.

DREAMS SHIFTED before Dryston's eyes, dropping away and changing so quickly that it took him longer to realize the sounds he was hearing were actually in the room with him, and not in his hallucinations only. His eyes sprang open, but he didn't move an inch. A breeze came in through the open window and a person along with it. She was soft footed and near silent as a mouse.

She padded across the wooden floor, swift and sure, heading toward him. He lay still, observing, waiting.

What in the darkest pit was Onora doing here?

Standing next to the bed, she looked down, taking intentional, steadying breaths. She was nervous—he could hear it in the staccato beat of her heart and her uneven breaths. Her hand moved, reaching to her thigh and pulling out a knife, the moonlight catching the glint of the blade.

Her hand came up, and he grabbed her wrist, pulling and flipping her onto the bed, straddling her. A muffled groan escaped her as his hand wrapped around her neck, his body pinning her firmly in place. A blond braid fell to the side, and Onora looked up at him with a snarl. His wings loomed out behind him, adding more intimidation than was perhaps necessary, but he didn't miss the way her eyes darted to them, wincing.

"Normally, when a female tries to sneak into my room, I'm in for some fun," he said. "But I have a feeling I won't like what you were planning, will I, Onora?"

In one swift movement, she took a dagger and sliced his stomach. It was a shallow cut, and he had her in a hold in an instant, his arms locking hers at her side, his blood dripping onto her shirt.

He grunted and grimaced in pain. The cut burned, then turned cold as ice as his vision became blurry. "What the fuck, Onora?"

"I know what you did to those people," she growled in his ear. His grip loosened slightly. Dizziness made his vision swim and he couldn't tell up from down. "You'll get what's coming to you."

"I don't know what you're talking about."

"You're a manipulative liar," she spat.

He tried to say more, but his eyes drooped and his arms fell away from her. The last thing he remembered was Onora standing over him, looking at him with betrayal in her eyes.

## CHAPTER 10
# ONORA

Clouds cast shadows on the sides of the mountains that rose on either side of the valley. Thunder whinnied under Onora, the leather of the saddle creaking as she pulled the horse to a stop, and the group behind her followed suit. She glanced back. Dryston hung limply over the pack mule, black hair hanging off the side, arms tied behind him with enchanted shackles digging into his wrists. The poison on the metal made his wrists blister red and ooze. She looked away, stomach twisting.

It had been ages since they'd had any fights with demons. While they trained, the ones that came through were few and far between, and she'd been so busy as a ranger in the elf lands that she hadn't encountered any since Dryston's father had deposed the Cruel Lord.

She'd forgotten how much the poison affected them, how much their bodies rejected it by harming them.

His head swayed, and he looked up, bleary eyes blinking as they searched, stopping as they landed on her with a keen rage.

*"Are you okay?"*

She shook her head and looked forward, that rage in his eyes reflecting the erupting volcano in her. She realized now how much she'd trusted him. Perhaps it had only been survival and necessity on their travels, but she'd trusted him, nonetheless. The images of the burnt farms and dead bodies flashed through her mind, and her hands ached from gripping the reins too tightly.

Dryston would see his justice soon enough.

She signaled, and the group turned off to the side of the road, finding a clearing under trees to set up for the night. Dismounting, she began pulling out supplies to help the others cook. Brayden and two other large men dragged Dryston off the horse, tugging him to a tree. He stumbled with every step, but that didn't stop his gaze from finding hers and leveling her with a look that almost made her demand they untie him and let her fight him right then.

He was angry with *her?*

She wanted to shout at him, hit him, make him feel the pain that whipped across her soul every night as she went to sleep, every morning as she woke. She wanted him to experience all the horrors every human had experienced at the hand of any demon.

Instead, she drew in a breath and turned toward the fire Jin was building. The other Hunters were giving her sly and tentative looks, no doubt clocking that exchange. Had they seen the passion of anger and mistaken it for something else?

Scuffling and struggling made her look back. Brayden had Dryston by the hair, head yanked back, and another Hunter, Leo, slammed his fist against his face.

"Leave him be," Onora barked. "I want him delivered in one piece for the trial."

"He doesn't need a trial," a woman snarled back. "We know what he did. Let's give him the justice he deserves now, no point in delaying it."

Murmurs of agreement rose from the others.

"The next person I see antagonizing the demon," Onora said, voice dangerously low, "will have their hand cut off. We follow the creed. There's no justice without due process, only a cold vengeance. Don't be a fool."

She felt all eyes on her, boring in, examining her every word, her every move. She stood taller, meeting all of their gazes one by one, letting the cold wrath that always coiled inside of her out, altering her face and expression. Each one looked away, startled as she looked at them, going back to whatever they'd been doing.

"If anyone wants to challenge me, feel free to draw your sword and see if you can beat me," she said, her words ringing in the clearing.

There was only one who stood a chance, and he was the only one who held her gaze when she looked at him.

Brayden. His fist still clung to Dryston's hair, his other hand resting on the dagger at his side, a cruel playfulness in his eyes as he calculated what she'd said.

Then he smiled, releasing Dryston so suddenly that the male stumbled to his knees, barely stopping himself from slamming face-first into the dirt.

"Right as always, Onora," Brayden said, then went back to helping the others chain Dryston to the tree.

She settled by the fire, adding water to a pot and helping the others make a quick meal from packets of dried food. When they'd eaten, she made a plate and handed it to Jin.

"Feed Lord Dryston," she commanded.

He stared at her hand, hesitating, then frowning at her with pursed lips. She pushed the plate toward him, raising her brows.

"I'm not trying to disobey, Lieutenant, but I can't stand the thought of helping him," he said, swallowing.

Onora let out a heavy breath and turned, stalking toward Dryston. She'd have to be the only one keeping him alive until they reached Venatu and could give him a trial. She knew how they felt, the horror of helping someone who had done atrocities. But if they didn't follow the creed, if they didn't uphold justice and give a fair trial, then were they any better?

No, they weren't.

She knelt in front of him. Dried blood made a trail down his nose and over his lips, dark rings circling his now dull eyes that tried to blink away a red dryness. The cut she'd given him bled slowly, his healing powers trying to combat the poison. The chains wrapped around his torso three times, poisoned ropes twining over his shackled wrists for good measure.

"They certainly are afraid of you getting loose," she muttered, taking the spoon of food and putting it to his mouth.

He kept it shut, his eyes slicing into her.

"You need to eat."

"Is it poisoned?" he asked, voice rough as gravel before he let out a rasping laugh. "Never mind, you wouldn't let me go so gently."

He took a bite, chewing and swallowing quickly, and she gave him more, until it was gone. Then she pulled out a waterskin and took his chin, tilting it up. The touch felt electric, some charge of magic going between them that left her lightheaded and his breaths coming out heavily. Shadows danced lightly on his shoulders, and his eyes darted to hers.

"You might want to hide that," he rasped out.

Panic tightened around her skull, and she jerked her magic back in, glancing over her shoulder. No one was paying attention, which was a nice break for once.

"Drink," she said, putting the waterskin to his mouth and carefully letting it fall in, giving him several drinks that he gulped down greedily, light returning to his eyes.

She put the stopper back in as he said, "Does that happen often?"

"What?" Although she knew what he had probably seen.

"The shadows caressing you like you're one of their own."

"Why? Does that mean something to you?"

She desperately hoped it did, that he had some answer for her. But she couldn't show him the tattoos, not here or anywhere. He could turn her in—out of spite or in an attempt to save himself.

"I just think it's curious. Usually sinks have to channel the magic of a specific type. This seems so natural to you."

She scoffed, and he clenched his jaw. "More lies?"

"Why would I lie about that? And pray tell, Onora, what have I lied about to you, ever?"

What indeed? It felt like he had, as if he'd betrayed her on a deep, deep level.

"You pretend to want peace and alliances with those of us in Nemus, but then you do this?"

"You take an awful lot of care for someone you believe is guilty."

"The court will decide if you're guilty or not. If, by some miracle, you're acquitted, then my hands will be clean and my honor intact."

"What is it I'm being accused of?" he asked.

She scoffed. "Don't play dumb. You can't manipulate me with your thrall while you have velin in your system."

"I'm not manipulating. I genuinely don't know."

"Oh? Are there too many crimes to choose from that you don't know which one specifically?" She came close to his face, wanting to see a crack in this facade he had. Something to show her she wasn't crazy. Some proof of something, anything. He only stared back, defiant, resolved. She pulled away, letting out a disgusted huff as she stood and walked away.

She needed to get to Venatu quickly. He had an effect on her that made her lose all sense. She wanted to kill him outright. She wanted to leave him tied to the tree, slowly bleeding out.

And part of her wanted him to tell her it wasn't true. That she hadn't been wrong and foolish. That she hadn't let her guard down or been held captive in a thrall. Part of her wanted him to convince her with foolproof evidence that it hadn't been him.

Even though she knew that thought, in and of itself, was foolishness. Dryston was the Lord of Shadows. And he had destroyed those farms as an act of war. He had killed those people as if they were expendable, their lives meaningless. As the demons had done to her family all those years ago. With each passing moment he wasn't in a jail cell in Venatu she came dangerously close to discarding the creed and her morals and taking out justice herself.

She stalked angrily to Thunder, sifting through the saddlebag to find her own packed food as her emotions kicked up like dust in a storm, refusing to settle.

"Hey," Jackson said, coming up beside her. "How are you doing?"

She sighed, pulling out the flatbread wrapped in cloth and taking a bite. "I'm fine."

"Do you think he truly did it?" Jackson's gaze slipped to where Dryston sat against the tree, face contorted in pain.

"There's apparently evidence that he did." She wanted to say a sure *yes*, to tell Jackson that it was obviously demonic work at play and that it was Dryston. But a needling feeling wouldn't leave the pit of her stomach, no matter how hard she tried to shove it down. Jackson stared at the demon lord, deep in thought. "Do you think he didn't?"

Jackson opened his mouth, then closed it again before finally speaking. "It seems out of character. But I don't know him well. Only you do."

Silence fell between them, and that needling feeling became stronger, razor sharp, the point pricking her conscience over and over again.

"Did I ever tell you about when I met Kaemon and Melina?" he asked, lowering his voice so no one could hear.

She stepped closer to him, shaking her head.

"It was when we captured them to bring him in and take her to a temple for purification."

She'd heard about that. They had escaped, killing all the other Hunters except Jackson. Everyone had surmised they'd left him as a witness to tell others how easily they could kill them.

"Kaemon was gentle, and Melina was in her right mind. They insisted it was a thrall, but . . . I just couldn't believe it. She was fully in control of herself, and she loved him dearly." Jackson swallowed, giving her a nervous side glance. There was something he wanted to tell her but wasn't, and she felt the omission like a blow. What would he not trust her with?

Jackson shrugged and stepped away, laughing nervously. "But I don't know Lord Dryston. And he will get a fair trial . . . right?"

Onora nodded. Him getting a fair trial was the only thing holding her fraying emotions together right now. She needed to know that justice would be met. One way or another.

THEY ARRIVED in Venatu the next morning. A few people milled here and there, the early birds up before the others came awake.

Those in the streets stared at the winged male slung over a horse's back, gasping in horror and stepping farther back. Onora led the procession to the guild, the grates opening loudly in the morning silence. Brayden, Jin, and she escorted Dryston to the dungeon, the jailers roughly throwing him into his dark, musty cell. He stumbled against the wall, breathing heavy, his hair matted to his face, clothes ripped and bloody. He slid to the ground, staring up at the ceiling, a calm look of acceptance on his face.

"Make sure he's given food and water," she told the jailer, who looked at Brayden for confirmation. She grabbed him by the jaw, yanking his attention back to her, his eyes going wide in shock as she came close with a snarl on her face. "Obey me, or I will hand out your punishment myself."

"Yes, Lieutenant," he mumbled, and she let him go, following Brayden out.

"You certainly give the demon a great deal of care," he said.

"If I have to repeat my reasons again, Brayden, I'll have to take my anger out on you," she seethed.

Their footsteps echoed in the dungeon and up the steps to the main office of the guild.

"I always like it when you do," he said, letting his voice go lower, his eyes looking her over.

"You won't this time," she said with a growl. Gods, she was tired of this. The trial couldn't come fast enough.

They found Amherst in his office, always up early and looking over the never-ending reports and complaints that came across his desk.

Since demons weren't common in Nemus anymore, Hunters had become a specialty group for any number of issues humans and their allies faced.

He looked up over his glasses at them and then stood swiftly, motioning for them to enter. "I take it you've been successful?"

"Lord Dryston is in the dungeon now. We can get the legal proceedings ready for his trial."

"I already have, he will be held accountable later today."

She blinked, shocked. "So early? Doesn't he need someone to defend him in court? It may take time to find someone willing to."

"He will have a defense. You don't have to worry, Onora. I've been getting this together while you were gone. Everyone is eager to get to the bottom of this and hold him accountable."

She nodded. It was early. So early. Usually, it took several weeks to set up trials to ensure fairness. But perhaps with the scale of this, it had been easier. Amherst came around, checking the healing scratch on her cheek.

"Did he do this to you?"

Onora sighed. It had happened when he tackled her. "Yes, but it's nothing."

"He won't get away with it, none of it," Amherst said, a cool anger in his tone.

Dryston had done it in defense, but she wouldn't say that. She didn't need Amherst giving her that look again. She didn't need Brayden spreading any more rumors about her.

She just needed to get through this trial.

## CHAPTER 11
# DRYSTON

Venatu looked exactly the same as Dryston remembered from the first, and last, time he'd visited. It was all the same: the spires of the castle, the blue and white flag waving over the bailey. Memories haunted him as Onora and Brayden led a host of guards to escort him to the trial. How he'd walked the same cobblestone streets with his parents and the human politicians, laughing and joking, making peace. How those same people had let his whole family be slaughtered in the woods as retribution against the Cruel Lord his own father had deposed.

His guards were stiff, an icy chill from each person piercing through his skin straight to his bones as they wound around, outside the barracks, leading him out of the dungeon toward his trial.

Breathing in, he tried to quell his rising anger, tried to remember what he'd learned from his parents all those years ago, here in this city, his first excursion acting as a diplomat. He'd been desperate to emulate them in every way. He'd seen them expertly handle tense situations, rub elbows with charming nobles, and each night they had answered all his questions and given him tips on diplomacy.

A lot of good that did.

Dryston had never been built for it.

In battle, he was an excellent leader. In politics? Less so. He was angry all the time, too strict, too tightly wound. He couldn't tolerate disrespect, and he hated when people tried to lie and manipulate him. Which was half of politics. He was too straightforward, too brash.

That's why they'd had so few alliances until King Leeth. That's why he'd been so desperate to keep in the Elf King's good graces. He wanted to build alliances with the humans, but that felt like a distant hope now.

The realization hit him in the stomach. He thought of his niece and how he had two sisters-in-law now. How his family was growing.

What if he wasn't around to see it?

What if this launched them into a bloody war that affected his loved ones?

He would have to keep his wits about him and make sure that he didn't piss the humans off further. Perhaps he could reason with them. Convince them to do the trial with the orcs, who were neutral. At the very least, he had to keep his family and his realm out of all of this, whatever it was.

They entered a stately building and climbed the marble steps that led up to a porch with tall white columns and carvings of humans, Hunters, and gods. They came into the foyer and more guards surrounded him, creating a veritable wall between him and the people here to watch his trial.

"This all seems a bit overkill, don't you think?" he asked, dipping his head to all the surrounding guards. Onora slid him an icy glare.

"We know demons are not to be underestimated."

"I would come freely to my trial, Onora," he said, his voice going soft, pleading. "I know I'm innocent."

Her jaw tensed as she gave him a long, questioning side glance. She shook her head and continued walking.

They wound through dark gray halls with light bouncing off them, lending a sterile atmosphere. They finally came to a large courtroom, the benches lined with humans, so many of them, all looking at him with hate in their eyes. A man he recognized as the chief of the Hunters sat in the middle, flanked by three humans on each side, all wearing white and blue robes, ready to decide his fate.

Onora led him to the middle of the room, to a dais facing Amherst.

"Lord Dryston," the chief said.

"Chief Hunter," Dryston said, bowing reverently. "It's a pleasure to finally meet you, though I would prefer it to be under other circumstances."

"I would as well," Amherst said, a bite in his tone. "But it seems there's no point in hoping for anything better from demons."

Murmurs of agreement rose, and Dryston stiffened his shoulders.

"How do you plead?"

Dryston frowned. "I do not know what case is being brought against me. But in my own estimation, I'm not guilty of anything warranting a trial."

"While I doubt you don't know why you're here, let's hear from the witness."

The chief gestured, and a young woman walked forward. She wore plain clothes and an apron, like that of a farmer or working hand. She looked nervously at Dryston before taking a seat next to the chief.

"This is Marigold Sumner," the chief said. "She is the daughter of the late Holden, a farmer in this community. Marigold, tell us what you saw."

Marigold swallowed, wringing her hands. "It happened not that long ago. I woke to screamin', yer honor. It was the middle of the night. I ran outside to see the farm was ablaze. Full of black shadows, licking like flames, bursting like lightning, consuming the whole farm. My pa tried to stop it, but the water was no use against it. He . . ."

Marigold's lip trembled, and she looked down, her face contorting in pain.

"Take your time," Amherst said.

She swallowed and took a deep breath. "He died, along with my mother and brothers, trying to stop it from consuming the land. But it took it all, including the house."

"How did you escape?"

"I ran, yer honor. Into the woods. And that's when . . ."

Her face went pale, and she looked at Dryston, then down at her lap again. Dryston frowned, shifting uncomfortably on his feet.

"What is it, Marigold? You won't be judged."

She spoke, each word trembling. "That's when I encountered a demon, yer honor."

"And what did this demon do?"

Marigold covered her face with her hands, drawing in deep breaths. "He put me under his thrall and . . . I'm so ashamed, my lord."

"There's nothing to be ashamed of. You can't control yourself under a thrall."

Dryston glanced at Onora, his jaw clenching. They couldn't be serious, could they?

"He made me his own. And I'm . . . I'm with his child."

"And who was this demon?"

Marigold looked at the chief, then to Dryston, her hand flinging up and her finger pointing directly to him. "That's him. That's the demon right there."

The observers in the room erupted in a cacophony of indignation and anger. People shot to their feet, rushing to the center, stopped only by the Hunters holding them back from getting to Dryston. A shoe hit his head, and he whipped around to see more poised to be thrown.

"Silence!" Amherst shouted and the room slowly quieted again, though the hostile energy still thickened the air.

Dryston quelled his anger as best he could, trying desperately to hold it all in and keep himself together.

"That's not true," Dryston said, his voice echoing.

"Why would she lie?" the chief asked.

Dryston shook his head. "I'm not saying she's lying, per se. Maybe she's only mistaken. I did no such thing. I was meeting with Lord Killgan during that time, nowhere near the human lands. And how would you know you're pregnant in a few days?"

"A demon baby grows quicker," Marigold said, defensive.

"Not that much quicker. It's not adding up," Dryston said. "Regardless, if a demon did this, I will work with you to find justice."

Amherst removed his glasses and rubbed his forehead. "It's not just this. We've had reports for months of women going missing, or turning up pregnant, all claiming demons. All matching your description."

"I think we can find justice here and now!" someone shouted from behind him.

The chief rubbed his eyes, then looked at Onora. "Onora, you've spent time with Lord Dryston."

The room went silent, tension building in the air, and Onora shifted on her feet. "I have, Chief."

"What is your reading of his character?"

She glanced at him, their eyes meeting for a brief moment that seemed to span an eternity, his heart pounding in his ears as she took him in, assessing. She looked back at the chief, her face a wall of stone.

"I saw no great evil in him, though I'm sure he's capable of it."

Dryston scoffed, his anger getting the better of him. She shot him a warning glance. "A glowing recommendation."

"Am I wrong?"

"Every living being is capable of great evil, but I have never and will never participate in it."

"Enough!" Amherst said. "We have an eyewitness, with no reason to lie. That's more than enough for us to decide."

"Talk to Lord Killgan, I was with him, in the opposite direction of these attacks," Dryston said, trying, and failing, to keep the bite out.

Amherst scoffed. "Why? So we can delay for days, weeks, maybe a month to pin him down and get his testimony? Giving you and the demons time to attack us? No, your reign of terror ends now. Besides, we know that you didn't meet with Lord Killgan. Lieutenant Brayden followed you. Stop spinning your web of deceit."

Dryston's stomach plummeted. Only one witness. That's all it took to convict him. The jurors next to the chief all came together and whispered. He sharpened his hearing.

*Fuck.*

They were only pretending to deliberate. They all found him guilty already.

*Fuck.*

"Onora," he whispered. "I didn't do this."

She kept her gaze forward, nostrils flaring. "You're a liar."

Anger consumed him, and small tendrils of smoky shadows wrapped around his wrist. Someone cried out and suddenly something large knocked into him and he fell back, slamming into the stone floor. Men were on top of him, holding him down.

"Lord Dryston, you're convicted of rape and murder, destruction of property, and violating the treaty signed by your father. You will be sentenced to death, to be taken out by one of our select Hunters in a few days' time."

He stared at the raging face atop him, a man with eyes full of bloodlust. He glanced at the others, finding a similar hatred burning in their eyes.

He had no allies here. He had no one to help.

Onora stepped forward. "Chief, allow me to kill him."

Dryston drew in a breath, swallowing as his mind scrambled to make sense of what was happening to him. Surely, he'd heard that wrong. But she looked back at him, a cold rage in her eyes that chilled his blood even more.

"I want to be the one to end his life."

# CHAPTER 12
# ONORA

Onora stared into the mirror, her stomach in knots. Today was the day she'd been waiting for all these years. She would take down the demon lord and be a step closer to toppling the entire House of Shadows.

So why had she woken up so anxious she'd vomited? Her skin seemed to stretch against her muscles tightly and her heart wouldn't stop pounding. She gritted her teeth and splashed cold water on her face. She would get over this and then kill Dryston—make him pay for his horrible crimes.

She grabbed her ax and donned her dusty blue cape, tightening the clasp around her neck and letting it flow behind her. The color had always filled her with pride, a symbol of hope and resilience, of her skill and honor.

Her stomach only turned again as memories of Dryston flashed behind her eyes. Every moment with him came forth, and she turned it over, looking for any clues, any imperfection in the prism that had captivated and fooled her.

She came up with nothing.

Which was even more infuriating. The witness yesterday was

confident in what she said. She'd been shaking in fear. She'd recognized Dryston.

Her stomach turned again, and her anger reignited.

She walked down the hall to the prison cells. So many people were here, ready to see this, ready for retribution against the demons.

Dryston sat against the stone wall when she arrived. Head hung low, his hair falling in soft waves about his face. He looked up, a cold resignation mixed bitterly with anger.

They opened the cell door, and she grabbed his chains. "Come along easily and I'll make this quick."

He stood slowly, looking down at her with a mixture of betrayal and pleading. He was insane if he thought that she would let him get away with what he'd done. She yanked on his chains, making him stumble a step, and his face came down close to hers.

"You'll get what you deserve, bat, and it will be by my hands."

He leaned forward more, his lips by her ears. "You will regret this until the day you die, Onora."

The words tumbled out like a threat, as if he would exact some form of vengeance on her from beyond the grave. How could she regret it? This would be the fulfillment of her vow to herself, the beginning of the end of what she'd been training for since that night all those years ago.

She led him down the halls, out into the courtyard. People lined the sides, Hunters circling the middle where she would kill him. The crowd shouted and cried out, yelling profanities and threats at him as they came to the center.

Brayden hit him on the back of the knees, making him sprawl forward, catching on Brayden as he fell, and the Hunter gave him another kick for good measure. Her heart thumped in her ears, but her rage screamed louder, and she gripped the hilt of the ax.

"Any last words?" she asked.

He gazed at her for a long moment, unnerving, unyielding. Then he shook his head, defeated.

She stepped forward, raising the ax high. Brayden grabbed him by the hair, yanking his head back to expose his neck, and Dryston swayed into the man, nostrils flaring.

She readied herself for the blow and his eyes rose to meet hers, piercing through black hair, filled with a cold, cold rage.

Onora steeled herself against the wave of emotions that crashed into her. She needed to know that this feverish, aching want was just the thrall—and that she could overcome it. She hesitated, his verdant gaze penetrating into her soul and, like a song, it twined its shadows and sang, "this is wrong."

Like crashing into icy water, that memory hit her again:

*"Are you okay?"*

She hesitated only a moment, just long enough to see a shift in his attention and long enough for him to move. A shackle fell off his right hand, and that hand reached up, grabbing her left and slapping the shackle onto her. In seconds, the world was pure darkness. She couldn't see or hear anything, except Dryston's careful breaths next to her ear, the feeling of him wrapping his hand around her throat and holding her against him.

"How the fuck are you doing this?" she gasped out.

But it didn't matter. She tried to yank free, but his grasp tightened, and she expelled a hard breath as he clamped her lungs. She knocked her elbow into his ribs, and he grunted, his hands loosening for a second as she brought her head back, hitting his nose with a loud crack.

Shouts rose up outside the darkness, calling for Hunters to jump in and save her, but no one did. They were too scared. Before she could move, before she could say or do a thing, his arms braced around her again, harder this time, and her feet lifted off the ground as they moved upward, flying in the air with the beat of his wings. She screamed as the darkness followed, the world around her black as night.

"Let me go!" she growled.

"If I did that, you'd die," Dryston said. "And while I have half a mind to return the favor, I need you for now."

"How are you using your powers?"

He shouldn't have been able to with the shackles on his wrists. Even though he removed one, the other should have left him weakened.

"I have no idea, but I thank the twin goddesses that I can. And I think you will too, when you realize I'm not lying."

"Innocent men don't need to flee."

"How simple your life must be to live in a world that requires so little nuance."

She struggled against him as the darkness fell away, disappearing like smoke in the breeze. The earth spanned out, leagues and leagues beneath her, fields and rivers and forests. She screamed again, but his arm tightened around her, his other grabbing below her legs. She was too terrified to do anything but cling to him, her mind reeling from the height, terror gripping her.

When she adjusted, her wits coming back to her, she let go of his shirt, looking pointedly away. Fighting was no use. She would die if he dropped her now. Or, because she was still chained to him, she would dangle, her shoulder dislocated, bruises and harm befalling her.

"I'm going to fucking kill you," she growled.

"Yes, you've made that abundantly clear. So far, no dice, though."

She whipped her head to look at him and his gaze found her again, fixed on her with the fire of a thousand suns. The anger felt like a physical blow, and she blinked, her body tightening anxiously from simply a look.

"I didn't do what I was accused of, Onora. Did those months of traveling together mean nothing to you? Did I not show an ounce of my character during that time?"

She drew in a deep breath, her own anger rising. "You certainly presented your character one way. Now I know it's different."

"How so? Based on one eyewitness, who was so grief-stricken and crazed that she's reliable? Is that more real than the time I saved you?"

She brought a dagger up to his throat. His eyes shot up in surprise and she smirked. "If I have to tell you one more time that you didn't save me, I will kill you right here and plummet to my death to defend my honor."

He ground his teeth, jaw flexing. "You might actually be insane."

They flew over the woods and finally dipped down below the tree line. Her heart pounded loud in her ears with anticipation as his feet hit the ground, his strong arms carefully letting her stand. He made no move to harm her as he looked at his surroundings. In complete control. Unafraid.

She gripped the hilt of her dagger holstered next to her hip. He was paying little attention to her, clearly not seeing her as a threat. All the better. She'd never needed others to accept her prowess or see her as dangerous. She'd learned long ago that the more an opponent underestimated her, the better the outcome for her.

He was only wearing trousers and a tunic, his boots having been abandoned in his room at the inn. His clothes hung tattered and dirty, but his muscles showed through the holes, and she hesitated for a moment.

It had been ages since she'd gone head-to-head with a demon. He had a solid eight inches on her and she was tall by human standards. His shoulders spanned a ridiculous width, his biceps easily twice the size of hers. If she wasn't careful, even without his magic, he could harm her easily.

She unsheathed the dagger, quiet and swift, as she took a step toward him.

His head whipped to her, eyes filled with a wrath that made every one of her instincts light up in danger. She thrusted the dagger but missed as he dodged, sliding it into his shoulder. He grunted, clamping his mouth shut to mute the noise, and grabbed her arm, throwing her against the tree.

Her ribs popped and she let out a yelp, loud enough she hoped it carried to any Hunters looking for them. Bringing her knee up, she slammed into his crotch. She didn't hit where she needed and while he winced in pain, it wasn't enough to keep him from cracking his forehead against hers.

Pain radiated across her skull as they stumbled away from one another, swaying and dizzy. But he missed a step, falling back and the chain yanked, pulling her off her feet, and she slammed into him, hitting the ground in a loud crash, sticks and stones scraping her face. He moved to get up, but she swept at his leg, making him fall back with a groan before flipping over and on top of her.

"Onora, I swear to the gods if you don't—"

She yanked the dagger out of his shoulder and rammed it into his stomach. Shock rippled over his features as she wrapped her legs around him and twisted, flipping him over so she was on top now. She pulled the blade out and brought it to his throat, letting it slice enough that a bead of blood bubbled onto the sharp metal.

He grabbed her wrist, twisting, and she cried out as agony rippled up her arm. He had her flipped over again, his legs holding hers in place, his hands gripping her wrists so hard they ached.

Blood from his wounds dripped on her, but even the one on his shoulder was already healing.

Godsdamnit. She needed more velin. The earlier doses were already wearing off. She wouldn't be able to make any headway without it.

She rammed her forehead to his nose, the satisfying *SMACK* making her grin. His face contorted into rage, and panic hit her at the same moment his hand gripped her neck, slamming her into the ground with a force that made her gasp, her eyes watering. Against her will, her body shook as scenes and visions danced behind her eyes of all the times Varek did something similar, of all the times she'd seen a human neck snapped as if it were nothing.

His grip loosened, a wary—but worried—look coming over his face.

"I'm not interested in harming you," Dryston growled, his face dangerously close to hers, his hot breath hitting her skin. "But I will if I have to. Play nice, and when we get these shackles off, I'll let you go."

She barely processed his words as her whole body became rigid, her breathing labored. She couldn't move, she couldn't do anything, and if he decided, in a split second, she'd be dead.

It would all be over. This was how she met her end. How she'd always feared.

Chained and under a demon, at his mercy and finding none.

"If I let you go, you won't try to kill me?" he asked.

She didn't respond. She couldn't respond. Her mind was flooded with terror, and her body was about to start shaking again from the horror of it. This had happened only a few times before. Usually, her response was only to fight. On the rare occasion that it was clear she wouldn't win, her body took over and froze.

He removed his hand, keeping it close, looking her over as she shuddered and she closed her eyes, hating the pity, hating the concern. What in the darkest pit did he have to be concerned about her? What about all the innocents he'd killed? What about the woman who had testified against him?

She managed the slightest of nods and he stood, staring at her warily. She rubbed her neck and stood shakily, embarrassed by how terrified her body had been, how every inch of her felt tense and worn out from the encounter. His eyes dipped to her neck, something like shame replacing his rage, and he hastily looked away.

She pressed against her skin and knew that bruises were already visible there.

He gestured forward. "Let's go west."

## CHAPTER 13

# DRYSTON

They traveled for hours, Onora in front and Dryston following behind. Dizziness buzzed in his head like a bee, but he shook it off and kept walking. He'd had barely enough food and water the last few days, and with the poison and lack of sleep, he wasn't sure how he was still walking.

He supposed it was fear. Though he couldn't properly feel it. No, it felt instead like this deep, dark cavern that echoed beneath the raging sounds of his anger, which was the only thing he could truly feel at the moment.

Anger at himself for getting caught again. Anger for even hoping the humans might give him a fair trial and hoping they'd want to one day have an alliance. Anger that Onora had not only had a hand in it all, but also that she so readily wanted to be the one to kill him.

And finally, anger that he very well could, and probably would, die soon. He hadn't given up, evidenced by the fact that he still walked ahead of her, trying desperately to find where exactly they were in the woods and how far they would be from Orc Haven, but he knew the odds weren't looking good.

He could still feel Onora's neck in his hands, how small and fragile she was. He could still taste her fear that had soured the air.

For all he knew and had experienced, he hadn't expected that much fear from her. He also hadn't expected her to attack him so viciously. His shoulder and stomach still ached from the stab wounds, even if they were healing fast.

He drew in a steadying breath to calm himself enough to think. He'd done very little canvassing of the woods in his time in Orc Haven. But he could tell from the sun what direction was west and he, at the very least, knew that was the best direction to go. If they were lucky, they'd cross the river and not be too far from Silenus, who would help.

The day wore on and they slowly made progress, stopping at creeks to drink, grabbing fruits and nuts along the way. She gave him a handful of red berries he didn't recognize, and he looked at them skeptically.

"What are these?" he asked.

"Raider berries," she said.

"I've never heard of them."

"They're native to this area and not particularly fun to eat because of the tartness, so that's not surprising."

He handed them back to her. "You eat them first."

She gave him a dull look. "Are you serious?"

He nodded, staring at her, waiting.

She popped them in her mouth, exaggerating her chewing, swallowing, then pulling back her gums and shooting out her tongue to show him that they were gone. He hesitated a moment, wondering if it was a ploy, but her teeth and tongue were stained red and there truly was no sign of her being poisoned.

He ate them, harvesting more along with her as they both greedily ate. His stomach still rumbled, starving, but this would have to do for now.

The forest was overgrown, a thicket of thorns and bushes making his steps stumble. His foot caught on a root and he launched forward, yanking on the chain by accident, tugging Onora back, slamming her into a tree. She shot him a glare, and he shrugged.

She drew in a deep breath and followed him, lithe over the rough terrain in a way that showed how much time she'd spent in the wilderness. He paid attention to the chain, keeping it slack and not letting it swing too much, but otherwise, he was lost in his thoughts and focusing on the trail ahead of him.

What in the darkest pit was he going to do about her?

He didn't want to kill her. He told himself it was for many very impersonal reasons. First being for alliances. He didn't think any hope remained with the humans now, but he didn't want to harm his chances with the orcs or anyone else. Second being that while he was often angry, he wasn't violent. He had killed when necessary, and he'd do it again, but it was an odious thing.

He ignored the voice in his head that kept reminding him of that moment, months ago, when he lay almost dead before the witch, Hevena. When Onora showed up and helped him, saving his life. She'd said they were even, but she'd torn a piece of her cloak and bandaged his largest wound, knowing that he had swift healing and wouldn't need it.

It had been a precaution to ensure he lived, in case there was anything she hadn't accounted for in his healing.

It was a sign of care that he'd been unable to shake from his memory.

He knew it was her honor that she had cared for her natural enemy, for a being she'd trained her whole life to fight and destroy. A being she had been taught to hate.

Yet he remembered, as his mind fluttered in and out of consciousness, how she'd knelt and wrapped the cloth around his wound, telling him not to die.

He shook his head, trying to shake the memory off as he hiked through the forest. Perhaps he couldn't quite shake that hope. Perhaps he didn't want to.

The morning slipped away into the afternoon and his stomach

rumbled angrily at him, deep pants he couldn't stave off with berries alone. He wished he knew where they were, but he'd landed in a hurry. He knew they'd have Hunters on his tail, and he couldn't fly fast enough while holding Onora to get out of range of their arrows.

How long until they canvassed the forest? How long until they found them? He reached deep within himself, tugging and pulling at the magic that had always felt so easy and constant before. Not now. Not with these shackles on and the velin still in his system. It felt like poking someone dead asleep, unable to wake it, only rouse it.

Yet he'd been able to when he'd flown away. Shadows had engulfed them, his panic enough to snap it awake. Somehow, he was able to tap into his abilities still, but minimally.

The chain between them shifted slightly, just so slightly. He turned to see what was happening when he was met with the edge of a dagger coming straight for his face. He narrowly dodged it, the knife's edge grazing his cheek, blood bubbling up and sliding down his face as Onora stumbled forward, past him, and then caught her balance.

She stared at him, angry, nostrils flaring, eyes narrowed, ready to fight.

Again.

"Gods-fucking-damnit," he spit out as she lunged at him again.

He blocked the hit, the cut grazing his arm this time, the pain radiating up his shoulder. He twisted, grabbing her wrist, and slamming her against a tree. She grunted, bringing her knee up and hitting him square in the groin. Pain lanced through him, weakening his grip and making his vision blur just enough that she slipped out, thrusting the dagger at him again. He hooked his leg and swept it under her, making her fall back with a cry, and then he was on top of her. He grabbed the dagger, sticking it in his trousers with the other one, and held her down by her wrists.

She glared up at him. "Fine then, kill me."

He raised a brow. "I have no interest in that. But if you don't behave, I will find a way to tie you up."

Snarling, she said, "As if you wouldn't enjoy that."

"Oh, you'd love it more than me, darling. You'd be begging for more."

She scoffed, turning her head away. He stood and gestured for her to go in front.

"You'll lead the way from now on," he said.

She'd just tried to kill him.

Again.

For the third time.

If he could just make it out of this forest alive, he'd count himself blessed by the gods.

# CHAPTER 14
# ONORA

The raider berries hadn't set in yet. She wiped the blood off her mouth from their tussle and led the way. The attack from behind hadn't done her any good. Her body ached with every movement now—her fatigue and her bruises combining in a horrible cocktail of pain.

The attack wasn't her most strategic decision, but she'd been desperate. He'd been eating raider berries all day. Normally, demons and many other magical sources didn't have any issues with them. Because their magic healed them so fast. With velin in the system, it should have slowed him down, making him tired and eventually putting him to sleep.

He had used his magic before, though. Something was amiss—she just needed to keep feeding them to him. She had to be a lot smarter. He could kill her so easily, even without his magic. She couldn't risk pissing him off.

Why he was keeping her alive, she wasn't sure. Maybe as a bargaining chip in case the Hunters caught up? A hostage to hold against his body and take the arrows for him?

She had to be nice, compliant. Gain his trust and then use it against him.

And she needed to find the key to the shackles. She'd been looking him over, trying to find where he kept it. She came up with only a few spots it could be, and all would be incredibly hard to pickpocket.

She stepped on a fallen branch as she led the way, cracking it as she'd been doing periodically, stealthily enough that she hoped he didn't notice. If any Hunters were on their trail, then they would see it and know she was leaving the tracks. Any mark she could make would only help her in the long run.

It had been too long since she'd been in this forest, and she hadn't spent too much time here. Still, she had a decent idea of where they were based on old maps. She'd heard the ocean waves of the southern coast and seen the water when they were flying. She'd been so dizzy and focusing on the tilting of her stomach in flight that she'd unfortunately not gotten as much information as she wanted about where they landed, but she knew they were closer to the shore than not.

If Hunters were looking for them, and didn't know where they had dropped down, then it would be most likely that they would start on the northern side of the forest. She needed to lead him that way.

She suddenly was glad for all the time she'd spent in the wilderness. For all the things throwing her off right now, that wasn't one of them. Her feet felt sure as she traversed the branches and brambles, having to slow her pace for Dryston, who was clearly not as accustomed to this way of life.

She wondered what he was accustomed to. She'd heard plenty enough stories of The Darkened City and their debauchery. The moon rites and orgies, the bloodlust and torture they loved.

Yet . . .

She tried to shove the thought away. The image of demons she'd had for so long had been effectively shattered from her time with Dryston, Enid, and Kaemon. They didn't feel so different from her. They'd even been kind, if arrogant—Dryston—and she was having a hard time reconciling all her experiences, all the things she'd been taught, all the ideas she'd had, into one cohesive picture.

Dryston had done the attack on the farm. He'd decimated innocent people's lives as an act of war. Like the Cruel Lord before him.

She could still picture her family home, the farm where she'd grown up. The chickens would run about the house all day, cozying up in their coop at night. Her mother had a garden she tended, always full of moonflowers that she said helped the veggies grow better. Onora would often take her little brother, strapping him in a carrier on her back and go for walks in the woods, showing him the plants. He couldn't understand her, but his laughs and giggles and cooing babbles had made her keep talking, even if it meant nothing.

Jackson used to bring her family bread that his parents baked and traded for other goods. They'd take it to the beach and eat it on hot days, dipping their feet in the water, collecting shells and weaving bracelets for one another.

Her chest tightened, aching like a fresh wound. All of that had been robbed from her in one night. In one swift moment.

And Dryston had done the same to someone else. To that woman she'd found at the farm, crying over her loved one's emaciated corpse. She clenched and unclenched her fists. She could try to kill him again, make it work this time.

She took in a steadying breath, focusing on the trail in front of her. She had to be compliant, gain his trust.

It was the only way she made it out of this alive.

And it was the only way she could ensure she would be able to kill him—giving him the justice he deserved.

## CHAPTER 15
# DRYSTON

They came to a small stream, stopping to take big, gulping drinks. The water slid down Dryston's throat, ice cold, pricking and slicing at his hollow stomach, unsettling it as it growled again. Trout swam in the stream like his head swam from hunger.

Onora stood and pulled the chain, but he held firm, making her stop.

"Give me a moment," he said, eyes focused on the fish. He hadn't done this since he was a child, messing around with Kaemon and Enid in the streams that fed out of The Darkened City, but he was too desperate not to try.

He heard rumbling from Onora's stomach and knew that while she had most likely been eating better than him the last few days, she had to be getting weaker, too.

The trout moved against the current, content to make no progress and instead flap their fins and grab whatever bugs fell down the stream and into their mouths. It was harder to see them from the rippling water, but he could make out enough. The occasional flash of rainbow in the filtered sunlight let him know they were there. Poising his free hand up, he stepped into the icy cold water, waiting, waiting . . . Then he plunged his arm down, clamping around the slimy fish and pulled up, quickly securing it with his other hand.

Standing, he turned to Onora. She regarded him with a look of surprise and—dare he say it—approval. But she quickly schooled her face with ennui. He held the fish out to her, and she pulled up the edge of her shirt, grabbing the fish with it so it wouldn't slip away as it flopped desperately.

"One more," he said, and focused again. It went quicker the second time around and he pulled a larger fish out, gripping it firmly, his mouth watering as his stomach growled again. It opened its mouth and closed it, gasping for water that wouldn't come.

They sat by a tree and Dryston looked down at the fish, wondering how he would get to the meat without just biting into it like a wild animal. He was about to, when Onora nudged his leg with her foot and held out a small carving knife. He frowned at her and she shrugged. Why was he not shocked she had another blade on her? Thankfully, this one was small and not sharp enough or big enough to cause a fatal wound without him noticing first and stopping her.

He cut the fish open and removed the innards that they couldn't eat uncooked. Then they both laid into it hungrily. The raw fishy taste had never been something he was either opposed to or drawn to, but in that moment it tasted like sheer bliss. He could almost weep from the clarity that returned to his mind with each bite. He cleaned it of any meat and edible parts, careful not to take the fine bones and swallow them. Then they washed their hands in the stream.

Onora gave him a sideways look and an almost imperceptible nod of thanks. He would take it, take anything from her at the moment. He wasn't delusional enough to think it meant she wasn't currently plotting his demise, but maybe it was a step in the right direction.

He gripped the knife in his hand, debating, knowing it was foolish to give it back to her. But she'd given it to him freely, letting him know she had it, and in this moment there was some small semblance of camaraderie.

She shook her head. "Keep it. For the next fish we catch."

He tucked it away in his pocket, shocked at how easily she was complying. How easily she had been complying since their last fight. Maybe her mind was changing—unlikely. Most likely, she'd come to some realization that they needed to work together for the moment.

They continued on, Onora picking up raider berries and handing them back to him, her mostly lithe, though her feet sometimes stumbled, cracking limbs or brambles, and he instinctively held an arm to steady her, pulling back before she could see. Not only did he think she would hate his offer of help, but he hated that he still had that instinct with her.

It was something he had for most people. Born from not only being the oldest sibling and trained from a young age to be heir to the throne of The Darkened City, but also from taking over as leader and parent when he was only nineteen. He often wondered what he would be like if all that responsibility hadn't been thrust on him so young, before he knew who he was or what he wanted. He'd been the only thread holding Enid together, his colony together, and his realm together.

The weight of it still bore down on him. Kalen desperately wanted him to find a mate to help ease the burden. The Lord of Shadows's mate always bore an equivalent title—lady or lord of shadows—and while their roles would be a bit different, it was equal in the honor and the trammel.

Dryston also wanted to find his mate, for many reasons beyond that. Seeing Enid and Kaemon with theirs filled him with an aching void, a loneliness he couldn't assuage with the lovers he took. Yet, he'd never found one. The moon rites, which were close upcoming, were a time for people to meet with other clans and colonies in hopes of a mate bond presenting itself.

Yet it never had for him, and he was growing weary of trying.

Now, he wasn't sure if he would have to again. He was no fool. His odds of coming out of this unscathed were small. If he could only get word to Silenus, or another ally, letting them know that he didn't want the demons to retaliate, he would consider it a good ending.

He couldn't have his people flung into another war. He couldn't have their shaky reputations further tarnished.

Onora halted, throwing her hand up, and then crept to the side. He followed silently behind her, sending out his hearing.

Humans were talking.

He hunkered in closer to her by the side of the tree, looking around. She looked up at him, annoyed, but said nothing about his proximity. He listened carefully. They were Hunters which was shit luck for them.

"Can't find the tracks," one of them said.

"We've been canvassing the whole area, and nothing," another said.

"Can you hear them?" she whispered.

He looked down, her eyes rising to meet his and catching, stilling as the world seemed to fall away from him. Her proximity was like a drug, filling his lungs and making his head empty.

"Well?" she asked, frowning, and he came to again.

"Yes," he whispered back, focusing.

"We saw him dip into the woods here," one said.

"They can't have moved that quickly to be out of the forest. Send a raven asking for extra Hunters to cover more ground."

It was silent for a beat and Onora said, "What are they saying? Is it Hunters?"

The men began speaking again, but Dryston only heard the last part. ". . . he said to kill her, too."

Onora screamed.

The sound made him stumble back, grasping his ear as she screamed at the top of her lungs, then started yelling for help. It took him a moment to realize what was happening. That she wasn't hurt or in danger, but that she was crying out for the Hunters to help her get away from him.

He jumped on her, tackling her to the ground and clamping a hand over her mouth, the other wrapping around her torso. She struggled, kicking and trying to bite him, but he pressed her harder against him, locking his legs around hers. She bucked and wiggled but couldn't get free; her screaming was muffled to almost nothing from his hand.

He sent out his hearing again.

"Was that her?"

"What's he doing to her?"

Dryston knew he didn't have time to formulate any real plan. So instead he stood, having to let her loose for a minute, enduring her bloodcurdling scream, then he swung the chain around, pinning her arm and wrapping it around her neck. She gurgled, her eyes going wide in shock as he tugged her against him, then threw her over his shoulder, keeping the chain tight enough that her scream was reduced to nothing but a faint, pained noise but loose enough to not cause harm.

Then he ran.

# CHAPTER 16
# ONORA

The cool iron bit into her neck and her screams died, turning to grunts and moans as each jolting stride yanked on her shoulder socket and pressed around her neck. She didn't know how long they'd been running, but she could feel the skin bruising, and her arms were pinned against him, her legs held by his arm so tightly she couldn't move.

Consciousness threatened to leave her, but she blinked, trying desperately to stay awake and mark her surroundings. When they finally stopped, he pinned her against a tree, his hand clamping on her mouth. The light was dim, twilight hedging the world in, but she could see the wild panic in his eyes. A panic so normal and feral that he looked like nothing more than a deer caught in a trap.

"If I remove my hand, will you stop screaming? One noise too loud and I'll snap your neck."

He was far too strong to fight and leave. She needed to be clever about this and get the key for the shackles from him. She didn't know why he hadn't killed her yet, but she felt it coming. There was only so long he'd put up with this behavior, and only so long she'd feel safe being with him.

It had to be tonight.

So she nodded her head, and his hand slowly fell away as he unwrapped the chains and let them fall between them. His chest rose and fell heavily, exhaustion sagging on his body, his wings tucked in, less bold and daring than she'd ever seen them.

There were berries nearby and pinecones that they washed in the stream and ate in silence. Her mind buzzed, looking for any opening, any opportunity. But he kept his distance, his eyes watchful, his movements careful. She tried to spy where it could be hidden. His clothes were simple, meant to be slept in only, so there were only the shallow trouser pockets. Could that be it?

He leaned against the tree, looking up at the sky. "Go to sleep. I'll keep watch."

*Fuck.*

He was too far away, so she moved closer, shrugging as he gave a raised brow.

"You're keeping watch, so closer is safer," she said.

He said nothing—he just looked around, focusing and letting her lie down.

She eased her breathing and kept her eyes on him stealthily in the dark. He was trying to stay awake, but exhaustion was evident with every breath in and out. If he would only go to sleep, she could get it off him.

She closed her eyes, listening intently around her, waiting for a change in his breath, or for him to lie beside her. Time passed slowly, every hitch of her breath feeling like a rock falling on cobblestone, and she thought surely he'd know what she was up to.

Then she heard it.

The change in his breath. The slowing down of sleep.

She moved closer, swallowing and praying that he didn't wake or hear her. But nothing. He was out cold.

Drawing in a deep breath, she reminded herself that she'd done this many times before and, while rusty, surely she could still pickpocket effectively. She reached first in his right pocket, slow and careful. He shifted, but didn't wake, and she held her breath in harder.

Moving her hand, she felt nothing, so she moved to his other pocket.

His hand flew out, clamping on her wrist.

Godsdamnit.

Even the increase in raider berries hadn't worked, had they? What in the pit was going on?

He opened one unamused eye. "What are you even doing, Onora?" He sounded so, so tired.

She debated what to say. This avenue wasn't getting her anywhere. She needed to check him, but if he caught her, it was over. He might even kill her. Probably would.

Heart racing, she racked her brain for what to do. What could she do to explain this?

She could only think of one thing.

Convince him she was under his thrall.

She shifted her hand on his thigh, slipping sensually up, and his eyes widened right before his face contorted into rage. Panic hit her at the same moment that his hand gripped her other wrist and he jumped over her, pinning her to the ground.

"What in the darkest pit are you doing?" he gasped out, confusion lining every feature.

"I . . ." Maybe she could still convince him. "I want you."

It sounded unconvincing even to her own ears, and he flexed his jaw, nostrils flaring in annoyance. "Don't lie to me like I'm a fool, Onora. What the fuck were you doing?"

His grip tightened, and she winced.

She was going to die.

She brought her forehead swiftly to his, just enough that he let her go as he grunted in pain.

She grabbed another dagger, hidden at her side, and whipped it out, cutting his arm. He grunted, but he had the advantage and quickly took it, flinging it in the stream. Then he straddled her, taking her arms and pinning them under her body so she couldn't move.

She breathed heavily, terrified, her throat closing in, the world closing in. He held her down as his hands searched her, carefully and slowly rubbing over her body, his eyes not meeting hers, his brow furrowed.

"I'm sorry," he mumbled. "I have to get any other weapons off of you."

He hated this as much as she did. His hands were deliberate, clinical, sure. There was no heat, no lust in his grazes. He was a male on a mission to keep himself safe, and she hated that her racing heart calmed, feeling, against all reason, safe here, under him.

"Why haven't you killed me?" she whispered.

She couldn't reason with it. It made no sense to her.

"I have no desire to kill you, Onora," he said, finding two more daggers hidden in her boot and tossing them in the stream as well. She had a few more that he wasn't locating and she hoped he couldn't. She always kept a few well hidden, and she was thankful she'd decided to fully kit up the day of his almost execution.

She swallowed. Maybe honesty was the best route. "I was looking for the key to the shackles. If you let me go, you can even chain me to the tree and flee. I won't say anything or tell them where you went. Just let me go."

He blinked twice, then let go of her wrist, sitting on the ground away from her and rubbing his temple.

"There is no key," he said.

Silence.

"What?" she demanded.

"There is no key."

"How did you get this shackle off of you, then?"

Had it been an inside job? Was there a human working with him?

He sighed. "I *had* a key. I took it off your boyfriend—he's an idiot, by the way. I dropped it when you struggled against me and I had to flee before we were both skewered by a hundred arrows."

That's why he hadn't killed her yet. He couldn't. With the shackles being enchanted, as long as they were still both attached, he couldn't kill her or even break her arm to get them off and leave her behind. She'd be a dead, rotting corpse attached to him until he could get free.

She gave a crazed laugh, and he raised a brow at her.

"What, exactly, has been your plan this whole time?"

"I know a blacksmith in Orc Haven. We would get there, get these off, and I'd send you on your way."

So he never intended to kill her. Maybe because there would be repercussions for him. Also, if he showed up with her corpse attached to him, good luck getting anyone to help. He needed her.

What would happen when they were free, though? He *would* kill her, then. No doubt about that. He may say otherwise, but he needed her—he couldn't show his full hand just yet.

She had only two options. The Hunters find them before he could harm her or play along to get him to Orc Haven and try to get help there.

"I can get us to Orc Haven," she said.

He eyed her warily. "You know where we are?"

She nodded. "I'll get us to Orc Haven, and when the shackles are off, we both go our separate ways."

Holding her breath, she hoped it was convincing—hoped nothing gave her away.

He gave her a pensive look and then sighed. "Okay, but get some sleep now. And no more groping me."

Her nostrils flared in annoyance, and she thought she saw a hint of a smile on his face as he leaned back, gazing up at the bit of sky visible through the tree. No use fighting. She needed him to trust her. She could rest now, knowing that he needed her alive at the moment. So she laid down, falling asleep as she schemed a way out of this.

## CHAPTER 17
# DRYSTON

He'd shown her his hand. Maybe he should have kept it a secret about the key. Maybe he should have let her believe he still had it and the power to let her go.

At least she hadn't tried to kill him over the last three days since he'd told her. No, if anything, she'd restored her stormy silence, her livid glares, and her sniping remarks.

Because she needed him alive, and he needed her alive. So she didn't have to obey. She didn't have to comply. Unless he harmed her.

Which he wouldn't do except in self-defense. He already saw the bruises on her from their fights, and he winced every time he looked at them. He beat himself up about it internally. Hurting others wasn't something he relished, certainly not ones who were smaller and weaker than him.

Though he wasn't certain Onora was weaker than him—or at least her other strengths greatly made up for the apparent weaknesses. She'd come so close to harming him so many times. He could have been dead if it weren't for the chain that alerted him—and that was only because he'd been on high alert since they'd escaped.

She was leading him northwest and from what he vaguely remembered of the map, that was the direction toward Orc Haven. They would have plains, a river, then more forests before getting there. Silenus was in those woods and if they could get to the river, he could find Silenus's house.

They'd encountered no Hunters since she'd screamed to alert them, and he didn't know if they'd gone the wrong way, or if they were always just a step behind, drawing ever closer.

They broke for the day, eating more fish as she'd admitted that the berries were a sleep aid and she'd been trying to drug him. He'd had to let his anger go, let it slip away because there were more important things to worry about at the moment.

The wind whipped through the trees, the cool breeze making Onora shudder, hunching in her shoulders. He wrapped his wing around them, blocking out the wind, and she glowered up at him.

"Do you want to be cold, then?" he asked.

"I don't want you any closer to me than you are," she spat, finishing off her fish and striding forward, yanking the chain so he followed.

Anger ripped through him, tendrils of black smoke coming from his wrists as he did. "I didn't do it."

He didn't know why he still tried to convince her of his innocence. He didn't know why he cared.

"I saw it, Dryston," she said, glancing over her shoulder with a new look—betrayal.

It felt like a slap, and his ire boiled hotter. "How? What could you have seen to convince you it was me?"

"I saw the destruction. Blackened earth. Bodies drained of their life. Who else could have such dark magic?"

"That doesn't sound like demonic magic to me."

She scoffed. "There were eyewitnesses."

"Maybe it was a demon, Onora. It wasn't me. I would never do something like that."

She stopped, turning and coming close, pressing a finger into his chest, her face full of fury. "You know what I hate the most? That you fooled me. I defended you to Chief Amherst after we went to Evolis. I've been harassed, told I'm under some thrall put on by you, all because I refused to say that you were evil. That I saw some honor in you yet."

He hadn't known she'd done that. His chest ached. She hadn't hated him. She hadn't thought he was a perverse murderer. What had changed so swiftly?

"I'm not saying your witness is a liar. But she could have mistaken me for someone else, or she could have been enchanted to believe she saw me. And if she is a liar, she could have been paid a handsome sum. One eyewitness is not enough for a conviction."

"Enchanting someone's memories is too difficult. That's entirely unlikely." Her brow furrowed, and she swallowed. He could see something in her wavering, and he wanted it to tip, to fall over in his favor. "You left Orc Haven before the attacks."

"I was meeting with Lord Killgan."

"No, you weren't." That doubt disappeared into a steely resolve.

"Ask Lord Killgan."

"Brayden followed you. You didn't go south. You went north, toward the attacks."

He blanched. That was a lie. She had been told by Brayden that he saw him do that. And she'd believed him. A new anger coiled with the others, something that felt dangerously close to jealousy.

"What's between the two of you?"

She frowned. "What does that matter?"

He stepped closer until there was only a breath between them and she craned to look up at him, refusing to back away. "Are you lovers?"

It shouldn't matter. It *didn't* matter.

Yet . . .

She scoffed, turning and stepping away, but he grabbed her by the wrist, tugging her back against him. She glared up at him again.

"Let. Me. Go."

He pointed ahead to the ground, where her foot had almost stepped.

A bear trap.

She jolted.

"Oh."

That was the most thanks he would get. He released her. "Do you trust Brayden enough to say that he would never lie to feed his own ambition?"

She blanched, swallowing. That had hit a mark. She didn't answer him, she just kept walking, looking down at her feet more often, sometimes back at him, curious and tense.

# CHAPTER 18
# ONORA

Onora woke before dawn on their fourth day of traveling to Dryston nudging her shoulder with his foot. She startled awake and stood quickly, the chain tugging and making Dryston stand swiftly as well. He scowled at her, then gestured for her to lead the way. They trudged for hours, and she looked for markers of the direction they were going, heading west toward the merchant city. They saw no signs of anyone in their vicinity, just thickets of vines and wildlife throughout the wood.

Walking in the woods always gave too much time to ruminate. In the past, she'd appreciated it. The solace and the wild had always given her a way to process everything going on inside her.

At that moment, she hated it.

She had no clue what to make of her conversation with Dryston earlier. She could detect no lies from him. He could almost convince her he hadn't done the things he'd been accused of.

But Brayden had seen him go north.

Did she trust him, though?

She'd never known Brayden to be a liar, not that he hadn't. Maybe he had, and she'd never known.

She needed this trip to end. She needed to be home and talking to Amherst and Jackson and making sense of all of this. Amherst wouldn't lie to her—he was like a father to her. Dryston had to be the one lying.

A loud horn blew in the woods, long and insistent, making birds scatter.

Onora halted, her heart aching with a keen hope she'd hadn't felt since Dryston captured her. The sound of a Hunter's horn, and nearby at that. She knew better than to scream—he would fight her again. But she had to go toward the horn. So she jetted forward, going in a way that she knew wasn't directly toward it, diverting enough that Dryston would trust her and follow her headlong into it. The sound drew closer with each blow of the horn.

So close, so close.

"Onora," Dryston said, halting and making her stop as well, stumbling into a tree.

She didn't dare look at him, didn't dare make a sound. Freedom was so close.

"You're leading us toward them," he ground out.

She turned, her mouth bobbing open and shut, her mind scrambling for any excuse to give as fear seized up her limbs again.

But she didn't have to. At that moment, an arrow whizzed past her head, and in a second he had twirled her behind him. Protectively. Her mind was too slow to understand what was happening, why he had done that. Hunters emerged from the trees, bows nocked with arrows and swords at the ready.

She stepped around Dryston and held up her hands. "Don't shoot. He needs to be given more poison and—" She grunted, her words halting as an arrow lodged in her shoulder. She stumbled back several steps and looked up in shock. "I'm on your side," she hissed.

The Hunter at the front shook his head. "Our orders were clear. Kill the demon and the Hunter with him."

"Who would have given that order? It's ridiculous."

The Hunter, a man she vaguely recognized from around the barracks, grimaced. "The chief did."

Her heart stuttered to a halt, head swimming. "Liar."

He shrugged, a conflicting emotion on his face, something like regret as his hand hesitated, holding the arrow back, poised to hit her. "You're under his thrall and aided in his escape. We have to kill you both on the spot."

Under his thrall? Aided in his escape?

"I am not under his thrall. I was taken as his captive, and under the rule of Archan, number 235, you must give me a trial and allow me cleansing before you kill me."

The Hunters exchanged a tense glance. The front one looked back at her. "I'm sorry, but the command of the chief overrules that."

Her head spun. This couldn't be true. The chief wouldn't have ordered that.

"I was tricked," she said calmly, holding up her hands. "Let me help you get Dryston back to the barracks."

The man pursed his lips, hesitating for a moment, just long enough that Onora didn't see it in time. The other man loosed his arrow and she couldn't move, couldn't dodge. Shock filled her as she watched it unfold, but she felt a heavy yank of the chain, Dryston tugging her arm to the side and making the arrow lodge in her shoulder instead of her heart.

The Hunters held up their bows. Rage filled her, and before she knew it, she'd flung daggers, hitting two in the throats. Another arrow hit her thigh, but in the tension she barely registered the pain. The others stood in shock, immobile, terrified, while she slashed at another one, watching him drop dead.

Dryston moved in tandem with her, using his fist and shadows, taking out two while she used her dagger on the other two. She ducked and parried, blocking the blows that came at her. She finally got in a hit and sliced up the abdomen of one, and then she heard a cry and turned to see that Dryston had flung the other away from her, crashing him into the tree, his neck cracking.

She breathed hard, looking them over. Their blood covered her hands, coated her cape and leathers. She moved, wincing at the pain of the arrow in her shoulder, and bent to the first Hunter. Rummaging in his pockets, she finally found what she was looking for—a letter. She pulled it out, carefully examining it.

Her stomach plummeted. It was the chief's signet, which she desperately wanted to believe had been used against his will to sign this decree. Then she looked at the scroll.

It was his handwriting.

She felt sick, like she might vomit, as her world tilted. She folded the letter and stuck it in her breast pocket. Something was wrong here. It had to be. This couldn't be true. Someone had to have forged his handwriting. But who? There were human spies who knew how to do things like that, but Hunters were less about finesse and more about brute force and fighting.

Dryston knelt before her. A torrent of emotion roiled in her, but in that moment, all she knew was that he had saved her, even if it was to be her damnation.

Voices shouted in the distance, and she stood, swaying on her feet from the pain. Wasting no time, Dryston grabbed her by the waist and tossed her over his shoulder. She let out a yelp, but he darted deeper into the forest at a speed she couldn't match on her own. Her stomach twisted, his tight grip on her other leg making her body tremble. His wings fanned out behind them, his tail looping up and her body heated in a confusing mix of terror and . . .

She wouldn't think about that. She closed her eyes and breathed in and out.

*"You're my special little girl." Varek ran the flat side of a knife across her face, a vile look of greed filling his eyes.*

Onora scrambled against Dryston, hitting his back until he halted and set her down. She pulled a dagger and pressed it against his chest, her own rising heavily. Something softened in his gaze, a keen understanding that she despised.

"How many of those do you have?" he asked, his large hand closing around hers with the dagger, gentle but insistent.

"Silence." He shut his mouth and she didn't know what to say, what to do.

"What is it you want, Onora? To kill me? That won't help you now."

"I want answers to my questions."

"What questions?"

Her nostrils flared. "Why haven't I heard about the missing women?"

Things weren't adding up.

It was silent as he waited for her to continue.

"I'm close to the chief. I would think he'd tell me if we had a demon problem again."

"I didn't do it," Dryston whispered.

She pressed the dagger tighter against his chest. "I didn't say I believed you. Only that I don't understand what's happening. That doesn't mean I still don't want to kill you."

"Kill me. Then you can drag my body around until you find a mage that will get these shackles off."

"I'll drag your corpse back to Venatu."

"And you'll be killed."

She gritted her teeth. "That was just those Hunters."

"You killed them. Don't you see how that will look?" He paused and swallowed. "You helped me escape—"

"I didn't."

"In their eyes, you did. Because I wasn't supposed to be strong enough to be able to do that, was I?"

A band tightened around her chest, her breathing constricted and labored.

"You helped me escape, then you killed two of your own men and escaped with me."

"If I can just explain to the chief what happened . . ."

Her voice trailed off. It had been his signet.

It had been his handwriting.

He hadn't believed her before when she said she wasn't under Dryston's thrall, and he certainly wouldn't now.

"Fine," she said.

She had no other choice than to work with him for the moment. Until she could figure out how to convince Amherst that she was a woman free from any spell or influence.

He stepped forward, gesturing to her shoulder, and she was suddenly aware of the wounds again. Her body was lit up like a lightning storm from the battle, and any pain that should be there was muted to where she barely noticed it. Jackson had always marveled at her ability to block things out, to discard pain or unwanted emotions in favor of pushing on and surviving. He called it a strength. Sometimes she wondered if it wasn't just more proof of her brokenness.

"Let me take care of those."

She hesitated, hating that she needed help, but finally nodded. His hand gently pressed in on her shoulder, and she gave an involuntary yelp. His other hand flew to her mouth, gentle yet firm. The nearness of him, the looming strength, the way his wings curled around them—it should have frightened her. It should send her senses whirling, her fear spiking.

But it didn't. She felt all too safe with him.

"Shh," he said.

She nodded, and he pulled his hand away.

"I'm going to count to three, then yank the arrow out," he said. "One . . . two . . ."

He didn't say three, he just yanked, and as she tried to suppress crying out, he pulled her against him, burying her mouth in his shoulder so she could. Breathing hard, she inhaled the musky scent of him, pine and smoke, and her racing mind calmed a fraction more, the pain in her body easing, the tension loosening. She could stay here forever, pressed against him, hearing the beat of his heart and breathing him in.

So she found it particularly startling when he drew back, disrupting her reverie abruptly, making her sway. His hands found her hips, steadying her, and flame coursed through her, blood and pain and comfort and desire a muddied mix.

But hadn't it always been? Her life had been marked by waves of pain and blood, followed by a deep and aching desire she couldn't name and rarely slaked.

Then Dryston knelt, his hands slipping down to her thighs, and she caught her breath, hating what the sight of him kneeling like that did to her. If her pain had been muted before, it vanished entirely as she gazed down at him, his large hands encasing her thighs, fingers tracing the arrow wound. He looked up, and she went as still as she could, afraid that the slightest movement, the slightest hitch in breath would expose her traitorous thoughts and feelings to him.

He was her enemy.

Wasn't he?

He'd done terrible things.

Hadn't he?

The voice in the back of her head seemed to wake, brushing against her consciousness with a chuckle.

Demons are confusing creatures, are they not?

She slammed the voice down, swallowing, focusing on the pain, how it radiated up her leg, making her tremble and sweat.

"Ready?" he asked.

She nodded, afraid of speaking, and then she closed her eyes as his hands pressed in and then yanked out the other arrow. She clamped a hand over her mouth as pain came over her anew, the sensation washing away to a dizzying euphoria.

He was standing now, a hand on her waist as he helped her lean against a tree, and every touch from him felt like a hot brand. She looked away, unable to meet his eyes. This all felt too vulnerable.

She'd had plenty of battle wounds before. Plenty that had needed treatment in the field. She knew that pain was something she could handle and, much to her dismay, was something she'd found long ago brought her a certain level of pleasure in certain contexts. This wasn't the context, though, and she wanted to curl up and die from the way that his care, coupled with the pain, was making her feel . . . things. Things she didn't want to unearth. Things she didn't understand about the nature of him and her.

His hand pressed on her shoulder again, and she snapped her attention to him with a glare, a nasty remark waiting on her tongue. But she was silenced by the clinical look of focus he gave to her wound.

"Let's see if this works . . ." he said, then started muttering in old *entailish*, his words slow and halting.

She felt nothing at first, then a dull ache, then the pain like a fire spreading through her veins, and she writhed, but his hands steadied her until the pain subsided. All of it. She grasped for the wounds and felt nothing.

"What in the darkest pit did you do?" she demanded.

"I healed your wounds," he said. "You're welcome."

Which was amazing, frankly. She was curious what else he could do.

"Don't ever use your fucking magic on me again," she said, standing upright and pushing away from him as best she could. Which wasn't much. His hands still held her up, and she markedly refused to acknowledge it.

"Don't worry, I wasn't using my magic," he said. "I used yours. You're a conduit, but you don't have to just use my magic as it presents in me. You absorb magic and can use it as you will. Your body has been trying to heal, but it's just been coming out as shadows. So I used an old healing chant the elves taught me, and your magic responded."

"How is that possible?"

He frowned. "I'm not certain. I've only seen it work with colony members when one's abilities tie into medicine, but I've rarely dealt with conduits, so I suppose that's why."

"I don't like you using my magic."

He only raised a brow and she sighed, begrudgingly admitting only to herself that she was thankful for it. She felt better.

Gesturing to his arrow, she said, "Let me."

He nodded, and she moved to get a good angle, pressing against his wings, then counting down before pulling it out. A small grunt was the only noise he made. She smelled the tip of the arrow. No sign of poison, which was good. She wasn't certain they'd be so lucky next time.

"We should continue on," she said, and he followed her deeper into the woods.

## CHAPTER 19
# DRYSTON

Signs of Hunters were scattered throughout the forest as they carefully covered their tracks. Dizziness bubbled in his head, and he didn't know if it was hunger or the events of the last few days catching up to him.

They stopped to drink by a stream, taking a moment to rest, and he let the cool water run over his hands. The winter air bit at his skin, and he closed his eyes against it, thinking of The Darkened City and its cool cave passageways. A pang pressed against his chest, a needling question: Would he ever return?

Onora looked haggard but focused, her brow furrowed in concentration as her keen eyes took in their surroundings, looking for any small details of their pursuers, as she'd been doing for hours. Seeing her in her element was a marvel, and he begrudgingly admitted that if he were to be chained to anyone, she was a very good companion to have in the woods.

They came to a small worn path by late afternoon, following it carefully, hoping it led to some marker he recognized. The clouds turned gray, a deeper chill penetrating his bones.

Then the birds stopped singing.

The set of Onora's shoulders became more rigid, and Dryston sent out his keener senses, probing for anything amiss. All he was met with was silence. No other sounds of wildlife followed them. Only the breeze through the leaves filled the air, no birds overhead except vultures. His mouth went dry. That was never a good sign.

Dawn light filtered through the leaves when Onora stopped. A clearing appeared before them with black soot coming out like a burst toward them. She stepped forward, carefully looking about. The trees' leaves were black and warped, the trunks turning around and twisting up.

A clear line delimited the foliage from the sudden and blackened earth that stretched on and on. In the distance was what looked like a structure, rising above it, but it too was so dark that it felt like he was looking into the void.

"Is this what you saw at the farm?" Dryston asked, a keen and primal fear slithering inside him.

"Yes." She stared in horror, the color draining from her face.

"I've never seen anything like it." He knelt, running his fingers over the blackness. It was powdery but stuck like slime, and he quickly wiped it on his pants. "We need to get a better look."

"It could be dangerous."

"I need to know."

She frowned, watching him carefully. Something flickered in her eyes, a challenge, then confusion, before she nodded, following him farther into the clearing. An eerie feeling whispered across his skin, the hair standing on edge, a familiarity that he couldn't shake.

The lines of lighter black rippled out like a stone dropped in water as they followed them in farther, a growing dread tightening in the pit of his stomach.

In the center were bodies, laying out as if they had been praying, prone, in a sun pattern. They were orcs, hands and feet chained, their skin thin and stretched over their bones as if they'd been drained of all blood, their faces twisted in expressions of horror.

"What is this?" Onora asked.

Dryston shook his head. It was clearly magical in nature, some force that seemed to sweep from this center point outward, warping everything in its path. And if he had to guess, it looked like a ritual sacrifice. The hair on the back of his neck stood up, something like a whisper of a breath blowing there, and an uncanny awareness filled him—something watched them. And it wasn't Hunters or any normal living being.

"We should go," he said. "I don't think any good can come from lingering on this evil for long."

Dryston followed behind Onora throughout the night, honing all of his senses, listening for any odd sounds, and looking for any odd sights. There were none. There were virtually no sounds. No insects buzzing, no creatures stirring. The dead quiet filled him with more dread than the blasting of a Hunter's horn ever could.

They stopped to rest, and he stared up at the sky, drops of rain settling on his face in a fine mist.

She asked, carefully, "Did you see anything odd when we were in Evolis?"

He raised a brow. "Everything was odd about Evolis."

"No, I mean . . . like spectral figures at night. Or voices calling to you."

"No, did you?"

She drew in a deep breath. "Yes, and so did Enid."

"Have you seen that here? Or since leaving Evolis?"

"I don't know. The woods are off. My vision in the dark isn't as good as yours, but it felt like there was always something hanging in my periphery, but when I look, it's gone."

A chill ran up his arms. "I've felt something but haven't seen anything."

He could see the fear in her eyes as she looked away, pensive. "We should find shelter soon. I don't want to get caught in this storm."

He was wont to agree—he especially didn't want to be caught in these woods at night with whatever lurked and watched, no covering to hide them.

The wind howled, sending hollow echoes around them, the empty branches rattling against one another. The rain picked up, and he knew they would have a fitful night's sleep wherever they rested. They came across another small clearing, nestled near the base of the mountain, and an old, worn-down cabin stood there, the front door rattling against the wind.

They waited a moment, hiding in the trees, observing, until Dryston said, "I think it's abandoned."

There were no signs of people inhabiting it. No worn paths shooting out from it in any direction, no care given to it, moss growing on the roof and ivy tangling amidst the front porch. Getting closer, he kept his senses honed for any danger but perceived none.

It was a simple, one-room cabin. Dust and cobwebs covered every inch of it, a slow leak in the corner tapping out a tune as the rain fell even heavier now. There was a small fireplace with a bit of wood and lots of soot and ash. In the middle was a pile of old furs and a blanket, a makeshift bed.

He knelt by the fireplace, muttering a prayer of thanks to the twin moon goddesses, making a sign over his heart, as he found flint and enough wood to at least get them a bit more dry.

He began stacking the wood, and Onora placed a hand over his, stopping him. "Like this," she said, rearranging the wood in a crisscross fashion, stacking it so there was a hollow spot in the middle where she placed the starter. She held out her hand, and he gave her the flint. It took several strikes and a few annoyed curses from Onora, but finally the spark took, and she coaxed it into a full flame, lighting up the wood and hitting them with glorious heat.

"We need to put this out before the rain stops," he said, "so the Hunters don't see the smoke.

She nodded, just staring into the fiery blaze, then her gaze flicked to him, scrutinizing, questioning.

"What was that blessing you said?" she asked.

He leaned back, savoring the sound of the embers snapping and popping. "It's just an old blessing to the twin moon goddesses. Thanks for watching over us and providing what we need."

"You're religious, then?" There was a note of derision in her voice, and he rolled his eyes.

"No . . . I mean, sure? I always loved the tales of the gods and goddesses growing up. And I like the rituals. I take it you're not religious?"

She leaned back on her elbows, wiggling her boots off and flexing her feet in front of the fire. His gaze trailed down the length of her, admiring her strong form, the dips and curves, before he looked hastily away, internally cursing himself. She was not his friend, not his ally, she was a reluctant accomplice. He didn't need to be distracted by her right now.

"I don't think I ever really have been, but most humans in Venatu attended rites and ceremonies for the Holy Mother. But, well . . . She turned out to be terrible, so no, I'm not religious anymore. I'm surprised you are."

"I don't seem the religious type?"

"You hardly exemplify the virtues associated with religion."

"Oh? Like what?"

She smirked and he flexed his jaw, trying to ignore what that cocky expression did to his thrumming blood. "Humility, chastity, honesty."

He wanted to quip back, to flirt, to say the words waiting at the ready in his arsenal to disarm her, but instead he looked back at the fire. *Honesty . . .*

It shouldn't hurt. Her opinion of him shouldn't matter. Yet it did, and he didn't know what he could do to win her over.

Or why he so desperately wanted to win her over.

She cleared her throat. "Tell me about your religion."

He frowned, casting her a suspicious side glance. She shrugged, waxing innocent, and he narrowed his eyes. Why in the darkest pit was she suddenly interested in the myths of demons?

"We worship the twin moon goddesses, who are said to have gifted demons the power of shadows during the great trials of the gods."

It was her turn to frown now. "That's it?"

"What else do you want to know?"

"Anything interesting. Rites . . . rituals—"

"The last time demons trusted Hunters with information about our rites, my entire colony was slaughtered before my eyes," he growled, and Onora paled, shifting a little farther from him. He swallowed, looking back at the fire to quell his anger.

Silence stretched between them, long and tense enough to suffocate him. But he didn't know what to say to make it better. Onora wasn't his friend, and he had no interest in laying out everything for her to then weaponize against them. People already knew too much.

"What do you mean by that?" she asked, voice soft.

She stared at him, tentative, curious, but guarded.

"By what?"

"That information was given to Hunters and then your colony was slaughtered?"

"Don't play stupid."

"I'm not. I don't know why you said that."

He glared at her, only to see genuine confusion in her eyes. "You know about my family being killed in Venatu?"

"Yes."

"Then what more is there to say?" She had to be playing a game, trying to get some extra information from him, find some chink in his armor.

"You seem to believe that the information given to the Hunters was what caused them to be slaughtered. That's not true."

He gave a bitter laugh. "My brother told an advisor he trusted that when we perform a ritual, our power leaves us, and then returns. He told the advisor exactly when the power leaves us. At that moment, Hunters ambushed my family, slaughtering them when they couldn't protect themselves."

The room darkened with his anger, his shadows swirling around him, around her, and she sat up, startled, as her own swirled out in response. But they didn't attack. Their shadows played, twirling and dipping, twining and hugging to the point that where one ended and another began was impossible to tell. He felt something odd—a connection to her that filled him with a swell of emotions that overwhelmed and knocked out his own—fear, anger, and confusion.

Her breathing became rapid and haggard, dismay contorting her features as she looked at the shadows. Then her breathing became too shallow, the breathing in too painfully ragged. He moved without thinking, taking her face in his hands and forcing her to look at him.

"It's okay, just breathe, just let it out," he said calmly, quietly. "Don't fight it. They'll come back inside you soon enough."

Stroking her face, he was hit over and over again with her fear, her panic. It tasted bitter, some old wound that was bleeding out, and it felt like it had a name. A demon one. Her panic was raw, slicing against him, and all he could do was weather it as he stroked her face, then her hair. Her hands gripped his wrists, nails digging in. He was sure it would hurt later, but he couldn't care at the moment. All he felt was her feral panic, like an animal caught in a snare, or a rabbit facing down a fox's maw.

Then he was hit with a heady knowing, as if something inside himself were linked to something inside her, a connection that left him laid bare. Shame and fear filled him, and he knew it was his own, those feelings that followed him always, coming out in angry bursts.

It felt as if she were riffling through his wardrobe, seeing everything inside of him like it was a garment she pulled out and held up. How he never felt he was good enough or doing enough. His fear for his family, his colony, his people. His fear here—that he would die, and that she would also die.

She blinked, the dismay turning to something that softened her features, and she also reached up her hand, brushing her fingers against the side of his face, and his breath caught in his throat.

Then she suddenly pulled back, yanking free of him and sitting as far from him as she could, a flush of red rising from her neck to her cheeks.

Neither said anything. What more was there to say? He felt as if he'd shown her every intimate thought and emotion he'd ever had, and he felt as if he'd peered into her deepest darkest fears.

They sat in silence until the storm ended, long into the night.

## CHAPTER 20
# ONORA

Onora couldn't find any adequate words for the rest of the night. The storm raged outside, and the one inside her had become eerily silent. Calm. A beast tamed that had always roared in her ear. She glanced at Dryston often, watching as he gazed at the ceiling, body tense and alert. Because of keeping watch, or whatever the fuck they had just shared? She didn't know.

All she knew was that Dryston sincerely believed he was innocent. He believed that his family had been killed unjustly. And he had been truly, genuinely concerned about her while panic had seized her senses.

She fucking hated him for it.

The voice inside her roused, chuckling softly at her racing thoughts, and she scowled, pulling her knees up to her chest.

*You're awfully active tonight,* she whispered to it, expecting no response in return.

We're so close. I can feel her.

Onora swallowed, startled. It had purred earlier, when Dryston had said the blessing to the twin moon goddesses, but try as she might to coax it out, she'd been unable to get it to respond. Even now, the voice seemed to fade like an echo in her mind, sleepy and soft.

It tugged inside her, drawing her attention to the window. Rain still splattered against it, softer now, and Dryston had put the fire out a few hours ago. It was cold, but the furs helped. She stood, going to the window and letting the chain hang taut between them. Only darkness met her gaze as she looked out the window.

Then something glowed, nestled in the trees, moving slowly. She squinted, but it was no use, she couldn't make it out until it came closer. The glowing were eyes, some being enshrouded in shadows, a spectral hand raised and beckoning.

She gasped, stumbling back and running into Dryston. She flipped around and his hands were on her arms, steadying as he looked out the window.

"What is it?" he asked.

She looked back, but it was gone.

It looked exactly like the being she'd seen in Evolis. When her gaze found Dryston again, he was staring down at her, eyes searching, open, pleading. His hands on her arm felt like a fire brand, and she stared dumbly at him. Everything was off-kilter. She didn't know how to feel about anything right now. She detected no lies when Dryston spoke to her, but then that meant Amherst was lying, or the Hunters were mistaken or . . .

Her mind reeled with the information. She needed to get these shackles off and talk to Amherst. She needed to see the Hunters again and explain to them everything and re-investigate the farm. Something was wrong. It had to be.

Nothing made sense anymore.

She moved out of his arms and stepped away, rubbing them. "The rain has slowed. We should keep going."

THEY ENCOUNTERED nothing amiss that night or morning. Animals and insects skittered about, having returned to the forest. No spectral beings slithered through the trees, beckoning, no Hunters pursuing them. The storm had likely washed their tracks away, which was good.

Or she supposed it was.

She turned over the contents of Amherst's letter with every step, her mind recalling the curve of every letter and punctuation perfectly, trying to find some error in it.

But it wasn't there.

The handwriting was his. The tone of the letter was his. The signet was his.

If she encountered Hunters she knew well, then she'd have a better chance at them hearing her out and getting to the truth of it all.

What would happen to Dryston, then?

The attack they'd seen in the woods—it couldn't have been him. Not only because he had been with her, but also because she'd felt it. His horror, his rage, his confusion.

He hadn't known about that attack, and it was too similar to the farm to be done by different sources.

She felt untethered now. She had no idea what to do, so she would just keep going forward until she could figure it out. Part of her wondered if Dryston could still be tricking her—if perhaps other demons had done the attack in the forest at his command.

But to what end? And why had she been seeing things like she'd seen in Evolis?

They broke through the trees in the late afternoon and stumbled out onto a road. She cursed, not wanting to be out in the open, but it was too late.

Only a little ways down the road was a wagon and several humans on horses. All wearing leather armor and carrying an array of weapons.

She swallowed.

They could dart into the woods, but the people were too close, they'd catch them quickly, and they'd already seen them.

They stared at them with curiosity, and she said to him, quietly, "Play along."

She reached into her boot and pulled out a dagger, and Dryston made a huffing sound.

"You have another one?" he asked, incredulous.

"Be quiet. I need them to think you're my prisoner."

The group came close, most on horses, two on a cart.

"Hey ho!" the man in the cart called out, looking between her and Dryston, a keen gleam in his eye.

She evened out her breathing, trying to look nonchalant, praying, hoping—desperately needing Dryston to keep his mouth shut and play along.

"Hello, travelers!" she said, somehow succeeding at cheeriness, despite her thundering pulse.

"What have we here?" he asked, taking them in. "A Hunter chained to a demon."

Onora nodded. "I caught him lurking in the woods."

"There's a bounty out for a demon," he said.

Onora flashed him a grin. "I'm hoping this is the one."

Dryston stiffened next to her but said nothing. She willed her face to stay neutral, to give nothing away, hoping Dryston could trust her a little. There were many things she didn't know at the moment, but she did know she needed Dryston alive, and she knew she couldn't let them be taken in by anyone who wasn't a Hunter she knew well.

"We appreciate you keeping our lands safe and free of their kind. Are you headed to Venatu?"

Their eyes bored into her, their attention so keen she could barely breathe.

"A little north of here, actually. I'm to transport him to Venatu eventually, but I'm meeting with others to take him there."

"Do the chains inhibit his magic?" The man looked them over warily.

She nodded, pulling the shackles up for him to see. "Indeed."

The man nodded. "Very good, very good. Those elven tools are amazing." The man stuck a finger to the back of his cart. "Get in and I'll take you to Norlein. I'll even pay for you to get a room at the local inn and some food."

Sweat stuck to her palm, and she desperately wanted to look at Dryston, to verify he'd play along, but that would blow their cover. The good news was that these people didn't know they were being hunted.

"That would be greatly appreciated!" she said. If she refused, it could be worse for them. At the very least, this would get them one more night. They could get to the city, keep their cover, and then leave in the night.

She walked to the cart and another man dismounted, coming over and offering his hand to help her up. "I'm Max," he said.

She took it, giving him a smile as she stepped up, hazarding a glance at Dryston as she did. His attention was narrowed on the man—where their hands touched—his jaw flexing.

Max glared at Dryston. "What are you looking at, bat?"

Dryston flashed him a smile. "Care to help me in the cart as well?"

Onora gritted her teeth, nostrils flaring. Anger flashed in his verdant stare, a veritable storm as he held her gaze, challenging.

"I have half a mind to make you walk behind the cart," the man growled, stepping up close to Dryston, drawing his sword.

Onora yanked on the chain, catching Dryston off guard and making him stumble against the cart, glaring up at her. She knelt down, holding his gaze, desperately hoping he could read her intentions, that he would play along.

But why would he think she was trying to help him?

She'd screamed before. To get the Hunters' attention.

Shit.

She swallowed, desperately needing this to work, begging her shadows to behave. Grabbing his hair, she made a fist, letting her knuckles rest against his skull and she willed him to understand, to see that she was trying to help, that they were still on the same side.

Something flashed in his eyes, and the anger abated to confusion and wariness.

"Get in the cart," she said, her voice a cool command. "And stop mouthing off."

There was a brief moment where they stared at each other, his jaw flexing and her fingers tapping on the hilt of her dagger. Then his eyes darkened, dipping to her lips.

She released his hair, and he climbed into the cart, laying back against the hay, smiling devilishly at the man, who got back on his horse, snarling.

"You have him well trained," Max said with a sinister chuckle. "But let me know if you want me to give him a little pain to keep him in line. I don't mind."

Onora shivered at the look in his eyes, sitting back, giving Dryston a long, warning look, begging him to behave. His hand discreetly brushed against hers and she felt an emotion—positive—a confirmation that he would, and she breathed a little easier.

They just needed to make it to a place they could escape.

Onora kept up small talk with the mercenaries all the way there, playing a part—one that now felt so dichotomous to who she was, but wasn't so far from who she had been a mere week ago.

"I'm Vernon," the man driving the cart said to her, casting a look back at her here and there as the horses clopped along, "and this is my crew. We were hired to protect Norlein and the farmlands around it after what happened outside Venatu."

"Do you know what happened there?" she asked.

"Aye," Vernon said. "No doubt about it. The attack was demonic. The whole farm was lit up in a fire black as night, with flashes of lightning inside it. Looked like a host of shadows with a storm in the middle. I've never heard of such a thing or such magic. I didn't see it myself, but it got everyone in a tizzy. Seems that Lord of Shadows is trying to invade again. But we won't let him, and certainly not with fine Hunters like you on our side."

She gave him a tight smile as Max pulled out bread and dried meat, giving it to her to eat. That description sounded oddly familiar. Sounded oddly like what she woke to often enough and nothing like what she'd seen a demon do before. She gave a roll and some meat to Dryston, and the man frowned.

"You should let him starve," he said.

"Unfortunately," she said, taking a bite out of her roll, "he managed to shackle me to him before the poison took full effect. If he dies, I have to lug his body around until a magesmith can take this off. So I need him at least strong enough to walk about."

Vernon nodded. "A right nasty business, that is."

"Is there a magesmith nearby, perchance?" she asked, hoping against hope that there was.

Vernon shook his head. "Only ones are in Venatu, where I suppose you'll be heading. And the elf lands of course."

She nodded. It was the opposite of true, but she'd play along. "I need to get him back for a trial."

"If we had a magesmith here to get you free, we'd give him the only kind of trial he needs," Max growled.

A swash of anger whipped through Onora. "Justice isn't to be taken out at random. There are proper channels to pursue it."

The man narrowed his eyes, and Onora flexed her hand around her dagger. That was clearly the wrong thing to say. Even if that's all things she would have said, regardless. Even if she'd trained her whole life to fight demons, she couldn't believe that they were all inherently bad. She'd always seen their rulers—the lords and ladies and chieftains—as the ones causing evil. Surely, they weren't born that way. Not any more than a bear or wolf was bad but still killed when needed. Not any more than any being was—but perhaps life taught them to be vicious and evil. Perhaps many of them were taught to be that way, to oppress others. But surely they weren't terrible from the start, not a baby.

Not Kaemon and Melina's baby.

Her mind dipped to a dark place, rattling her. Kaemon was not bad. She could feel it in her bones. Yet he'd been hunted, imprisoned, tortured by Hunters.

Enid had been helpful, kind even.

Dryston had been honorable.

All lies. It had to all be lies.

But who was lying? The Hunters? Or the demons?

"Honor is the only thing in life holding justice together," Onora said, giving Max that narrow-eyed gaze back. "And if you pursue justice based on feelings, you have no honor. There is evidence and trials to determine if justice is required, and I will not betray my own honor based on feelings."

Vernon smiled. "You're a good one, miss. I can see it. Max is a bit of lightning strike. Ignore him."

Onora nodded, thankful for Vernon's clear head. She laid down on the hay. "Mind if I nap?" she asked. "Sleeping in the woods isn't exactly peaceful."

Vernon nodded. "Sleep as much as you need."

Onora closed her eyes, happy to avoid any more conversation. But she didn't sleep, she stayed alert, listening, waiting for any warning of danger.

They came to Norlein by evening and rolled up to a small, dingy inn. People gaped at Dryston, but said nothing as Vernon and the others escorted them in.

He stopped right inside the door, turning to her and placing a fatherly hand on her shoulder. "Listen here, we'll escort you to Venatu. We'll take you there so you don't have to be alone with him any longer."

"I'm supposed to wait for my counterparts here. Norlein is our rally point. They should be here tomorrow, so I'd hate to hold anyone up."

Vernon patted her shoulder. "Very well, but we will stay with you until they show up. We'll get a room where several of us can keep watch over him while you sleep."

She pursed her lips. "I appreciate it, but that's not necessary."

"You'd sleep alone in there with him?" Max asked, incredulous.

She cleared her throat, desperately grabbing at the fraying ends of her deception. "Again, he's docile. I think this one is a bit addled in the brain, and the poison has made him pliable. I give it to him each night and I've had no issue."

Max watched her with an unnerving fervor, and Onora looked away, focusing on Vernon.

"I think one of us should be in there with you," Max said, voice low and dangerous.

*Fuck.*

"I fear that I can't allow that, as much as I appreciate it," she said, keeping her voice steady. "Too many would try to circumvent justice by killing him outright. They won't care for the proper channels, nor for the fact that I will have to haul a rotting corpse on my arm until I can get it off. While you seem wonderful, I have an oath to uphold, and I must lock and bar my door tonight and protect this prisoner from any vigilante justice."

It was silent for a moment, and she thought they wouldn't buy it. They would call her bluff.

The problem was, she believed every word she said. She knew Dryston was in great danger here. People would gladly kill him and let her clean up the mess if it meant they got to take out their own warped justice.

Finally, Vernon nodded. "You're honorable. I can see that and appreciate it. I can also see the truth of your words. What we will do is take turns patrolling the inn and making sure he doesn't escape, and if he attacks, you can scream and we will find a way to get to you."

She dipped her head in thanks, but also to hide the clear relief that washed over her. "I thank you. That's more than I can ask for."

She walked forward, yanking Dryston roughly for good measure. "I'd like some rest now. I've had a long day, and I need my strength to keep up the journey."

Vernon purchased her a room, handing her the key and then they bade them good night. She led Dryston up to the room, feeling every eye on her, feeling every bit of anger and fear that followed them up.

This was bad.

This was very, very bad.

## CHAPTER 21
# DRYSTON

"What the fuck, Onora?" he hissed as she locked the bedroom door.

This was bad. Catastrophically so. They weren't going to let her and him out of their sight. She'd said to play along, so he'd trusted her. But this had been a ploy to get him back in the Hunters' hands, hadn't it?

She placed a finger over her mouth and gestured for him to help her move the heavy chest in front of the door. He frowned, eyeing her warily, but helped her push it forward. She listened at the door and he sent out his senses. There was someone at the end of the hall chatting with another person, but no one was directly outside their room.

She came close to him, and he could smell that leather and coal smell that was familiar to her. "Let's get some rest, wake up early, and sneak out the window. We are on the first floor so we can get out and run. Let's take the moment to recover our strength and make a plan."

"What is your plan here, Onora?" he asked, stepping closer in. "Lull me in and contact your Hunter friends to come pick us up?"

Her eyes took in his chest, lingering as they swept to his biceps and then up to his face in a scowl. "I'm trying to keep us from being killed."

"By bringing me into the heart of a human city and regaling them with how much of a simpleton I am? How *docile*. How pliable?"

She scoffed and stepped to go around him, but he moved again, trapping her against the wall. "It was an act, Dryston. I'm trying to survive, and I can't fight off that many people. Certainly not trained mercenaries."

"I think you enjoyed commanding me around down there," he said.

She was silent for a beat, the corner of her mouth hinting at a smile. "I think *you* enjoyed it, *Lord* Dryston."

Her voice was low, sultry, and every syllable felt as if it were a stroke on his cock.

Godsdamnit.

"Now move," she directed.

Part of him wanted to. To fold to that sure voice, that cool command. Another part of him felt a keen level of anger toward her, one that didn't want to make it easy for her. One that didn't want her to think he'd roll over and just show her his belly, hoping she wouldn't slice it open.

So he stepped closer, his knee between her legs, encasing her against the wall. "Watch your tone with me, Lieutenant Onora."

Crimson flooded her cheeks, and he felt as feverish as they looked. He wanted to kiss them, lick them, take his time tasting her skin.

He felt cool iron against his throat, pressing in. "I told you to move," she said.

In a swift movement he had it out of her hand, clattering to the ground, then he grabbed her, pinning her back against him, a tight hand against her throat.

She drew in a deep breath, struggling against him, but he had her held in such a way that it was damn near impossible to get out of. He felt the shape of her throat under his hand, how perfectly it fit. How his fingers twined around it effortlessly, able to grip assuredly.

Her pulse thrummed under his fingers, the *thump, thump, thump* like a siren's call. Her chin tilted, face looking up so their eyes met. She glared at him with steely, murderous resolve.

He could get drunk on kissing them, abandoning his senses in the wilderness of her touch. He pressed his fingers in on either side of her throat. She drew in a sharp breath, eyes darkening.

He released her with a swiftness that left her stumbling forward, and he turned away.

Her eyes conjured thoughts that he had no business having.

"Let's get some sleep," she said, out of breath.

The bed was big enough for both of them, but it would be cozy. He climbed in and she looked at him, wary. He shrugged.

"You're welcome to sleep on the floor if you're so averse to it."

She sighed and climbed in, falling asleep quickly, to his astonishment. He wished he could sleep so peacefully with danger lurking outside the door. Though, he supposed, the danger wasn't for her. He stared at the ceiling, his mind a swirling tempest. Onora was helping him now, though he had no doubt that she would kill him the moment the chains were off.

He listened to her soft, sleeping breaths, glad she was able to rest. She'd endured a lot the last few days, and he needed her alert. If it had just been him on that road earlier, he would have been killed by the mercenaries. He begrudgingly admitted that her wits had kept them safe. Even if her words from earlier still chafed. She said they were a lie, but did he believe that?

It was getting late, but sleep still evaded him. He closed his eyes, trying anything to calm his thoughts, when he heard Onora moan.

He stiffened. Did she have a wound she hadn't told him about?

She moaned again, and he realized she wasn't hurt at all.

She was having a very, very good dream.

Her hands gripped the sheets, her brows furrowed as she arched slightly, rocking her hips, and he looked away, his cock twitching awake.

*Fuck.*

He tried to think about anything else, to think about the sight of her bringing an ax over his head, ready to kill him—but she moaned again, soft and breathy, and all his thoughts emptied out.

He groaned into his pillow, wishing that he could dull his sharp senses. Every harried moan that escaped her lips seemed to scrape down his ear, into him, stroking over his aching member. Her scent of arousal grew, and his head spun from the visions flashing in his mind —of him between her thighs, lapping up her sweet cunt with his tongue.

He clenched his fists, resisting the urge to stroke himself at the sound of her. It felt like a violation, something she'd never consent to if she were awake.

"Oh, oh," she groaned, and he flexed his jaw.

Who the hell was she dreaming about? Jealousy ripped through him and his shadows darkened the room at the thought. He remembered the smile she'd flashed at Max when he helped her into the cart and his eyes shuttered closed as he breathed deeply in, trying to banish the thought.

She let out a muted cry, her body arching and clenching, and Dryston gripped the sheets, his own cock spending only a little.

He was in agony.

Her eyes fluttered open, darting to him, confused. Then reality crashed into her and horror replaced the confusion.

He chuckled. "You were having a great dream."

She sat up, glowering at him. "No thanks to your thrall."

"My thrall?"

"Putting sex dreams in my head."

His mouth twitched as he tried to remain serious. "You certainly seemed to enjoy it."

"This is your fault."

He shifted over her, and her breath caught. Her arousal washed over him again, and he inhaled deeply, certain he could get drunk on the scent of it. "If it were my fault, Onora, you would have come undone with a cry loud enough to wake the entire city. Not that quiet noise you made."

They stared at each other, desperate, heaving breaths hitting bare skin in an erotic caress. Her eyes dipped to his lips and up, her own lips curling in a snarl, even as she tilted her head a little closer.

*Fuck.*

He moved nearer, their noses almost touching. Her hand fisted the sheets harder, and he closed his eyes, trying to calm his rattling breaths. He dipped down, inhaling as he passed her jaw along the column of her neck, where her pulse beat furiously. He was barely able to focus as he breathed in her scent more deeply, his nose pressed to the skin of her throat.

She pulled her hand away, scrambling to the other side of the bed. Her mouth opened and closed, then she turned over, curling up as far from him as she could.

Any heat in him washed away with the cool wind that whipped inside him. It felt bitter and biting, a shame that lanced through his skin to his bones.

He leaned against the headboard, staring at the ceiling, washing down the hollowness that formed inside him. Closing his eyes, he watched his breath, trying to forget about what he'd just experienced, trying to forget the scent of her arousal that followed him

Onora woke him early the next morning, dawn far off. She shook his shoulders, clamping a hand over his mouth and placing a finger over her own to keep him from startling. The pressure of her hand, the feeling of her curves against his body as she leaned over him, the shape of her face—all of it made heat flash through him as he remembered the encounter from the night before.

He also remembered how quickly she had retreated from him.

Dryston braced his hands on the bed and slowly sat up, a sound of alarm coming from Onora, before he felt her slam into his arm, grabbing his thigh sharply to steady herself. He looked to the side, seeing her pressing against him, her face inches below his, her chest heaving and eyes frightened as a cat.

"Easy there, Hunter. I know your dream got you excited, but you need to at least ask first." He tsked and her eyes narrowed.

"We're chained together," she spit out. "Maybe try to be aware of that next time you yank around wildly."

Her eyes were a swirling blue-gray before a storm strikes—clouds billowing and mixing with salt air over a violent sea, water above and below ready to swallow him whole. The only thing he was aware of in that moment was her heaving breasts against his bicep, of her uptilted chin and parted lips that haunted his waking and sleep, of her hand still clenched on his thigh. His eyes darted there, arousal flooding him at the sight, and he clenched his teeth, begging his body not to respond to the glorious feeling of the pain and pressure of her hand.

She pulled it away hastily, stumbling back from him on the bed, yanking him this time so that he jerked, falling over her. His blood thrummed through his veins, his groin, filling him with a heat that threatened to consume him. She'd always been able to get under skin. Even when he didn't want her to, even when he wished he could forget how those beautiful eyes measured him and found him lacking. Even if he wanted to forget how she'd saved him in Evolis.

But what had that been? Only her honor? Perhaps, but that didn't make him any less irritated. She had a spark of good in her that was uncommon amongst any living being. A steely resolve and integrity that made him feel small. A calmness to her rage that made his own anger feel too alive and unpredictable.

Her hand pressed against his chest, and he was lost in examining her face, the contours and lines of it, the shape of her nose and mouth and eyes. The way her hair fell in dirty strands, still beautiful.

The hitch in her breath pulled him out of his reverie. It wasn't a hitch of someone aroused or surprised—but scared. Panic lit her eyes, her body stiff, arms pinned under him. He pulled away swiftly, his stomach plummeting.

Dryston was angry, he knew that, but he thought that he had a lot to be angry about. It didn't make it any better that most of the people who he encountered saw him as a threat, a predator, a volcano about to erupt. And he was the face of the House of Shadows and how others perceived demons.

And he hated seeing how frightened she was of him.

He hazarded a glance in her direction, and she was staring out the window, picking at her nails, face neutral save for her heavy breath and the heartbeat that slammed into his ears with every quickened beat.

That was a very real reaction to him, not just bravado and threats, but genuine fear that made his gut sour. He hadn't done anything, yet there was something in her estimation of him that made him terrifying.

It felt more damning than his death sentence.

Dryston slowly got out of bed, mindful of the chain between them, standing next to the bed as she crawled out. She tripped when she stood, and he grasped her elbow. Her heart rate picked up again, and he removed his hand the moment she was steady.

She walked stiffly ahead of him, and listened at the door, letting out a low curse.

"Someone is keeping watch," she whispered.

"We'll go out the window then."

She nodded, and they opened the window, taking their time to keep it from creaking too loudly and waking others. Then they climbed out, Dryston first, using his tail to balance him. Then he placed hands on her hips to help her out easily. He tried to ignore how that simple touch lit him up, how the way she grasped his biceps made him want to pull her against him. When her feet hit the ground, she released him with a harsh swiftness and moved away, leading him onward.

They wound through the streets, toward the edge of town. It was much smaller than Venatu, but the paths were winding, and a few people still milled about, giving them odd looks. They would be telling others about this soon enough—they needed to get away as quickly as they could.

~

NORLEIN ABUTTED the forest and mountains to the east of Orc Haven, so they slipped quickly and quietly back into the wild, heading west. If they could find the river, then he could find his way back, or at least to Silenus, not too far from Kaemon's old cabin.

They continued on through the morning and day, weakness growing on him, hunger buzzing like flies on a corpse. They hadn't eaten since the cart ride the day before, and that hadn't been much. Still, the hours kept stretching on.

He was so weak and hungry, his steps becoming more and more erratic, his focus shifted to just staying upright and trying to follow the path correctly.

A glint of sunlight flashed before his senses caught up, gleaming off a blade, coming face-to-face with Onora. She backed into Dryston, and his wings flared out instinctively, but it was no use. They were surrounded by Hunters.

Shit.

He hadn't been paying close enough attention, even though he'd been focusing as hard as he could. It was only a matter of time, though, since they'd been in the city. No doubt someone there would have heard about the bounty for Onora's head as well as his and would have contacted the closest Hunters. It was also no wonder what direction they would have gone. Any other and they would have been too out in the open, forced to go through human farmlands around the mountains before hitting the neutral orc territories.

Brayden came forward and took Onora by the chin, forcing her to look up at him. Dryston bristled but was keenly aware of the crossbows marked on them, making him go still.

"Such a pity to lose you," Brayden said. "You always were a wildfire in all the best and worst ways. But the chief has made it clear that he can't stand a demon's whore in his presence."

A low growl rumbled from Dryston's chest, and Brayden looked up at him.

He tsked. "I see you've already got him possessive of you. Only out for less than twenty-four hours and you've already spread your legs for him."

Onora shoved her knife at him, but he blocked it.

"What's going on, Brayden?" she demanded through clenched teeth. "You know the chief wouldn't actually approve of this."

Brayden raised a brow. "You know the policy for monster fuckers."

"The policy is to purify them at the temple."

Brayden pursed his lips. "And now we don't use the temples. We now know that they are a lie."

"But killing innocents because they've fallen victim to a demon's thrall? How is that just and good?"

"It's the best option for them. The shame of it without the opportunity for cleansing . . . Can you imagine it?" Brayden took a step back and gave her a placating smile. "Anyway, I am sorry to do this, Onora. I'll miss you."

He gave a signal, and the others brought up their crossbows. Instinctively, Dryston grabbed Onora and twirled, covering her with his wings, taking the brunt of the hits. He cried out as three arrows lodged in his wings and smoke curled around him in black tendrils. His magic felt as if it were pouring from him with a vengeance. He barely knew what was happening, only that he heard struggles and screams, and he turned to see that most lay on the ground. Some were unconscious, some dead. The others stared at them in shock, hands shaking.

Onora grabbed his wrist, turning on her heel and running. He followed her as more arrows whizzed past, her breakneck speed a shocking thing.

Sounds of the Hunters behind would catch up to them, then fade, in and out, in and out.

Then the barking started.

"Shit," she cursed, sparing a quick and horror-filled glance over her shoulder before picking up her speed again. "The hounds . . . they have the hounds."

The words were punctuated with heaving breaths, terror or exhaustion he didn't know.

A horn sounded, followed by nearby shouts and rallying cries. The Hunters were catching up.

There were so many of them now.

Onora tripped, quickly catching herself, then kept going. Fatigue wrapped around his limbs, seeping into his bones. The same weary lines draped over her sagging shoulders and jerking steps. How much longer could they continue on like this? He racked his brain for a way out and saw none. What would he do when they caught up? He would beg them to leave her alive, he knew that much. Why? Perhaps it was for honor. Perhaps because he could see the confusion in her eyes.

Perhaps because he'd seen the look of desire, the look of her icy regard melting, and he knew that she was a victim like he was. Because he knew they were more similar than different. He had little hope of surviving this, but perhaps she could.

Rushing water filled the air, and he craned his neck to see them rapidly approaching the bank of a river.

*Shit.*

They were about to be cornered. Onora came to a halt at the bank, and he stretched out his wings instinctively to protect them, the left one shuddering from the arrows sticking through it.

Hunters came from all sides, hounds rushing toward them, yapping and barking with a fury. He tried to find any opening, any way to survive this. The only way out was the river—deep and wide, roaring and raging.

He took her by the chin and forced her to look at him. He could hear her racing heart, how the panic beat in tandem with his own. Her stormy eyes met his with a wild desperation. "Hang on to me."

She shook her head, understanding what he planned. "No, it's too dangerous."

"There's no other alternative."

"We could die in the river," she said. "We're both injured. The current will take us."

"I can swim. I know I can. If we stay here, we're dead. Take hold of me."

He opened his arms, and she stared at him, then looked at the hounds coming their way. The Hunters with crossbows poised. She turned back to him, hesitating only a moment before wrapping herself around his torso. He encased her, holding her tight, before jumping into the river.

# CHAPTER 22
# ONORA

Onora closed her eyes and braced as they hit the water, the impact making her teeth clatter. The water rushed over her head and she held her breath, desperate for another gulp of air, for anything to help. His body was over her, also submerged, taken by the current and dragged under.

She stuck to him, knowing that if she didn't, she would be dragged by the chain on her arm and pulled under, possibly dashing her on the rocks.

When she felt like she couldn't hold on any longer, when she thought that she would pass out or welcome the water into her lungs, her head broke through. Dryston swam with the current, his wings and tail helping direct him. The sounds of their pursuers faded as the distance and the roar swallowed them up into the growing darkness. A cold chill swept through, making her shiver as her breath came out in puffs.

She lost track of time as they floated along until finally, they washed ashore, under a cave. She clung to Dryston as he got them safely on land, then he collapsed, breathing hard, face contorted in pain. Her limbs were so stiff that she could barely move. She tried to stand but collapsed—the feeling gone. Dryston caught her, placing an arm under her knees and pulling her in his arms.

She hated needing his help, but her whole body shook, aching with every breath in. He took her into the cave, so dark she could only make out his faint outline as her eyes adjusted. Water crashed against the walls, a slow trickle in the back reverberating.

Dryston sat her down, taking her shivering hands between his and rubbing them. A small warmth returned to her fingers, bringing a prickling sensation that made her groan in pain, the sound rhythmic as her teeth clattered.

She held up a shaky hand and pointed at his wings. "Th-the, a-a-rr-rrows."

He kept rubbing her hands. "I'll be fine."

She shook off his grasp, stumbling to her feet and placing her hands against the cool wall for support. A bit of feeling and warmth had returned to her, and she managed to walk over to examine him, able to see as her eyes adjusted in the darkness. The chain clanked between them, an ominous sound in the echoing cave.

The arrows were bent and broken, some just jagged stubs coming out of bleeding wounds.

"I-I'm g-going t-to pull them out," she stammered.

He nodded, and she grabbed the first one, wrapping her hand around the shaft. But it only slipped, wet from the water and blood. Grabbing her shirt, she yanked it out of her trousers, feeling the sturdy cotton and then taking a rip of it and wrapping it around the shaft. It was still slick, but this time she was able to pull it out swiftly, the sound of it ripping through flesh surrounding them as it bounced off the walls. Dryston let out a grunt, bracing against the rock wall as she took out the others.

She used her hands where her eyesight failed her, feeling the wounds for any sign of infection or anything that would need special attention. Nothing met her wanting hands, only hisses from Dryston, and she felt confident that his speedy recovery would help if there were anything lingering.

They slumped to the ground, the cold seeping in deep, frosting her nose and body. It was the kind of cold that made logic flee in the despair of never feeling warmth again.

"You're still shivering," he said, and the concern in his voice was almost as loud as the raging river outside.

"Well," she said, annoyed but sounding funny between the clacks of her teeth. "It's freezing."

"Fuck."

He moved closer, pulling her into his arms. His heat wrapped around her, his strength engulfing her, but she pushed, thrashing against him weakly.

"What are you doing?" she hissed.

"I don't have the means to make a fire, do you?"

Silence.

He continued. "We have to use body heat to get warm."

She could feel his warmth against her hands. Delicious, enticing. If she hadn't been under a thrall before, the promise of that heat would pull her right into one.

"Fine," she said through clenched teeth and reluctantly pressed against him, the small bit of warmth taking the edge off. Still, she shook against the bitter cold, teeth clattering, her bones chilling.

"We need to take off more layers," he said quietly, reluctantly.

She groaned but knew he was right. Their clothes were too wet—icy in some spots.

Standing, she turned from him. It was dark enough she could only really make out his outline and faint movements, but she knew a demon's vision in the dark was excellent. How much could he see, though? She carefully removed her pants, wanting to leave her undergarments, but they were soaked through, so she carefully peeled them off as well.

She told herself not to look. She couldn't see anything anyway, right? But her eyes were adjusting and some needling part of her wanted to know if he was looking away, too. It was merely to ensure her own chastity—that's it.

Glancing over her shoulder, she was surprised by what she could see. The outline and shadows shifting around his imposing frame, his biceps and shoulders rife with muscle. His chest and abs were well-defined, dipping to a dramatic V above the soaked trousers that clung to him. She swallowed, blinking at the outline she saw there. It shouldn't be shocking that he was large there too when he wasn't small anywhere else.

"I'll have to start charging you for the viewing, Lieutenant," he drawled, a smug humor in his voice that made her eyes snap up to his in disgust. "I think it's customary to give coins for a strip."

She scoffed. "I would if there was anything impressive to see."

His jaw flexed, and he let out a sardonic laugh. "Deny it all you want, darling, but I—"

His voice trailed off, expression slack. Onora didn't know what had come over her. Perhaps it was the competition of it all, perhaps it was his constant teasing. Perhaps it was because she had known it would have this reaction, and she loved the thrill of power that raced through her veins at the sight of him shocked into silence.

She finished pulling her shirt over her head and unclasping her bustier, letting it fall away. His throat bobbed, mouth shut, as his eyes roved down the length of her.

One part of her felt fear. He was so much larger than her, his horns imposing and his body lethal.

But another part that she hated to admit was much, much larger, felt a deep swell of satisfaction. Triumph.

Desire.

The cold nipped harder at her bare skin and her nipples peaked, his eyes snagging and pausing there before meeting hers again with the expression of a man ready to beg for mercy.

And she would smile as she commanded him to beg for it if it weren't for the cold biting into her bare skin and making her shiver harder than before.

He came forward in an instant. No more flirtation, no more competition. He tugged her against him and slid to the ground, laying them down.

His arms were strong and wide, his forearm the size of her neck, his biceps almost the size of her thighs. She swallowed, placing her hands on his chest to provide some space for her breasts to him, but he adjusted, pulling her arms and placing them on his side, tugging her against him, the hard, muscled planes of his torso tight against her body, making her swallow. Warmth would come to her one way or the other. His wings wrapped around them, insulating her, and soon the heat halted her shivering.

He rubbed her back, the gentle but firm strokes returning a bit of heat to her, and she nuzzled closer, desperate to melt the persistent chill that seeped to her bones. His body was like a blast of heat from a fireplace, and she shifted, moving her legs between his to get warmer.

He stiffened, his hands slowing slightly as if distracted, but she was too cold to care. She pressed against him tighter, the feeling of his skin on hers almost hypnotic in the comfort of it.

Gods, how long had it been since she'd cuddled anyone?

Brayden had never been overly affectionate, though. Once he was done, he put clothes on or rolled away and fell asleep. He had little interest in cuddling, and Onora had always thought she was the same.

Dryston's body was a comfort. Despite the hard muscles, his skin was soft and comforting. He smelled like the moonflowers and a cool summer night. The feeling of skin against skin seemed to calm her racing mind and let her drift.

She shifted again, bringing her hips against his to get even closer.

His hand reached around, grabbing her thigh, and he tugged her up so her body and hips were against his torso. He shifted his hips so his top leg came over hers, fully covering her. His hand still gripped her thigh, though, and her heart pounded, a dose of extra heat flooding her from head to toe, bursting like lava between her legs.

"Is this uncomfortable for you?" she asked, unsure why he had her at such an odd angle. She was comfortable, fully so, but surely he wasn't.

He was silent for a beat. "Yes," he said, voice husky. "Go to sleep, Onora."

Her senses thrilled and tingled at his deepened voice—the roughness and rawness there.

Was he . . . ?

She shook her head, nuzzling it against his chest to hide from the cold. Surely not. This wasn't sexual.

It was survival.

He held his breath as her face pressed against his pecs, and a wicked thought consumed her. How would he react if she ran her hand up his torso?

No, she wouldn't do that.

But she flattened her palm against his lower abdomen and his chest rose and fell suddenly with a sharp intake of breath. His leg shifted again, clearly hiding something. She swallowed. There was her answer, and she could lie here and stew about how he was turned on when she was shivering and they were being hunted, and she could be angry with him.

If she weren't so consumed with how large his hand was against her thick thighs, of how it hadn't left, of how his fingers wrapped around and between her legs, so close to the spot that was now aching.

No, this was a slippery slope. It was the thrall, and that was it. If she gave in a little now, she would be consumed by him.

She looked up, barely able to make anything out in the dark.

Yet, she could feel his gaze on her, hot as a brand, focused and intent. She buried her head again and curled her hand into a fist, tucking it into her side.

She would go to sleep and forget this had happened. They had to work together to survive. Nothing more.

## CHAPTER 23
# DRYSTON

Once upon a time, Dryston had entertained a fantasy of there being something between Onora and him that wasn't animosity—something sexier—but right now there were only conflicting emotions muddying any common sense.

Sleep evaded him as he listened to the raging river outside and Onora's soft, sleeping breaths. It had taken her a bit to fall asleep—he'd heard her low harried breaths, careful as if she were trying to keep them under control. The image of her face as she pressed her hand to his lower abdomen flashed in his mind on repeat. Dark, shy, full of lust. His raging hard-on had barely disappeared even as her breath evened out and she fell asleep in his arms. Even though she was his enemy.

She'd tried to kill him.

Onora felt so small in his arms, though, so fragile. Part of him couldn't blame her for the threats and anger. The lashing out like a frightened animal.

She was also snuggled up against him, the strong and unflappable Hunter in need of his warmth, his protection. Some primal part of him loved it. He wanted to hold her tighter, to pepper her in gentle, thorough kisses, to stroke her body carefully and show her how safe she was with him.

The scent of her arousal met his nose and hit his system like a drug. He knew it didn't mean anything. People's bodies responded to stimuli without desire. And just because she was naked in his arms, pressing her hand against an erotic spot and aroused herself didn't mean she wanted it.

Or wanted him.

The thought stung for a reason that he had no desire to figure out.

This wasn't sexual.

It was survival.

As attractive as she was to him, as much as the thought of a passionate hate fuck with her made his cock stir again, he wasn't about to make her think for a second she wasn't safe with him.

He didn't want her to give in to a high stress, highly emotional moment and then regret it later on, feeling as if she'd been out of control or felt coerced in any way.

She somehow managed to light his rage hotter and faster than anyone had before. But in this moment he felt a cold fear he couldn't quite name. She shivered against him until he lost track of time, her body slowly resting, but soft moans and restless whispers from her lips throughout the night echoed in the cave.

And one name repeated with a tinge of horror. "Varek."

A demon name.

She buried her face in his chest, her breath hitting with a staccato intensity. He rubbed her back, unable to sleep even as fatigue overcame him in waves. His wings still ached, a shot of pain lancing through them with the slightest movement. Usually he healed faster, but usually he was well-fed and able to rest after serious wounds.

She stirred against him, and he rubbed her back in soft, full strokes until she finally calmed. What in the darkest pit was he going to do? The Hunters had all their resources dedicated to this, it seemed, and they were determined to kill him. If they could get the shackles off, would he even be able to fly to The Darkened City without getting shot immediately?

And what of his family? He feared them looking for him or retaliating and coming to harm. He swallowed the knot in his throat at the thought.

What of Kalen and Maria? He hadn't seen them, so he'd assumed they were fine, left behind. Had they been killed? Taken?

He needed to find out as soon as possible and get word to his family to not retaliate. The tensions were too high here. If he died, he needed to ensure the demons wouldn't set back the work he and his father had put in.

He'd spent so many years working up an impossible hill to gain trust with their allies, to rebuild the farmlands and refineries of the shadow realm to ensure they had goods to trade. Kaemon would keep a level head, and he knew Enid was a fine leader, but she was also fiercely protective, as was the rest of the colony. He could remember her agony all those years ago when they'd left their family behind. The attack that had happened outside Venatu.

They'd been on a peacekeeping mission to shore up alliances with the humans after the Cruel Lord's occupation. They'd been attacked when vulnerable, and all had been killed except Dryston, Enid, and, as they learned not too long ago, Kaemon. Their brother, who had been captured and tortured by Hunters for years after the attack, and presumed dead. Dryston had sent so many scouts to find him, to no avail. Until Enid had heard a rumor and knew in her heart that it was their brother.

He could still feel the blood on his hands as he'd carried Enid away to safety, as he'd chosen to save her and left their mother and brother to die.

He drew in a deep breath to calm himself. The memories still assaulted him in moments of weakness and terror. Every day since then, he'd lived by casting glances over his shoulder to see if another plot was being schemed.

Light filtered into the front of the cave, soft and golden, and he drew in a deep breath. They'd made it through the night. He thought they should stay until the next evening, though, to travel by the cover of darkness. He'd have to lead the way, but maybe her encounter with the Hunters had swayed her more toward him. They had crossed the river and there was too much chaos for him to see properly, but if he could get a decent grasp of his surroundings, he felt confident he could find Silenus's house in the woods.

She stirred, and he looked down, finally able to see what he hadn't the night before. Black twining ink that wrapped up and around her arms and torso. Ones that looked suspiciously like a demon lord's markings.

His blood ran cold. He knew of the Hunter's practice of taking them as a sign of disrespect, but he hadn't thought she'd have one. Shadows swirled out of him in anger, engulfing the faint light.

He knew how they'd discovered those tattoos. His father's body. Shortly after his father's death, he'd heard of Hunters taking the markings as a sign that demons were nothing and they had defeated their most powerful demon.

It was demeaning as fuck. He knew Hunters hated all demons with an indiscriminate fire, but he had thought Onora a more tolerant one. Someone more willing to challenge her perceptions.

She stirred, blinking, and he pulled his shadows back in, letting the light come back around them. Her eyes and face were soft and vulnerable in a way he'd never seen her. Her gaze tracked his face, and she opened her mouth to speak. He moved away, sitting up swiftly and letting her go abruptly. She jolted, having to brace on the ground to stay up. Her expression immediately turned to stone, any openness gone.

"You're well?" he asked, voice ragged from holding in the curses he wanted to lob at her.

"Yes." Her voice was raw, dry.

He drew in a breath and forced himself to look at her. Confusion swam in her eyes, but her lips were set in a hard line. "Come here."

He stood, offering her his hand. She eyed it warily, then took it, moving slowly and painfully, stumbling as she stood, slamming into him.

He wanted to push her away, get her tattooed body far from his, but he needed her alive.

"You need water. Me, too."

She stood on her own, her eyes taking in his tattoos, but he turned, not wanting to see it or think about it anymore. His shirt hung on the chain between them, as did hers, and he pulled it up, tugging it over his head, and he felt her follow suit as they wandered to the water's edge, kneeling and taking a drink.

His brain cleared some as the cold water hit his hollow stomach, making it ache even more, and he swallowed down the nausea of hunger, thankful that he could think again.

They sat in silence, drinking water as they felt the need, staring at the river as the sun rose, casting orange and pink hues across it.

"We can't go to Orc Haven," she finally said.

He turned, looking at her. She was bedraggled, hair askew, clothes cut up and stained, dark circles under her eyes.

"We need a blacksmith to get these chains off."

She shook her head. "We need a magesmith. There are none in Orc Haven. And none that I know of in any of the orc lands. These chains are specifically enchanted by elves. We need someone who knows how to undo those specific enchantments."

Dryston ran a weary hand over his face. "So we have to go to the elven lands?"

That added more time and danger to their journey. More sneaking and surviving. At least he had good relations with the elf king.

He used to, at least. There was no telling what King Leeth had heard and now believed about him.

He shook his head. "I wouldn't even know where to find one in the elven lands, and the journey is too long."

Onora sighed. "I know of one. He'll help us."

"You're certain of this?"

"Yes. And he's on the outskirts, close to Port Arro, so less time traversing the elven lands."

Could he trust her? He looked her over, his gaze harsh and assessing. She met his gaze with her own steel, and he saw her resolve there. Her honor. Her sincerity.

Maybe it was an act, and she was a good liar.

But what choice did he have?

"Very well then. What happens after the shackles are off?"

She met his gaze, a searching look there, a maelstrom of emotions flashing in a moment before she replied. "Then I finish what I started."

# CHAPTER 24
# ONORA

Onora tried to keep her face blank, to hide the fear that roiled under her skin. Dryston only raised a brow, letting that arrogant smirk she'd always found so aggravating come to the corners of his mouth. She truly didn't know what she meant by that. She only knew that she'd always had one goal since her family died. And if she didn't have that, then what did she have?

"What if I kill you first?"

She scoffed. "If you can manage that, then you win."

"Not really," he mumbled, looking back over the water, his brow furrowing.

She wanted to ask what he meant by that, but it died on her tongue, swallowed by her fear like the many other questions she had.

Like why their tattoos were identical. She knew he had tattoos—he was the Lord of Shadows. And she knew her tattoos were different from the normal mocking ones the other Hunters got.

What she couldn't reason out is why hers were exactly like his.

Had the magic, when Enid unleashed it in Evolis, put her under his thrall?

It would explain her hesitation in killing him. It would explain why, for all her threats, she wanted to believe that he was good. Despite all the evidence she had to the contrary.

Or at least, the evidence she had once had.

She glanced stealthily at him as he gazed out over the water, lost in thought. He was handsome. She was able to think that without her stomach dipping in horror, without her mind fighting it.

Because she knew he wasn't behind the attacks. And she knew that he had been protecting her—caring for her this whole time.

She didn't quite know what to do with that.

No one had ever treated her that way.

He had every reason not to. A tight band wrapped around her chest, constricting as she tried to parse out how she should feel about him. About all of it. The chief commanding that she was killed on the spot left her untethered, flying loose. Nothing felt right, and she wanted to take her anger out on someone. But she couldn't use him as a proxy anymore. No, her ire needed a new target.

Darkness covered their tracks, but so did Onora as they wandered on, Dryston leading this time. His wings twitched when he fanned them out, stretching, only to shudder back against him.

"Are you okay?" she asked.

He nodded, waving a dismissive hand. "It's nothing."

They came to a bend, taking them away from the river. She followed him dutifully, not questioning him as he often stopped, looking around and examining the surroundings for clues of their exact whereabouts.

It was noon the next time he stopped, leaning against a tree, his breathing labored. She came in front of him to see his face pale and skin clammy. Her hand flew to his forehead. It was hot as a brand.

Fuck.

"Tilt down," she said steadily, examining his wings.

He obliged, and she kept her face blank, free of worry that could upset him.

They were infected. And bad.

Which shouldn't be happening because of his demonic healing powers.

Unless the arrows had been poisoned.

She could curse herself for not checking more carefully. They hadn't used the velin on the arrows before, most likely due to the sudden nature of needing to pursue them. The poison had to be made only an hour before using.

"I know," he gasped out, his accepting gaze meeting hers.

"You know and you didn't say anything?" she hissed, shadows puffing like smoke from her hands and shoulders. She didn't even bother trying to pull them back in.

He gave a mirthless laugh. "What can we do about it?"

"We need to find silver fern."

Though she'd seen none. She'd been looking for it in case they did need it. They would need a lot, considering the state he was in now. She'd have to make a tea and poultice and possibly bleed the wounds.

"I've been looking," he said, shaking his head. "We have to keep walking."

He stood to keep going and stumbled. She caught him, pressing him back against the tree.

"You need to rest." Panic wrapped around her throat, humming through her limbs.

"Why? So I can die, lying in the forest, with you chained to me?"

He stood again, grimacing, and kept walking. "Silenus lives near here. I can find him."

She acquiesced, following behind him, keeping a careful eye on the state of him. It wasn't looking good. His steps were sloppy and slow, his eyes blinking in and out. Hallucinations and panic would overtake him before the poison killed him.

She searched her mind and memory for any way out of this. She looked at every bit of greenery they passed, hoping the next one would be a large crop of silver fern. But it was no use. Winter was setting in and had already killed off so many plants.

A horn sounded through the woods, low and ominous, making every bit of her come alert. Shortly following it was the sound of dogs barking.

Dryston shook his head, blinking as his chest rose and fell rapidly in terror. His arms wrapped around her waist, strong and sure despite his weakened state, and he lifted her, jumping into a dizzying sprint. She couldn't comprehend how he was able to go at this speed with the poison in his system, but he seemed to have gotten a second wind. His face paled more, his veins turning black before her eyes, the poison spreading faster and faster as his blood pumped harder from the exertion.

"Stop!" she said, her fear carried on the wind as he continued on.

He didn't stop. He either didn't comprehend what she was saying, or he didn't care. She pressed her hand to his cheek, trying to get his attention. His bleary eyes darted to her only a second before he focused forward again, giving the slightest shake of his head.

"Dryston," she pleaded. "Dryston, stop. Stop!"

"I . . ." His breathing was labored and painful, each inhale seeming to barely fill his lungs. ". . . can't . . ."

"Dryston, you have to," she said. "You're making the poison spread in your blood faster."

He shook his head and kept forward, stumbling but catching himself. The wounds in his wings were bubbling, jagged holes that made her stomach churn.

"You won't be able . . ." He stopped, slumping against a tree and blinking his eyes rapidly. "You can't carry my body alone . . . I have to get you to someone who can help you."

She furrowed her brow, taking her hand and pressing it against his forehead. He was even hotter than before. Shit. This was spreading too fast.

"Just stop. Let me try to find silver fern and maybe it will slow down."

He shook his head again. "No. I'm dying, Onora. You won't be able to carry my body. You'll be captured and killed. I have to get you to Silenus."

Her chest constricted painfully. He wasn't running away to get them both to safety. He thought he would die.

And he wanted to ensure she wouldn't.

*Fuck.*

She whipped her head around, looking for silver fern, but she couldn't see any. Dryston kept going, slowing bit by bit as the hounds' barking came closer. She looked at their feet as they fled, trying to see any sign of silver fern, or anything that could abate the poison.

He thought he was dying.

She swallowed the lump in her throat at the thought.

He *was* dying.

Shit.

A few days ago, she'd been the one volunteering to take his life.

Now the thought made her want to vomit.

Then she saw it. The glint of soft, silvery foliage in the forest.

"Dryston, there!" she said, pointing toward it.

His head whipped around and he came to a stuttering halt. She wriggled out of his arms, tugging him along to the creek bed where it was. So close, right in reach. Just a few more steps.

She felt the tug first, the yank that popped her shoulder out in a flash of pain so keen she had to bite down on her other arm to keep from screaming. She fell back then, on top of his body, heaving and immobile. He'd passed out.

She shifted, coming to his side, checking his face and pulse. He was alive, but if she had to bet, the delirium was setting in. Her arm ached and dangled at her side. She grabbed a nearby stick, shoving it in her mouth and clamping down on it. She positioned her body against him, lining up her arm and then, on the count of three, she shoved her shoulder back into the socket. Another flash of white-hot pain washed over her body, starting at her shoulder and spreading from head to toe.

She spit the stick out, panting hard, her jaw aching. She looked down at him. Well fuck, this wasn't good. He was enormous.

The barking grew louder behind them and an eerie calm came over her. If she was going to die, she would at least go out with a fight.

She looped her arms under his shoulder, wincing and gritting her teeth, then pulled, able to drag him painstakingly slowly. Bit by bit she accomplished it, bringing him to the edge of the creek, taking all the silver fern with her and shoving it in her pocket. They came to the water, and she sat in it, pulling his head onto her lap as his wings were washed in the softly flowing water. The iciness pricked at her, but she took a bit of her shirt and ripped it, dipping it in the water and placing it over his forehead. He stirred, his eyes moving behind the lids, and she hoped it eased some of the pain.

Was this all she could offer him? Some relief in death? A bit of company?

*"Are you okay?"*

The memory came to her again, and her eyes shuttered closed. His body over hers, shielding her, protecting her. Putting himself directly in harm's way to do so. A light burst in her chest, fiery hot like a forest fire, brighter than the sun, burning, burning and eating away inside of her.

*"Let me come play, Onora."*

She was tired, too tired to tell the voice to hush. She was furious, too furious to even listen to it. And she was scared—far too scared to just sit here and wait for them to die.

She moved, getting on her knees and inspecting his wounds again. Her vision was framed by blurry flecks, her world tilting and turning slightly even as she stayed still. She was in bad shape herself. But his wounds—gods, the wounds were terrible. Festering and sizzling, oozing blood and puss, his veins blackening and spreading.

"Fuck you for trying to die on me!" she hissed with a venom and anger that could shatter worlds.

That voice within her chuckled, a heady and alluring thing that she didn't have the strength to ignore. It wrapped around the shadows in her, the magic in her, threading it with sparks of lightning, flashes that resounded off her arms.

She placed her hands on his shoulders. His eyes fluttered open, and a stupid, boyish smile came over his face.

"Always frowning," he said.

"I need you to say that incantation again. Use my power and heal yourself," she said, livid.

His fingers found her braid, touching the silky soft strands. "By the goddess, it's unfair how beautiful you are."

"Stop your nonsense," she barked, "and say the godsdamned incantation, Dryston."

"Absolutely gorgeous when you're angry." He was crazed from the fever. What in the darkest pit was she supposed to do?

She slapped him across the face.

"I swear by your twin goddesses that if you compliment me again, I'll kill you and drag your corpse along with me until I find the mage-smith myself."

He raised his brows and closed his eyes. The pain was receding some, but the poison was settling in. He'd lose consciousness soon.

Her hands laid over his heart. "Gods-fucking-damnit!" Then she started muttering the words she'd heard him say, her tongue slipping over the syllables, the rough-hewn consonants something that seemed to escape her.

"Your accent is terrible," he muttered.

She shot him a glare but didn't stop speaking, her mouth furious and her eyes ablaze like lava. She kept going, so blind with the rage of her emotions welling up that she couldn't see anything until she was done. Slumping to the ground, body wiped and drained as she looked down at him. The wounds were healed and his skin was cool. He had passed out, but the black veins were gone now.

Her legs and arms shook as her emotions calmed and her body became aware of every ache and pain in her.

Water splashed, and she swiveled around in an instant, her dagger out and ready. A nymph sank down below the water. Only her eyes and the top of her head were visible. Her finger pointed up, though, and a soft, flutelike whistle sounded. She was alerting someone, and Onora tried to stumble to her feet, tried to tug on him, but she only fell in the water again, too weak.

Twigs snapped and leaves crunched in the forest, and she gripped her dagger. Nothing readily presented itself and tension coiled in her gut.

*Shit.*

Something else shifted, and she stood, stepping up to the edge where she'd heard it. There was silence and she evened out her breathing, honing her hearing. The faintest sound of breath was directly in front of her, hiding in the dark. Thrusting her hand out, she hit flesh, and she wrapped her hand around it and yanked, making the being yelp as she pulled it into the clearing.

Moonlight colored his pale skin blue, his amber eyes seeming to glow golden as he stared at her. The jewels on his antlers tinkled and his long, delicate fingers wrapped around her wrist.

"I mean no harm, my dear," Silenus said. "Naida told me friends were in trouble. I'm here to help."

She swallowed back the sob of relief forming in her throat and nodded, unable to form the words of fear and relief that mixed like bitter herbs and sugar on her tongue.

Silenus walked up and examined Dryston, grimacing. "He was shot with poisonous arrows, I see."

"I can't tell if all the poison is gone," she said.

Barking passed in the distance, but it was farther away, growing fainter with each yelp of the hounds. Had the dogs caught another scent?

"If you'll help me carry him, my house is a little way away."

Onora helped Silenus pick up Dryston. Unconscious, it felt like trying to move a boulder, but they managed—slowly.

Silenus lived in a hollowed-out tree. The door opened up to a cozy scene, a living area with a fireplace decorated with crafted items from the woods, a pleasant seating area with blankets and stacks of books, and off to the side, a generous bed. She helped Silenus take Dryston there and lay him down, collapsing on the bed with him, his head falling in her lap. Then Silenus went to his counter and washbasin, gathered herbs from a jar, and began making a salve.

Onora chewed her lip, guilt washing over her. This was a simple male, living a cozy life. She could very well be bringing the wrath of the guild on his head.

"We're being hunted," she blurted out.

Silenus gave her a smile over his shoulder and nodded. "I gathered as much, from the wounds and chains, etcetera."

"They may come for you."

Silenus shrugged. "I doubt it. I have my house warded and the surrounding woods. They'll never be able to find me. No offense, but the humans of Nemus are not very adept at identifying magic spells."

Onora knew that was true. Having no magic until recently had meant they were at a severe disadvantage from everyone else.

"Is that why the hounds didn't follow us to the river?"

Silenus mixed the herbs together. "Most likely."

She let out a sigh of relief.

Silenus brought the salve over, along with water and rags. He began cleaning Dryston's wounds, then tilted his head back to help the tea he brewed go down.

"What happened?" Silenus asked, taking a damp rag and placing it on his forehead.

She drew in a deep breath, the events of the last few days stretching in her mind like years. So much had happened, and so much had changed in her heart and mind. She told Silenus all that had occurred.

"I . . ." She chewed her lip and looked down at Dryston, his eyes fluttering behind closed lids, his breathing even now, but his skin still clammy and more pale than she'd like it to be. "I volunteered to execute him."

She couldn't look at Silenus for that confession. She didn't know why she felt confident telling him these things, but she did. He had a gentle way of looking at her that made her want to blurt every thought to him. Shame wormed through her body, and she couldn't bear to see his reaction, as much as she still felt the need to utter the words out loud. To clear the air. To let Silenus know who he was helping.

Silenus chuckled. "Well, I don't think he deserved it for what he was accused of, but I can't say I blame you. He can be lethally tiresome at times. However, the poets say love and hate stem from the same vine of passion."

He flashed her a sympathetic smile, a look of knowing in his usually playful eyes, and the shame fell away to an oddly tender feeling. Like a wound healing, and she looked away again, launching back into the rest of the story.

"They're hunting me as well," she said.

Silenus pursed his lips. "That's a very curious thing . . . Something is afoot here. Some scheming I don't care for."

The chaos they'd been through hadn't lent her much time to think it all through, but even now, she couldn't comprehend it. What scheming could be happening? Why order her to be killed? And more importantly, why lie and make Dryston and the demons the scapegoat?

## CHAPTER 25
# DRYSTON

*Dryston was nineteen again as he held Enid in his arms, blood soaking her clothes from the arrow lodged in her stomach. Another stuck out of his wing as he flew. He could feel the poison setting in, but stopping wasn't an option. Enid's life hung in the balance. He had to find a safe place for her and then go back to save the others. He searched his mind frantically for any clue where he could go. But there was no sanctuary nearby. After taking the Cruel Lord down, the orcs and elves had expressed no interest in an alliance with them. Only the humans did, and that had been a trick.*

*A lump formed in his throat. He couldn't make it. He couldn't do it. He needed to get Enid to Medeis, an entire continent over, which was a day's journey flying nonstop at his highest speed. He didn't know when the poison would fully settle in, and he didn't want to be flying when that happened. Only the goddesses knew what would happen if he became delirious over the ocean.*

*"Kaemon. Mother," Enid repeated, sobbing.*

*She was already delirious. Her skin was so pale. Gods, was she dying?*

*Terror shot through his veins, his heart racing, returning a bit of clarity to him again. He wouldn't be able to save his family. He would have to leave them and try to save Enid. And he wasn't even sure he could save Enid. She was dying in his arms.*

*He kept going, blinking his eyes, shaking his head, trying to stay lucid, to keep his mind above water as he flew.*

*But pain lanced through him, every inch lighting up like a flame was taken directly to his skin. He cried out as his muscles clenched. It took every ounce of his remaining focus to hold on to Enid and stay in the air. The poison was setting in, but he had to keep going. He had to keep flying and get Enid to safety.*

"Easy there, easy there," a soothing voice said.

Dryston was aware first of how raw his throat was, then of the screaming that filled the room. When he blinked awake, it was blurry at first and he felt hands clasped around his face, others tangled in his hair. He settled, his vision clearing, and he realized he'd been the one screaming. He was soaked in sweat and smelled awful, and the face above him looked at him with sympathy.

"Kaemon always had nightmares, too," Silenus said softly. "I'd hear him sometimes in the woods, and he told me once about it. But I had to get him very drunk. Which is difficult. The male has the constitution of an alcoholic, but don't let it be said that I can't keep up." He gave a devilish wink.

Dryston let out a weak laugh, thankful to see a familiar face. Perhaps everything before had been a dream. A terrible, terrible dream.

"If the Hunters were having trouble finding us before, they certainly won't anymore with that hollering," Onora bit out.

Never mind. He was still with Onora, who was her usual grumpy self. He tilted his head up to look at her, realizing his head was laying in her lap and it was her fingers tangled in his hair, her other hand under his head. She frowned, fierce and angry as always, but something else shone through her eyes as they scanned him furtively—worry.

"Thank you for healing me, Silenus," he said.

Onora let out an indignant huff.

"Onora did a fine job of trying to save you," Silenus said, leaning over to examine Dryston's wounds, his long, soft hair falling around his face.

Onora made a grumbling sound. "It would have worked if you'd said the incantation."

"I have no idea what you're talking about, Onora," Dryston said, enjoying how much it riled her. Her scrunched-up face and squinted eyes had a certain effect on him that was dangerous. He looked away, back at Silenus, who gave him a sly, knowing look.

Dryston narrowed his eyes in a threat. He knew Silenus had a meddling tendency. He'd heard and seen enough in regards to Melina and Kaemon to know he'd say the wrong thing at the wrong time.

His wavy blond hair fell around his bare, chiseled chest as he dotted his wounds.

"You're very good at this," Dryston said.

Silenus fluttered his lashes down for a demure smile. "Don't praise me, Dryston, or I'll fall in love."

Dryston smirked. "Don't flirt with me when you're still in love with my brother."

Silenus shrugged. "I could love you just as easily, I'm sure."

Dryston shook his head, chuckling. Onora examined them with a raised brow.

"She's wondering if we've ever been together," Silenus said.

Onora let out a protesting whine. "No, I'm not."

Dryston fixed her with a disbelieving look, and her lips flattened into a thin line.

"Onora was very, very worried about you," Silenus cooed, and another indignant huff came from her.

"Of course I was," she replied coolly. "If he dies, I have to drag his carcass around."

Silenus made a humming sound, unconvinced.

"It's survival," she bit out.

Dryston tilted his head back again, and she looked down, meeting his gaze. An uncommon vulnerability was on her face that made his heart stammer and his chest constrict.

"That's all," she added quietly, unconvincingly.

"Of course," he said softly. "And it was just survival when you convinced me to strip naked and keep you warm."

Her nostrils flared. "That was your idea!"

He flashed her a grin and adjusted to lean on his elbows and sit up. His body felt like every muscle had been pulled taut and abused, every joint aching and his head still pounding. Her hand flew to his bicep, steady and strong but unhelpful, and her words belied what her expression screamed—concern. He didn't know what to do with that. Or the way it made his heart pound a bit louder and his blood race.

Maybe it was just honor. Maybe it was just survival and necessity.

But how could it be when he felt a magic between them as striking as a bolt of lightning? He couldn't be the only one feeling it, could he?

"We should leave soon," he said.

"Not so fast," Silenus tutted. "You'll need a few days of rest to get the toxins out."

"But the Hunters . . ."

"The house and forest are warded," Onora replied, her hand urging him to lie back down. He placed his hand over hers, gripping it with a firm squeeze. Her eyes stuck where their hands met, then they carefully came back up to his, darkening. He had to look away or he might do something truly stupid with her. She was still a Hunter. She was still the person who had captured him and volunteered to kill him.

He swung his legs to the ground and gripped the bed to stand shakily. Onora let out a grunt of protest and Silenus just raised his brows.

"Being obstinate won't make you heal any faster," the satyr said, crossing his arms.

"I need to relieve myself," he replied.

"Oh, well . . ." Silenus unfolded his arms to gesture for them to follow.

Onora scooted to the edge of the bed. The giant feather mattress all but swallowed her up as she tried, making her stumble at the edge, where he caught her under her arms, pulling her against him. She pushed away hastily, refusing to make eye contact, and when she stood, she made a sound of alarm before her legs buckled underneath her and he quickly grabbed her again, holding her in his arms. Every bit of him ached from the effort, every muscle tense and pulling, but the instinct to protect her was overwhelming, too strong to ignore. He would rip every muscle and tendon in his body to keep her safe and comfortable.

Which was a horrifying thought. Where had that come from?

She weakly beat against his chest. "Let me down. You need to rest."

"You can't stand."

"I just need to get feeling back in my legs—let me down."

He frowned, setting her on the edge of the bed amid her protests, then he knelt before her, placing his hands on her calves, silencing her. He slowly rubbed them, slipping up to her knees and the end of her thighs. She drew in a sharp breath, and he tried to ignore what that did to his senses. Tried to ignore how touching her felt sacred and how he wanted there to be fewer layers of clothes between them. He wanted those thick and strong thighs wrapped around him.

Then the scent hit him like walking in a rose garden—her arousal. Warmth spread up his cheeks, down his chest, straight to his groin. He spread his hand along her thigh and dug deeper, looking up at her as he did, noting how her chest rose and fell heavily.

"That's enough!" she growled, swatting his hand away.

He flashed her a grin.

"Move," she said, voice commanding and dark—almost as dark as her eyes had become. "Why are you lingering?"

"Sorry, I thought you enjoyed the view."

Her eyes turned to slits, and he stood, chuckling as he ignored the bark of pain that lanced through his limbs. He offered his hand to her, and she stared at it, pursing her lips. It was a simple thing, yet it felt as if the whole world hinged on how she reacted. Would she shove his hand away? Would she take it limply? Reject it softly and politely? It shouldn't mean anything. It shouldn't be a big deal.

That's what he told himself repeatedly in his head for the seconds he waited.

Her gaze shifted to his, tentative, curious.

She took his hand, her fingers curling around it firmly, and he thought his heart might stop.

It shouldn't mean anything.

Somehow, it meant everything.

He helped her stand, her hand lingering in his for longer than propriety demanded.

"Are you two coming?" Silenus called from the room.

The moment disappeared like the exhale of a breath, but it would stay in his mind for a long time to come.

DRYSTON'S MOUTH watered at the smell of cooking herbs that filled the cabin as Silenus prepared them dinner. He pulled bread out of the stove and Dryston shifted in his seat, ready and desperate to rip into the whole loaf even as the heat wafted off it. His stomach rumbled and Silenus cast a glance over his shoulder.

"It will be ready soon enough, but don't gorge yourself, Drys. I don't want to deal with you having a bellyache."

"I fear I won't have much control over my impulses," he said. "We haven't had a proper meal for days."

Longer for him. Prison food was notoriously bad, but what the Hunters had given him should be a crime.

Silenus finished preparing the food and brought it over, placing plates in front of them. "What's the plan to get out of this situation?" he asked, gesturing to the chain hanging between them.

Dryston didn't have time to answer as he grabbed the bread, ripped off a large piece and stuffed it into his mouth, devouring it so fast he barely had time to breathe. Before he could choke on it, Onora slid his water closer to him, nodding for him to take a drink and he did, giving her a sheepish smile, an uncommon moment of embarrassment washing over as she witnessed him act like a wild animal.

"We're heading to a farmhouse near Port Arro," Onora said, taking calm and steady bites of her food.

Dryston swallowed his next bite, ignoring the gnawing impulse to shove more food in his mouth. "Have you heard anything about Kalen and Maria? Or my family?"

Silenus shook his head. "I hadn't heard anything until I saw Onora with you in the river."

Dryston's stomach sank. He hadn't asked Onora about Kalen and Maria. He hadn't seen them imprisoned and assumed they'd been left, but had they been killed?

As if sensing his question, she shook her head and said softly, "We didn't do anything to them. Or I didn't. I don't know what's happened in the days since we escaped."

He breathed a small sigh of relief. Anything could have happened since they were captured, but at least they'd last been known alive.

"How do you plan to get to the farmhouse?" Silenus asked.

Dryston shrugged, taking the bread and dipping it in the soup and managing to take a small bite that he properly chewed. "I guess stay in the woods and sneak like we've been doing." It was a terrible idea and would most likely lead to their deaths. "Silenus, can I have parchment to write letters to my family? If I don't return . . . I need to get word to them."

He could feel Onora's gaze on him like a brand, and the way Silenus stopped his spoon midair, blinking at him, made his chest ache.

Silenus set the spoon back in the bowl and nodded slowly. "I'll give you provisions and guide you out of the woods in a couple of days. Then I'll take the letters to Orc Haven."

~

THEY LAID in bed the rest of the day, passing it mostly in a tense silence. Silenus was in the other room, working on his art, leaving them to rest. Dryston read a couple of books. They were shockingly mild in nature, considering how flirtatious Silenus was. Onora shifted her shoulder, trying to rotate it and wincing. Dryston cocked his head to the side, curious, but she ignored him, trying again and unable to fully bring it up, her eyes crinkling in pain.

"What's wrong?" he asked.

"It's fine. It's an old injury that flares up sometimes, and it was just dislocated, so now it's stiff." She rubbed her shoulder with her other hand, wincing.

"I can do that for you," Dryston offered.

She sighed, dropping her hand and angling her body. "Okay."

"No arguing?"

"Why would I argue?" she growled.

"You love arguing with me."

She ground her teeth, her jaw ticking. "You don't have to help me. I didn't realize you only offered to piss me off."

He bit down the quip ready and waiting to be lobbed at her. "I wasn't. I want to help."

Her accepting his help felt like a boon. A gift from the gods. When had the dynamic between them changed so much? When had she started trusting him? He didn't know, but he had a feeling it was when he'd passed out, recovering from the poison. He wanted to talk to her about it, to know what was going on in her mind, but it was too soon, too delicate.

"Okay," he said, settling next to her. "I've done this for soldiers under my command. Plenty of old injuries and flare-ups amongst warriors. Often on campaign when you can't easily get to a professional. Not to brag, but I'm quite good at it."

"All you do is brag."

"It's difficult not to when I'm good at so many things."

She rolled her eyes. "Just get to it already."

The chains clanked as he brought his other hand around and pressed on her shoulder. "Tell me when I get to the spot."

He moved deftly, pressing just enough that it hopefully felt amazing without being too rough. Her muscles were so stiff, her body so rigid, she could use an entire body massage. Which he'd gladly offer to her. She glanced at him sheepishly, then she looked away and he could suddenly hear how loud her heart was racing.

"What are you thinking about?" he purred, and she glared.

"How I'm going to kill you—ow!"

"There?"

She nodded, and he adjusted his pressure, massaging deep but slow and pressing out. She winced and clenched her jaw.

"What have you come up with?" he asked.

"Huh?"

"What's your plan for my death? I might have some pointers for you. I'd prefer to go out in style."

She let out a mirthless laugh. Glancing over her shoulder. Their faces were so close now, and her eyes took in the lines of his face, the movement feeling like a physical caress, lighting him up. Then she lowered her brows in a snarl.

"Beheading is a classic."

"Hmmm," he hummed. "It is. But is it a bit cliche? I'm sure you can come up with something cleverer than that."

"Drawn and quartered is next in line."

He grimaced. "Still too cliched, please, Onora. If the bards are to sing of my death and your heroism, shouldn't it be something far more inventive?"

Her mouth hinted at a smile, but she pursed her lips and schooled a frown on her face.

"Perhaps I'll flay you alive," she breathed.

He adjusted her arm up, pulling it out and massaging from her shoulder blade to elbow and then back down over her torso.

"Now we're talking." He focused on the muscles of her rib cage, and she groaned in pleasure. Her muscles were so tight, but godsdamnit, did her groan have to sound like *that?* He had to look away from her, focusing down where his hands were. Keeping it chaste.

"Perhaps I'll even place your head on a pike."

"So you can stare at my beauty every day?"

She scoffed. "As a reminder to anyone what their punishment could be."

"Keep the skin there, at least. It would be a tragedy to deny the world of my glorious face, even in death."

"You're morbid."

He brought his face up, inches from her own, and her heart hammered in her chest, echoing in his ears. "You started it, darling."

Her hand found where his rested on her rib cage and softly, so softly he could almost convince himself it wasn't happening, she moved it up, right below her breast, a question in her eyes.

Fuck.

*Fuck.*

All chivalry fled his mind. Any ounce of reasoning that had once prevailed was nowhere to be found. He'd lay her down here and taste every inch of her, touch every inch of her, caress her until she was screaming his name and her body turned to liquid from pure bliss.

Her fingers ran over his hand, his forearm, her eyes never leaving his, daring him, teasing him, almost commanding him. She stared at him, scared, tentative, her eyes full of lust.

*Fuck.*

Her pulse beat furiously in her neck. He could kiss her, taste the beads of sweat on her skin, lap it up like a dying man in the desert. What was the difference, really? He thought he'd do anything for a taste, beg, degrade himself, anything.

The floorboards creaked loud enough to wake the dead as Silenus moved in the other room, and Onora scrambled away from Dryston, shock and embarrassment washing over her features, the look like a douse of cold water on his fiery desire.

## CHAPTER 26
# ONORA

Dryston slept most of the next day and Onora sat at the farthest edge of the bed, staring out the window. Soft flurries of snow fell here and there as the wind howled outside and she was thankful for the warm cabin. Silenus had gone out, looking for food and to ask Naida—the nymph who had found her—if she had any news for them.

Fear coiled around her. Would they make it to the magesmith in one piece? Was it all a fool's hope?

Hello.

She shoved that little voice away as shadows burst out of her, twining around her face, then sweeping down and caressing the sleeping demon beside her. He looked so gentle in rest, even if he was large enough to take up the majority of the bed. He mumbled in his sleep, turning over, his arm flipping over her thigh, his head resting against her legs, shooting fear up her spine. But not because he was a demon.

Instead, because of the horrifying way his simple touches sent a blazing heat between her thighs that she was fairly certain he could somehow sense. He seemed to earlier, much to her mortification. She could still picture him, kneeling between her knees, his hands on her thighs, strong, firm, sure.

She rubbed her thighs together, swallowing away the image and staring out the window, trying to think of anything else but him. Anything but how handsome he looked in the position. How she had the strongest urge to touch his horns. How his horns would be wonderful things to hold on to tightly while he . . .

She shook her head, biting her lip, trying to calm the way her heart thumped against her ribs.

His hand gripped her thigh, his face pressing against her, and she groaned inwardly.

Fuck him and fuck this thrall.

His hand moved up her thigh, an innocent enough motion, but the location was too much. Far too much. Desire washed over her like a flame, and she stared down at him, horrified and angered that he was blissfully sleeping while she was tormented by his demonic thrall.

She tried to yank her leg away, only for him to hold firm, the strength in his grip enough to send her mind dipping to imaginings best left uncovered. Drawing in a breath, she yanked her leg away with enough force that he woke up, blinking his eyes in confusion as she tried to stabilize herself from the overcorrection, her body tilting toward the window with a frightening speed.

Dryston moved in an instant, reaching to grab her, but the movement of his body shifted the bed so instead she toppled the opposite way and fell against his chest. His arms caught and held her. She looked up and the top of her head connected with his chin, his teeth clattering loudly.

"Fuckkkk, Onora," he hissed.

"Well, maybe you shouldn't fucking touch me, Dryston," she spat.

"*You're* the one who fell into my arms."

"You say that like I wanted to." She pressed against his chest to sit up, but her hair tangled in front of her face and her arms were too interlocked in front of her to be of much effect.

"I don't think I'll ever forget the look on your face while you watched me fully undress in that cave."

She scoffed, pushing off him, only to fall back on him from the shifting bed. "I loathe touching you, Dryston. Don't get any high ideas. That look I gave you meant nothing."

His grin widened. "That wasn't the only time."

She scowled at him and he only chuckled, which infuriated her more. "Any look has simply been to find vulnerabilities."

He raised his brows. "Have you found any?"

She pulled her dagger out and pressed it to his ribs. "Just the normal ones, Dryston. Demons fall as easily as humans do, and I know all the ways to kill you in a matter of seconds."

His eyes darkened, his hand going to hers, not removing it, just resting there. "I'll be sure to not anger you then."

"I think that would require an act of divinity."

His thumb traced the back of her hand, never removing the dagger, letting it rest against him, poised for a kill strike. Breathing became difficult and focusing damn near impossible.

"Do I annoy you? Or does your attraction to me annoy you?" His eyes danced with a mischief that made her see red.

"I would have to find you attractive for that to be true, so you can erase that theory from your mind."

His hand left hers, forefinger tracing a delicate line on her forearm, sending a shiver through her. His eyes darted to hers, darkening, and she knew she was in real danger now.

Real danger of letting this male do as he pleased with her.

And possibly begging him to do so.

In a swift motion, he gripped her hips, flipping her over, so he was on top, unhanding the dagger and tossing it to clatter on the floor.

No. *Definitely* in danger of begging him to have his way with her.

Which made her feel out of control—more untethered than before. The past few days had only been a constant free fall. Every new piece of information warped her perception of reality until it was unrecognizable.

The heavy rise and fall of his chest as his gaze raked over her wasn't helping. Not one bit. His wings fanned out behind him, a show of strength, a challenge to her threats, but his hands gently gripped her waist, a devastating desperation wrecked his features, a longing so deep she felt like she were drowning in it, gulping and desperate for air.

She suddenly understood why the thrall was said to be so all-consuming, why humans were warned time and again of resisting it. She'd be damned if she were so easily pulled under his thrall.

She wrapped her legs around his waist, making his eyes go wide, his jaw tensing as he swallowed hard.

Then she pressed up, noting the barely aborted grunt he swallowed before she twisted her hips, bracing against his shoulder, and flipped him over so she was on top now.

Surprise lit his eyes but was quickly chased away by a heavy-lidded lust. "This works, too," he choked out and damnit if that didn't send a thrill through her.

She had to keep her wits about her, though. They were alone for the gods knew how long. Silenus could walk through the door any minute, and Dryston would be entirely too smug about having a witness to her straddling him. She had no business giving in to him. She needed to let him know she wasn't interested. Because she wasn't . . .

His hand trailed up her thigh, and she couldn't remember what she'd just been thinking. Suddenly her clothes were too much, too constricting. She was desperate to feel his skin on hers, to feel his rough hands all over her, to run her hands over his horns, to feel his lips on every part of her.

"Dryston . . ." She fisted his shirt, unsure what to say, how to act.

His hands moved up to her hips, gripping them, and she swallowed a groan. Then he gently adjusted her, moving her off him, setting her aside and sitting up, rubbing his forehead and shooting her a grin as if none of the last few moments had happened.

Left reeling, she tried to gather her thoughts, barely managing to compose her face as she realized that had been a joke for him. A power play.

“We should eat,” he said, scooting to the edge of the bed.

She nodded, feeling like a fool, swallowing the bitter taste in her mouth. Silenus came in then, carrying more firewood.

“Naida said that Kalen and Maria are safe, and the Hunters have moved north, wary of the orc lands,” he said, smiling. “We leave tomorrow morning, bright and early.”

## CHAPTER 27
# DRYSTON

Silenus followed them out of the clearing and took them to the river's edge the next morning. He'd packed homemade tarts and smoked fish, with an assortment of berries and nuts, to last them the rest of the way. Dryston handed him the letter he'd written for the other demons and Silenus stowed it away in his crossbody.

"You'll be careful?" Silenus asked.

"Of course," Dryston said. He gave the satyr a hug before parting ways.

They wandered up the river, hiding just inside the forest until they couldn't anymore, then they scrambled down along the river's edge, hiding amongst the rocks and crags. Plains spanned out around them, grains waving in the wind for miles.

They stopped on the riverbank at midmorning to eat. The sun bore down hotly on them, and Onora threw off her jacket, closing her eyes against the cool breeze. She looked so calm, so at ease that he marveled at it, his musings tangling as his eyes drifted to her arms and the tattoos there.

A burst of anger lashed inside him, and he swallowed, tamping it down. She noticed his face and grabbed her jacket to put back on, but he grabbed her arm, stopping her, and looked closer.

Her breath hitched, but he ignored it as he truly looked at them for the first time. He'd thought they would be swirls of black ink, faded under her skin, but instead he saw an intricate design that swirled and dipped, patterns rippling out with scrolls and dots and lace. The ink was fresh as the day a tattoo was laid, an intense black.

"These tattoos are magical," he breathed, finally meeting her gaze again.

She shifted uncomfortably, her expression hardening in a challenge. "What did you think they were?"

"I know it's customary for Hunters to get tattoos reminiscent of the Shadow Lord's," he said, unable to fully keep the anger out of his voice.

"I would never," she said, shaking her head. "That's a barbaric practice. These marks are magical."

"But it's demonic . . ." He rolled up his sleeve, placing his bare arm next to hers, the pit of his stomach falling away.

They were identical.

Magical tattoos were always unique. Mating tattoos, acquired during the joining ceremony, were similar, but unique. He'd only ever seen something like this one time before.

She cleared her throat and asked, "Do you know what it is?"

"How long have you had these?"

"It happened when Enid opened the well of magic in Evolis. My skin burned for days after. It felt like a tattoo but my whole torso, all at once."

He blinked, astounded, scrambling for any other explanation. "That may explain some of it. You're a conduit able to take in extra magic, and she's a demon who was using her powers, so it may have jumped to you somehow."

"Does branding normally happen when conduits use their powers with another?"

"No." He stood, clearing his throat. "Let's keep on."

DRYSTON TURNED over this new information about Onora's tattoos in his mind, searching for any new way to look at it. Whatever it was with Onora's tattoos, it had to be a mistake. Some magical mishap.

She sure as the darkest pit couldn't be his mate.

That would be catastrophic on so many levels. Least of which being their deep-seated hatred for one another.

His eyes drifted over her backside as they walked along the river's edge, the afternoon light hitting her golden hair and making his breath cease for a moment.

He shook his head. She was objectively attractive, and they were in a dangerous situation. It wouldn't be the first time someone had developed a slight fixation on the person they were surviving with.

That's all it was.

Not because she was his mate.

Besides, he'd been around her for a while now. Traveling here and in Orc Haven. If she was his mate, he would have felt the effects of her fertility and the mating frenzy already. He would have been driven mad with lust for her.

And what he felt was normal lust.

Maybe slightly elevated levels of lust.

Nothing too far out of the norm.

The morning drifted by without incident, though they both startled at every little out of place sound along the way. A bridge rose up in the distance, strong and wide with the flags of the human realm on one side, and flags of the largest Orc Clan—Lord Killgan's—on the other. The marker of where the human lands ended and orc territory began.

"We're close," Onora said, excitement shading her voice. "We'll cross the bridge and a few miles northwest we'll see fields—after that, the farmhouse."

They stuck to the river's edge until they came to the bridge, carefully scrambling up the rocks to pass over it, when they heard the clatter of horses' hooves. Dryston peeked over the edge, cursing when he saw a troupe of Hunters approaching in the distance. He grabbed Onora around the waist, pulling her against him and pressing her into the side of the riverbank under the bridge. She let out a yelp, but he covered her mouth with his hand, shushing her. He clenched his jaw, terrified of removing his hand and her betraying him again. She'd helped so much recently, but was that because he was the safer option?

She stared at him over his hand, hers resting gently on his wrist, firm, but not threatening, not fighting. She gave him a begging look, curious, wanting an answer.

He had to trust her. He let his hand fall away, sending up a prayer to the twin moon goddesses for protection.

She stared at him, confused, but stayed silent. He leaned forward, whispering in her ear and trying desperately to ignore how her scent called to him, made his head dizzy and his senses leave him. "Hunters."

"Shit."

She tried to crane her neck to look, but neither could see from here. Then she leaned forward, her lips to his ear, the breath hitting and making his cock stir, and he bit back a groan. "What can you hear?"

He closed his eyes and focused. He could hear her hammering heart and hitching breath to an agonizing level of detail, but he needed to focus. The horses came closer with a few footmen, their armor clanking. It took several minutes before he could make out much else, but then a man asked, "Do you think she's helping him?"

The man was shushed by a woman. "No, of course not. She's being held captive."

"But there's been another attack. How could he have gotten there so quickly without her help?"

Dryston's blood ran cold. Another attack.

"What is it?" Onora asked.

He placed a finger over her lips and her eyes darkened, her breath hitching and making his mind scramble for control. He closed his eyes again.

"Even with her help, how?" the woman asked. They were talking low, as if they didn't want the others to hear them speak. "It's in the elf realm this time. We've been tracking them for days with better resources. How could they have gotten there?"

"Flying?"

"We would have seen him."

"Onora wouldn't have done it," another male voice said, also low. "She wouldn't sit idly by while he murdered all of those people."

"What if she *is* under his thrall?" man number one said.

"She's not," the woman replied. "She's not, I can feel it."

"The chief said he has evidence. He said he's been trying to rehabilitate her, but this was the final straw and she's a threat to everyone." The man's voice sounded tortured, scared, unsure.

What in the darkest pit was going on?

They moved over the bridge, only snippets of conversation coming here and there that were mostly inconsequential. He stayed pressed against Onora the whole time, afraid of moving and anyone seeing them. Her curves met his hard planes in a way that made it difficult to breathe. He was painfully aware of how his hands gripped her hips, holding her steady. He wanted to sink his fingers in, to press her against him, to feel her body as close to his as possible.

He dipped his head, coming close to hers, and she tilted hers up.

Fuck.

This was a bad idea.

A terrible, horrible idea.

But his logic and reasoning were faulty—nonexistent at the moment.

He moved his hand up her side, to her ribs, and her breath caught. Their noses brushed and his cock stirred, throbbing, aching.

Fuck.

A cart clanked over the bridge, rattling it and making both of them startle.

He came back to his senses as she seemed to as well. She looked up, carefully avoiding his gaze.

"What did they say?"

He told her, and a myriad of emotions crossed over her face.

"They were defending you," he said quietly.

It might have been unwise, possibly giving her more reasons to confront Hunters later, knowing she had backup, but the sight of her immense relief made it feel worth it.

## CHAPTER 28

# ONORA

They followed along the riverbank, keeping low and watching for signs of scouts. The roar of the river muffled any sounds they made. The sun beat down on them, chasing away the chill of the morning.

"How long have you been a Hunter?" Dryston asked after a while.

She raised a brow, and he shrugged.

"We have nothing else to do while we travel. Humor me."

She looked out over the water. "I started when I was thirteen."

He gave a low whistle. "A bit young, don't you think? Is that normal for the guild?"

"No. It is young and inadvisable. But I was orphaned and had nowhere else to go. The chief took me in, and I begged him to let me train. He refused at first. Said I should go to school in Venatu and learn those skills. To be a child for a little while longer."

"What changed his mind?"

"I wouldn't stop training. And he . . ." She closed her eyes, trying to chase her memories away with the whistling wind as it hit the windowpane. He'd all but refused. But she'd woken early every morning and trained, joining with the recruits on their morning run and, while slow at first, she eventually kept up with them. That hadn't convinced him, though. It had been the screaming nightmares, the way she flinched when anyone raised their voice, the way she would shut down, and freeze, the way she would then shift into a rage. "He realized I hadn't been much of a child for a while. And he let me train."

It was silent for a beat, and she refused to look at him. She could feel his eyes on her, boring in. She didn't know why she was telling him all of this. Maybe because it didn't matter. They would eventually part ways. And maybe it felt nice to admit her weakness to someone. To not have to be strong and invincible.

"How did your parents die?"

"The Cruel Lord killed them. He killed all the adults in my village and enslaved the kids who didn't fight back." She choked out the last words, hating herself anew.

*Didn't fight back.* She'd hidden under a bed, watched as her family was slaughtered, too afraid to do anything. She would have died, yes, but at least she would have still had her honor. Maybe she could have saved her baby brother if she'd at least tried.

As if he could sense her thoughts, he said, "I ran when my family was attacked. I took Enid and flew away. She begged me for hours to return and save our mother and Kaemon. They were still alive when I left. But I didn't. I said it was to save Enid, to protect her. But I was also terrified. I was a coward."

She met his gaze, and a kindred brokenness looked back at her. "You would have died."

"Oh?"

She swallowed. She remembered that day, all those years ago. "I didn't realize you were there. My mentor, who was like an older sister to me, was called out to help. Said that the demons had attacked Hunters patrolling the woods. They sent so many Hunters in response. You would have died. And so would Enid, if she'd come with you. Your instincts—your fear—saved you."

"Doesn't mean I wasn't a coward."

She shrugged. "I'm sure your parents would disagree. I'm sure if they saw you and your siblings were alive, they would be thankful you ran. They would be angry if you hadn't."

"That's true for you, too, Onora." His voice was soft, too soft.

She fiddled with the buttons on her shirt as a distraction. It was silent again and finally she said, curiosity overwhelming her, "You were truly in Venatu that day? You and your siblings?"

She'd heard that delegates had come, and she supposed Dryston would have been old enough to come along. But hadn't Enid and Kaemon been young?

"We needed the colony to complete the ritual in the temple. Our magic is tied into one another and in order to remove the enchantment on the ley line, we need as many from our colony as possible. My father had been talking for months to the human lord and was convinced it was safe. He'd visited so many times prior to that. We had meetings all week long with humans, dining in the great halls, drinking together. I truly thought it had worked."

Onora frowned. This was so different from the story she'd heard. She knew they'd been there a week, but she'd thought it was only adults. The Lord and Lady of Shadows and their delegates. They had gone to visit a temple in the woods and slaughtered Hunters patrolling as part of a demonic rite to gain power. Then Hunters from the guild had been sent and killed all of them.

Except Dryston and his siblings. Which the stories had always left out were there.

She'd traveled with Kaemon, too. He'd said he'd been held captive for years by Hunters. She'd refused to believe him, or at the very least believe that he'd been held captive when he had done nothing wrong.

But why would Kaemon have lied about it? And why would Dryston be fabricating this story now?

"You're saying that they attacked you?" She didn't like it, she couldn't believe it. Because if that were true, then the chief would have ordered it. And if *that* were true, then he had been lying to her.

Which would mean that there were increasingly fewer reasons to believe he hadn't written the decree for her death.

He gave a bitter laugh. "I suppose you heard another grand tale? About us spending months and months brokering peace as a scheme to kill more humans?"

She didn't respond, unsure what she could say. "Demons endured tragedy at the hands of the Cruel Lord, too, Onora. I remember the years of my family hiding out in a village, trying to keep our heads down from his soldiers, my parents doing whatever they could to protect us."

Everything felt as if it were shifting, the world slanting, and she was trying to stay upright. She wanted to tell him he was a liar, to shut up, that he was manipulating her. Because that's what she'd experienced of demons all those years ago. The little and big lies they told her, making her question her reality. The way they tried to groom her and make her into something that was perfect for them.

*Choose honor before all else.*

Her father had told her that integrity and honor should be clung to, even in the face of death. Even when it would get you killed. She'd lived her life that way. Where would her integrity be if she didn't listen? Try to understand?

"How did your father overthrow the Cruel Lord?"

He blinked, clearly surprised by her question. "The Cruel Lord took a special interest in my mother. He took her to be his bride. That's unheard of. My parents were mates and married. That's a bond that's respected above all else. So my father told him that he could have my mother if he challenged him and could defeat him. The Cruel Lord was arrogant and agreed. My father was so enraged and desperate to protect my mother that he killed him quickly. It was a shocking thing, but it also meant he was suddenly the new Lord of Shadows."

Onora didn't know what to do with this information. She'd heard nothing about the demons not supporting the Cruel Lord. She'd heard he'd died and had a successor, Dryston's father, but she hadn't realized he'd oppressed the demons as well.

"I didn't know all of that," she said.

Dryston stared at her, a look of challenge in his eyes. As if he expected her to fight, repudiate what he said, or worse—laugh at him. When she didn't, he ran his hand through his hair nervously and frowned.

"A lot of people don't believe it."

They stared at each other a moment—charged, like the shift of a tide, something tilting, tipping, turning over.

"I believe you," she said quietly.

His throat bobbed, jaw clenching, but there was emotion in his eyes—deep and welling. A relief that made her chest constrict. As if she'd cracked open some vault in him and behind it were a trove of truths and treasures for her to find out about him.

And she was startled to realize that it felt like the entire world had just opened up to her.

FIELDS OF CORN hid their way from the river on, providing cover amidst the otherwise open area. They came to the house at dusk. It rose like a beacon amidst the plains, crags and rocks falling off far in the distance where it met the ocean, surrounded by woods to the side.

She peeked around the sturdy stocks at the house, looking for signs of anyone else present. Smoke rose from the barn and the smell of metal met her nose. The forgery.

Finally, a tall elf male, slender but strong, came out of the barn, a leather apron on his body and a helmet in his hands. His skin was pristine despite the heat that filled the barn. He went into the house, then came out, dressed in a casual sweater and trousers, then sat on the porch, drinking tea.

"Is that him?" Dryston asked.

She nodded.

"So, what are we waiting for?"

"I . . ." Her voice trailed off.

"He seems to be alone."

"Yes . . ."

Dryston glanced down at her, confused. She chewed her lip nervously, then finally sighed. "Okay let's go."

The elf didn't notice them at first, but when he did, he stood quickly, frightened, before squinting his eyes, seeing Onora. His expression turned stormy.

Her shoulders stiffened but she powered on. She'd told herself that his ire couldn't be worse than what they'd just endured, but now, face-to-face with it, she barely had the energy for it.

"Tannin," she said as they came close.

"Onora," he said, a haughty tone lining the edge of every word. His gaze swept over them, a brow raising in amusement when he took in the chains on them. "Who arrested who?" He waved a finger between them.

Onora let out a heavy sigh. "Can you help us get free? They're magically sealed."

Tannin let out a bitter laugh. "Funny how you can suddenly remember my existence when you need something, Onora."

Dryston shot her a quizzical look, but she ignored it.

"Tannin we can talk, privately, after the chains come off."

"And what do I get out of this deal?" Tannin crossed his arms. "It seems you two are wanted, and I may be getting myself into trouble by helping you."

Onora's nostrils flared. "You're awfully good at making sure everything is about you, Tannin. Always have been. What—"

Dryston cut her off. "Tannin, right? I'm Dryston." He put his hand forward, having to yank hers along with it.

Tannin took it, flashing him a smile. "Lord of Shadows?"

"The one and only."

"My oh my. I'm infinitely curious about how this all came to be."

"We'll tell you whatever you like. I can see there's an interesting history between the two of you, but regardless, I can offer tempting compensation if you get me free."

"Onora? What can you offer me?" Tannin asked.

She rolled her eyes. "What do you want, Tannin? For me to apologize? I'm *sorry*. Are you happy?"

Tannin's nostrils flared. "You don't mean it at all. And after you left me, high and dry."

"I left you? You slept with the tavern wench!"

Tannin's face was a study in shock. "Why, I—well, I . . ."

Tannin looked at Dryston for help and he threw a hand up. "Count me out of this fight, friend."

Tannin sighed and shook his head. "I was in love with you, Onora. I think we should just part ways and never speak again."

"Gladly," she growled. "Once you take these shackles off."

"There are plenty of magesmiths in Elf Glen."

"We need you. We need discretion."

Tannin pursed his lips.

Dryston stepped between both of them, placing comforting hands on Tannin's shoulders. "I want you and Onora to hash things out, but I am currently being hunted to be killed. If you can get these off me at least, I can get out of your hair."

An indignant noise came from Onora as she gaped. So much for their moment of bonding earlier. Tannin cocked his head to the side, giving Onora a satisfied smirk. "Oh, so he lets you go and then he just keeps me here shackled?"

Dryston shrugged, casting a backward glance over his shoulder. "That's between the two of you."

Her gaze narrowed, and he flashed her a mischievous grin, winking.

Tannin sighed. "Fine, I'll take your shackles off." He looked at Onora and held up his hand at her mounting protest. "Even yours. But I need something in return."

"Tannin . . ." Onora growled.

Tannin tsked. "It's obvious you're both in danger. And that danger could follow me if I choose to help you and not turn you into the law. I need to get something out of this."

Onora clamped her mouth shut with a grumble. This would create more danger for them, but she couldn't deny it made sense. Tannin was putting himself in danger by helping them.

"What do you need?" Dryston asked.

Tannin looked toward the forest to the east. "There have been odd happenings in the woods and the area beyond. I haven't heard from my friend in two weeks. He was supposed to come by two days ago, but he hasn't. It's not like him. I fear he's become lost in the woods or injured. Can you search for him? He always follows the same path. You'd only need to do that and go to his house. If you don't find him, you can stop and come back."

"Why haven't you searched for him?" Onora asked.

Tannin chewed his lower lip. "I'm no fighter, and I fear the things I've been seeing in the woods."

Dryston glanced at Onora, but she wouldn't look at him. Her skin crawled with an eerie premonition, and she looked at Tannin warily.

"What have you seen?" she asked.

Tannin shook his head. "It's nothing. Probably just fanciful dreams. Regardless, there are also bandits in the deep woods, and I'm not particularly sturdy. I would appreciate the help, and I will release you of your shackles before you go."

"You trust us to not flee in the night and leave you high and dry if you get our shackles off first?" Onora asked, wary.

Tannin sighed again. "You are many things, Onora, but a liar is not one of them. When you give your word, it's ironclad. More secure than any enchanted bindings." Tannin waved for them to follow. "Come along."

TANNIN SET up herbs and other components of the spell on a bench, stoking the fire and adding them carefully to a pot. Sparks filled the air as he chanted words in elvish, each addition to the small cauldron making the air shift and turn colors.

Finally, he had them place the chain on a bench and he poured a bit of the liquid over it. There was a jolt, a zap that made Onora lurch forward in pain, then sparks ran along the metal—blue arcs like lightning, branches coming out and snapping along her skin. Then it stopped, and another sensation flooded her.

Magic.

It felt like she had been dying of thirst, gulping down water under a waterfall. She gasped and clutched her chest, heart racing like a hundred wild horses.

Then it stopped, and she finally took in her surroundings again. Pitch black darker than the night. She tried to pull the shadows back in, tugging and yanking, pulling and coiling them back inside of her.

But the darkness remained.

Hello.

The lightning arced around the room, hitting off the metal and clanging like thunder. Then a coldness, ancient and old, terrible and furious, ripped through her bones, seeping into the marrow, engulfing every part of her. Arms wrapped around her, but the touch only stung, sending the sensation throughout her body as she screamed in pain.

Hello.

"Onora!" Dryston cried out.

She tried to respond but couldn't get anything out through the clanking of her teeth. He grasped her face and the shadows suddenly fell away, the lightning cooling and slithering back along her limbs. She blinked her eyes rapidly. Dryston held her against him, cradling her head from flopping around.

He wiped the hair from her brow, the strands wet and sticking. Her hand clung to his shirt, fisting it weakly.

"What happened?" she gasped out.

"Our power returned."

"Did you hear it?"

"The thunder?"

"No, the voice."

Dryston stared at her, cocking his head to the side.

She pulled herself up, standing shakily, then falling back, letting him catch her. Their eyes met, a moment more intense than the lightning and thunder passing between them, rippling along every surface of her skin. Then she looked hastily away, down at her wrist, now free of the shackles to him.

Now free of him.

It felt strange somehow. Too light. Too free. And oddly, she almost missed it.

She tried to stand but she swayed, and he had her tucked under his arm in an instant, steadying her.

Tannin took his helmet off. "Rest up tonight—tomorrow morning you'll keep your end of the deal."

# CHAPTER 29
# ONORA

Onora splashed the water in the tub, making the bubbles pop and float in the air. It had been a long time since she'd taken a bath like this. Usually, the showers at the guild, made from enchanted waterways in the building, were quick and practical. But having a ready source of water and elven enchantments to keep the water the exact right temperature was too tantalizing to give up. Her aching body was enjoying it immensely.

She needed to get out and give Dryston a turn, but in addition to the comfort of it, she was none too inclined to face the two males downstairs. Her time with Tannin had been a whirlwind. He was overly romantic and a talker, and she'd been lonely as the pit. They'd both made mistakes they weren't proud of.

And Dryston . . . she didn't know what to make of him or what to do about him. She'd been promising to kill him this whole time, and now was her chance. Well, after they looked for Tannin's friend, at least. She was nothing without her word. That was for sure.

Now she didn't want to. When she'd vowed to destroy the Lord of Shadows all those years ago, it had seemed so straightforward. But Dryston put a real kink in those plans. He clearly wasn't guilty, and something in her rioted at the thought of harming him. Perhaps it always had. Perhaps that's why she had hesitated.

She scrubbed her body and dipped her head under the water, slowly emerging and then stepping out. Grabbing a towel, she dried herself off, wrapping it around her. She'd left the clothes Tannin found for her in the room next door where she was staying, cursing herself now as the cold nipped at her exposed skin.

As she left the washroom, she halted, coming face-to-face with Dryston as he ascended the stairs. Every part of her hummed, the too keen awareness of her nakedness sending a thrill and a flush through her. He'd seen more of her before, but that had been out of necessity, and this felt somehow markedly different. Maybe because their dynamic was changing.

Maybe because part of her wanted to let the towel fall to the ground, see how he would react. Yet . . . she remembered in Silenus's house, how he'd swiftly put a stop to her straddling him and how that had made her feel. She squared her shoulders, stepping toward her room at the same time he moved forward, into her path. His eyes took her in with a heat that set her own body aflame.

She swallowed. "Stop looking at me like that."

"Like what," he purred.

She gestured wildly. "Like *that.*"

"I'm sure I don't know what you mean." He took a step toward her and she stepped back, hitting the wall. She cursed under her breath, scowling up at him.

"It's too intense."

He only hummed, stepping in closer and she almost reached out to feel his hard pecs, but she curled her fists into balls instead.

"I think you like it."

"I do not." Her breathy voice betrayed her, though.

Dryston's eyes traced a line along her jaw, his hand coming up and his knuckle following that trail. She moved along his hand, her lids falling heavy with lust. His scent filled her nostrils, dancing along her body and twining with her own, making a new smell.

What was wrong with her?

She snapped out of it and jerked away. He winced slightly, as if she'd struck him, and her chest tightened.

Fuck.

What *was* wrong with her?

"This thrall of yours is obnoxious," she said.

He chuckled, his face coming close to hers as his eyes blinked and darkened, full of desire, his breath heavy and uncontrolled, like he was fighting some deep, primal impulse. His thumb traced her lower lip.

Then he placed his lips close to her ear, the whisper of his words sending a pulsing ache through her whole body. "Everything you're feeling, Onora, is all your own."

"Fuck you."

He tsked. "Now, now. Where's your manners? Say please and I'll consider it."

Her breath caught as his thumb moved lewdly across her lips, his tongue licking his own, and she longed to feel that inside her mouth. Without thinking, she moved closer, leaning in for a kiss.

Then he stepped away, a smirk spreading on his face. He turned and chuckled, self-satisfied. Rage poured through her like molten lava. Before she thought, she brushed past him and when she did, she flung her leg out, hitting the back of his knee, grasping his shoulder and flipping him to the ground. He fell with a thud, a groan, and a curse. She looked back, smirking at the rage in his face.

"Careful, it seems to be slippery there," she crooned, walking to her room, shutting the door tightly.

THE FIRE CRACKLED in the hearth, a tense silence forming between them all after dinner. They would set out at dawn to look for Tannin's friend, but she didn't know the protocol for how to act in her ex-lover's house while sitting next to another male that had inspired lurid fantasies to run rampant for the last few hours in her mind.

Tannin took his lyre off the wall and tuned it up, slowly playing it. "Do you remember this song, Onora?"

She had little interest in a walk down memory lane, but she nodded her head, resting it against the cushion of the couch, watching his lithe fingers on the strings.

"I sang it to you that first night," he said, his voice thick with emotion, his eyes wandering off to that distant time and place. "I always thought that's what drew you to me."

Onora groaned internally. Another point they'd been incompatible with: his errant romanticism and her rigid practicality.

"It's a lovely song," Dryston said.

She cut a glance at him and saw a pleasant smile on his face, despite the tense lines running underneath. Was he . . . ? Onora cocked her head to the side, and his nostrils flared as he looked away from her.

She leaned over, whispering so only he could hear as Tannin continued playing, his voice humming the song low. "Are you jealous of my ex-lover?"

He gave a mirthless laugh. "Hardly. If anything, I pity him."

"For what?"

Dryston's eyes met hers again, their faces close, too close, and the heat in his gaze stole her breath away. "He had the dishonor of knowing you intimately."

"Don't act like you haven't been itching for the chance yourself."

His tongue licked his bottom lip, the movement so sensual she thought she might lose her mind. She sat back, staring ahead, trying to calm her racing heart.

Tannin stopped playing, adjusting the tuning of the lyre. "I wrote a song for you." Tannin looked at her, and she gave him a flat-lipped smile.

"Oh, there's no need to show us," Onora said, grimacing.

"I want to hear it," Dryston said, flashing a devilish grin at Onora.

She promised him death with her eyes, which only made him grin bigger.

Tannin began playing, the sound lovely and his voice lovelier, but the words made her cringe, wanting to pass away and die. He swore his love for her, undying, eternal, stronger than the jaws of death.

Dryston tapped his foot along, hands behind his head, too much joy on his face. Onora had a mind to cause him great levels of pain for that. He kept stealing glances at Onora to see her reaction, and he suppressed a laugh each time.

"Tannin, I haven't been this entertained in ages," Dryston said as Tannin keyed up for another song.

Onora drew in a deep breath, smiling broadly and turning to Tannin. "Me, either. It's making me remember all the good times we had. Here. In this house. Upstairs."

Tannin's brows shot up and Dryston's grin faltered, turning to one of annoyance.

To say she felt buoyed by his reaction was an understatement. He *was* jealous.

Tannin's eyes narrowed on her and he stood, putting his instrument away. "Don't play with me, Onora. I'm going to bed. As both of you should, too."

He left the room, shaking his head, and Onora sighed, sitting back.

"You don't have to be cruel to him," Dryston said, still annoyed.

"I'm not being cruel to him. All of this bluster is a male who romanticizes what's not right in front of him and forgets what he has when it is."

Dryston just raised his brows and she shrugged.

"Tannin has many great qualities, but being anchored in reality isn't one of them. He's going to forget what I said the moment he's asleep." She turned, facing him and drawing her legs up against her. The fire cast flickering shadows on his face, giving his already strong features even more definition.

Gods, but he was perfect.

Which was annoying as the darkest pit.

"If anyone was bothered by my words"—she said, taking her foot and poking his leg—"it's you."

He scoffed but didn't lean away from the touch. Instead, his eyes fixed there for a moment before finding hers again. "Hardly. You keeping your lusty gaze on another is giving me a break."

He leaned back, putting his hands behind his head.

She rolled her eyes. "Oh please. As if you haven't been staring at my ass for days."

"It's nothing to be ashamed of, Lieutenant. Many a female has fallen prey to my charms, and plenty of males, too."

She let out a sarcastic laugh. "Yes, because of your thrall. Don't get cocky just because you have a magical thread pulling others to you."

He was silent for a moment, a look passing across his face she couldn't read. Then he leaned forward, taking up the space on the couch and making her lean back against the arm as he braced on the back, coming over her.

"Do you want in on a little secret?"

She blinked, barely able to take in his words and process them. But she nodded in agreement, unable to speak.

"There is no thrall. That's a lie. What you're feeling for me is very real, and very much on you."

It was her turn to scoff. "Don't be ridiculous. I—"

But his thumb found her mouth, tracing the bottom of it, silencing her in a deluge of desire. His nostrils flared, drawing in a breath, and he closed his eyes, breathing hard.

Fuck.

If the thrall wasn't real, then what was this?

"You're lying," she whispered. "Besides, I'm not interested in you or attracted to you."

He leaned closer, whispering in her ear. "I can hear your heartbeat. I can smell your arousal. I can see it in your eyes. Don't bother lying to me."

He smiled, all smug arrogance, and rage lit in her chest. In a moment, she had her legs wrapped around his waist and she flipped him, tumbling him back to the other side of the couch, laying back, straddling him—her hands on his chest.

He opened his mouth to speak, and she placed a finger over it, shaking her head. He slammed it shut, watching her intently. She ran her hands up his chest, his heaving breath an erotic melody. Then she ran them up his neck, through his hair, finding the base of his horns.

His cock twitched and he tried to shift under her to hide it, but she pressed down against it, and he drew in a deep breath. She ran a thumb up the length of his horn and he gritted his teeth, his cock fully hard under her.

Fuck, he was huge.

She shifted her hips, grinding against him, and he let out a strangled moan.

"Onora," he gasped out, and she thought she might come just from the way he said her name.

His hand flew up to her hips, sliding up her waist and breasts, palming them, and everything in her lit on fire.

Fuck.

She was losing control. She'd meant this as a tease, as a competition to show him just how much he wanted her too, to wipe that smug look on her face.

But if she let him keep touching her, she'd also let him ravage her on this couch.

She pulled back, standing, leaving him staring at her confused. And she smirked.

"Don't pretend you don't want me, too." Then she turned and walked up to her room.

## CHAPTER 30
# DRYSTON

"I never have," Dryston muttered under his breath as he watched her walk away.

He lay there for a bit longer, steadying his breaths and bringing his mind back from that precipice it had been teetering on. That ice-cold feeling doused him again, shame and a keen unworthiness. Her body responded to him, but he also knew that didn't have to mean anything about actual desire. And if she was actually his . . .

He shook his head, shutting down that thought.

Onora being his mate would be politically terrible and very unlikely. But on a personal level, her being his mate meant he'd get to spend the rest of his life being rejected by her like he was just then. Being deemed unworthy.

He trudged up the stairs to his room, lying in bed, mind racing and replaying the image of her straddling him, stroking his horns and grinding against his cock.

He was rock-fucking-hard right then and he closed his eyes, trying to shut the scene out, forget about her, and go to sleep. But his cock grew harder, aching, as he recalled her harried breaths with perfect clarity.

The expression on her face when his hands had palmed her breasts had been euphoric. He wanted to chase that feeling.

No. He shook his head and buried it in the pillow. It had felt like ages since he'd given himself any release and it had been actual ages since he'd had a partner. Months. And traveling chained to Onora hadn't helped with that any.

He could relieve himself, get it over with, and think of anyone but Onora.

He stroked himself, thinking of anything else but her, some vague and nebulous idea of a partner. She knelt before him, taking his cock in her mouth, swiping her tongue around as she sucked hard and pulled him in and out of her. He moaned into his pillow, the pleasure mounting, rising.

But it wasn't some vague female anymore. The wings he'd been imagining morphed and shifted to nothing, the hair turning from dark brown to the color of sun hitting wheat stalks. Gray-blue eyes gazed up at him, those lips that had entranced him from the moment he met her wrapped around him, her deft hands stroking the shaft.

And before he could stop himself, before he could change the image in his mind's eye, he spent himself, biting the pillow to muffle the groan as his cock twitched in his hand.

He stared at the ceiling for a long while, exhausted, but unable to sleep for the pair of blue eyes that haunted him late into the night.

Night still blanketed the world when they awoke, a darkness so vast that the moon overhead felt like a beacon, the stars scattering and dotting the sky. Dryston met Onora downstairs, her eyes taking him in slowly.

Heat flashed over him too, the memories of the night before flooding him. He wanted her, right then, right there, on the kitchen table.

She offered him a mug, steam curling in the air and a floral fragrance meeting his nose. "Tea?"

He took it, giving it a sniff. "It's not poisoned, is it?"

The corners of her mouth tugged up, mischief in her eyes as she turned back to the boiling pot of water to pour over her mug. "I suppose you'll just have to try it and find out."

He walked to the counter, leaning against it and encasing her, looking over her shoulder. Her movements slowed, her eyes flicking up to him for a moment before looking back at the dried tea leaves she was placing in a bag.

"Do you need something?" she asked.

He looked her over for signs that she was afraid, but he saw none—only the fresh color on her cheeks.

"No," he said, shifting so his chest pressed against her arm, savoring the contact, wanting more. "I'm just looking at the ingredients."

She made a low humming sound, then picked up her mug and shifted to face him.

"You're awfully comfortable in Tannin's house," he said, trying—and failing—to keep the bite out.

"I've spent plenty of time here."

He felt like he'd been lanced through the heart, and he gave a rueful laugh. His body felt possessed, something primal coming over him that wanted to meet the challenge in her eyes, in her words. He stepped forward, pinning her against the counter, leaning over her.

"What would he say if he knew you were straddling and stroking me last night?" Dryston wanted—needed—her to face that moment they had shared, have her admit that she also wanted him—to some small degree. Something that rumbled deep in his chest wanted to claim some part of her, even if it were only her desire.

"That's none of his business," she said and casually took a sip of the tea, commanding, in control, unbothered.

Which was infuriating. He hadn't imagined it last night or all the other times. But she could stand here and act like it was nothing?

He thought he might be going insane when she placed her palm on his chest, making his heart race and he almost crumpled, willing to fall to his knees and beg or do whatever else she wanted. She slowly and carefully drew her hand down, down, finally resting over the top of the band of his pants, a single finger tracing a line there.

Nothing mattered or existed anymore. He pressed against her, grabbing her hips and pulling them against him, eliciting a sharp intake of breath from her. He would have her right here, moaning and crying out his name for all to hear.

But footsteps coming down the stairs made them halt, and in a moment she pushed him away, stepping so far from him that it felt like a slap across the face.

Tannin appeared around the corner and Dryston leveled a glare at the elf before he could compose his face. He raised a brow but said nothing, floating over to Onora.

"Here's a tracking crystal," he said, placing it in her hand. "He and I often used them to meet up in the woods."

"You two are very close?" she asked.

He swallowed, brows pinched in sadness. "Yes."

Onora's face softened for a rare moment, her hand on his shoulder, and gave him a squeeze. "We'll find him."

Tannin followed them to the edge of the woods, locating the path, then waved as they continued on without him. It was odd traipsing through the woods with her but not tied to her. He didn't think he would have missed it, but he did miss her proximity.

What in the burning and flaming pit was wrong with him? He felt like a moon-eyed lad, obsessing over his first crush. Or a panting dog desperate for water.

As they trekked, he slowly noticed that the birds stopped singing and no other sounds of wildlife followed them. Only the roaring of the river filled the air, no birds overhead except vultures. His mouth went dry. This was all too familiar.

Dawn was just peeking through the leaves when they saw it. A ring of black soot bursting out, coming right to their feet.

## CHAPTER 31
# ONORA

Onora held her breath, carefully looking about as she continued on. The trees still stood, their leaves black and withered, the trunks turning around and twisting up.

It was the same as the others—a clear line marking the healthy fields from the sudden and blackened earth that stretched on and on. In the distance was what looked like a structure, rising above it, but it too was blackened so dark that it felt like she was looking into the void. Dizziness overcame her from the sight, the sheer destruction.

"It's the same as the other," Dryston said, a keen enough horror in his voice that she turned back to see his eyes wide with a primal fear.

The first attack, then the one in the woods, and now this? They were all the same so far, and fear crawled along her skin like bugs.

"Do you think there are bodies here, too?" she asked, quiet, frightened.

"We should look. See if anyone is hurt or in danger."

They came to the edge of the black, kneeling to look at it. It was soot, but the color felt void, as if they could step onto it and into another realm entirely. But when they did, the ground crunched with the brittle, scorched grass like normal. As they walked, lines in the ground became clearer, rippling like waves out from the middle. In the center was a home with two barns, modest and barely standing. Roosting atop the rafters were vultures, and the smell of burnt flesh stung her nose as she gagged.

A noise came from the home, indistinguishable at first, but as they came closer it was clearly someone crying. They spared a half glance at each other before both broke into a sprint, keeping pace with one another as they ran up to the house, halting outside, and sidling next to the wall. Onora peeked around, into the doorway, her heart dropping into the pit of her stomach.

A little girl knelt, the one bright spot of color in the blackened world, her legs and cheeks stained. Tears came down her cheeks, a look of shock there as she clung to the arm of a woman's corpse.

And in that moment, Onora was transported back. Once again a little girl, clinging to her family's body, shocked and desperate. Crying.

*The demon walked up to her, grabbing her by the arm and dragging her to her feet. She wailed and cried, screaming to the sky in her anguish and despair. But she stopped when a large hand connected to her face, turning her head to the side and making her teeth clack together.*

*"Stop crying, you bitch," Varek said, a look of delight on his face that she would only learn to recognize later as someone who enjoyed the pain and tears of others.*

*So she did, and when the chief took her in, he also told her to stop crying. So she had. All that pent-up emotion roiled within her, strangling her like a noose.*

She stepped forward without thinking, reaching her hand out to the girl, desperate to help, to comfort. Dryston grabbed her arm, holding her in place. She tried to yank free, looking up at him with a snarl, but his face made her falter.

Devastation. Anger.

He was just as affected by this.

"There could be traps; wait," he said, then began examining the doorway. The girl was too occupied with her sobbing to notice them. When he was satisfied, he stepped into the building.

The girl finally looked up, a squeak of terror escaping her. In a moment, Dryston knelt down, his wings tucking all the way in, his palms up and out. Onora watched in fascination. The usually brooding, preening male had instantly adjusted to look, somehow, nonthreatening.

Her wide eyes took him in, afraid at first, then curious, her gaze flicking to Onora before back to Dryston.

"We just want to help," Dryston said.

"Who are you?" she asked, a hiccup following her sniffle.

"I'm Dryston, and this is Onora. What's your name?"

"Anna."

"Anna, is this your home?"

She nodded, and Onora closed her eyes, taking a deep breath. She'd known it was, but seeing the little girl confirm it didn't make it any less devastating.

"Is this your family?" He dipped his head to the bodies.

She nodded again. "But not Momma or brother."

"Where are they?"

She sniffled again, rubbing her nose with the back of her sleeve. "I don't know. They were in town, and I was playing in the woods when it happened. I don't know where they are."

"Do you know anyone nearby?"

She shook her head. "They're all dead, too. All the farms. I checked."

Onora's stomach turned as Dryston looked back at her, his expression mirroring her horror.

"We want to help you—to get you somewhere safe. Will you come with us?"

She looked them over again, silent for long enough that Onora thought the girl would say no. And then what? Would they force her?

Finally, Anna stood, stepping toward him. He stood slowly to his full height, and the girl looked up at him, more curious than afraid, and swayed, blinking her eyes tiredly. Her body was weak, perhaps she hadn't eaten for a couple of days.

"Can I carry you?" Dryston asked.

She nodded, reaching to him, and he picked her up. Her face immediately crumpled as she pressed it to his shirt.

"I can't stop crying," she said, and Onora's heart broke at the distress.

"It's okay," Dryston said softly, holding her tighter. "You don't have to. It's okay to cry."

Onora stared at the scene in front of her so similar, yet so foreign, from all those years ago. A demon finding a young girl amongst the decimated remains of her family and taking her. Only this time, the demon had been gentle, showing the little girl kindness in a way Onora had rarely known. Certainly not from those who held power over her.

A brief and fleeting thought ran through her head: What would life have been like if the person who found her had been gentle? Who would she be?

But she let that slip away in the tides of thought, for she knew it was no use wondering.

They walked along the farm for a few miles, watching for any signs of life. Anna fell asleep against Dryston's chest, the scene so foreign and comforting to Onora that she couldn't stop staring at it. Dryston met her gaze, cocking his head to the side in a question, and she looked away hastily. Too many emotions asked to be seen in that moment, too many asked to be acknowledged and felt. She couldn't do it. She needed to hold herself together for a while longer.

For she feared once she let one out, the whole dam would crack and flood her.

The sun set over the horizon, and they could see two people off in the distance. Onora placed a hand on Dryston's shoulder, stopping him.

"We have to be careful. Hunters will be on the way to investigate this."

He nodded. But where could they go? The fire had destroyed any natural cover they had. They could sprint to the river, but then what? They couldn't jump in again, not with the little girl.

So they trudged on as the other figures still approached. As they came closer, it was evident it was two humans, not armed, and Dryston tried his best to keep his wings tucked. When they finally saw him, the woman let out a cry and stepped back. The young man with her grabbed her arm and said something, clearly trying to calm her.

Anna perked up at the sound, her head whipping back. She, too, let out a cry. "Momma!"

The woman made a sound like a sob and began running. Dryston set Anna down and the girl sprinted, almost falling in the dirt. The young man, whom Onora presumed was her brother, began running, too. Dryston stayed still, about ten feet away, and Onora knew it was to not spook them. He was so careful, so aware of that, and something bloomed in her heart, something tender and aching for him.

In the cabin she'd felt emotions that weren't hers, ones that flooded her senses. Fear and shame. She wanted to reach out to him, to let him know she saw him and his efforts, saw his care and thoughtfulness, and it was good. But instead she watched the reunion in front of her, swallowing the lump in her throat.

The young man looked at his surroundings, eyes landing on them. "Do you know what happened?"

Dryston shook his head. "No clue."

"I've heard tales of it happening elsewhere, too. People say it's demons." He gave a scrutinizing look at Dryston.

"It's not me or my people if it is demons. I've never seen anything like it before."

The young man nodded. "I wasn't accusing. I believe you."

Dryston's brows shot up. "You do?"

The young man gave a rueful smile. "I know what people say about demons, but one saved my life years ago. In the woods outside Thon. He looked like you, actually. I was caught in a bear trap and had been for a few days. I was going to die. But he got me out, found a satyr friend to help heal me up, then carried me to my doorstep and left me there, flying away. I never got his name."

"Kaemon," Dryston said, emotion in his voice. "That was my brother, Kaemon."

"I owe him my life." The young man gestured to Anna. "And I think now I owe you for hers."

Dryston shook his head. "Think nothing of it. Kaemon would say the same."

The man smiled. "Regardless, if anyone comes asking about demons in this area, just know that we didn't see anything."

"Thank you."

"Do you know anyone by the name of Elgin?" Onora asked.

The man nodded. "Yes. He helped us when the attack happened. A good male. He headed to Orc Haven—said he had a friend there he needed to talk to about everything he'd seen."

Onora let out a sigh of relief. They hadn't found Elgin, but they did have news of where he was and why he hadn't met up with Tannin.

# CHAPTER 32
# DRYSTON

It took much of the evening and later into the night to trek back to Tannin's. Tannin—who Onora had once had a fling with. Her old flame. Something white hot and raging coursed low in Dryston's belly, a furious rage he had to calm down. Tannin had helped them. While he and Onora were nothing.

Onora took a break, taking a drink from her water skin, then turning and handing it to him. He took it, their hands grazing, and a jolt like lightning raced up his arm and he yanked it away too forcefully. She raised a brow but said nothing, and he took a hefty swig from it, wishing it was alcohol or something to calm his racing mind.

She pulled out the map and compass Tannin had given them and came close, showing him the forests and other markers.

"I think we're a little off from where we need to be. We should head north for a bit and see if we can find this grove," she said.

He leaned down, drawn to her like gravity, clearing his throat and staring at the map to pretend that's what he wanted to get closer to. Then he was hit with it—the scent of her fertility.

Fuck.

Fuck.

*Fuck.*

Visions of her sitting on his face, him lapping up the taste of her cunt, ran through his mind, consuming him.

He drew in a deep breath and straightened, calming himself. If she truly was his mate, he'd have to find a way to quell the mating frenzy until it was over. Maybe forever if she didn't want him.

He stepped away from her—one long step, then another. She gave him a questioning look, but he ignored it, heading north, moving fast. He wouldn't leave her behind, but if he could get some distance between them, that would be best for his sanity.

Onora kept up, her lithe feet doing well in the woods, despite the size and strength advantage of demons. She was faster than many of them, and Dryston found he'd have to go comically and suspiciously fast to get the desired distance between them.

Well, fuck.

"You're keeping up quite well," he said, trying desperately to ignore all of his senses that were pointed toward her. She was fertile. He could smell it like the nectar of the forest, and it was making him insane.

She rolled her eyes. "I'm a ranger. I think I should be able to. Besides, don't underestimate humans."

"I'm not. I'm just surprised at how fast you are."

"I'm faster than you."

"Okay," he conceded like one would to a child, smiling.

Her nostrils flared. "I am. I'm certain of it."

"Of course, of course," he said again, placating. "You're a fast little one."

"You're so fucking patronizing," she spat as he laughed.

"A very fiery little thing." His voice was deep and full of humor and her brow furrowed deeper.

"Fuck you."

"As I already told you, only if you ask nicely."

Her cheeks colored, and she took in a heavy breath.

"Or should I make you beg for it?" he asked, knowing he was treading dangerous territory and completely unable to stop himself.

"I'm not into your sick foreplay, bat."

He smirked. "I'm not so sure about that."

"Race me."

He frowned, having to backtrack. Hadn't they been flirting? "What?"

"Race me, unless you're scared."

"I'm not scared of you," he said, rubbing his jaw.

"First one back to the house wins," she said, checking the laces on her boots.

His pulse thrummed, and he swallowed. "This isn't a good idea, Onora."

"Why?" She stepped close, looking up at him, her eyes full of mischief. He could smell her well and good now, the scent enough to knock him to his knees. "Is your ego too fragile to handle potentially losing to a woman?"

"It's not that, it's—"

She scoffed. "Then let's go."

"Excuse me?"

"Race me. Now. Let's see who's faster and more agile."

Images of her running from him filled his mind and, quite against his will, his blood started pumping faster, his cock warming.

Fuck.

"Do *not* run from me," he growled.

"*Excuse me*?" Onora mockingly threw his words back at him.

She took a step forward, but before she could take another, he grabbed her wrist. "I'm being serious, don't run from me."

She yanked her arm free. "Or what?"

He didn't have time to formulate a coherent response that didn't make him sound terrible—insane, horrible. Because in a flash, she was off, running away from him, fast as a deer.

And he was following, his mind bent on one thing—tackling her.

Then claiming her thoroughly.

# CHAPTER 33
# ONORA

Onora sprinted through the forest, her feet sure, nimble over brambles and bushes. Dryston wasn't far behind her, but for now, she was keeping pace far ahead of him. The breeze hit her cheeks, and she savored it, loving the feeling of being free, of running with abandon.

She didn't know where this was coming from. Maybe from his possessiveness earlier, to him acting like she wasn't a threat at all. Maybe she wanted to show him that she could best him and shouldn't be underestimated. Maybe because, once again, she felt wildly out of control with him, and she needed some sort of a win.

She curved around trees, ducking under branches, leaping over fallen logs. She gained more ground, leaving him farther behind until she couldn't hear him, and she grinned.

Typical.

She would never let him hear the end of her win. She'd hold it over his head and—

Something came from above her, hitting her mid-stride and tackling her to the ground, pinning her there. She struggled and yelped, only to realize it was Dryston over her. His eyes were dark, the moonlight hitting his hair in hues of blue, highlighting his horns. He was angry, or determined or . . . she didn't know, but it was a dangerous look. It should frighten her. It should make her scream.

Instead, heat coiled in her lower belly.

"Drys—"

He silenced her with a kiss. Fierce, coarse, and demanding. His lips bruised hers as they moved roughly, biting, nipping, claiming, as a growl escaped him. She whimpered and his lips trailed a line to her neck where he groaned, kissing her softly now, his nose pressed to her skin, inhaling.

Then he pulled back, looking at her, shame washing over his features.

"Fuck . . . I'm sorry . . . I shouldn't—" His words were cut off with a hiss as she maneuvered her pinned hand to hook over the top of his trousers, tracing a line there. She shifted her hips as much as she could, rocking them, rubbing against him. His cock twitched, and she drew in a sharp breath.

His eyes became heavy lidded with lust, his throat bobbing. His hands gripped her tightly, and he pressed down on her, grinding, his lips trailing up her neck again.

"Onora," he gritted out.

She rocked against his erection again. "Yes?"

"This isn't . . ." He swallowed hard, falling on her neck, taking in a long, languorous inhale of her scent. "Fuck, you smell amazing."

Her head tingled, and she could barely think for the scent of him so close, the weight of his body on hers.

She tilted her head, opening her neck in an invitation for him to kiss her there. His lips came close enough she could feel the featherlight brush against her skin before he tugged back a fraction, his breath hitting her in heavy pants.

"Tell me to stop," he commanded. "Tell me to get off you and I will."

She said nothing, she only ground against him again, making him groan, his teeth clamping down on her neck as his hips met hers, matching the motion, his hard length pressing against her core.

He licked up the column of her neck, taking her earlobe between his teeth and grazing it.

"Tell me to stop, Onora," he pleaded, voice gravelly. "If you don't want this, tell me to stop."

She turned her head, meeting his gaze, seeing a wild desire there. Her whole body lit up, and she whimpered. A low growl sounded in his chest and in a moment his lips were on hers again, devouring, biting, pulling.

He sat up, straddling her, then quickly and with fumbling fingers he unbuttoned her jacket, then ripped the blouse off her. Her corset was a maze of laces and she began undoing them, only for him to grab a dagger, gently pushing her hands away as he cut them in one swift movement, removing her top. She reached for his shirt, and he hastily flung it off, revealing his muscled chest.

He ripped her pants off with a speed she could barely comprehend.

Then he stood, unbuttoning his trousers, and she could already see the imprint of his cock , hard and long and twitching. She throbbed at the sight, and she thought she might resort to begging if he didn't hurry. Then he slipped his pants off and his proud length springing out, hard, and thick and long. She knew he was large. She'd felt it enough times on their travels. But seeing it erect and swollen, at her eye level, she was shocked by it.

He pressed her back to the ground, his hand reaching for her core. He grunted in satisfaction when he touched her, lighting a spark from her head to her toes.

"You're so fucking wet for me," he whispered in her ear. "Good girl."

She placed a hand on his, stilling his deliberate strokes. "Normally, I'd like the foreplay, but I want you inside of me. *Now*."

Or she'd go insane.

She might even die.

This wanting was too much, too intense. She could barely think, barely breathe, for the wanton need coursing through her.

He smiled, lining himself up over her, and she felt him at her entrance, nudging. But he didn't thrust in. He encased her face with his hands, running a thumb along her cheek.

"You really want this?"

"*Yes,*" she ground out, every one of his touches scraping across her with intense pleasure.

"Say please."

She frowned, pursing her lips.

He nudged her entrance again, and she swallowed a groan.

"Say please, Onora. I need to hear it." His voice was a command, an order.

"You're cruel," she spat, unable to just obey so easily, even in the face of her raging desire, even as his persistence sent a thrill through her.

He grinned, kissing her fiercely, and she met the strokes of his tongue with the same fervor.

"Say it," he demanded, his voice going low.

She fixed him with a look of challenge, grinding her hips against him. His eyes flashed as he grunted, and a wave of heat washed over her. He gripped his hard cock, running it along the length of her, pressing the swollen head first against her apex, then carefully inside of her. She gasped, and he pulled out, pressing the tip in again, the thickness of it already stretching her.

"Say please, Onora," he growled.

"Please, Drys," she finally whimpered.

He thrust in, unable to go all the way, and both groaned from the sheer bliss of it. He came out, then thrust in again, a few more times until she was able to take him fully. A moan escaped his lips with each one. He gave her two hard strokes, slow and deliberate. Then he stopped, his breathing desperate and hard.

She couldn't take it, the pause, the edging. It was too much. She needed more, more of him. She rolled her hips against him, and he sucked in a sharp breath.

"Fuck, fuck, fuck, fuck, *fuck*," he muttered, each word hitting with each breath against her neck as she rolled against him. His hand pinned her hips down. "Onora stop, *stop*."

"I want this," she gasped out, needy for more friction, for anything to satiate the ache between her legs. "I want this Dryston—we don't have to stop. I trust you—I feel safe with you."

He swallowed, his labored breaths hot against her skin as he sank his teeth into her neck, making her thoughts scatter and her body come to the edge of that sweet oblivion. It had only been seconds since he'd been inside of her and she was already this far gone?

"Onora, one more bit of friction and I'll . . . I'll finish." He gritted the words out, clearly embarrassed.

She cupped his face and forced it up to hers. He looked like a man starving. Tormented. Anguished.

She rocked her hips once, then twice. He fell on top of her with a groan so deep it rumbled his chest, his wings shuddering as he twitched inside her.

She hadn't finished, but knowing that he'd only been able to last inside of her for thirty seconds made her feel smug as the darkest pit. He looked at her, that clarity washing over him, and she smirked. His nostrils flared.

"Do you come so quickly with all your lovers, Lord Dryston? Haven't you been bragging this entire time about how you'd make me scream? Did you mean from frustration?"

"Godsdamnit, Onora," he growled, then thrust his hips again, his cock still twitching, his hand gripping her hair. She tried to hold it back, not wanting to give him an even ounce more of satisfaction, but a muted whimper still escaped her.

He grew harder inside of her as he thrust into her, filling her with a blissful agony.

Dryston ran a thumb along her bottom lip. "That won't happen again. And I will make you scream, Onora. I'm going to fuck you absolutely senseless."

"Don't make promises you can't keep," she gasped.

"What was that, darling?" he drawled, leaning over her, not losing his rhythm. "I couldn't hear you over your loud, desperate breathing."

"Fuck you," she whimpered.

"Only because you asked so nicely earlier."

He leaned up, on his knees and thrust hard into her, slow, deliberate, making her feel every inch of him, and she arched off the ground. He looked so smug now, and she glared at him but it was short-lived, because she gasped in ecstasy as his thumb moved to the apex of her thighs, slowly making circles as he drove into her.

She lost all sense but the ones that felt his every ravaging but careful touch. He was above her, his wings out, his chest heaving and covered in sweat, and she wasn't certain she'd ever recover from the sight—the feel of it all. Shadows burst from both of them, dancing and twining, caressing one another and adding to the intensity and pleasure.

This coupling was so unlike any other she'd had. Something in her seemed to snap into place—a piece of a puzzle she'd never known had been missing and she wanted him closer, nearer. She reached up, clasping his neck and pulling him over her. Their lips met in a slow dance, ardent but controlled. Their breaths mingling, their sweat mingling, her very self mingling into his. She could hardly grasp where she ended, and he began. They were two bodies moving as one, climbing, running, reaching that climax together.

And when she came, he followed her over that edge only a second after, both of their cries echoing in the forest.

He toppled on top of her, heaving as he peppered her in kisses, his cock twitching inside her for long after, moans and soft whimpers escaping both in the long-lasting aftermath.

He wrapped his arms around her and flipped over, taking her with him as he held her tightly. She gave him a long, languid kiss, then fell against his chest—sleep finding her quickly.

# CHAPTER 34
# DRYSTON

The world around him was muted orange light. Confused and disoriented, Dryston blinked awake. His wings curled around them, and Onora's face rested against his chest, her soft and steady breaths feathering against him. Her skin against his was like a drug, the scent of her heady and intoxicating.

Heat and desire flooded his body as the memories of the night before crashed into him. It felt like a fever dream. He remembered waking up and quickly she was kissing his neck, grinding against him. He took her another time, and they fell into slumber almost as quickly as it had happened. Then that happened several more times.

He'd come so many times the night before, and he felt sore all over. She shifted, and he moved, allowing her to sit up as he grabbed his shirt, pulling it on.

She blinked her eyes awake, a soft expression there that laid him bare. He'd never seen her so calm and open around him. She'd told him last night that she trusted him, that she felt safe, and he thought he'd do anything to keep it that way.

Her eyes darted up, and he followed them to his curled wings.

*Curled wings.*

His stomach dropped, heart racing. The telltale sign of a mate bond—curled wings to protect the other person. He shot her a glance, worried. She stiffened, her face hardening as she looked away and cleared her throat as she stumbled to her feet. The shock of the rejection rippled through him, and he stood too, pulling his face into a calm mask. She opened her mouth to say something, then closed it, turning to grab her clothes and pull them on.

So they wouldn't talk about it. That was fine. Regret sullied his racing blood. They had built a rapport, and he'd managed to shatter it in one night.

One glorious fucking night.

He was never getting over it.

"Listen, I think we both had fun last night," she said, not looking at him as she buckled her trousers. "But it was a mistake. It won't happen again . . . If you can control yourself."

His nostrils flared, and he drew in a breath. She grabbed for her shirt, hastily pulling it on as if her words were nothing. As if they hadn't fucked over six times the night before. As if they hadn't fallen asleep in each other's arms.

As if she wasn't his godsdamned mate.

"Good," was all he said, then stood and began dressing.

His mate. She was his mate. Which explained a lot. But he'd just consummated the bond with her without even telling her that they were mates. Without a wedding or any type of formality. With other demons, they would feel the bond keenly, and consummating the bond without a discussion wasn't done.

Fuck.

She finished dressing by sheathing her dagger in her boot and finally looked up at him. Amusement danced on her features—completely unfazed by the fact that he was now bonded to her. She couldn't feel it—surely.

"You seem distracted," she purred. "Do you need more rest? Did I wear you out last night?"

He flexed his jaw and flashed her a grin. “Hardly. Want to go another round, Lieutenant?”

She huffed an incredulous laugh, but her cheeks colored and her eyes dipped to his lips. “No—that’s not happening again. We got it out of our systems. It’s done.”

Dryston kept grinning, walking past her, even as his stomach dropped away at the realization.

He had a mate.

And she wanted nothing to do with him.

TANNIN EYED them suspiciously as he poured tea into their cups, setting the steaming mugs in front of them on the kitchen table. “But Elgin is safe?”

Dryston nodded, taking a drink. “As far as we know. He’s in Orc Haven, safe.”

Tannin gave them a weak smile. “I hoped to see him in the flesh, but I’m glad he’s safe. What’s your plan now?”

Dryston looked at Onora, who seemed to be looking pointedly away from him.

“Can I stay with you for a few days?” Onora asked. “Just until I figure something out?”

Tannin nodded. “Stay as long as you need.” He looked at Dryston then.

Dryston drew a weary hand over his face. “I’m meeting other demons along the coast, if everything goes well, and then heading back to The Darkened City.”

Port Arro, to be exact. He’d told Kalen and Maria in his letter to meet him there and to leave at the first sign of danger, or if he hadn’t found them in a week’s time. That was coming close. Only a few more days and the sooner he could get out, the better.

But that meant leaving Onora.

His mate.

"Are you going to be safe here?" he asked her.

She quirked a brow. "Of course. I have plenty of friends to help me." Her eyes darted to Tannin, and he smiled. It seemed whatever bitterness had existed between them was entirely gone now. A stab of jealousy shot through him, and he gulped down more of the tea.

"Stay the night, Lord Dryston," Tannin said. "I'll give you provisions, and you can leave in the morning."

"Thank you," Dryston said.

DRYSTON TRIED to sleep early that night. Tried to not picture Onora's flushed face and sweaty, matted hair as she panted her desperate pleas for his cock the night before.

And well . . . he was failing horribly. He wanted to see her, talk to her—anything. They didn't have to fuck, even if he had a raging hard-on that didn't want to leave.

Fuck.

The mating frenzy was no joke—he'd known this, and yet here he was, still shocked by the overwhelming desire to fuck her senseless, to claim her—to make love to her over and over and over again until he couldn't anymore.

Dryston rubbed his face. He needed to get a grip. He stood and began pacing when the scent of desire and arousal hit him in a wave that nearly knocked him over. He recognized that scent of arousal, sweet and musky, and his cock tightened against his trousers.

*Fuck.*

Onora?

He groaned. Was she with Tannin right then?

Images of the two of them flashed in his mind, and a keen rage filled him. He should go next door, knock it down and investigate. Teach Tannin a thing or two.

He shook his head. What in the pit was he thinking? That wasn't like him. Not at all.

He attuned his hearing, sending it out so he could better grasp what was happening in the next room. Much to his dismay, he could hear her labored breaths and soft moans, stifled, trying to stay quiet. His cock throbbed harder against his pants, and he clenched his jaw, agony rippling through him.

Not thinking, he stood and padded to the door, tapping his knuckles loudly. A muffled groan was heard, and he was simultaneously turned on and annoyed. If Tannin was in there, he had no idea what he would do. He knew what he should do—which was leave and let them make their own choices. What he wanted to do was throw him out. Or tell him he could stay and watch to learn a few things.

Which was insane. He was going insane.

She moved about, cursing quietly, and it sounded like she was putting on clothes.

The door opened and Onora stood in the crack, her cheeks flushed, eyes glazed with lust, and her breath caught when she saw him, eyes darkening.

Well, fuck.

That made his knees feel weak, and his cock stirred even more.

"What do you want?"

"Was I interrupting something?" He tilted his head to look into the room behind her.

She glowered at him, stepping out and closing the door more so he couldn't see in. "That's none of your concern. What do you want?"

What did he want? He wanted to press her against the wall and fuck her so hard she screamed his name and everyone within a hundred-mile radius heard it—especially Tannin.

"What do you *want*?" she snapped, her heavy breath as subtle as a sledgehammer.

His brows raised as he flexed his jaw. "I thought I'd see if you wanted any company." He stepped forward, coming close to her, too close. His eyes flicked into the room, trying to see anything.

"I have quite enough company, thanks," she crooned.

*Control yourself.*

Easier said than done. He looked down at her, knowing that he was leveling a glare that would make a lesser person cower. Instead, she crossed her arms, standing her ground, sending the glare right back.

"Who's in there?"

"That's none of your business. Now go," she said, pressing a hand to his chest.

The scent of moonflowers hit him like a drug. His nostrils flared as he looked down at the hand on his chest. *Oh.* She'd been pleasuring herself.

She started to yank her hand back, but he caught it, bringing it to his nose and inhaling slowly. Poets and priests alike talked of the nectar of the gods, a drink so divine it would render a person inebriated for a century just from a sip of it. Dryston knew he'd just found something better—for just this faint scent was heady enough to make him lose all sense, all inhibition.

His tongue shot out, dipping between her forefinger and middle finger, licking up, the taste of her sweetness making him groan as he then brought her fingers into his mouth and sucked.

She stared at him, shocked. "What happened in the woods stays there. It was a one-time thing."

Still, she didn't move away from him.

The corners of his mouth tugged up. "I think it was at least six times for you."

She pursed her lips, and he stepped closer and she retreated into the room a step.

"Who were you thinking about?" he asked, voice rough and gravelly.

"That's . . ." She gulped, taking a deep breath that shuddered out as he put his hands on her hips, "That's none of your business."

He pulled her hips to his, pressing his hard length against her stomach and she let out a soft whimper, the sound like a death knell to any leftover sanity he could have claimed.

"Was it me?" He grinned, leaning down and brushing a kiss along her cheek.

"I would never. I have far better prospects than a scowling, arrogant bat."

His grin only widened as he took another step in, pivoting both of them so he was bracing against the wall as her back pressed into it. He could see her restraint slipping, twisting out of her grasp as she shifted, letting her legs fall open so his knee came between them.

"Then what were you thinking of? What was this man doing to you to make your cheeks so flushed and your heart race that much?"

She placed her hands on his chest to push him away, but he leaned into it harder and she drew in a sharp breath.

"Why in the darkest pit would I tell you?"

His knee came against the apex of her thighs as he dipped down to her ear, inhaling her scent deeply. "Because then I can do it to you, but better, and erase your memory of whoever you were thinking about forever." He could hear the jealousy in his voice, he could hear the danger that shaded every syllable. He should pull back, collect his thoughts—calm the fuck down. Instead, he pressed his fingers into her hips deeper and relished how it made her face twist in a look of desperate pleasure. "I'll make you forget any touch you've loved before."

"You're a brute." Despite those aggravated words, she rubbed against his thigh, pressing harder against it.

"That's right, darling, do what you need," he whispered, peppering her neck with soft kisses, ending with an even softer bite. "Tell me what your fantasy is."

She swallowed, silent before answering. "Your hands, inside of me," she croaked out.

"So, you were thinking about me?" He growled, gripping her hips tighter, his fingers sinking into her soft flesh. He wished it were his cock sinking into her warm heat, but this would have to do for now.

"Don't press your luck, Dryston, or the only way I'll be thinking about you is how to best display your severed head on a pike."

He chuckled, taking a quick bite out of her earlobe. "You're so feisty tonight. Did your fantasy of me get you that wound up?"

She slipped her hands in his hair and tugged hard. He grunted. "I said, don't push your luck, Dryston."

He pulled back and looked at her, grinning, before he brought his lips down to hers. They met like a comet streaking across the sky, burning up in a blaze of blues and reds and oranges. Her lips were so soft, so damnably kissable. He devoured them, their tongues tangling, swiping inside, needing more, more, more. If she devoured him whole, he'd die of bliss. He only knew that the clothes between them—any space between them—was too damn much.

He pushed up her nightgown, then he knelt down, kissing below her belly button, over her tuft of hair, before he hiked her leg over his shoulder and pressed his lips against those soft, perfectly wet lips of hers. She tasted like midnight, like the scent of moonflowers drifting on a cold winter wind. He sucked and licked like he was dying of thirst, like this was his only sustenance, the only thing that could bring him back from the brink of death.

Maybe it was.

Her groans made him grow tortuously hard and when she grabbed his horns and started rubbing, he whimpered so loud he had to stop, just pressing his face into her cunt, breathing and trying to form any thought or process of the mind to continue.

"Oh," she said, her breathy voice like a direct stroke to his cock. "*Oh* . . ."

He grabbed her hand, looking up at her, the glorious sight of her curves on display making him lose his train of thought again. "I'm trying to focus."

She smirked. "It looks like I'm more likely the one to make you scream tonight."

"We'll see about that."

He pressed his face back to her folds, sucking hard, and she moaned, rocking her hips and he pressed two fingers inside of her. Hooking his fingers, he gave a pulsing motion as she arched her back against the wall, her hands grabbing his horns, holding herself in place and sending a rush of pleasure through him. He added another finger, then another as he continued licking carefully in a circle. Then he brought his tail up, slowly adding it in, and she let out a cry that she quickly aborted, clamping her mouth shut.

He looked up as he moved his hand and tail inside of her, watching her come undone, her face twisted in a beautiful agony, her hands gripping his horns like it were the only thing keeping her upright.

"Don't—don't stop," she gasped. When he didn't respond, she added, "Please."

He flashed her a wicked grin, sucking hard and swiping as he moved his hand in and out as she whimpered, the noise peppering him like a direct stroke against his cock. Her legs began to shake and his other hand steadied her. She clenched around his hand, her body going rigid as moan after moan escaped her perfect mouth and she rippled around his fingers.

He stood, drawing her to him as she gripped his shirt, looking up at him with face flushed and eyes clear, her body practically limp. He kissed her, and she sucked on his lower lip, their noses brushing against each other as he drew back a fraction.

"I need you," he whispered.

She only nodded, her lips trailing to his neck, kissing him and making his wings shudder. Every inch of his skin felt on fire, every nerve exposed and her every touch about to send him over the edge.

He swiftly removed his pants, grabbing her by the ass and lifting her up, propping her against the wall. Her eyes went wide in surprise and he kissed her, bringing his cock up to her entrance and thrusting in. Her head fell back, her eyes closing as her hands flew back up to his horns, rubbing this time, taking her time to brush over the ridges, making him grow harder inside of her.

"You feel so fucking good," he moaned against her neck.

He thrust into her at a ravaging pace, trying to hold back and entirely unable to. Her hands, her bare body, her scent—it all mingled to make him lose complete control, unable to stop even as the wall shook, the pictures falling off and clanging to the ground. But he didn't care. He only cared about this—being inside of her, being one with her, feeling every part of her on him.

He came with a moan that he buried in her neck, clamping down on the skin. Picking her up, he carried her to the bed as she let out a yelp of surprise. He'd laid her down, ripping back the covers and crawling in next to her, gathering her against him. His hand traced her face, and she looked at him with a keen vulnerability that wasn't lost on him. She'd said she trusted him. And he wouldn't do anything to hurt that.

"This is the last night we spend together, Drys," she whispered, closing her eyes against his touch.

He knew it was. He'd tried to stay away, but that was impossible. As long as she was near, he would want to be next to her. They would part soon, and then what? He'd have to recover himself and try to go on without her.

"I know," he said. "Just tonight."

She opened her eyes and nodded, then he leaned down and kissed her.

# CHAPTER 35
# ONORA

Onora woke to the morning sun, a pair of green eyes staring at her like she was the only thing that existed in the world.

Then she heard the loud and obnoxious clanking of kitchenware.

"Is that—"

"I think Tannin wants us to wake up and come down for breakfast," Dryston said with a chuckle.

The sound sent her lower stomach fluttering, and she hid her face in his chest again, afraid he'd see every tender thought now racing through her mind.

Neither made a move to leave. He'd fucked her over and over again throughout the night. The frenzy of it left her sore and aching. She needed a reprieve, but still her body craved his. His every touch and caress had felt like touching a raw nerve and igniting it with a fire of passion.

More clanking sounded through the floorboards and she groaned.

"Should we help him with breakfast?" she asked.

Dryston nodded, taking a lock of her hair and tucking it behind her ear.

The way that made her chest ache wasn't good. The sooner he left for The Darkened City, the better. She didn't need to catch feelings for him.

She rolled out of bed at the thought, grabbing a towel from the washbasin and scrubbing herself down before putting her clothes on. She turned to see Dryston watching her with appreciation as he buttoned his shirt and she turned away, unable to stop the grin that slid across her face. Maybe she could enjoy just this—this morning, this last bit of time together. Then she'd lock it away like a keepsake.

Yeah, she really needed him to leave.

She'd seen his look in the forest, the morning after. Like the realization of what they'd done had hit him.

She knew regret when she saw it.

She practically fled down the stairs, desperate to have someone else present to help break up her insanity. She came to the kitchen, breathless, to see Tannin aggressively scrambling eggs.

"Good morning," he said with a lofty air.

She groaned inwardly.

"Need any help?" she asked.

He shook his head, gesturing for her to sit as Dryston came in and Tannin looked him over, lips pouting.

"Good morning, Tannin," Dryston said, sheepish.

Tannin narrowed his eyes. "I'm glad *you're* having a good morning."

Onora decided to ignore that statement and instead grabbed the newspaper from the table. It had been ages since she'd gotten her hands on a copy of *The High Flyers*—a gossip page from Lesern, that somehow found out every sordid detail of obscure situations. Usually, she didn't care for it at all. Today she just wanted anything to keep her from engaging with Tannin's madness.

*Lord of Shadows still missing as Hunters scramble to find the one responsible for heinous attacks on farmlands.*

She swallowed. Dryston had been trying so hard to garner a better reputation for himself and for demons. How far would this set them back? She glanced up to see him chatting amicably with Tannin, who was trying, and failing, to ignore the demon's charm. Dryston picked up a knife and began cutting vegetables, engaging him in story after story easily.

Onora couldn't deny that Dryston had a gravity to him. Maybe everything she felt for him was nothing more than that. Maybe it was natural and inevitable that she'd be nursing some faint blush of feelings for him.

He was—aggravatingly—impressive. He'd taken over as ruler so young. He was fair to her, even when he didn't need to be—even when honor shed the burden of that guilt from him.

He was good. Inarguably so.

How had she ever thought he could be behind those attacks?

He glanced over his shoulder, giving her a wink and then he halted, staring at her with wonder, a soft smile spreading over his face, and that's when she realized she was smiling, too. Like a godsdamned idiot. On display for anyone to see.

And she couldn't stop.

This wouldn't go anywhere. It couldn't. He would go back to The Darkened City and find a wife—or didn't demons call it a mate? Have a brood of kids with her and be a wonderful ruler. Onora's face and name would pass from his memory like grains of sand out to sea. She would be someone that he'd had a wild time with, that he'd been attracted to passionately for a moment and nothing more.

She feared she'd remember him on her deathbed. And not just the perfect caresses, or the way he studied her pleasure like it were his vocation. No, instead she'd remember this. The way he'd looked at her like she was worth something.

Worth anything.

*Are you okay?*

The memory flashed behind her eyes, and they shuttered closed.

They'd been fighting the void creature outside Evolis. She'd been cornered, holding her ground, realizing that she would die. Then he came in and tackled her, blocking her from any blows by the beast. He would have died. Surely he had to have known he would die to save her. Enid had distracted it, pulling the fight to her, and that's the only reason they both survived.

But he'd saved her.

He'd covered her body with his, ready to take the blows and die to protect her.

Why had he done that? He owed her nothing. She'd been brusque at best with him, nasty at worst. She'd justified it because he was a demon. Because his kindness had to be an act. A facade.

But it wasn't.

It was who Dryston was. He would use his body as a shield to protect anyone who needed it.

And what's worse? It hadn't stopped there. He'd seen her later that night, in the hall, and his hand had brushed a stray lock out of her face, concern—true concern—lining every corner of his face as he asked her that haunting question.

*"Are you okay?"*

Because no one had ever asked her that. She was unflappable, indomitable. She was always fine. And if she wasn't, they danced around it until she was. She had to be strong—for everyone else.

*"Are you okay?"*

The tenderness and care of those words had single-handedly wrecked her. She'd hated him for it. He'd found the only chink in her armor, her only vulnerability. It had been a pricking wound that opened her up, bleeding her out like a flood.

She blinked away an odd moisture in her eyes and swallowed a foreign lump in her throat. He cared. And she couldn't pretend it was special for her. She saw the way he looked at Tannin and others and had helped that little girl. It's who he was. Maybe that was better. He would always be that way regardless of who he was interacting with.

She wanted to fall toward him like gravity. She wanted to always be near someone so safe.

But she couldn't. His home was in the Shadow Realm and hers was . . .

She didn't know where. But not there. Not with him.

"You and Onora . . . ?" Tannin let his voice trail off, his brows pinched painfully high as he looked at Dryston, his voice bringing her out of her reverie.

Dryston swallowed. "I'm . . . I'm sorry. I knew how you felt and I still—"

Tannin raised a hand. "I understand." He let out a heavy sigh. "I'll write a lament."

Dryston patted his back, giving his shoulder a tight squeeze. "That's probably the healthiest way to handle it."

Tannin nodded, then left the room, grabbing his lyre on the way out. Dryston brought two plates of eggs, potatoes, and vegetables to the table and slid it over to her.

"You two are good friends," she said, taking a bite.

Dryston shrugged. "He's a nice guy."

Tannin's voice rose outside, beautiful and cold, singing the lament of a woman who ripped his heart out. Onora groaned and Dryston chuckled.

"Even if he doesn't have the firmest grasp on reality," he said.

She grinned, eating the breakfast and savoring these last moments together. He'd be leaving today. She was a little surprised he was still here, but she wouldn't complain.

She should say something—anything, about their time together. That she didn't still hate him. Though she supposed he knew that well enough from the last two nights with him.

"Onora . . ." Dryston started, giving her a long, searching look.

"Yes?" she asked hastily, wanting him to say anything, to voice anything that was between them.

They didn't have the chance. Tannin's singing stopped and he rushed through the door holding a letter addressed to Onora. She took it, looking down at the seal.

The Hunter's Guild.

Her blood ran cold.

When she opened it, though, it was Jackson's handwriting.

. . .

Ornery,

I hope this letter finds you alive and well. You told me long ago about Tannin and I haven't breathed a word to anyone else. But I want you to know that the commander has called off the bounty on both your heads. He realized that you're not to blame and wants to talk to you. If you're interested, meet me at midnight by the border bridge. Just you and I to talk.

Love,

Jackson

That odd lump returned, and she swallowed it down again. They weren't being chased anymore. Their names had been cleared and she could return home.

She had a home now.

# CHAPTER 36
# ONORA

"Who is that from?" Dryston asked.

"Jackson," she replied. "He says they realize you aren't the cause of the attacks, and the warrant has been called off."

Dryston frowned. "How does Jackson know we're here?"

"He knows about Tannin, and he knows that Tannin would be who I would suggest seeing to take the shackles off. He's the only one who knows, though."

"Do you trust the missive?" He rubbed his jaw, worried.

"It's in his handwriting." She stood. "I have to get ready. He wants me to meet him at midnight. Tannin, do you have a horse I can borrow?"

Tannin nodded. "I'll get her ready for you."

Dryston grabbed her arm as she went up the stairs. "Are you certain it's safe?"

"Yes. Jackson wouldn't send this to me if it wasn't. And maybe I can help figure out what's happening with the attacks."

It was silent for a moment, his eyes swimming with questions.

"Don't go back," he said.

"They're my people," she said quietly.

"I don't think it's safe."

She clenched her jaw. "What would you have me do?"

There was nowhere else to go. If she didn't have this . . . She had nothing.

"Come with me," he said fervently.

"To The Darkened City?" she scoffed.

"You could."

She frowned, crossing her arms. "And be killed on sight?"

"They won't—I won't allow it."

She chewed the inside of her lip. "I can't . . . Dryston. I just can't."

She believed he would protect her. But at what cost? He had loyalty to his people, and would they truly accept her? Be comfortable with her? A human in the cave city of the Shadow Realm? It was laughable. Besides, she would have to watch him find his mate and the thought of that made her stomach turn.

"Or stay with the elves or orcs. Just don't go back to the human lands yet," he added flippantly. "Just be careful. Make sure it's truly safe."

His care warmed her heart in uncomfortable ways, but it was only that—his general care.

"I will. Jackson wouldn't summon me if he thought there was any chance of endangering me."

She went up the stairs, grabbing the few items she had. She'd need to leave soon, and she wanted to carry light. Tannin had a few of her old daggers she'd left here, and she carefully placed them on her, then headed back downstairs. Dryston waited for her in the kitchen, arms crossed, chewing his lip as he stared out the window at the fields in front of the house.

There were so many things to say—too many. The words tangled, collapsing in on themselves until they were nothing. So instead, she pulled out her favorite dagger, the only one she'd kept on her this entire time and handed it to him. He stared at it in her hand before taking it, turning it over, the etchings glinting in the light. It was a demon dagger, one she'd taken during the occupation and had become a comfort to her. She been able to hide it and keep it secret and it had always felt like a small protection.

Because of that, she never actually used it. She just kept on her for good luck. She'd always seen it as a sign that she'd used their weapons against them, that she'd overcome the demons. But handing it to Dryston colored a new meaning. It meant she felt free of that old fear—mostly. She was certainly becoming free of it, and was when it came to him. He'd made her feel safer and more protected than the dagger ever had.

But she didn't tell him any of that.

"You'll need some form of protection on your way to Port Arro," she said stiffly. "I have plenty enough."

"This is a demon-made dagger," he said, frowning.

"I took it long ago, during the occupation. It's good luck."

He gave her a faint smile, concern and many other emotions swimming in his eyes. She wanted to say all the words that bubbled up in her, but she shoved them down. It was no use now.

"Goodbye," she said.

"Goodbye."

Then, she left.

~

It took several hours to reach the bridge, but she had plenty of time to wait and think before it was midnight. The cool night air bit at her cheeks and she nuzzled against Tannin's horse, shielding herself from the wind. She supposed Dryston was already in Port Arro by now, perhaps making plans to fly far from Nemus, back to his home.

She would probably never see him again. Their goodbye had been brief, succinct, barren. There were many unsaid words between them, but the two nights of bliss would have to be enough. The thought hurt more than she cared to admit, so she just looked up at the moon, wondering about the moon goddesses of the demons. She wondered if

Dryston would have shared more with her if she'd gone with him. It would have been foolish, but part of her wished she had taken him up on it.

Stupidity. She hadn't survived this long by being impulsive and driven by her emotions. The demons would want her killed. Dryston would grow tired of her, and she'd truly have nowhere. She just needed to speak to Jackson, to see him and hear his voice and her mind would be righted.

Finally, she heard horses approaching, and she frowned, looking to the other side of the bridge. There were so many Hunters coming toward her. Hadn't Jackson said it would be just them? Or had he said that only she should come?

Scanning the faces of the Hunters, she didn't see Jackson, but she did see Brayden. An oily feeling slithered in her stomach, some primal fear that made her almost mount the horse and run.

But Jackson had said that the bounty was called off. Maybe Jackson was at the back and she couldn't see him.

Brayden dismounted as he came closer, walking toward her. She took a step back as other Hunters rode swiftly to the front, surrounding her.

Shit.

"You came," he said, a calculating smile spreading across his face.

"Where's Jackson?" she asked.

"Good question. We hoped you could tell us," Brayden said.

"He sent me a letter and—"

Brayden laughed.

"Gods, I forgot how grating that noise is," she spat, and Brayden snarled.

"I sent you that letter. I was afraid you'd be able to tell it wasn't from him, but I suppose you are easily fooled."

Her heart stuttered. "It was in his handwriting."

Brayden waved his hand dismissively. "That's an easy enough spell."

"For who?" Tannin had told her once that forgery required a great deal of care and skill, and many were unable to perform spells like that. Too much precision. It was easier to do it by hand.

"I think you know her, but I don't want to spoil the surprise. She's very excited to see you again."

"Who?"

He tsked, waving his finger. "Now, now, patience is a virtue, dear."

He came next to her, grabbing her arm. She recoiled, but his grip was strong and there were too many arrows poised to fly at her if she tried to fight him.

What in the darkest pit was going on?

"Where's Jackson?" she demanded again.

"Where, oh where? See, no one has heard hide nor hair of him for about a week now. We thought perhaps we'd draw you both out with this. But it seems he's less gullible."

She cursed under her breath. The letter hadn't sounded like Jackson, but she hadn't even bothered to question it because it was in his handwriting.

A fool. She'd been a damned fool.

Brayden grabbed her sleeve, pulling it back. He looked over her tattoos with disgust, then held her arm up for all to see. Hunters grumbled and cursed, and she yanked her arm back.

"He's marked her as his mate!" Brayden said, pointing at her in horror.

Onora glowered at him, but the protest died on her lips.

*Fuck. Oh. Fuck!*

She had to get out of this. They would kill her. Put her up for some sham trial before killing her. Full circle, as she'd done to Dryston.

But if she fought him, she could die.

It didn't matter, she wouldn't go down without a fight—without her honor.

She brought her elbow down forcefully, hitting him on the nose, the crack filling the air. He cried out and lunged at her, but she brought her dagger up, slashing at him, cutting his arm. He drew his sword and circled her.

Well, fuck.

This wasn't good at all.

He slashed down at her, and she ducked under as the other Hunters surrounded her. She slashed at one's leg and he cried out as an arrow flew, grazing her cheek.

Fuck, fuck, fuck.

Another slashed at her and sliced her arm, the warm, sticky blood dripping as she rolled to the side, away from them. Then another arrow flew, hitting her in the shoulder of her dominant arm.

She would have to give up. But then she'd be subjected to the gods knew what.

Let me out to play, Onora.

She didn't push the voice away this time, she didn't shut it down. What other options did she have?

*Yes?* she asked it.

Let me make them pay.

Onora breathed in heavily, her fear of whatever this was overtaking her. What was she unleashing? What was she doing? This phantom voice that had followed her since childhood. So she closed her eyes and let it take over.

First, the world became black. A pitch blackness the likes of which she'd only seen one other time. In Evolis, when she'd been fighting Hevena. Everything shifted, tilting, things warping like noodles on a fork.

That's right. Let go. Let me take care of you.

She'd lost control before, losing track of time and space, and she tugged on the reins.

Okay then, I'll let you see.

The shadows shifted and she could see—but it felt different. As if it weren't her eyes perceiving it, but instead her whole body became aware of things in front of and behind her, as if she could feel it and then her mind could see it clearly. The Hunters were shouting in fear, but every sound was swallowed up in the intense blackness, dying away as it sank away like water in a drain.

Brayden ran, fleeing somehow, and the voice inside of her didn't care, letting him go.

A cold seeped in, more intense than winter, greater than the ice caps of the mountains, a cold that pierced the bones and wrapped around them like a blanket. They turned to ice, and she knew their veins were cracking and breaking, their faces fashioned in an eternal scream.

Onora's powers were shifting, growing, pulling until she was unaware of herself, of time, of anything but cold darkness.

When she came to, their bodies lay on the ground, their lips and skin blue. She shuddered out a cold breath that drifted on the air. Her shoulder ached, her head dizzy. She'd lost a decent amount of blood and there was poison in this arrow. Regular poison, not the velin that only affected magical beings. She stumbled to the horse, and carefully climbed on her back. She rode her over the plains, her vision blurring and her heart racing. Where could she go? Tannin's place was compromised, and she didn't know where Jackson was. She had nowhere to go —no one to trust.

Except Dryston.

Where was he now?

Something inside of her tugged and pulled, like a cord of gold. And in her muddled mind, hazy with each thought that slipped away, she followed it. Because what else could she do?

# CHAPTER 37
# DRYSTON

Port Arro was a bustling city even at night. Dryston knew that he had an alliance with King Leeth and, assuming that was still held, he should be safe in the elven territories. But he didn't want to take any chances. He'd asked Silenus for the name of an inn in Port Arro that would provide discretion, then he'd told Kalen and Maria to meet him there.

He hoped he hadn't missed them already.

Lights shone from streetlamps, lighting his way past taverns bursting with sailor songs and the sour scent of ale and rye bread. He kept to the shadows, knowing that it was futile to try and sneak. Elves were larger than humans, but their physique tended toward slender and willowy, not stocky like his. Not to mention his wings, horns, and tail.

No one seemed to notice, though, as he passed by drunken patrons and an assortment of other people who seemed more than happy to turn a blind eye if he returned the favor. He came to the inn, The Fish and Net, and stared at the outside. It was worn down, the sign cracked and fading to the point that he had to stare for a while before piecing together what it said. An enchanted light flickered inside, old and worn. He opened the creaking door and entered. The tavern was crowded as well, but the people here only gave him wary looks and then turned back to their tables, sticking to strict cliques.

He pulled his hood down and came to the bar. The barkeep, an older satyr, tall and strong with a slashing scar over his chin, was filling tankards as he approached. When he finished, he came up, looking Dryston over with a quick, scrutinizing glance. Thankfully, he had no chains on him and was wearing clothes Tannin had scrounged up for him. They were ill-fitting, but that wasn't apparent under his cloak.

"What can I do ya for?" the satyr asked.

"Have two other demons come through here, a male and female?" Dryston asked.

The satyr gave a curt nod. "They're upstairs. Arrived two days ago. I suppose you're the one they've been asking about every day?"

Dryston gave a flat-lipped smile. He'd hoped for more caution, but Silenus had assured him that the innkeeper used discretion and enforced it lethally because otherwise his business would dwindle to nothing.

"I suppose I am," he responded.

The satyr reached under the bar and grabbed a key, handing it to him. "They're in this room."

Dryston thanked him, sliding several gold coins to him that Silenus had given him. "Silenus says hello."

The satyr's features softened a bit, but all he gave was an approving grunt before turning back to his work.

Dryston made his way up the stairs to the room carved on the key ring. Coming to the door, he fingered the dagger Onora had handed him. She'd placed it in his hand, telling him that he needed some form of protection. She'd said it brusquely, quickly, not looking at him. But he felt the weight of the gesture even as he touched it at his waist now.

He hoped she was safe and happy. Now reunited with her people. The thought felt bitter but he tamped it down. The way she'd said they were her people—as if she and him were worlds apart, unable to bridge that gap. Maybe she was right. Maybe the mate bond had been some magical mishap. Some binding that had slipped through, ancient and strong, from that portal Enid had opened up.

She was a Hunter, trained from childhood to kill his kind. And he was a demon—a being she hated. Even if those two nights had shaken his belief in that. Even if he couldn't claim hatred for her anymore. She'd left, acting like his offer to come to The Darkened City was ridiculous.

Shaking his head, he knocked on the door. It did no good to dwell on it. He'd have plenty enough time to try and fill that aching, bruised void of his mate's absence when he was back home.

Scuffling sounded in the room, hushed voices, then the door cracked open and Kalen's face appeared before him, harsh and calculating, falling away to a mad relief. He flung the door wide and yanked Dryston in, shutting the door behind him and locking it, then shoving a trunk in front of it.

"Well, hello to you, too," Dryston said.

Kalen pulled him into a hug and said with a voice thick with worry, "Gods, we feared the worst."

Maria was close behind, her eyes lining with tears as she gave him a quick hug and pulled back, turning to discreetly wipe a tear away. Dryston swallowed down the emotion that lumped in his throat.

"I did, too," he said, voice cracking.

"We'll leave in the dawn hours," Maria said, already beginning to pack up their items. "We can't tarry here much longer."

"Tell me what's happened while I've been gone," Dryston said.

Kalen closed his eyes, shuddering out a breath. "A lot. The human king has declared war on the Shadow Realm. He's said that anyone who aids you or demons will meet his wrath."

The hair on his arms stood up. "Were you safe in Orc Haven?"

Maria nodded. "Yes. Lord Killgan has issued a warning to the king that if he tries anything in the orc realm they will retaliate."

Dryston rubbed a hand over his face. So much strife caused by this all. "And King Leeth?"

Kalen shook his head. "He's been silent. Pointedly so. We can't make out what it means."

"He could be holding off, not wanting to start a war until he can talk to you," Maria said. "For now, the Hunters haven't been able to cross the borders into orc lands without being arrested."

Dryston let out a sigh of relief. "The sooner we can head home, the better . . ." He rubbed his jaw. "Onora received a letter from a friend saying that the chief Hunter had called off the hunt. Saying they realized it wasn't us."

Kalen scoffed. "Did she fall for that? That's not true in the slightest. This morning in the market someone told me to leave soon, as the Hunters would start killing any demon indiscriminately. The chief sent out yesterday a decree to kill any demon on sight, and to bring Lieutenant Onora in dead or alive."

Dryston's blood ran cold. "The letter was a farce?"

"Yes, and good riddance, I suppose," Kalen said with a growl. "If I ever see her again she'd better pray to any god she worships because I'll take her and—"

Kalen's words gurgled to a stop as Dryston's hand wrapped around his throat, lifting the demon off his feet. Shock filled his features as his wings tucked in and he grasped at Dryston's arm.

"You'll what, Kalen?" Dyrston's growl was lower and filled the room less, but somehow it was far more threatening. He dropped the male and Kalen stumbled back, grasping at his throat. Dryston's chest rose rapidly. His nostrils flared as shadows burst from around him, threatening and poised toward Kalen. "You'll do what to her?"

Maria placed a hand on his arm and he drew in several breaths, calming himself. Kalen rubbed his throat, a twin look of hurt and anger in his eyes.

Dryston was silent for a moment longer, both of them waiting patiently for an explanation.

"She's my mate," he said through gritted teeth.

Shock rippled over their features.

"Oh shit," Kalen spat under his breath.

"Where is she, then?" Maria asked.

"She went back to the Hunters. The ones who apparently want to recapture her."

Fuck.

"I have to find her."

Kalen grabbed his arm before he could leave. "She made a choice, Drys. You have to let her go."

"She didn't know. She was fooled by them," he said gruffly, and Kalen drew his hands back, throwing them up in defeat.

"It's folly to leave now. She will be captured and taken, and you have a realm to lead. You have a family and colony who need you."

Dryston rubbed his jaw as his mind reeled. He had no clue where she was. He had no idea how to find her.

Yet something tugged in his gut. Like a rope tied around his waist, pulling him in a direction he could almost see. He jolted, turning to the door the moment he heard a commotion below them.

He yanked the trunk out of the way and rushed down the stairs. The innkeeper was holding someone limp in his arms, a head full of blond hair and an arrow sticking out of her. Others crowded around him, a man coming to help lift her. Dryston shoved through the others, carefully taking her out of their arms. She blinked, grasping his shirt weakly.

"I didn't know where else to go," she croaked out.

"You came to the exact right place," he said, holding her tighter against him.

"She's poisoned," the satyr said.

"I can help," the man said. "I know healing spells."

Dryston snarled, and the man threw up his hands.

"He's overprotective of her," Kalen said, his words clipped in annoyance.

"I don't know if I can trust you," Dryston said to the man, ignoring Kalen.

"You can trust anyone here, son," the satyr said, crossing his arms. "As long as you keep your own mouth shut."

Dryston looked at the faces staring at him, every muscle in his body tensing. It was a gamble, but she needed healing. Finally, he nodded, the man grabbing supplies from the satyr and following him up the stairs.

The man worked a while on her, taking out the arrow with Dryston's help, then cleaning the wound as she babbled incoherently, her skin clammy and pale. Then he muttered a spell, slow and soothing. When he finished, he turned to Dryston.

"She'll probably sleep for a few days, but she should be good."

"Thank you," Dryston said.

"Can we transport her?" Maria asked.

Dryston shot her a glare, and she shrugged.

"We need to leave—soon."

The man nodded. "Yes. She's fine, but the spell puts the person to sleep for a while so that the healing isn't painful. Once that wears off, she will wake. It's different for each person, and humans usually take longer. But she won't be harmed by traveling."

Dryston pulled out a few more gold coins and handed them to the man. "That's all I have now. But I can get you more and—" He pushed Dryston's hand away.

"No, thank you," he said. "We take care of each other here. I beg your discretion in exchange for the services rendered, and I'll keep your secrets as well, Lord Dryston."

Dryston nodded. "I thank you."

The man stood. "You don't have to worry about anyone here reporting you, but she was riding a horse through the streets, muttering loudly. I don't know the state of things too well, but conflict is brewing and it's best if you all get back to the Shadow Realm before it reaches a boiling point."

"We leave tonight," Dryston replied, looking down at Onora.

Hopefully she would like The Darkened City. Because she had no other option now.

# CHAPTER 38
# ONORA

*Varek yanked her close, his alcohol-soaked breath hitting her face. "You're turning into quite the beautiful prize," he said, his eyes darkening. All she could see were his horns above his head, the brown of his wings looming out about her. She'd feared this day coming. When he would stop seeing her as a funny little pet and start seeing her as a woman. She was still too young. Far too young.*

*His finger came along her cheek, and she shuddered.*

*"There's no need to fear, sweet thing. My thrall means you'll enjoy every minute of it."*

*She pulled back, whimpering in fear and seeing, to her dismay, that he enjoyed that more. Racking her brain, she tried to find a way out, a way to escape.*

*He laughed. Cruel and heartless and terrible as he let her go. She stumbled back a step, holding her arms against her. Then he backhanded her so hard she fell to the ground. He removed his belt, and she wondered this time, as she did every time, if the removal was for a beating or something worse.*

*He came close to her ear, his hot breath hitting it in a way that made her want to vomit. "But you see, the lord says I can't do anything like that to you.*

*Yet. He needs his special little human for something, and when that's done, he said I can have you all to myself."*

*A lump formed in her throat, but no tears came. They never did anymore.*

*"But I can discipline you."*

*She became lost in the pain and the sound of leather hitting her flesh.*

Onora woke with a gasping, hard breath. She sat up, heart racing as she looked around the room. She was in a large bed with dark-blue silk sheets and a heavy velvet blanket. Checking her body, she saw that she was completely healed. The room was dark, with a few mage lights creating a dusky glow that glinted off cave walls. There was a dresser and side tables to match with ornate carvings on the mahogany wood, and next to the bed was an oversized chair with an even more oversized demon sitting in it.

Black hair fell over his face, moving with his puffing breaths and soft snores.

Was this a dream? Had she died and now she was caught in the afterlife, given visions of Dryston to sate her soul for eternity?

She moved closer to the chair and he shifted, rousing slowly, then smiling when he saw her.

"You're awake," he said, relief evident.

She nodded. The last full thing she remembered was the dead Hunters in the woods. After that it was a blur of riding on horseback, memories slipping in and out of reality, then being held in his arms.

"How do you feel?" he asked.

"Good, surprisingly. I didn't think I was going to survive that."

"You were attacked by Hunters?" His voice was a low growl, the words more a statement than a question.

"Yes. It was a trap. They forged Jackson's handwriting."

"I'll kill them all."

She coughed. "I already did . . . mostly."

He raised a brow.

"Well, the ones there. Brayden escaped—he's slimy like that."

"Then I'll kill him."

"Don't you dare."

"Or what?" He came to the bed, putting a knee down and leaning over her. She had to resist the urge to grab him for a kiss.

"It's unwise."

"I'm afraid I'm only capable of imprudent behavior when it comes to you."

"Oh?"

His eyes raked over her, and she leaned toward him, right as the door opened. Dryston moved in a flash, standing away from her, and she swallowed, hiding her disappointment. A demon entered the room, one that she faintly recognized from Orc Haven, a male with a sour disposition. His eyes flicked to her briefly, lips tightening.

"Hello, Kalen," Dryston said.

"The council wants to see you," Kalen said.

Dryston groaned. "Of course." He turned to Onora. "Do you feel up to coming to the council meeting?"

"Is she needed at the meeting?" Kalen asked.

Onora agreed with his sentiment, but the way he said it made her narrow her eyes at him. He gave her a quick glare, then fixed his face as he looked back at Dryston.

"Yes," Dryston said. "They want to discuss what our reaction to the declaration of war against us is. I think Onora has a vested interest in that and could have valuable insight."

Her stomach dropped. "King Olan did what?"

Dryston grimaced. "He wants any demons in Nemus killed on sight and has declared war against us."

She felt the blood drain from her face as she gripped the sheets. This was bad. Very bad. She stumbled out of the bed, taking her boots that Dryston handed her from elsewhere in the room, and carefully made herself as presentable as she could. She still looked haggard, but it was to be expected. She wasn't going to fuss about looks when there was a war about to break out.

She followed Dryston and Kalen out the door. The Darkened City was a marvel. Onora's eyes swiveled all around them as they walked through the intricate passageways of the cave system. Mage lights hung in sconces on the wall, giving soft glowing light of varying colors.

The first area they came through was clearly the business district. Demons stood at stands, bartering and bargaining, several sailors and merchants of varying races bringing in goods of all kinds. Bards played the lyre and sang, their voices carrying in the hall and twining with one another as they played off each other's songs, harmonizing and creating a melody that felt like magic itself.

Next, they came to an area that she assumed were schools, as children ran and played, adults keeping watch, while others sat in circles and listened to stories. Then they dipped down, following a winding trail deeper into the cool caves. A waterfall fell on the opposite side, the sound a soothing echo around them.

She heard music on one level, and then work on another and so on and so on as she followed Dryston and the others deeper and deeper into the caves. She received many curious looks, but none hostile—yet. She was certain once they knew who she was and what she'd done, she would need to watch her back.

Dryston and Kalen chatted with the head of the guard as they walked, briefing him of all that happened. Though, Dryston gratefully kept any mention of her part in his capture and almost execution out of the story. She wondered at that, the careful phrasing of everything he said. But she wouldn't bring it up. She didn't need to volunteer any of that information.

Finally they came to a set of large double doors and Dryston looked back at her. "This is the council. Let's see our fate."

Their fate indeed. She had a horrible feeling that the council would take one look at her and see her guilt. She drew in a deep breath. Cowardice had never held her back before, though, and she wasn't going to start now.

# CHAPTER 39
# DRYSTON

The council room was loud as they arrived, even standing outside the doors. That was never a good sign. The most opinionated demons in the city convening and demanding his presence was not his favorite activity to begin with. An urgent request followed by this buzzing? He already had a headache.

The double doors opened, and they walked in, Onora staying close to his side. He knew it was apprehension, maybe even a little fear, but he liked it. Liked how it made him feel needed. Wanted.

The room was full of chieftains, business owners, and his cabinet, as well as many of the royal guard. Kalen and Maria followed behind him, and the room fell silent as he entered. An older demon stepped forward, a smiling relief lighting his face. Salen was Dryston's closest advisor and had been his father's as well. He was sometimes stuck in his old ways, but Dryston was always able to get him to the middle and listen to reason. His wisdom and experience had been invaluable to Dryston.

"Lord Dryston," he said, striding forward and then pulling him into a tight, unceremonious hug, despite his formal language. Then his eyes darted to Onora. "You must be the Hunter."

Dryston turned back in time to see her stiffen, her face becoming an impassable wall of stone, the same look she'd had so often before. The last few days it had been gone, though. Seeing it again was upsetting, and he had half a mind to threaten Salen for making her feel that way.

Murmurs rose in the room, and he cursed under his breath as his shadows twined around him and poised, ready to strike. He pulled them back, inhaling a deep breath to calm them.

Salen's eyes darted between him and Onora, and Dryston noted that he wasn't the only one. He swallowed, ignoring it. He knew what they were thinking, and they were right.

"Welcome," Salen said, looking at Onora. "I've heard tale you helped Dryston escape."

She opened her mouth, but Dryston answered for her. "She saved my life. I was dying from poison arrows, and she was able to use a healing spell on me."

She gave him a curious look, but he looked back to the crowd. They had no business knowing the full scope of what had happened. It was in the past. Things were different between them now.

"We have a lot to discuss," Salen said, ushering them to the large round table in the middle of the room. It was the table for him and his advisors, the cabinet, and the chieftains of the different regions of the shadow realm.

Dryston went to the head of the table, looking behind to see Onora had stashed herself to the side, standing with the others who were not official spokespeople for the realm. She looked nervous, rigid, with her hand resting on the hilt of her dagger. Her eyes darted around the room, noting the weapons on everyone. Demons were a warrior culture. Even bards and farmers were known to be strapped with weapons at any given time.

He didn't want to leave her in a crowd of demons by herself, and there was a seat next to his, one that had gone unfilled since his parents died. He knew what it would look like to everyone else, and he hesitated a moment, before beckoning for her to come. She did, and he took the seat out and pushed it in for her to sit.

Others exchanged more glances, but he ignored it. He had no time for their idle chatter. Then he sat down and the room fell silent, save for the scrape of wooden chairs on the stone floor as the others sat.

"I, Salen, Vice Lord, call this meeting of the colonies to order." A few other demons sounded their agreement, others yawning and stretching comfortably in their chairs. Salen liked to be formal, but most demons preferred a more informal atmosphere. "Lord Dryston, let's get you up to speed."

Another older demon, Makel, cleared her throat. "There's not much we need to tell him. He's experienced it. Now let's move the motion to retaliate against the Hunters."

Murmurs of agreement rose, and Onora sat even more tense in her seat.

"There's an order to all this, Makel," Salen said. "Do not get ahead of yourself."

"They killed the first Erebus Lord and kidnapped our current one!" another chieftain cried out, banging his fist on the table. "What is there to discuss?"

"We need to hear from Lord Dryston and the human first," Layla, a younger demon chieftain, said. "There was a trial, and the Hunters claim they had good reason."

"Do you believe that?" Makel asked, incredulous.

"I believe that many Hunters most likely did believe it," Layla replied. "I don't believe our Lord did anything of the sort."

And so the fighting continued on in that fashion. Dryston drew in a deep breath, rubbing his forehead, and shot a glance at Onora. She looked by turns angry, amused, and scared. He reached under the table and placed his hand on her knee, giving it a squeeze. She met his gaze, a question there.

"You're safe," he whispered, and she nodded, still tense.

He stood, finally, and cleared his throat. "Will any of you let me speak, or will you continue your prattling?" His booming voice echoed through the cavern. The people stopped and looked at him, those who'd stood to engage in a passionate debate sitting down. "First and foremost, we will not be retaliating against the Hunters. If they want a fight, they can bring it to Medeis. We are not attacking them." Angry dissent rose, and he held up his hand, his shadows bursting around him in fury as his wings flared out, shutting down the voices. "Now, let me tell you what happened, and we can discuss after." So he did. He left out Onora being the one to kidnap him and her volunteering to execute him, but because of various questions he couldn't avoid the fact she'd been the one to try to execute him. She sat with a straight back, meeting the looks of suspicion with her own steely glare. Then he told them about the attacks, what he'd seen and heard. "It seems some lying amidst the higher ranks is occurring in the human realm. We're not going to hold individual humans accountable for their leaders."

"What of this human?" Makel asked, pointing to Onora with a snarl. "Can we hold her accountable?"

"If you wish to hold me accountable," Onora said, her voice low, commanding, and dangerous. Not a single person in the room moved or uttered a sound as she spoke. "Then challenge me. Let's fight it out and see who the gods decide needs to be held accountable."

Makel sat back, her face going sheet-white as she looked at Dryston with the same shock he felt.

Not because she'd so openly challenged a demon to a fight in a room where she was the smallest and weakest. But because that command had tugged on something primal in each one of them. It had made him want to sit and obey her every command. It had silenced a room. It had brought every one of them to attention.

And he only knew of one reason why that could be.

"My apologies," Makel said, sincere, her voice trembling, and now it was Onora's turn to look confused.

Well, she would just have to stay that way. He was in no place to have his heart ripped to shreds by her at the moment—he had a war to avoid.

Dryston leaned on the table, his eyes meeting each person's as he said, "If anyone touches Onora, I will personally skin you alive."

The room was silent, deadly so. The Lord of Shadows had spoken, and many bowed their heads in agreement, obedience. He stood upright again.

"I've just returned. Let me gather more information before anyone makes a rash decision."

Makel nodded, swallowing. "As you wish, my lord."

"We're adjourned for now." He turned, looking for Enid. She leaned against the doorframe with the swaggering grace she was well known for. "I want to speak to Avenay."

Enid's brows shot up, but she nodded, coming closer as the others dispersed, talking amongst themselves or leaving.

"Should we let Onora have a bed to rest in and . . . bathe?" Enid asked.

Onora rolled her eyes, which only made Enid grin.

"I want her to talk to Avenay with us, but after, yes," Dryston replied, motioning for Kalen and Maria. They trotted over, and Kalen's eyes shot from him to Onora, the usual calculating reasoning visible behind his eyes. "I want both of you to find servants and oversee them setting the room adjoining my own for Onora. Clothes and food and whatever other comforts she needs. You'll be her personal detail while she's here."

"The room . . . adjoining *yours?*" Kalen asked, an edge to his words.

Maria nudged him, coughing awkwardly, and he stood straighter. Enid looked at Onora with that same curious gaze as before, but this time with something more knowing.

Shadows twined around his arms again and he was getting really, really tired of it at this point. "I can trust you, can't I, Kalen?"

He knew he could. Kalen's suspicion and pushback was from love and a loyalty that ran deeper than brothers. Still, he needed to remind him on occasion that he had no business questioning him on certain things.

"Of course," Kalen replied, something like hurt passing briefly across his face. "We will protect her with our lives."

"And make sure that her nest is comfortable," Maria chirped, barely concealing the grin on her face.

Dryston leveled a glare at her. He didn't need rumors like that running around. He needed to figure out what was going on between them and talk to Onora before all the gossiping biddies of The Darkened City got to her first.

Enid motioned to Onora and Dryston. "Follow me. Avenay will be excited to talk to both of you."

AVENAY WAS IN HER STUDY, nose deep in her notes as she leaned over the desk, fingers dirtied with ink. The room was small, but the cave walls were covered with books and maps and parchment and scrolls. He wondered how she found anything in the room.

"Lover," Enid said when Avenay didn't notice them standing before them.

She jerked up, her dark curls bouncing and her brown cheeks tinged in red. "Enid," she hissed. "Not in front of your brother. We've had this talk."

Enid chuckled. "Sorry, I didn't realize lover was one of the salacious names you asked me to not call you in front of others. I only thought it was sweet ti—"

Avenay shot to her feet. "Hi, Dryston! Welcome back. You're all in one piece, which is always preferable."

"Indeed," Dryston replied, grinning. "I'm personally very thankful to be in one piece."

"Drys has something he wants to talk to you about, sugar as—"

Avenay held up her hand, glaring at Enid and silencing her—save for the laughter—and turned to Dryston.

"What is it?"

"Nothing good, I'm afraid," he said, then told her about the attacks and what they'd seen.

Enid sobered up with each word, and Avenay picked up an enchanted quill and parchment, making it write with a flick of her wrist. He could see what she wrote, mostly just jotting down what he said verbatim, but occasionally he noted things like, "related to Evolis?" and "because we opened the well?".

He finished by saying, "I can see you're already thinking what we are by your notes."

"Can you tell me where these attacks occurred?"

"Not precise locations, but I can give you a general idea. Onora may know better."

She grabbed a map and pencil. "Please."

They showed her roughly where he thought they must have been, conferring with one another to get a more precise idea of where they could be.

"I need to speak to my father," Avenay said. "And I'll ask seraphs to investigate and see the locations of these."

"What are you thinking?" he asked.

She sighed, shaking her head. "It's too soon to say. But what the witches in Evolis were up to . . . it was nothing good, Dryston. They were into dark, dark magic. Straight from the blackest pit. I'll keep investigating, and when I know more, I'll tell you."

# CHAPTER 40
# ONORA

"These should fit you well enough for now," Maria said, handing Onora a stack of folded clothes. "I'm sure Dryston will order a custom wardrobe to be made for you soon enough."

Onora frowned. "Why would he do that?"

Maria flushed, smiling and shaking her head. "No . . . well, no reason, really."

"Maria!" Kalen barked from the hallway. "Let her be."

Maria shrugged, exiting the room and giving her a small wave as she did. Kalen was a bit prickly, which she couldn't really speak against, as it was similar to her, but Maria had always put her at ease. Even if her words left her confused.

A lot was leaving her grasping for any sense.

Why would Dryston be ordering an entire wardrobe made just for her? How was that his business?

And why was it so odd for her to be in the room adjoining his? To be fair, at first she'd thought it would be an awkward arrangement, some small offshoot that would lead into his space. But it was entirely her own. It was an apartment, really. There was a bedroom, a sitting area, a small kitchen, and a bathing room. She'd barely had time to take it all in when she'd awoken, but now she saw the extravagance of it.

There was a door that could be opened wide enough that the two sitting rooms became almost like one. She hadn't dared peek into his room or explore it, even if she wanted to.

Even if Maria seemed to think she would and that it would be an okay thing to do.

She had the horrible, sneaking suspicion that they all assumed she was his paramour.

Which was a horrifying thought that she hated.

Or should hate. There was a thrill that coursed through her at the idea of how possessive and protective he'd seemed of her earlier. Of how he'd taken care of everything. When he demanded she be put up in the room next to him, it had felt like he was staking a claim on her.

And she hated that—of course.

This thing between them was a dead-end—a fling.

She shook her head. There was no reasoning about it now. She was exhausted, and the bath was calling her name. Kalen had found a servant and already told them to bring her a spread of food and drinks and whatever else she needed. She wanted mostly to eat and rest, but she also really, really wanted to take a bath.

She went into her separate bathing room, and drew water, delighted that it was heated. There was a small glass bottle of liquid next to it, blue and enticing, and she poured a bit in, shocked when soapy bubbles burst up, filling the tub, smelling like lavender.

She sank below the water and came up, brushing her wet hair back. What was she going to do? Going back to Nemus wasn't an option—she'd be killed if she ever stepped foot there again. Her chest tightened. She'd never see her squad again. She'd never traipse the foothills outside Elf Glen. She'd never wear that dusty blue cape with pride again.

Her eyes smarted, so she dunked back down below the water, coming up and scrubbing soap into her hair, watching with horror and fascination at the dirt and other debris coming out of her hair. Damn, she'd been filthier than she realized.

What could she do? She couldn't stay here . . . could she? Dryston had said she could, and said she'd be safe, but was she?

She couldn't bet on it. She'd need to make a plan soon. Avenay was here—maybe she had connections in the realm of light, and she could find mercenary jobs there. She'd never been to Medeis before, though she'd looked over the maps many times. She could travel the continent, picking up odd jobs and exploring new realms.

While Dryston stayed here, ruling.

The thought gave her a pang that she pointedly ignored.

She finished cleaning and got out of the water, quickly dressing in the nightclothes Maria had given her. They accentuated every bit of her assets.

She heard Dryston's door click on the other side, and she looked at herself in the mirror again.

The clothes clung to her curves, her peaked breasts, a cutout in the back and maybe, just maybe, she wanted him to see her like that. She so rarely wore anything like it, and she wanted to see his reaction. Even if part of her was afraid to. Even if part of her had spent so long protecting herself that even the thought of this small rejection made her heart race like crazy. Normally, men came to her, obsessed and ready to conquer, and she didn't have to dance around the delicate land of feelings.

Now that there was something between them—maybe only one-sided—she had no clue what to do. The thought of kissing him or seducing him and being rejected made her want to flee. Yes, they'd had two glorious nights, but now they were back in his home. Would he entertain her as a lover? Would she even want that?

She stood in front of his door, trying to talk herself into it. But what did she need? Why would she be knocking on his door? There had to be some plausible excuse for her interrupting his evening. She shook her head. She should just head back to bed.

But then the handle turned, and the door opened. Dryston stood before her, a look of surprise on his face.

"Hello," he said.

"Hi," she responded, stilted.

"Were you about to knock on my door?" The corners of his mouth hinted at a smirk and her old rage lit.

"Well, that's the normal thing to do, instead of just barging in. Do you normally just fling the doors open to females' bedrooms?"

"No," he responded, "usually they open them with great excitement."

She let out an exasperated huff. "Why are you trying to creep into my room?"

He chuckled. "You're wound up. I thought you were gone."

"So you were just going to come in and riffle through my things?"

Picking a fight with Dryston hadn't been her plan, but somehow those were the only words that came out of her mouth.

"What things? The handful I gave you? Do you think I want to rob you?" He was full-blown grinning now, and she could hit him. "Okay, okay. Sorry. I wanted to make sure you had everything you needed—clean bedding, clothes, whatever. Now, fess up, why were you about to knock on my door?"

A smart retort rested on her tongue, but she bit it back with a swallow. "Do you have any tea?" That wasn't why she'd been knocking, but saying "I wanted you to look at my ass in these clothes" felt stupid at the moment. And he would look at her ass, but then he'd send her along the way, and she'd be left alone dreaming of how good he looked right now in that tight shirt.

His brows shot up in surprise. "I do."

He walked into the room, beckoning her to follow. A fire blazed in the hearth, casting glowing light in the room, creating a soft warmth against the cave chill. On his sofa was a blanket and a stack of papers on the table in front of it. He put on a kettle over the stove and leaned against the wall, facing her. His eyes trailed down the length of her, tracing every curve and line, snagging on the parts she'd wanted him to look at. The slow perusal left her breathless, heart picking up its pace.

"You have new clothes," he commented, voice gravelly.

"Is that a compliment?" she quipped, wishing she hadn't. She didn't need to fish for compliments from him, even if she felt feverish for his attention.

"Oh no." He shook his head. "Just an observation."

She pursed her lips, ignoring the dip of disappointment in her stomach. What was she, a teenager?

"I'm afraid any compliment I can give to you in those clothes would be wildly inappropriate. Salacious, even."

His eyes darkened, the shadows cast from the firelight making his intent gaze capture her like a predator to prey.

The kettle whistled, and he turned, pouring it over tea in two mugs, bringing it to her. Their hands brushed, and a sudden nervousness came over her. He was a flirt. He liked getting the upper hand. It was all a power play to him. She shouldn't take his words to heart. He probably said it to a million males and females. What they had shared at the farmhouse had been nothing. He'd regretted it. She remembered his face far too well in the woods, and she didn't need to encourage her own entangled feelings.

"Thank you," she said, stepping back to leave.

"Sit with me," he said, the tone like a command, his eyes holding a plea.

She followed him to the sofa. He sat on one end and she on the other, curling her legs up in front of her. It was silent for a moment, comfortable somehow, even if she felt the need to break the quiet with anything.

"The Darkened City is different than I imagined," she said.

She'd never been known as a great conversationalist, and what was the point trying now?

"How did you imagine it?" He looked at her with genuine curiosity, maybe a bit of apprehension.

"I don't know. I guess I imagined it more like what I'd experienced during the occupation."

Revelry every night. Drinking and violence and abuse. Dryston wasn't that way, but she had thought there'd be a bit more of an edge to the place. Not the gentle scenes of children running and laughing carefree.

"What was that like?" he asked, voice quiet.

She took a sip of the tea, unsure what to say. "Bad. Really, really, bad."

He was suddenly next to her, his leg pressing against hers, a small contact, a simple touch, but it was enough. His gentle way of letting her know he was there and saw her pain. She took another swift drink to swallow the lump in her throat.

He saw her so clearly, so quickly. As if her every thought were on display for him. It should unsettle her. But somehow it was comforting.

She rarely spoke of her time under the occupation. If she did, it was to Jackson in quick, vague references they both understood. But Dryston drew her out. She wanted him to know. And she hated that she did. He was becoming someone she could lean on too much—more than she'd ever been able to lean on someone. The way he looked at her, as if his hands were open and ready to take all her fears and destroy them, to take all her anxiety and soothe it, it was too much. This couldn't last, and she couldn't get used to it.

But she tossed her normal caution to the wind for the small, faint hope that it would all work out. That this wouldn't be something that broke her more.

"I had a chain around my neck for five years," she said. "It felt weird when it came off. My neck was weak and got tired easily and sometimes I craved having it back." She closed her eyes, remembering those first couple of years of freedom. It had been almost worse than the captivity.

She could make her own decisions and she wasn't watched constantly and sometimes she missed her chains. Sometimes she missed having the object of her anger always before her. Without it, that rage came out in other ways, on other people. Like Jackson, who didn't deserve it.

Dryston's hand found her neck, wrapping around the back of it in a gentle squeeze, and she wondered how he knew that would be comforting and not awful. She looked at him and startled at what she saw: his nostrils flared, fury coiling around him in angry shadows.

"I'm sorry," he ground out. "I'm not upset at you."

She nodded, knowing he wasn't. His hand slipped down her back, his eyes finding her scars under the tattoos, and more shadows burst out around him, his jaw clenching.

"Who gave these to you?"

She rubbed her arms, looking down. "The demon who owned me."

His wings flared out, twitching. "And where is this demon now?" His words were a threat.

"He's dead."

"Did you kill him?"

Onora only nodded.

"I hope it was painful."

Her cheeks warmed at the intensity of his gaze, at the way his anger seemed to coil around her like a protective coat. "It was. I made sure of it."

"Good girl."

Her toes curled, and she held her breath as his hand rubbed her back.

"Was there anyone else?" he asked, a dangerous edge to his words.

She shook her head. "What would you do if there were?"

He drew in a deep, haggard breath. "I'd rip them limb from limb."

His hand slipped up her shoulders, trailing a line that made her shiver, then he cupped her cheek. "Go rest, Onora. You've earned it. Tomorrow I want to show you my city."

She nodded, standing and not saying anything, unable to form any words or thoughts after that encounter. She came to the door and turned to see him watching her with a tormented expression—as if her pain were his, even if he couldn't know the depth of it. Having her pain seen and heard made her feel like crying. So she just ducked her head, closing the door behind her.

She slept well that night, no nightmares or waking to a pitch-black void. She slept safely, knowing Dryston was nearby.

# CHAPTER 41
# DRYSTON

"I don't need an entire wardrobe," Onora grumbled as she pulled on her shoes.

Dryston waited patiently for her, raising a brow, looking over her clothes. They were basic linen, shapeless, and rough materials. They were youth-sized clothes made for patients at the hospital. They hit her in odd spots. Her body was more filled out than many youths, but her height was relatively similar, so it had been the closest they had.

She stood, waving a hand down her front. "It's not like I'll be wearing this forever, just while I'm here."

And how long would that be? He didn't bother asking. He hoped avoiding the question meant her stay would be prolonged, but he also feared she would bolt at the first chance. She was free to go now, but where?

"You need more clothes. Besides, there's no telling how long you'll be here."

"Are you planning on kidnapping me?" she asked, following him out the door and down the cavernous halls.

"No, I'll leave the kidnapping to you. You're much better at it."

They meandered to the business district, stopping every few minutes for someone to greet Dryston, and consequently her, then for others to ask him questions or bring their problems to him. He answered them patiently, often redirecting them to someone else or saying that they should set up a meeting for another time.

"You're busier than I thought a lord would be," she said after the tenth person waved goodbye, promising to stop by his office later.

Dryston sighed. "Yeah. Sometimes I wish I could run away."

"They trust you."

Dryston glanced at her. "Careful there. That sounded dangerously close to something like respect."

She rolled her eyes but didn't deny it, and Dryston would be lying if he didn't stand taller in the shine of her approval. If he didn't want to chase that feeling further, devoting himself to garnering more compliments like that.

They came to the tailor, a bustling and ornate shop with velvet couches, gold gilded mirrors, and oak wood imported from the realm of light. The owner, Talin, greeted them warmly with a kiss on each cheek. Dryston was shocked to see Onora endure it with nothing more than a blank look of shock. Behind him was Melina, who Dryston had heard was immediately snatched up by Talin after he saw her walking in the market wearing one of her own dresses. By the way they interacted with one another, Dryston could see they were getting along well.

"I hear that you need a new wardrobe," Talin said to Onora, who shifted uncomfortably on her feet.

"Not a whole new wardrobe, just some basics. Plain. Nothing too expensive or flashy," she said.

"She needs a new wardrobe, plain basics as well as whatever else you dream up and catches her eye," Dryston said.

Onora grabbed him by the arm, turning him around and whispering, "I can't afford that. I actually can't afford the basics, but I'm willing to pay you back once I find a way to earn it."

"You're not paying for any of this."

"Pray tell, who is then?"

"Me. And it's nothing. Anything you like, really, Onora."

"No. Just the basics, and I'll pay you back."

They stared at each other, her glaring and him unyielding. She crossed her arms, and he crossed his. Her nostrils flared but he turned back to Talin.

"She only wants the basics, plain and cheap and not flashy," he said and heard a sigh of relief from her. "I, however, would like to purchase a wardrobe of this quality and with these items." He pulled out a folded-up piece of paper from his breast pocket and held it out. He'd written a list of clothes he thought she'd need for various events coming up and ones that she'd perhaps like to have for comfort. "And if you can make them for her measurements, that would be wonderful."

She reached out to snatch the paper away, but he tugged it up, out of her reach, shaking his other finger with a tsk.

"I don't need all of that," she seethed.

"It's not for you, it's for me."

She looked him up and down. "And you're going to wear them . . . how?"

He smiled. "I'll find a use for them, I'm sure."

She clenched her jaw but just shook her head, not arguing further, and he grinned.

"Come here." Melina beckoned, and Onora stepped forward so they could begin taking her measurements.

Dryston flopped on the sofa, running his hand over the green velvet as they removed Onora's clothes, save for her undergarments. He told himself to look away, that he shouldn't leer. But his eyes trailed faster than his mind worked, and when he looked up and saw her smirking, he rolled his eyes, grabbing a paper from the side table and opening it.

It was a new issue of *The High Flyers*. A rough, and frankly unflattering, sketch of him graced the front, and he groaned. Did he even want to know what they were saying now? They'd spent many years unkindly dragging Enid's name through the mud. They had loved the rake of The Darkened City, but now she was mated with Lesern's darling, so they could only say glowing things about her.

Was he their new target?

He snorted at the title of the article: "Lord of Shadows Kidnaps a Hunter—and She Seems to Like It."

Straightening the paper, he held it up in front of him, getting Onora's attention. She squinted, reading the title, then giving him a weary look.

"I didn't realize you liked the gossip pages," she said.

"I don't usually, but who knew they were such credible sources? I might have to give them another chance."

She scoffed. "Credible? Not a single line of that is true."

"Not even one line?"

"No." She raised an imperious chin.

"Not even a little?"

"Not an ounce."

Melina carefully marked the measurements, keeping her head down as she worked hard, barely trying to hide her grin.

He grabbed a nearby pen and marked out the title, replacing it with his own: "The Dashing Lord of Shadows Rescues a Hunter—and She's Absolutely Besotted with Him."

"Is this better?" he asked.

She only rolled her eyes, looking away and ignoring him.

"She didn't refute it," Talin said in a singsong voice and Dryston grinned, then laughed as he saw Onora's jaw flex in irritation.

"I have no need to dignify that with an answer," she seethed.

"You just did," Dryston replied.

She whipped her head to him, glaring. "Don't you have lordly things to do?"

"Oh yes. Mountains and mountains of lordly things to do. But I'm clearing my schedule for the woman so besotted with me. Leaving you hanging is hardly the gentlemanly thing to do."

Fury whipped across her features and she turned on him, but Melina's gentle hand brought her back to the center, changing the subject.

"Will you be at dinner this week?" Melina asked, taking a pin out of the seam and tightening it.

Onora shot a confused glance at Dryston, but Melina answered, "The colony dinner. It happens once a week."

"Oh, I don't think a—"

"Yes," Dryston interjected from where he sat, trying, and failing, not to admire the shape of her ass.

She raised a brow, and he shrugged.

"You don't have to," he said, aiming for nonchalance. "I just assumed you would. Since you're our guest. It's fine either way."

She pursed her lips. "I think not, then. I'd hate to intrude."

Dryston bit back the retort because it did no good. He wanted her there, but if she didn't want to . . .

"I want you there," Melina said, her soft voice firm. "We need more girls, and I haven't talked to a human in months."

The women looked at each other, Melina smiling her saccharine smile and Onora's features softening in a way Dryston had never seen. Melina had that effect on people. He'd seen silent, curmudgeonly elders be unwound in her presence, offering up stories and laughter that had been most likely locked in the vault of their mind for ages.

"Okay then," Onora said.

Melina turned to Dryston. "If you do have lordly things to do, you can leave us be. We'll be a bit, and if Onora is up for it, I'd like to take her to the stables later."

Dryston's chest tightened, thankful, as always, for Melina. The way she loved so immediately, ready to calm others. He was glad Melina would show Onora around.

He looked at Onora, who gave him a curious glance, as if asking permission.

"If you're comfortable with it, Melina can give you the best tour of the stables."

Onora nodded. "I love horses."

Melina chuckled. "Oh, they're not horses."

Onora frowned in confusion, but Dryston stood, taking that as his cue. “Where’s Kaemon?”

Melina waved her hand to the door. “With Emilia in the market.”

IT WAS easy to find Kaemon in the crowds. So many people were drawn to him naturally, but with Emilia strapped to his chest, he was impossible to stay away from. She was already such a social baby, used to babbling and smiling at the citizens of the city. Kaemon’s face lit up when he saw Dryston.

Ten years of thinking he was dead. Ten years of mourning him.

But here he was. In the flesh.

“Doing some shopping?” Kaemon asked.

“I was mostly just coming to look for you,” Dryston said. “Melina thought you’d be here.”

“Did you visit her at work?” Kaemon said the words with pride, his eyes lighting with that special look of love he had for her. “Talin snatched her up immediately. Her designs are taking off so well, and I can’t go anywhere without seeing someone wearing something by her.”

“She’s brilliant. Talin would have been a fool to not bring her under his wing.”

“How is Onora?” Kaemon asked as Dryston locked into stride with him and they wandered the market.

“Good . . . I think. She seems calmer, but to be fair, we were running for our lives for a while there.”

Kaemon’s brow furrowed and emotion swam in his eyes. “We were so scared.”

“I know,” Dryston answered softly.

“I had to hold Enid back. She wanted to light up all of Venatu in shadowfyre.”

Dryston gave a wry chuckle. “I know.”

Silence fell for a moment, Kaemon chewing on his inner cheek. "Is it true?" he finally asked.

"Is what true?"

"That Onora kidnapped you and wanted to kill you, but you had to use her to escape?"

Dryston grimaced. "Yes. She had her reasons. There's a lot going on, and she's been through a lot."

"Can you trust her?"

"Yes," Dryston answered without thinking. Should he be more careful? Perhaps. But he knew, somewhere deep inside of himself, that he could. That things had changed between them, and she wouldn't harm him or the other demons.

"Very well then, I do, too."

Dryston let out a sigh of relief. Enid seemed amenable to Onora, but Enid was difficult to read. If she were told to give her last words before her execution, she'd tell the stupidest joke she could think of just to lighten the mood.

They came to a stall with daggers—finely crafted in the demonic fashion, with ornate handles. He found one with an inlaid sapphire, the hilt made of lava rocks, shimmering as he moved it in the light.

"I'll take two of these," he said.

"I didn't know you were that into daggers," Kaemon said.

"I'm not. Onora is, though, and I think she'd like these."

Kaemon eyed him curiously. "Yeah?"

"She's not a threat. And I know she's a bit on edge here, being the smallest and weakest."

"Oh, I didn't think she was a threat. I just think it's . . . sweet that you're buying her a gift."

Dryston waved his hand dismissively. "Well, I actually went to the forgery last night and requested they make her a set of axes as well. I know she'd feel a lot better with those on her side."

"Custom-made axes?" There was another question in Kaemon's words, but Dryston brushed it off.

"She needs them," he replied gruffly.

Kaemon smiled a knowing smile, a tentative look on his face. "Of course. Are you buying her anything else?"

"Just things she needs," he lied.

"Oh?"

"She needs more clothes. We didn't exactly have time to pack before we left."

Kaemon grinned. "Oh. Sounds like you're creating a nice little nest for her in the room adjoining yours."

Dryston cut him a look of warning, and Kaemon just laughed. Nesting was common mating behavior. Buying an abundance of things, making sure their living space was comfortable, doing anything and everything to show the mate they were cared for.

"Maybe I should get to know her better," Kaemon said.

Dryston shrugged. "Whatever you want. It doesn't matter."

Kaemon nodded, giving him that damnable knowing smirk, and Dryston ran a hand over his face. He'd forgotten how nosey everyone was here. He only hoped Onora would have no clue about it all—that everyone would leave her out of their speculations and hovering.

# CHAPTER 42
# ONORA

Melina had been practically a celebrity amongst the Hunters for a while now. The woman who people had thought was kidnapped by a demon, only for her to insist she wasn't, become pregnant with his baby, and be protected by the elves. Onora had expected someone different. Not this gentle, sweet creature.

It made sense, though. Kaemon was just as sweet. They matched each other well, and as they talked while Melina helped her get her clothes sorted out, it became harder and harder for her to believe it was merely some demonic enchantment that had brought them together. Perhaps initially, but from what she'd seen of Kaemon on their travels, and what she now saw of Melina, they seemed to just . . . fit. Like a key and lock. Perfect.

Talin and Melina conferred on designs for Onora's clothing, and she watched in wonder as they sketched and drew up designs she'd never dreamed of. Most were simple, but with some small flare.

Talin pursed his lips. "She'll need fighting leathers, but those take a moment."

Melina nodded. "Give her some pants that are not so loose—she'll trip if she's training. Also, I'm taking her to the stables after this. She needs something darker and more practical."

"I see, I see."

"Also, the rites are coming up—have you drafted any outfits that would fit her for that?"

Onora watched in surprise as both of them went back and forth, showing sketches, modifying, holding up scraps of cloth against her face and body and showing her the ideas for her approval. She had to admit, Melina had a much better sense of what she would like, and while Onora had never bothered with fashion, she found herself excited about the small details Melina added.

"Your jacket should have a gold bar over the breast to denote your rank," Melina said.

Onora swallowed the lump in her throat. "I'm not so sure I hold that rank anymore."

Talin tsked. "Lord Dryston will certainly appoint you to a similar rank here, I'm sure."

"Oh. I don't think I'll be here that long."

Talin frowned. "But, my dear, where will you go? Dryston can't leave us. We need him as a leader. And you will be a fine leader beside him. You have that fire in you."

"Oh, it's not like that between us." Her cheeks warmed at the thought.

"But you're in the room adjoining his."

So that *was* a big deal. Why? She couldn't tell. It looked like an additional room in a home, nothing too crazy, and she was too afraid to ask why everyone was having this reaction.

Melina looked at Talin and shook her head, and Talin and his assistant pursed their lips, a knowing look passing between them all.

Melina cleared her throat. "Talin, do you have any close-fitting trousers she could borrow for today?"

"I have just the thing," he said, going into the back room.

"Then we can go to the stables," Melina said with a grin.

Onora stared in shock. She'd heard tales of gryphons many times before, come across illustrations and even saw one flying overhead once. They were said to be slightly untamable. Creatures full of their own will and only obeying whom they pleased.

They were gorgeous creatures, though. This one was jet black, with a face like a raven, its head tilting to the side as it blinked, taking her in. Wings with feathers that faded from black to blue ruffled behind her, her body lithe and graceful as a cat's, with a long, deadly tail in the back.

"This one is feisty, Melina," the animal handler, Halst, said, giving her a side eye. "Do you think Onora can handle her?"

Melina put her hand out, palm up, and the gryphon came forward, nudging the hand with her beak until Melina gave her scratches under her chin. The creature made soft cooing sounds, its leg twitching in delight.

Halst chuckled. "You certainly have a way with them."

Melina smiled. "Onyx will love Onora. I can feel it."

She beckoned for Onora to come forward, and she did, placing her hand out too, palm up. Onyx tilted her head, giving Onora a wary look, then a questioning one to Melina.

"She's friendly," Melina said, and it didn't sound like a lie, even if Onora knew she'd never been described that way before.

Onyx came forward, tilting its head, examining her hand, then sniffing it. Halst plopped nuts in her hand and Onyx immediately picked them up, tilting its head back and chomping it down. Then she looked at Onora, cooing happily, and knelt.

"She wants you to get on her," Melina said.

Onora stared at the creature, who blinked its big eyes at her. Her hand trembled at the thought of sitting on its back and flying, but she wouldn't let Onyx see that, so she stepped up, placing her booted foot into the stirrup and swinging her other leg over. Halst came up, and she grabbed straps on either side of the saddle and showed Onora how to buckle herself in.

"Have you ridden a horse before?" Halst asked.

"Yes."

"Same idea, but gryphons like to be asked more nicely."

Then Halst gave a gentle slap on the gryphon's rump and Onyx made a loud caw, jumping into the sky. Onora swallowed down the scream that rose in her throat, falling away with the roar of wind that whipped around her as they launched into the sky. In moments, two other gryphons were next to her, and they all came to a cruising height, the gryphons leveling out.

Onyx's wings flapped gently next to her and the gryphon tilted her head back, cooing reassuringly at Onora.

"She does like you!" Halst called out, laughing.

"I told you!" Melina said, throwing her head back, closing her eyes against the wind as it carried her long, wavy locks trailing behind her like a flag. She grinned at Onora, and Onora found herself grinning back.

THEY FLEW for close to an hour, over mountains and forests and rivers and fields. The Shadow Realm was a sight to behold. Winter was just creeping along the land, frost freezing over the gem-colored greens and reds, sapphires and purples of the foliage, crusting them like diamonds and twinkling in the sunlight.

Halst pointed to a lake that was as blue as the sky and Melina nodded, whistling as they dipped down. Onyx perked up at the sound, then dipped, twirling and bringing her wings in, and Onora had to swallow another scream. She thought she could hear a cooing that sounded distinctly like laughter as Onyx glanced back, blinking her amber eyes, mischief hiding there.

They landed gracefully, the descent soft and easy, and Onora sat in the saddle longer than necessary, breathing heavily and getting her bearings. Finally, she undid her restraints and jumped down. Onyx moved close, nudging her arm affectionately, and nestling against her face, making her laugh. Onyx cooed her laughing coo again and Onora petted her neck, giving her a hug, then turned to her companions.

"She was apologizing," Melina said. "For scaring you."

Onora thought to protest that she wasn't scared, but what was the point? She had been.

Halst produced cheese and bread, and a skein of wine for them to share. They found a rock to sit on while their mounts splashed about in the cold water, playing with one another, then sunbathing to warm up.

"Has your family always raised gryphons?" Onora asked Halst.

Halst shook her head. "My parents were in the royal guard. I started a while ago. Enid saved a bunch of them from a cruel farm and brought them here. They were unruly and untrusting and aggressive when I first started with them."

"Was that hard to train out of them?"

Halst took her hand, palm out flat, and shifted it—so-so. "They were pretty broken. Many said it would be kinder to let them go, but they would be killed by ranchers for attacking livestock. The other option was to kill them, and let them finally get rest. I didn't like either of those options, so I asked Dryston to let me have some stables, supplies, and a year to make them better. He agreed. He also didn't want them to die. His mother loved gryphons."

"What made you want to put all that work in?"

"They weren't bad, they were just broken and needed healing. I was the same. My parents and colony had been killed by the Cruel Lord and I had been made a servant of his. He was horrible. I spent so many years just trying to survive that when he was gone and Dryston's father was the Lord of Shadows, I didn't know what to do with myself. I still worked for him, but I felt restless. So the gryphons came along and they needed rescuing. And, well, so did I. I think they did the real miracle work. I just made them feel safe enough to be kind again. They made me feel alive again."

Onora was silent, absorbing what she said, seeing the truth of her words in her eyes. Onora had always looked in the mirror and seen her old wounds staring back at her. Ones that wouldn't heal, that just kept oozing and bleeding. How could anyone recover from that much loss and abuse?

But she could see the healing in Halst's eyes. In Melina's, too. The past was not erased—it never could be. But the wounds were healed and in their place was just a scar. No pain, no turmoil. Healed—despite the proof of the horrors.

"You're a Hunter?" Halst stated more than asked.

"I was," Onora said. "I don't think I have a place there anymore."

"The Cruel Lord did terrible things to the humans of Nemus."

Onora took a swig of the wine. "He did indeed."

"If you don't have a place there anymore, you do here. I hope you know that. I know Makel has a sharp tongue, but most demons don't see you like she does."

Onora drew in a deep breath. Was that true?

"Do all demons know each other's business?"

Halst and Melina shared a glance, laughing.

"Yes," Halst said as they both nodded. "Unfortunately, we do. But it's also why we have so much respect for Hunters. Many demons suffered at the hands of the Cruel Lord. We know why Hunters came to be, and we have nothing but respect for them for fighting back. Your people helped us here, though you may not know it. The fight in Nemus, coupled with the demons fighting him here, split the effort and kept him from being able to take over any one place quickly."

Onora had never thought of it that way before. For the first time, looking at a demon, she didn't see someone that was so different from her. She saw a kindred soul looking back. A sister in spirit.

Perhaps, then, she and Dryston were not so different, either.

It was late when Onora returned to her room that night, having spent the rest of the evening in the stables with the two females, learning about gryphon handling from them, and just spending time with Onyx to bond. She found herself excited for tomorrow when she could go back and feed and care for the gryphon again, and perhaps talk to Halst more. She hoped to see more of Melina, but she didn't want to bother her too much.

Onora's door had a magic lock on it, one that Dryston had swiftly and perfunctorily tied to her handprint that morning. She ripped her gloves off, placing her hand over the smooth stone ball, covered in runes, next to the door. The lock clicked, and the door creaked open of its own accord.

Onora wasn't certain she'd ever get used to the common use of magic like that.

"You're out late."

She jumped, grabbing her heart and turning to see Dryston leaning against his open doorway. Shirtless. Gray night pants hugging him in a lewd way that made her shoot him a glare.

"Don't scare me like that," she said.

He threw his hands up. "Sorry! Didn't realize I was sneaking up on you. Did you have fun with Melina?"

She nodded, her cheeks flushing. Feelings stirred in her like a child, happy to make friends—feeling welcome. Being a Hunter, she'd developed a deep relationship with her squad. They were closer than a family in many ways, and she missed them terribly. But she'd never had to just make friends. The few times she'd had the opportunity, she'd done a shit job of it. Prickly, aggressive, mean, rude—people had a variety of words to lob at her and she supposed they were right. Even if she didn't always mean to be that way, it still came out that way.

But with Melina and Halst, it felt like second nature.

"Melina is kind—so is Halst." She didn't know what else to say, and she suddenly felt shy and tongue-tied around him. She didn't want to snipe at him all the time or be mean and rude. But that was their relationship, and she didn't know what to do about it. They stood in silence for a moment and she racked her brain for anything to say to him.

She came up with nothing.

"Want some tea?" he asked, sticking his thumb over his shoulder to his room.

She nodded. He already had tea going, two mugs set out, and she wondered if he'd been waiting on someone else. But no one else showed up as they sat on the couch and she recounted her day to him, wanting to spill every event, but holding back because she wasn't used to having anyone this interested in the small details. But he listened, attentive, asking more and more questions, as if he just wanted her to keep talking.

When she finished, he stood and went to the dresser, taking a cloth case and bringing it over, handing it to her.

"What's this?" she asked.

"A gift," he said, shrugging like it was nothing. "I found it in the market and thought you'd like it."

She untied the flaps and opened them, revealing a set of beautiful daggers. A sapphire set into the hilt, and she ran her hands over the lava stone, then the blade. It was fine craftsmanship—some of the best she'd ever seen and certainly better than anything she'd ever owned.

"This must have cost a fortune," she muttered.

He took a sip, shrugging again. "It was nothing."

"I can't accept this," she said.

"This is hardly the most expensive thing I've bought you."

He said it with a touch of pride, and she drew in a deep breath, holding the daggers out to him.

"I have my own on me. I can't afford these, and I don't want you buying me anything else."

She already owed him a fortune. Maybe he was so wealthy he didn't notice, but she knew the price of things—knew how extravagant gifts often accompanied expectations. What did he expect of her?

He gently pushed them back to her.

"Keep them," he growled.

Heat coiled in her lower belly at the command, and she pulled them back onto her lap.

"No more gifts," she said.

He smiled, taking another sip. "I make no promises."

"Why do you want to give me so many gifts, anyway? Don't you have someone better to give them to?"

"Who better than someone in need?"

"So I'm a charity case?"

"I . . . no, that's not what I meant."

She crossed her arms. "Are you trying to ingratiate me? Trying to lull me into some stupor so that I'll be compliant?"

Her chest tightened, her rage building again.

"Godsdamnit, Onora, no. No!" He rubbed his face. "I just want to do something nice for you. I care about you. Can I not do something nice for someone I care about?"

Her cheeks heated, and she blinked, staring blankly, unsure of what to say or do. He cared for her? She had thought at best he held a lusty regard for her, maybe some sort of camaraderie, but *care*?

She didn't know what to say. Brayden had once told her he loved her. It had been a lie, and she'd laughed and he'd never forgiven her—for calling him on it. He'd wanted to manipulate her with it.

But she couldn't see Dryston's angle here. They weren't fucking. Or they hadn't since those two nights, and Dryston was making no move to repeat it. She couldn't get or give him anything. He was just buying her shit. Making her tea. Asking about her day and being kind.

What the fuck was he playing at?

He *cared* about her?

Jackson cared about her. So did Andrea, Avery, and Jin. Maybe she shouldn't be so surprised. They had been through a lot, her and Dryston. They'd bonded like warriors did—in the fight to survive.

She swallowed, running her hand over the dagger again, not making eye contact. "Thank you."

"No thanks is needed."

"I want to repay you—"

"It's. A. *Gift*."

She shot him a glare. "I want to repay you in some way. Not with money, per se. I just—" She didn't know what to say, and she threw her hands up. "What in the darkest pit am I supposed to do now? I have no job, I have no way of taking care of myself. No home—"

"Stay here," he said, soft, tentative. He followed it with another shrug, and she didn't know if he meant it or if he had only said it to assuage her ramblings.

"What would I do here?"

"Join the guard. Train gryphons. Skulk in the shadows, hissing at people I despise—"

"Be serious."

"I am. You can be so frightening, and I have a few people in mind."

She crossed her arms, and he laughed.

"Really. You'd be good in the royal guard."

She drew in a deep breath, unsure if he was being serious or placating and too tired to argue more. So she changed the subject, asking him about his day and hearing a great deal about Emilia. Eventually she started nodding off and she must have fallen asleep, because she felt him pick her up, shushing her back to sleep, then felt the covers tucked in around her chin, warm and comforting.

# CHAPTER 43
# ONORA

Onora woke to a servant bringing her a massive amount of food for breakfast. She ate all of it, then looked around, unsure what to do. She and Dryston had talked late into the night—about everything and nothing, it felt like—but she didn't know what she was supposed to do with her days. Who she was supposed to be now.

Getting out of bed, she was determined to explore the city and find some occupation. As she stepped out the door, though, she saw a box of freshly made clothes waiting for her, with a note on top. She opened it to see a spidery scrawl, barely legible, and she squinted to make it out.

Your training leathers are here. I'll be in the training ring all morning if you want to come and check it out.

-Drys

She immediately grabbed the leathers, changed into them, and made her way to the barracks.

~

ONORA HADN'T BEEN this nervous since she'd tested to be a Hunter. She doubted this was an actual screening for her to be in the royal guard, and she doubted Dryston had been serious about her joining, but still, she wanted to impress them. Him, mostly. She wanted to show them what she could do.

When she arrived at the barracks, sparring sessions were already in full swing. She snuck to the side, taking it in. Off to the far side was a section where demons were practicing magic techniques on wooden dummies. Another area for weapons practice, the clank of metal punctuating the air. And closest to her was hand-to-hand sparring. Dryston was wrestling with another male that looked vaguely familiar.

Shirtless.

Sweaty.

His muscles rippled with each strong movement as he wrapped his arm around the other male, flipping him, then pinning him down.

A new fantasy danced behind her eyes, of Dryston pinning her down like that, his sweaty body on perfect display, his hands strong and sure.

His head whipped up as if she'd said that out loud, shouting it for everyone in the arena to hear, his eyes finding her as if he were a compass and she was true north. A grin split his face right before his sparring partner got a hold and flipped him again. Now Dryston was pinned and, well . . . damn. That also did things to her.

She shook her head, trying to focus as they finished out their fight, Dryston finally making the other male tap out. He stood, helping the other up and they patted each other on the shoulders, then, immediately, Dryston sprinted to her.

His eyes roved over the leathers, taking his time. They were demon-style leathers, black, with ornate pauldrons and a scrolling stitch down the front.

"The demon fashion suits you," he said.

She shrugged. "I think Melina is just a very good seamstress."

"That she is," he said. "Want to spar?"

She stood in dumb silence. Yes, she did. But sparring him? Right now? When he looked like *that?*

Nodding her head, she tried to get her brain in the right headspace for this.

But he turned, whistling to get someone's attention, and when a female demon looked at him, he beckoned her over. She was tall, but only a little above Onora's height, with a lithe, athletic body, icy blond hair, and piercing blue eyes.

"Lily, this is Onora," Dryston said.

"I know who she is," Lily said, her tone as cold as the shade of her hair.

Dryston frowned only a moment before saying, "Would you mind sparring with her? She seems eager to get back into it."

Lily's gaze didn't leave Onora's as she said, with a smirk, "Oh, I'd love to."

They met in the middle, Lily handing her weapons off to another demon, and Onora offered her hand. Lily only stared at it.

"Sorry, this is a human tradition. A sign of respect for the person allowing you to train with them," Onora said.

Lily smiled. "Oh. That's cute."

She didn't take the hand, and Onora dropped it, narrowing her gaze. Lily was trying to get in her head. For what, she didn't know, but she wasn't going to let it keep her from fighting her best.

A whistle marked the beginning of their match and Lily immediately lunged for her legs, but Onora jumped back, bringing the top of her foot up swiftly, connecting under Lily's chin. Lily let out a growl, throwing her hand out and sending a swirl of shadows to Onora, who, without thinking, sent out her own that swallowed Lily's. Lily stared at them, agape, and Onora lunged at her, toppling to the ground. They wrestled evenly, a tangle of arms and legs and elbows. Lily would get the upper hand for only a moment before Onora slipped out and took over, back and forth, back and forth. Then Lily got her in a lock, arm around her neck, and whispered, "You might be fucking Drys, but don't think you're special because of it. You're not the only one warming his bed, and you never will be. You haven't fooled anyone else. You're his little pet—for now. He'll get tired of you and send you on your way soon enough. So don't get comfortable."

Onora wriggled free, sending an elbow back and slamming into her nose with a crack, Lily letting out a string of expletives as her grip loosened.

They broke apart, Onora rolling away, and both stared at each other, panting hard. She didn't have time to think about what Lily said. Instead, she jumped her again, focused, intent, her mind razor sharp as she wrapped her legs around the female, toppling her down and getting her in a chokehold. Lily thrashed and hit, trying to get free, but she couldn't.

"Tap out," Onora growled in her ear.

Lily refused, her face growing redder, gasping for air.

Finally, Dryston whistled again, calling the fight, and Onora dropped Lily, standing swiftly away from her. Lily grabbed her neck and shot a glare at Onora. Onora offered her a hand to get up, but Lily only slapped it away, stumbling to her feet and then stalking off.

"She's a sore loser," Dryston said with a grimace.

Onora wondered if Lily was only a sore loser in fighting—or if she was sleeping with Dryston too, and that's what she'd been referring to. Her stomach dipped, a pain radiating in her chest at the thought, but she shoved it away. What did it matter?

"Well, well, well," the male who'd been fighting Dryston said, giving Onora an appraising look. "The Hunter has some chops on her. Lily is rarely bested in hand-to-hand fighting. She's a scrappy one."

"I've had the same sentiment said about me," Onora replied.

The male chuckled. "I'm Mandel, by the way."

She offered her hand to him and he took it, kissing the back of it and she flushed, swallowing hard. Dryston gave Mandel a sharp look but said nothing as the muscles in his jaw twitched.

"Let me show the rest of the barracks," Dryston said, stepping in between the two of them. "Mandel, you need to practice more. You're getting rusty."

Mandel frowned. "Oh?"

Dryston crossed his arms. "You telegraph your right hook too much. I can see it a mile away and your footwork is getting sloppy. Keep it up and you'll be a liability to the squad."

Mandel's nostrils flared. "I'll keep that in mind."

"Good, see you around."

Mandel narrowed his eyes, and Onora gave Dryston a raised brow as they walked off.

"That was a bit harsh," she said.

"That's how Mandel and I are. He prefers me to be straightforward with him."

"He seemed to be doing a fine job," she said. "Besides, you said nothing to Lily when a human bested her."

Dryston opened his mouth, then closed it, chagrined. "I'll apologize to him."

She hated how her stomach clenched at the fact that he didn't refute not telling Lily to work harder. Was Lily one of his paramours? She banished the thought, focusing on what Dryston was showing her, who he was introducing her to.

"General!" Dryston called to an elderly demon who stood at a desk, looking over letters. The male looked up, greeting them both warmly.

"Lord Dryston. And this must be Onora." The general offered his hand to her. "I'm Lionel."

"It's a pleasure," she said.

"Likewise. Dryston has told me you want to join the royal guard?"

She slid Dryston a glance and he rubbed the back of his head, shrugging. "It's an option."

"I am in the market for a new job," she said, not quite wanting to admit that a part of her liked the idea of training here, getting stronger and showing what she could do.

"Keep coming here to train and we'll find a place for you," Lionel said.

The words buoyed her, giving her a small glimmer of hope that perhaps she could have a place here.

"What does a colony dinner entail?" Onora asked as she followed Dryston down a new pathway of cave halls that went by vast apartments with families sitting out front, or with lights in windows showing different domestic scenes. So vastly different than she'd ever imagined.

They came to a door that unlocked from Dryston's touch and they walked in, down stone steps, past a receiving room to a large dining area. There were a few tables, seeming to separate demons by age, young kids at one lower to the ground with toys scattered around them. Another for youths that were chatting and horsing around. Then another larger one with adults buzzing around it, others coming in and out of a room she assumed was a kitchen with place settings and food.

She suddenly had the feeling that she was intruding on somcthing very special. It felt like the holidays she remembered as a child, celebrating the solstice with the village. Or the ones she'd seen celebrated through people's windows in Venatu on the nights she'd had patrol and wandered around, watching happy families, untouched by the horrors that marred her soul.

Dryston introduced everyone to her as they came up, each of them kind, taking her hand and chatting with her like she wasn't their enemy. As if she weren't a Hunter.

Which, she supposed, she wasn't. She wasn't anything anymore.

Dryston grabbed her gently by the elbow, navigating her to the kitchen. Kaemon stood in the corner with Emilia, playing with her while Enid and Avenay chatted with Maria in the corner. Kalen and Melina were cooking, moving around each other like it was second nature, handing each other utensils without having to speak. Kalen in an apron with a towel thrown over his shoulder was a jarring scene and when he turned, seeing her looking at him, he narrowed his eyes.

Melina halted, seeing Kalen staring at something and looked back, her face breaking into a smile. She wiped her hands then rushed forward for a hug and Onora stiffened, which made Melina stop short, wringing her hands. Onora didn't know what overcame her, maybe a protective instinct for someone so sweet and kind, but she stepped forward and pulled Melina in a hug, who returned it fiercely.

"I'm so glad you came," Melina said.

"I hear you're making homeland food?"

Melina nodded, grabbing her hand and pulling her over to a pot of cooking stew. Flavors hit her in a wave, familiar and comforting. Nutmeg and cinnamon, cardamom and green pepper.

"My mother made a similar stew," she said quietly, for only Melina to hear.

"Mine did, too," Melina said.

A body was suddenly next to her, peering over the stock pot and Onora looked up to see Enid crowding in. Always taking up the most space, unapologetically and loudly. Onora smiled, raising a brow.

"I heard you bested Lily in sparring," Enid said, crossing her arms and leaning against the counter. This was one of the few times she'd seen the female in clothing that wasn't something entirely functional. They were loose fitting silk pants with a sweater that hugged her neck. She somehow still looked foreboding. "You're sparring me next time."

"Oh? Do you like losing then?"

Avenay, Kaemon, and Dryston all chuckled as Enid rolled her eyes, still grinning.

Melina ushered them all into the next room, taking seats as the food was brought in. An abundance of wine, bread, stuffed mushrooms, and berries.

"How often do you have these dinners?" she asked, looking around at the full table, the loud room, and feeling a pang of loss.

"At least monthly, sometimes more."

"The colony is very important to demons?"

He nodded, taking the bread from the center of the table and breaking off a piece for her and him. "Very much so. We're all related by blood or mate bonds, somewhere along the way, but we are all tied into each other's magic. A colony together can cast spells in a way demons can't on their own."

"I didn't think demons could cast spells at all."

"Usually—we can't. But together, with the guidance of a priestess we can. I don't know why it's that way. But it's made us value the colony even more."

"It's nice," she whispered, absentmindedly.

The door opened, a cool draft rushing in, as did the sound of hurried footsteps. Mandel entered, looking around before spotting Avenay and coming to her.

"A letter for you. It's marked urgent," he said.

She took it, exclaiming softly at the seal and then ripped it open, reading fast.

"What is it?" Enid asked, coming close to her.

"My father," she said. "He says he has research findings he needs my eyes on as quickly as I can come. He doesn't want to write it down though . . ."

Enid and Avenay exchanged a look.

"I need to go to Lesern," she said, and Enid nodded.

"We both will."

"Right now." Avenay gave her a pleading look, and Enid took her face in both of her hands kissing the top of her head.

"Right now."

She came over to Dryston, kneeling down. "We're leaving. Don't get into any trouble while I'm gone. I'll keep you updated as much as I can on what her dad has found."

"There's a lot of strife in the world right now. Be careful."

"Aren't I always?"

"Rarely."

Enid grinned, patting him on the shoulder, then standing and saying their goodbyes as they left. Dryston called Mandel over.

"Sit and eat. We're down two and Melina makes enough food for an army."

"Gods bless her. She's the best cook in the city, too," Mandel said, taking a seat and rubbing his hands excitedly.

The main dishes came, and they ate, different people talking, everyone catching up, some moving around the table and coming to talk to Dryston, saying they were so glad he'd made it back. They all talked to her as well, asking about her life, and she awkwardly stumbled through the fact that she was a Hunter, but none seemed to care.

Except Kalen. He sat catty-cornered to her, his eyes often on her, narrowed. He eventually moved closer, coming near to Dryston.

"Will you be participating in the moon rites this year?" he asked.

Dryston raised a brow. "Why do you ask?" Dryston shifted uncomfortably in his seat, and Onora eyed him curiously.

Kalen shrugged, taking another drink of the wine. "Lily says you're escorting her."

"What are the rites?" she asked before thinking. She wanted to seem unaffected, cool, but she wanted to know what they were. Why Dryston seemed uncomfortable. Why was he escorting Lily?

Kalen smiled. "They're a special demonic ritual. They are . . . romantic in nature. It's often how demons end up finding their mates."

Onora told herself to be calm, to not react. So Dryston was escorting Lily to a rite to find his mate. She'd known something like this would come along. She just hadn't anticipated it occurring so quickly after she arrived.

Dryston drew in a heavy, annoyed breath. "It's an old tradition, and a bit outdated."

Kalen frowned. "You go every year."

Dryston waved his hand as if what they said was absurd.

"Every year," Mandel echoed, stabbing a carrot and eating it, grinning as Dryston shot him a glare. "Is Onora participating?"

Dryston's nostrils flared. "No."

Another stab of pain in her chest. Something romantic, and Dryston decidedly didn't want her there. It made sense. It made complete sense.

It still hurt like the darkest pit.

She scoffed, and he looked at her. "Oh? Do I not get to decide?"

"You'd hate it," he said dismissively, and she bristled.

"You don't know that," she said.

He smirked, that stupid, infuriatingly handsome smirk. "Yes, I do. You'd be out of your element at the moon rite. It usually turns into an orgy, Onora."

Her cheeks flamed. Oh. She hadn't caught on to the subtle innuendo.

But regardless, what did he mean by that? Out of her element?

Suddenly, she remembered his look after she'd woken in his arms in the forest. Regret. Perhaps even disgust? He'd looked so worried, so regretful.

She shoved the memory away.

"I don't know, Drys," Mandel said, a devious smile on his face. "I think she'd love it."

Dryston's knuckles turned white as he gripped the knife in his hand, staring at Mandel. He really, really didn't want her to go, did he?

"You should come with me," Mandel said. "Unless you think I should skip the rites to practice more, since I'm getting *rusty*." Mandel fixed Dryston with a challenging look over his wineglass as he took a drink.

"She's not going," Dryston said, his voice low, threatening.

"Aren't you going?" she asked, turning her cold gaze on him.

"I hadn't decided yet." He stared at her with a pleading look, begging her to not go. A wise person wouldn't. A wise woman would bow out and not participate in this.

Not that she hadn't had her share of group sex in the past. The elves had less proclivity to modesty and chastity than humans, and she'd spent enough time with them that she knew she'd enjoy it greatly.

"You always go," Kalen said. "And you can't put off trying to find your mate."

Onora stuffed another mushroom in her mouth to hide her disappointment. Mandel's gaze was on her like a brand.

"We're not talking about me right now, Kalen," Dryston spat. "I don't think Onora would like it. Obviously, she can answer for herself. Sorry I got involved."

He took a long, hard gulp of wine and she crossed her arms, leaning back with a smirk.

"It wouldn't be my first, or second, or third," she said, giving him a hard look.

Kalen coughed on his drink and Mandel grinned, giving a low whistle.

"You underestimate her," Mandel said.

"If I'm going to stay here, Drys, then maybe I should start participating in demon culture," she drawled, trying to call his bluff, get any reaction out of him.

"She makes an excellent point," Mandel said.

Dryston gave her a long, hard look before his expression melted away into that unreadable smile of his. "Well then, I guess I'll see you there."

"I guess you will."

# CHAPTER 44
# DRYSTON

Dryston buttoned the sleeves on his blouse and stared at the door that adjoined his room with Onora. Mandel was escorting her to the moon rite, which meant she would be going to the same one as him. They were carefully selected so no colony members were in the same room and things were rotated so demons had a chance to meet others they wouldn't normally. Bringing in clans from the outskirts.

He'd told her it was an orgy, but it didn't have to be. It just often descended into that in some of the outer rooms of the temple. Many demons came, drank, and talked to other demons and then left. If you found your mate or someone you wanted to be with you could leave and take care of your business privately.

The adage of finding a mate there was what was outdated. It rarely resulted in that. Perhaps it did a long time ago, when it was just a way to get the far-reaching clans together but now it was just a chance to mingle with others, potentially find a lover before you met your mate, and maybe have a wild night or two with a few others. Dryston did usually go, but that was partially because he hadn't ever found his mate and people hassled him to keep trying, and with his busy schedule it was a good way for him to meet others.

But he knew who his mate was now. And she was going with someone else.

He didn't know what to do. How to explain the bond to her? She clearly didn't feel it or she would be as insane as he felt right now. Instead, she was happily going to go to an orgy.

When they had barely touched each other for over a week. He'd been pleasuring himself every night to stave off the edge of the mating frenzy, to help in any way he could from pressuring her before he could talk to her about it.

Kaemon had told him to just tell her. But things were too tenuous. Last night, when she'd said she was going to participate in demon culture was the first hint he had that she was amenable to the idea of staying. Would him telling her about the mating bond drive her further away?

He had no clue and he couldn't chance it. He couldn't chance losing her. If she left, he couldn't follow. He had a realm to run. A realm that relied on him.

He would have to accept being forever separated from his mate.

He could skin Kalen alive. He knew she was his mate, but he was still taunting her, trying to convince him that it was something else, that the bond was wrong.

But Dryston knew that wasn't true. Every time he looked at her, the faintest brush of her hand against him, gods, even her absence, sang of the bond.

He paced his room, listening for the sound of her leaving, but it didn't come. Had she left earlier? Either way, maybe it did no good to linger and twist himself in knots. He had to make an appearance, drink an ungodly amount of wine to try and cope with the raging storm inside of him, and then leave. Let her do what she was going to do and be fine with it. Even if it didn't involve him.

As he stepped out the door, she did too, and they both stopped, staring, startled.

Fuck.

She was gorgeous.

And wearing barely anything. The dress had a low deep V that rested at her navel, her round breasts perfectly displayed, her back bare, the dress starting again right below the dimples above her ass. Those dimples he'd traced with his hand the last time they'd been together and she'd fallen asleep before him.

Those dimples that he imagined every night when he took matters into his own hand.

When his eyes finally snapped back to her face, hers were tracing over him, traveling from his cut chest that was on display up to his wings, dipping to his horns and down to his eyes. His cock stirred, and he drew in a breath to calm his racing blood. He wanted to pin her against the wall, take her into his room, bend her over, and fuck her right then.

"Where's Lily?" she asked, her voice cold, her face disinterested.

"She's meeting me there," he replied, his gaze snagging on her peaked nipples showing through the fabric of the dress. He rubbed his jaw, trying to focus on what she was saying. What *was* she saying?

"Oh. Mandel is picking me up just down the hall."

That bastard. He lived across the city. He would have had to pass by the very place they were now headed in order to come pick her up.

"What a gentleman," he growled.

She pursed her lips and he internally cursed himself.

"Mandel is waiting on me, I'm sure," she said hastily, stepping forward.

He grabbed her wrist, stepping up close to her, inhaling her scent as she looked up at him tentatively.

"I'll walk with you." He looped her arm in his and she raised a brow, but didn't protest. They walked down the hall in silence, but Dryston barely noticed. His every thought was spent trying to combat his instincts to touch her, kiss her, pull her into his arms.

They caught up with Mandel at a split in the pathway and he looked between them, a playful, knowing smirk lighting his face.

"I'm glad to see you got my date here in one piece," he said, walking up and removing Onora's arm, twining it with his. "Thanks, Drys."

Dryston rubbed his jaw and gave a mirthless laugh. "Of course."

Onora gave him a look over her shoulder as if she were going to say something, but instead she turned and walked with Mandel down the hall. He followed them, listening as Mandel chatted her up, making her chuckle here and there, and Dryston could think of a hundred different ways to give Mandel a painful death.

The moon was already high overhead when they stepped above ground, the black, shimmering lava rocks glinting in the light. Grooves in the rock made paths up to a black temple that rose high in the sky, with jagged spires and tracery windows of stained glass.

They waded through the crowds of people to the temple, walking into its cool atrium. Light filtered in through windows on the ceiling and spires, casting light in symmetrical lines that showed a pattern swirling to the center. Mandel led them to the right, to one of the first doors that led down a set of stairs, into another cave room, filtering light in.

Tables were set up with food and drink and leaf, music playing from a magical recording, and people milled about, talking.

Dryston broke from the two, clenching and unclenching his fists, trying to calm his mind, and heading straight to the drinks. He poured a full glass of wine and gulped it down, pouring another.

"You're starting the party early," a sultry female voice said, and he turned to see Lily coming toward him.

He and Lily had been partners for the moon rite more than enough times, and he'd tried to let it stay at that. But she had always still pursued him, and he'd been told she was convinced they were mates and he would realize it at one point. He'd stopped sleeping with her then but it didn't stop her advances, and he was barely in the mood to wave her off.

He glanced at Onora to see Mandel's hand had slipped to her lower back and he was introducing her to another male.

Rage coiled around him, a fury that he feared he wouldn't be able to fully contain. It had been a terrible idea coming here. Obviously, Onora was not new to this idea, but the thought of her coming undone with two others while he was absent . . .

He turned back to Lily, who looked from Onora back to him.

"Drys, I know you're going through a lot, so if you don't want to be here, you don't have to be," she said.

The wine was hitting his senses like a sledgehammer, and maybe that was better. Part of him cared a bit less about what he was seeing. He stepped forward and put a lock of hair behind her ear. If Onora was going to forget about him, maybe he should try to forget about her.

Lily blushed but stepped back. "I'm not interested in just fucking, Drys. You know that. And I can see that you really want to be with her." She jerked her head toward Onora, hurt lining every feature of her face. "So maybe go tell her that."

Dryston felt like he'd been slapped, and Lily poured herself a glass of wine, then walked off. Dryston stared as Mandel's hand made lazy circles on her back, slipping up on her rib cage and he gripped the glass so tight that it broke.

Yes, this had been a truly terrible idea.

## CHAPTER 45
# ONORA

Onora found it odd that Dryston seemed to be lurking in the corner, drinking and watching them, but she had to admit that she only noticed because the heat of his gaze felt like it was searing her skin. The hand that Mandel rested on her side was hot and heavy and she wished it was Dryston's. But he wasn't saying anything. She hadn't called his bluff. She hadn't forced his hand to tell her that he wanted her. Even if it were only sexual.

And now she was fairly certain she was being involved in plans for a foursome, and normally she'd be fine with that but she wanted Dryston. She wanted to feel his cock throbbing inside of her, she wanted his hands holding her down, his teeth scraping over her nipples.

She glanced back over her shoulder and Dryston had stopped cleaning up glass on the floor to gaze at her, nostrils flaring, as if he could scent her lurid thoughts about him.

She turned away, toward Mandel, placing a hand on his chest. Mandel smiled down at her, his hand tracing a line on her face, down her neck, her chest.

"You seem eager," he said, and his hand traced below her breast, skimming softly and making heat flood her core. Maybe she should do this, go through with it. Mandel was kind, assuring, and handsome as the gods. And Dryston seemed intent on forgetting about her.

She ran her hand down his chest, slowly, taking her time as his eyes darkened, his body pressing closer to hers. She traced a line over his lower abdomen, and Mandel let out a grunt, biting his lip as his hand skirted up from her rib, between her breasts, and grasped her neck, finally cradling her face. He tilted to kiss her, when a strong arm wrapped around her waist and she was tugged away. She yelped, and Mandel stepped back as Dryston grabbed her, throwing her over his shoulder like she was a sack of grain.

"What the fuck are you doing?" she hissed.

But Dryston didn't respond, and Mandel just gave her a wave and a tight-lipped smile as Dryston carried her off. She glared at him and Mandel chuckled, turning away, and she had the sudden, gnawing feeling that Mandel had planned this to get under Dryston's skin.

It seemed to have worked. Dryston carried her off, people watching and muttering, and she turned, speaking into his ear.

"You're making a scene."

"Good," he growled.

"It's embarrassing," she lied. Something in her thrilled at the display.

"I want them to know you're here with me," he said, his hand gripping her legs, her thighs in a way that made her core throb.

"Oh? I am?" she ground out, annoyed and thrilled in equal measure.

He met her gaze, a dangerous look there that made her almost whimper. She swallowed it instead. "Yes. You are."

She curled his fist around his shirt, and she could feel how fast his heart was beating. It matched her own rhythm—furious.

"Let me down."

He gave her an icy glare that made her stomach flutter. "No."

They came to a room in the back, and she craned her neck around to see people were talking, touching each other in soft caresses and turning when they saw them. There was a large bed in the back with a velvet comforter and enough space for several demons.

"Out. Every one of you. And let the others know that they aren't to come in here."

They all nodded, hastily leaving, bowing to him as they did, and he took her to the bed, sitting her on it.

"What the fuck was that about?" she demanded, standing, only for his firm hand to push her back down in a sitting position, gripping her shoulder.

His breaths were heavy, shadows curling around him in agitation. "I can't stand to see you with Mandel."

Heat flooded her, firing her cheeks, and she crossed her arms. His eyes darted to her breasts, and she realized she'd put them, somehow, more prominently on display.

"That's not really your choice."

"I know. Fuck . . . I know. I'm sorry. I just . . ."

His voice trailed off, and he paced. She stayed sitting, enjoying how rattled he seemed. Good. He should feel bad about his actions.

"I don't want you here," he said.

She rolled her eyes, standing and walking toward the door. "That's not your decision. Fuck you, Drys. Just because we fucked a few times, do you think you own me?"

He stepped in front of her, blocking her path.

"No, of course not. It's not like that. It's . . ."

"What? It's what?"

"I'm fucking jealous as the pit, Onora." He cupped her face with his hands, tilting it up, and she swayed toward him. "I think about you all day long. I think about all the things I did to you in the forest every night." He bent down and kissed her forehead and her breathing became shallow. "I think of your naked body, and I get so hard I have to take care of it myself so I don't knock that door down between our rooms and ravage you every night." He kissed her nose, and those butterflies returned, making her dizzy. "I want to touch you every moment of the day. I want to be inside of you." His hand slid down her neck, gripping softly, gently, commanding as his mouth peppered kisses there, coming up to her ear. "I want to feel your skin on mine." He bit her earlobe. "I want to hear those sweet moans you make right before you finish."

His lips found hers then, and she ran her hands up his chest, rubbing her thumb over his nipple and savoring how he groaned into her mouth. He pushed her back toward the bed, kissing her, the intensity of it increasing with each brush of his lips on hers, every soft bite. Their tongues danced against each other, his exploring her mouth in broad strokes.

They came to the bed and his hand slipped to her breasts, palming them as his other hand slipped to her waist, bringing her roughly against him. He was so hard, and she moaned, desperate to feel him inside of her. But he carefully took her dress off, caressing her as he did, sending shivers of desire through her body.

Then he laid her down, kneeling at the edge, hiking her knees on his shoulders. His horns came up proud and strong as he dipped down, taking one long swipe, making her jerk and whimper from the sensitivity of it. But he kept at his ministrations, licking, sucking, swiping, as she rocked against his mouth, finally reaching down to grab his horns and he grunted, the vibration sending a ripple through her that shot straight to her head, buzzing through her whole body.

She was lost to the sensations of his hands gripping her thighs when she felt something nudge at her entrance, and then go inside of her, and she gasped as it hooked and she realized it was his tail. She arched as he pulsed inside of her and she finished with a cry, gripping his horns hard as she rode out the wave of pleasure.

Then he was standing, taking his own clothes off. His erect length came free, hard, the swollen head already dripping as the veins bulged. He kissed her passionately, slowly, his hand caressing her face before it tangled with her hair. Then he positioned himself at her entrance and rubbed the tip of his cock there, his eyes closing as his body shuddered, and he moaned like he was dying. Then he thrust in, only a little at first, nudging, grunting with each thrust until he was finally inside of her, and she reveled in the feel of it, how he filled her.

He thrust slowly, taking his time as he touched her, and she returned his strokes. The exchange built up in her like light and shadows, as her hands explored his body, memorizing every imperfection and every perfection. They kissed until their lips were swollen and raw and her skin was peppered with the marks of his teeth, his hands pressing into her, his body marred with the marks of her nails on his back.

He picked up the pace, sweat gleaming on his bare chest, his hands gripping her thighs like they were his only anchor in a ravaging storm.

"Dryston!" she gasped out.

He stuck two fingers in her mouth, swirling around and bringing them out to massage her clit while he pounded into her. "Say my name again." He growled.

"Dryston," she whimpered.

"You're such a good fucking girl." His words were praise, a command, but his eyes held a longing so deep she could barely breath looking into those eyes. But she couldn't look away, didn't want to as the look of possession coupled with desperation accelerated the mounting rapture each stroke he laid into brought.

He moved inside her so long it became a constant for her, and her pleasure built and built, his harried breath hitting her skin until she contracted around him, biting down on his shoulder as bliss exploded through her with a force that made her whole body shake.

He pulled her against him, his strong arm holding her up as he thrust once, twice—then he came with a roar that echoed off the walls. He stayed inside her as they laid down, drawing the covers over them. She was tired, and his eyes blinked rapidly to stay awake, but his hand traced the lines of her face as she traced his chest, afraid of sleeping and waking to this being nothing more than a dream. Afraid of waking to his regret. Afraid of waking to them talking about how it wouldn't work, and she wouldn't have any more moments like this with him.

Because she wasn't certain she could bear that talk. Those words.

She wasn't certain she could bear not having him. He'd been jealous? So had she. The thought of this ending felt like a lance through the heart.

So she didn't. She banished the thoughts and nuzzled close to him as he grabbed her tightly to him, as if he too were afraid of letting it go.

# CHAPTER 46
# DRYSTON

"We strike now, before they have a chance to gather forces," Makel said, slamming her fist against the table.

Dryston rubbed his forehead, taking in a deep breath. It had been like this all morning. A meeting to decide what they were to do for the upcoming conflict. There were a lot of opinions. A lot that Dryston needed time to look over and think about. He also needed to talk to his allies. But he didn't know how to. He'd already sent missives asking for their feedback. What more could he do? He certainly couldn't step foot in Nemus again for a while. It was too dangerous.

He was also less inclined at the moment. Things were going well with Onora. He didn't want to start a bloody conflict with her people, potentially dragging in ones she loved. He wanted to wait and see. There was a good chance that all this talk of war and attacking from King Olan was just bluster. Someone trying to rile others up in an attempt to cause more issues for the demons.

"We need to think rationally," Salen said. "Let's start with the Realm of Light. See if we can't get a diplomat to go to Nemus and see what our allies there feel."

"That will make us look weak," another chieftain said. "Sending a seraph to do our work? It will show everyone that we doubt the strength of our bonds with our allies."

"We do," Dryston said, his echoing voice silencing all of them. "We do doubt it because King Leeth has remained silent, and Lord Killgan hasn't answered any of my letters. It would be foolhardy to send a demon there now. I don't have anyone I'm willing to sacrifice for it."

It was silent around the table, and he drew in another breath. Many sitting at the table had an old way of thinking. They believed he should do a show of force, convince others that they would simply crush them if they came against them. That would be effective to a point. But he needed to disband the bitter taste others had in their mouths at the mention of demons.

He needed to be a diplomat.

Which he was terrible at.

"Is Onora causing you to hedge your decisions?" Makel asked.

Dryston frowned, looking around and seeing the others not quite looking him in the eye. They had already discussed this, it seemed.

"No, she's not. I've worked for a long time to get other realms and rulers to trust us. It's been a hard road, and only recently have we succeeded in garnering the favor of other leaders. This is a huge setback. If I don't handle it perfectly, it may take many more years before we can get the alliances we need."

"Can we trust Onora?" the chieftain asked.

"Of course. She has more honor than anyone I know."

She'd been training every day for the last month with the royal guard. She kept up in most ways and made up in other ways when she couldn't. Kalen was still grouchy with her but had begrudgingly admitted that she was an excellent warrior and that she had a great deal of integrity to her. Mandel had had a glowing recommendation of her, and Dryston had slugged him, jealous and angry, only for Mandel to tell him that he was sorry for taking her to the rite. He'd been pissed by his attitude earlier and wanted to get under his skin.

So Dryston had quelled the urge to wail on him again and instead apologized.

Enid and Avenay still hadn't returned and he hadn't heard from them, other than a quick letter saying they were making interesting discoveries and they would tell him soon.

"She could be a fox in the henhouse, Drys," Makel said, uncharacteristically soft. "Be careful."

"I am. She's earned my trust. I know it will take longer to earn everyone else's, but she's working toward that."

"I've seen it," Salen said. "I can't say I fully trust her, but I trust you and I see the effort. It doesn't hurt that she's your mate. I'm sure that's a good motivator for her."

Dryston shot him a glare, and Salen threw his hands up. "I know—we aren't supposed to bring that up. You have to talk to her at some point. Regardless of her response, she has power over us because of it. It's in our nature to obey leaders, and even if she wasn't magically marked as ours, she has a leader's heart. People will fall behind her naturally, and she has a right to know about it."

Dryston clenched his jaw. "I know. All in good time. This isn't the most normal or ideal situation for finding a mate, and both of us are making the best of it."

Or he was. She'd been sleeping in his room every night since the moon rites. He loved it, and they'd fallen into a rhythm, but they hadn't spoken once about what they were, and he could tell she was still shy at times of being affectionate in public.

Was that her nature, or because she didn't see it as serious and felt the public display of it was too permanent? He didn't know, and he was too afraid to ask. He kept waiting for some marker, something to happen between them or for enough time to pass so that he felt confident talking to her about it.

But their couplings were so wild and passionate, their cadence so natural that he couldn't tell if it was just a burst of passion from her end that would inevitably burn out.

"We need to decide, and soon, what our actions will be," Makel said.

"I think we need to send scouts first. If seraphs will aid us, that's best. They won't be shot on sight," Dryston said.

"I'll talk to the Lord of Light," Salen said. "I'm sure he will be amenable to it. Enid has become the gossip pages darling now, and Avenay is their prize, so they have some motivation to keep us around."

"Thank you," Dryston said.

DRYSTON KNOCKED on the heavy wooden door and heard a baby cooing, then footsteps before the door opened with Kaemon and Emilia. They grinned on seeing him and he scooped Emilia up in his arms as she babbled to him, grinning like he'd hung the moon and stars, grabbing and holding the finger he offered her.

"She isn't helping my ego any," he said as Kaemon brought him into the parlor, where Melina was sewing a quilt by the fireplace. "I swear I can do no wrong with her."

"Well, she's just a baby. She doesn't know any better. Give her time," Kaemon said, and they both laughed.

Melina looked up and gave a wave. "Where's Onora?"

"She's training."

"She's very dedicated to that," Melina said, something like pride in her voice. The two women had been spending a lot of time together lately. Dryston would drop by and find Onora here, chatting with Melina and awkwardly waving at Emilia, who grinned at her but hated being held by her.

"She is indeed," Dryston said. "She's been impressing Kalen, even."

Kaemon whistled. "That's a difficult thing to do."

Dryston nodded. He had come here for a specific reason, but as Kaemon handed him a cup of warm tea, he found the words sticking in the roof of his mouth.

"You came to ask us something?" Melina asked. She somehow caught on to everything.

He cleared his throat. "How does the mate bond work between a human and demon?"

"Very similar to how it is with demons."

"Do you feel the same drive and desire that demons do?"

She shrugged, but Kaemon answered. "It's hard to know. But she does feel the bond and the drive. Your souls are connected, you'll feel that regardless of magical affinity."

"I started feeling it more strongly after the well was opened," Melina responded. "I think my magic responded to it, and I was able to locate Kaemon better with it."

Dryston rubbed his jaw. "So you do feel the desire to be with him because of it?"

Kaemon and Melina looked at each other, the love in their eyes so intimate that he looked down at his tea.

"No," Melina said. "I feel that because I love him. I know people think that's the bond, but it's not. I can feel the difference. The bond is a wonderful and heady thing, but it's not how I love him. I love him because of who he is and because I choose to. The bond just gives it different shading."

Kaemon squeezed her hand. "I feel the same."

"Are you asking because of Onora?" Melina asked.

He choked on his drink, and Kaemon raised a brow. "It's obvious to everyone, Drys. Especially after the moon rites."

"How the fuck do you know about that?" he asked, incredulous.

"The report was that you almost killed Mandel so . . ."

He rolled his eyes. "That's hardly even close to what happened."

He sighed, taking in another breath. "Yes, it's about Onora. I'm scared to tell her about the bond because she may cut and run if she feels like she has to be with me because of it."

"Then tell her you love her instead," Melina said.

He was silent as Melina looked at him as if it were the easiest thing in the world.

"That," she added softly, "is also very obvious to everyone."

There was no doubt about it. He was crazy about her and had been from the moment he saw her at The Tipsy Tavern. He knew that now. All those months of torment, his mind bent toward her—it had been his admiration desperately asking him to yield to love. Now that he had, it was the most obvious thing.

But how in the darkest pit was he supposed to tell her that?

# CHAPTER 47
# ONORA

Onora heard Dryston come into his room, and she stood from where she lay on the bed, reading, and walked to the doorway, peeking in. They left it open all the time now, and she sometimes wasn't certain where she should be, but when he was there, he always sought her out, wanting to touch her and hold her, even when they weren't having sex.

It was an odd but not unwelcome experience for her. She liked how much he wanted her, and she had never realized how calming it was to just lay in someone's arms, silent, reading or sleeping or just thinking. Her darker thoughts left her mostly alone now. She spent a lot of time training with the demon warriors, or helping Halst in the stables, bonding with Onyx, and she found that the rich life she had here, with all of the bonds and colony dinners and Dryston, was something that was slowly healing her old wounds. They may be scars, but she wouldn't want to lose the proof of all she'd been through. It had made her who she was—for better or worse.

Dryston was tense, his face that impenetrable wall he always wore. She felt a tightening around her ribs at the sight. She strode to him as he sat on the bed, bumping his leg with hers, so it opened and she stood between them. He looked up at her, a small, very small crack in that armor evident in his eyes. She brushed her hand along his cheek and he caught it, pressing it there and closing his eyes. He bore the weight of the realm on his shoulders, the weight of the maladies of his ancestors. The weight of his family, his colony.

"How can I help you?" she whispered.

He wrapped his arms around her and pulled her to him, burying his face in her abdomen and holding her tightly. She ran her hands through his hair, brushing her nails along his scalp, and he pressed harder into her. She ran a finger gently along the edge of his horns and a strangled groan came from him, followed by, "Onora."

She ran another finger along it and his wings shuddered. His breath changed as it beat against her torso. She placed her palm at the base and gripped, stroking, and his back rose and fell heavily with each breath. She gripped the other one and did the same. He pressed his face deeper to her stomach, desperately tugging at her shirt, pulling it out of her trousers and planting kisses all along her skin.

Would she ever tire of him? Ever tire of his touches and kisses? She didn't think she would. She knew when this inevitably ended, she would never have a lover like him again. But she could only enjoy it now. She would give him what he needed. She took a step back, and he jerked, catching himself on the bed from the loss of her against him, his eyes ravenous as they looked her over.

"Take your clothes off," she said, steadying her voice to the one she used as a commander.

His eyes flashed, understanding there, but no defiance. He stood, smirking as he removed his shirt slowly, revealing his well-defined chest to her, the trail of dark hair on his abdomen dipping below his waistline and making her gaze stick there.

"Do you like what you see?" he said, all male arrogance.

She placed her finger to her lips. "Shhh, Dryston. You will do as I say. Speak when I ask you a question. And come when I tell you to."

His eyes darkened at her command, and she knew she had been

right in her assessment of what he needed. Someone else in control. Someone else to take over.

"You've obeyed me so well," she cooed, running a finger along his cheek. "You've been so, so good for me."

He only stared at her, ready and waiting for her command. She walked around him, trailing a hand along his bare skin, taking in his tall and muscled frame. He shuddered, swallowing as she did, and she smiled, coming before him. She undressed, reveling in how his gaze became heavy lidded with lust. Then she stepped forward, placing a hand on his chest.

"On your knees."

He obeyed swiftly, his hands gripping her ass and sliding to her thighs, sending a wave of heat down her body.

She grabbed his chin, running her hands along his face. "Take your fill."

He pressed his face into her, licking and sucking, lapping up her cunt like it was the best thing he'd ever tasted, and her head tingled, dizziness making her sway into him, propping herself up against his shoulders. She stroked his hair, avoiding his horns, save for a few strokes at the base that made him groan against her, the vibration rippling against her sensitive nerves.

His hand came up to her breast, palming then flicking the nipple, and she groaned, gripping his shoulders tighter, tighter, her nails digging into his skin, when she finally came, the sensation rippling through her core and up her torso, sending shocks through her whole body.

He looked up at her, smug, licking his wet lips and she knew she would have to hold out on his pleasure, edging him, making him earn it. Making him so desperate for the command of relief that he would beg.

"Get on the bed," she said, and he obeyed, laying down, his proud length hard and twitching and on full display. She grabbed the ropes he kept under the bed and straddled his chest, taking his wrists and bringing them above his head, carefully and deftly tying him to the headboard. His eyes darkened more, and she smirked, leaning down to kiss him.

His lips met hers, their tongues clashing and teeth clanging in the passion of it, and she pulled back, placing a finger on his lips.

"Slowly."

He nodded, and she leaned down again, slowly kissing him, taking her time, his breaths more desperate, like a plea, with each stroke of her tongue over his, each bite of his lip. Then she kissed his neck, nipping and licking, making her way to his nipples, sucking and swirling as he writhed and groaned under her.

"Plea—"

But she stopped, shaking her head, and he shut his mouth, swallowing hard.

"Now it's going to take even longer, Drys," she said.

He nodded, pursing his lips as if that would help him keep the words in. She grabbed a bit of cloth from the side table and wrapped it around his mouth, tightening it so he couldn't speak.

She sat back, angling her body so he could see perfectly, then she slid her hand down from her neck, fondling her own breast, then down, down, between her legs. He watched, breathing heavier, licking his lips as she stroked her core, swiping from entrance to clit.

"Put your tail in me."

He shifted, his tail coming out from under him, and then he slowly brought it to her entrance, nudging as she rubbed her apex. Then he entered, and she moaned, shuddering against the sheer pleasure of it. She writhed and groaned, rocking her hips against it, and he grunted, groaning along with her, his cock growing harder and harder as he bucked his hips, as if trying to find any friction.

Fuck, she wanted to feel that inside of her.

But not yet. He was nowhere near ready for the release yet.

"Keep your hips still," she said, and he obeyed.

She palmed her breasts, thrusting in time with his tail, the sweet ache between her legs growing as sweat dripped down her forehead, her legs shaking. He closed his eyes, brow furrowed painfully, his cock so swollen.

She stopped, shifting and coming over, grasping the shaft and giving it a hard stroke. He groaned loudly, his hips jerking up with the movement. Taking it firmly in both her hands, she licked from the base, taking her time, making patterns and swirled up the shaft until she licked over the tip, met by a deliciously salty taste.

His knuckles were white from gripping the ropes, the veins in his arms matching the same lurid bulge as his member, his chest and legs misted with sweat.

He smelled amazing, like midnight and the smoke of a campfire, the fires of a forge. Dipping down, she licked his balls, feeling them tighten, and then she gently sucked on them. He couldn't control it anymore, couldn't contain himself, and she wouldn't stop him as he writhed against her passionate attentions. Finally, she came back up, giving another languorous lick before taking him into her mouth and sucking, pulling him in and out, his hips thrusting up into her and she let him, let him hit the back of her throat and she moaned, her cunt dripping wet, desperate to feel him fill her up entirely.

She couldn't let him finish before she felt that. So she stopped, and he stared at her, desperate, pleading, a male undone. Then she moved over him, running a hand down his chest and savoring how he undulated under her caress, before she took his cock and slowly sheathed herself over it.

His groan rocked her, his hips thrusting inside her, filling her, the sensation of his swollen cock making her legs quake, taking a moment to recover, taking a moment to try to remember her name or who she was in the wake of that glorious sensation.

He kept thrusting inside her and she rocked her hips, meeting his movements, and his breaths were harried, whimpers escaping him repeatedly, an anguished plea for release. She moved up and down, savoring how his eyes took in her whole body greedily, how his hands strained against the ropes, desperate to touch her and unable to. She reached forward, rubbing his nipples as she moved her hips in a way that her clit lit up, making her gasp, moving against him as desperately as he moved against her. He groaned, opening and closing his mouth, holding back the flood of words that threatened to spill.

She whispered a kiss in his ear, slowly removing the gag and reaching up to untie the ropes. "You may speak, Dryston. Say whatever it is you've been holding back."

Then she kissed him, his own mouth devouring hers, pulling her lower lip between his teeth and holding it there long enough she felt dizzy.

"I love you, Onora. I love you. Gods, I love you."

She stopped her motions, staring at him in shock. She blinked, trying to process it. He didn't mean it. They were in the throes of passion. He meant that he loved what she was doing to him. She swallowed as he stared at her, wide-eyed as worry lined his features.

She should have kept going, should have ignored it. Hearing him take it back right now might shatter her. She wished she had only tucked it into her heart to pull out like a prized jewel later. Now she would be confronted with the fact that she wanted to say the words back. She loved him, too. But he had just meant . . .

"You don't have to say it back, Onora. I'm sorry. I didn't mean to say it like that. Fuck . . . I'm an idiot. This isn't the time or place to say something like that. I know you don't feel the same way."

Her head spun with his words. "You . . . love me?"

He blinked. "Yes. I do." His words were precise, stilted. As if he were bracing.

"No. You don't love me." She let out a breathy laugh. How could he love her? Wasn't this just sex for him?

He shifted, sitting up and moving her so she was still on him, but they faced each other now. He grasped her face.

"I love you. No expectations. No conditions. I love you, Onora. I've been meaning to tell you. But I didn't know when was a good time."

She slammed her lips to his, and they kissed, long and hard. Her heart raced and ached and she wanted to cry for the first time since she was a child, but may the gods be damned, she wasn't about to start now. She pulled back, breathless. When she did, there was a tender vulnerability in his eyes that broke her. She didn't have words at that moment. Her emotions were a flurry, dust kicked up in a tornado, and she didn't know how or what to say. "I love you" was too simple. It didn't even begin to encompass what she felt for him.

So she rocked her hips, and he groaned again, twitching inside of her. She kept going, slow and deliberate, grinding hard against him and reveling in how he writhed under her, his expression of ecstasy. Shadows came from both of them, dancing and twining, playing and caressing as sparks of lightning jolted off her and onto him, not hurting, just sparking and lighting up the room. She rode him, bending to kiss him as they both tumbled over that edge together. They collapsed in one another's arms.

"We barely know each other," she finally said, afraid he would take the words back, afraid he had only meant them for the moment of passion.

He ran a thumb across her temple. "Here, yes." He dropped it over her heart. "Here, yes." Then he cradled her face, making her look into his eyes. "But our souls have known each other since the universe was only cold darkness. Our love has existed since before the gods thought to craft these bodies of flesh. Can't you feel it?"

She nodded, closing her eyes. "Yes."

He kissed her and then she pulled back, gasping out the words, "I love you, too. I don't know when it started. It snuck up on me, but maybe I always have."

A smile lit across his face and she thought he might cry, but he couldn't cry because then she would. He brushed a lock of hair behind her ear.

"You're my mate." He uttered the words as if they were precious, delicate, something easily broken.

His mate.

By the gods, she was his mate.

She'd been worrying all this time, and she was his mate.

"What exactly does that mean?" she asked. "I know that it's a strong soul bond, but I'm not sure I understand it fully."

His hand stroked up her arm. "It's a deep and never-ending bond between two people. We will always be drawn to each other and be connected. It also means that you're the Lady of Shadows."

She frowned, propping herself up to look at him. "Wouldn't that happen after marriage?"

He shook his head. "Magic isn't concerned about legalities. The markings on you are the markings of the mate of Lord of Shadows, and it marks you as the Lady of Shadows."

"What does that mean?"

"It means that regardless of if you want it, demons are naturally inclined to obey you. It's part of the colony's magic and instincts. We fall in line to the most powerful and follow them. The Lady of Shadows is equal in authority."

Her heart started racing. "A human?"

"My mate." He kissed her forehead, and she closed her eyes, leaning into it. "They all already know. They could tell when you challenged them at the council meeting."

She groaned. "Will this cause problems?"

He shrugged. "Some people have expressed concern, and some may be unhappy about it, but most are impressed with how you dedicate yourself to the royal guard. Kalen has begrudgingly sung your praises."

She felt a spark of pride at that. Kalen barked at her every day and never complimented her like he did the others. In many ways she couldn't keep up with the demons. She was smaller and weaker, but in other ways she was better. She could climb and dodge and react faster because of her smaller size, and the gryphons warmed to her easier because she was less of a threat.

"Let me keep working with them, I don't want anyone to think I'm here to rule over them without knowing anything about them."

He ran a hand through her hair, silent for a moment. "Does that mean you accept the mate bond?" His words were careful, and he wouldn't quite look her in the eye.

"Yes," she said and kissed him deeply. "I want to be with you, Drys. As long as you'll have me."

It took every ounce of her courage to say that, and she stared at him, swallowing hard as she waited for his response. Maybe he didn't want her as his mate. Maybe he would hide her away or send her away after this fever of passion broke.

He kissed her back passionately. "Then you will have me forever, Onora. Till our bones are dust and our souls become stars."

"I think even then, you will have me," she breathed against his lips.

"Good," he said and kissed her passionately, moving to be over her, ready for more.

## CHAPTER 48
# ONORA

The shores outside The Darkened City were bustling with merchants and artisans. A tall mountainous volcano sprouted from the ground, rising high with green foliage rolling down to the beach and giving way to black lava rock. Three large boulders came from the water, hedging in a tide pool full of shimmering black rocks. As she and Dryston wandered closer, she realized that the rocks sparkled with a pearlescent sheen, casting glinting rainbows.

Vessels came to port and went, as demons milled about along the sands, some fishing, some lounging, others hitting up shops or restaurants. Fried fish and potatoes greeted her nose and her stomach rumbled. Dryston squeezed her hand, guiding her to a grill where they were given fish on a stick and a basket of potatoes; then they sat down to eat.

It was the new year festival and the first day that the deep-sea fishers came home, bringing a variety of goods to be sold. It had been almost three months of being here and she was settling into a rhythm, making friends and slowly integrating into the community. It felt natural, as if she had always belonged here. Yet, she often marveled at it. A much younger version of her would have been shocked to see this scene. Sitting next to her mate, a demon, on a dock surrounded by demons she called friends.

A shadow darkened the dock, and she looked up, seeing two flying beings looping around in the sky. She squinted, then Dryston let out a cry of joy—it was Enid and Avenay. Enid spotted them, waving, then tucked in her wings and dove for the dock. She landed with a thud, shortly followed by a gentle landing from Avenay.

They rushed up to them, breathless and a look of urgency on their faces.

"We have a lot we need to talk about," Enid said.

THE COUNCIL HALL echoed with murmurs from the members who had been gathered urgently from all over the city. Avenay walked to the table, grabbing multiple pieces of parchment out of her bag, spreading out scrolls and smoothing them down.

Dryston came up on one side of her and Onora on the other, seeing that it was the map she'd marked the location of each attack. There were the marks made by Avenay and added in were marks in red, some over the other marks, others slightly offset.

"I showed my father this map," Avenay said. "He'd seen one with similar markings, that's what the red is."

"What are they?" Onora asked.

"They were other wells of magic," Avenay said. "They were said to be portals to the void, that if cracked open would flood the world with magic."

Prickles of fear ran along Onora's skin, her hair sticking up. "How bad would that be?"

Avenay drew in a deep breath. "Well, that in and of itself would probably be fine. The main problem is why someone would want to crack them open. It's an old fable, a horrible and specific spell that is said to have been sealed away in the grimoire of Evonin."

Dryston's skin paled. "That's the grimoire the Cruel Lord stole from the elves."

"The one we gave to King Leeth in exchange for protecting Kaemon and Melina," Enid said, voice dark.

"What's the spell?" Dryston asked.

"It's a spell to revive a being of great power."

As if stirred from a great slumber, the voice inside her purred.

Evoleen.

"Evoleen," Onora repeated out loud.

Avenay nodded. "That's what we believe it is. Opening the well in Evolis was the first step. It's the largest, the lock." She pointed to a red circle in the mountain range where Evolis is. "The map my father had showed Evolis as a location with a key symbol."

That's where she was sealed away. The voice filtered through her mind, ancient, cold, cracking.

*Who are you?*

Her twin sister.

"Did Evoleen have a twin?" Onora asked, and they all looked at her with a puzzled expression.

"The twin goddesses are different from Evoleen," Enid said.

No.

"Well . . ." Avenay said, pulling a face. "That's actually a theory I've been working on."

Enid crossed her arms. "What theory? You haven't told me."

Avenay shrugged. "Demons worship the twin moon goddesses. The one of light—the light side of the moon. And the dark side—the never-seen one. Well, there is some lore I've uncovered that mentions the dark one was in opposition to the light one and gave her life to seal the light one away."

"Where did you find that?" Dryston asked.

"The temple archives. It had a lot of dust on it, I don't think anyone had read it in a long time."

She wanted power. All of it. She would destroy the world to consume it.

A shiver ran through Onora as she repeated the words out loud, and everyone stopped to stare at her in shock. The voice continued and she repeated it word for word.

I had to lock her away. But in doing so, I gave up my corporeal body. I was saved by a witch. Your ancestor. She took my power and sealed me inside herself, to be passed down to the eldest daughter for generations. Sleeping, waiting, watching for any sign of magic.

The room became cold, their breaths coming out in puffs and darkness swirled with shadows, a pure darkness, cold as the void, a spark flicking across it.

*Will you kill me?*

No, my dear, i love you as if you were my own daughter. I saw your mother raise you, and I too raised you. As I saw her mother raise her.

The darkness twining with shadows came by and caressed her cheek.

"You have the power of the other goddess?" Avenay asked, gaping.

Onora swallowed hard. "I suppose so." Memories flashed in her mind, a flood of things that began making sense. Her mother called Onora her moon child. Being drawn to the mountain ranges where Evolis was, the birthplace of witches. "When the demons enslaved us, Varek, the Cruel Lord's first-in-command, kept me close by, not allowing anyone to touch me or harm me. He said the Cruel Lord had a special use for me."

Avenay chewed the inside of her cheek. "I think he intended to take the power inside you and use it to revive Evoleen. I think he occupied Nemus to crack open these wells and bring her back."

"The temples," Dryston said, his face pale. "He placed so many temples on ley lines in Nemus. He was trying to use them and the demonic power to bring her back. Fuck."

"Who is behind this, then?" Onora asked. "Is it the Hunters?"

Avenay shook her head. "There's so much chaos in Nemus right now. I can't say."

"What have you heard of Nemus?" Onora asked, fear gripping her for her friends.

"Nothing good," Avenay said. "There have been a lot of border skirmishes and more attacks. From what we can gather, the attacks are happening where the marks are, or very close."

"How many more remain?"

"Two."

Avenay's words echoed in the silent hall, an omen of doom.

"What happens when they are all opened?"

Avenay swallowed. "I can only assume Evoleen is fully revived, brought to her full power—perhaps even more so."

Death. That's what will happen, Onora. And only you have the power to defeat her.

"We have to stop it."

The room was silent again and she looked around, the council members shifting on their feet.

"We aren't welcome in Nemus, girl," Makel said. "How are we to stop it?"

"This will affect everyone. Not just Nemus. Evoleen won't stop there. She will grow in power until she consumes the whole world."

"Let's not be dramatic," Salen said, laughing awkwardly. "Do we really believe all this about goddesses and magic wells?"

"Yes," Enid said resolutely. "We've seen the magic, we've seen the people affected by it. Onora speaks the truth."

"We have to go, and we have to try and stop her," Dryston said. "My people will meet the challenge, who will join us?"

It was silent for a bit, Salen taking a step back, shaking his head and Makel following. But then several chieftains stepped forward, kneeling and placing fists over their hearts. The others gave pleading looks, unwilling to help. Onora drew in a deep breath. She had no idea what forces awaited them in Nemus. The demons kneeling weren't much. But it would have to do.

# CHAPTER 49
# DRYSTON

There was no time for fear as the demons flew to Nemus, staying over the orc lands and hoping that Lord Killgan still viewed them as friends. Onora rode on her gryphon beside Dryston, her keen eyes scouting the ground below. They flew for hours and as dawn broke, lighting up the lands, it was a grim scene.

Dark and death–marked land stretched for miles, the void a dizzying view from above, the veins of black soot spidering out across the plains, finally stopping a town over from Orc Haven. They arrived outside the merchant city by midmorning, the warriors setting up tents to camp in as Onora, Dryston, and several others braced themselves to enter its walls, uncertain what waited there for them.

Deserted streets, papers drifting on the wind, abandoned buildings. The Tipsy Tavern fared little better. The usually vibrant building was cold and dark. They walked up, entering to see it empty, the quiet an eerie omen. The back door creaked, and out came Jorah, a hefty axe in his hand, a fierce look on his face that fell away when he saw who it was.

"By Yeolah's grace," he muttered, striding forward.

Quickly after him came Aife, shock coming over her features as they hugged and greeted them all.

"What's happened here?" Dryston asked.

"Bad things, Drys," Jorah said. "It's been a dark time since you were taken."

"There have been more attacks, killing people in one fell swoop," Aife said. "Hunters pushed in and attacked a farming community, then the black soot appeared and the few who escaped were too terrified to speak of what they saw."

"They opened another portal," Onora muttered.

"Where is everyone in Orc Haven?" Dryston asked.

Aife shook her head. "Not many travelers so people have closed up shop. Some are going to Yeolent. Lord Killgan has been gathering warriors to attack the humans."

"We need to talk to Lord Killgan. If he plans to retaliate he doesn't know what he's up against," Dryston said.

"There's only one more portal left to open," Avenay said.

"What's this talk of portals?" Jorah asked.

"Come with us to Yeolent and we will explain on the way," Dryston said.

Yeolent was mostly how he remembered it. Sprawling plains, the first hint of spring evident in the bright green grass poking up through bits of snow. Smoke drifted up from chimneys, and tents spanned out for miles making an encampment. They were stopped by two big, burly orc warriors as they approached.

"What business do you have?" the first asked, looking over the odd arrangement of people in their party. They'd left most of their men outside Orc Haven, bent on traveling lighter and not coming with a show of force.

"I'm Lord Dryston, of the Shadow Realm. Tell Lord Killgan I seek an audience and hope to aid him."

The first gestured to a younger orc and sent the message with him. They stood patiently in silence as the orcs stared them down, unmoving, unwillingly to chat, when, finally, the young male returned and they were escorted through the tents and campfires to a large hall at the end. The giant double doors were opened by the guards, ushering them in.

Warmth hit them as they entered, orcs milling about and making room for them. In the middle was a large table with well-outfitted warriors standing around, and at the head, Lord Killgan poring over a map. He looked up, meeting Dryston's gaze with a grim smile, beckoning them closer, shaking his hand as he came near.

"I did not know the state of our alliance," Killgan said, "but I have to admit seeing your face gives me relief."

"Did you receive any of my ravens?" Dryston asked.

Killgan shook his head. "No, but that's not to say someone didn't. Too much has happened since we last spoke, and I've been roaming the plains, trying to protect my people."

"What's your plan here, with all these warriors?"

"We have to strike the humans. They've been encroaching on our land more and more, and the last attack was devastating. Those were the largest farmlands and right before winter properly set in, destroying the main stores of grain and food. We plan to strike their stores and take it, then head for the Hunter's Guild. They seem to be at the helm of this." Killgan dipped his head to Onora. "What of this one?"

"I'm no longer a Hunter," she said.

Killgan nodded. "I figured as much, when I saw your face plastered on wanted posters. Well enough, you're not the only one."

She frowned and he continued. "There's a band of humans we've given sanctuary to. They defected from the Hunter's Guild. They're led by someone named Jackson. They've been undermining the Hunters for months now. It's the only thing that's kept them from fully taking over."

"Where are they?" Onora asked eagerly.

"Up north somewhere. I haven't heard from them in a while. Truthfully, I'm not sure if they are still alive."

Onora's face paled and Dryston grabbed her hand, squeezing.

"We have information about these attacks," Dryston said. "Avenay, can you explain?"

Avenay stepped forward, pulling out her map, then explained it all to him. Killgan's eyes grew wide with each word she spoke, and more orcs gathered around the table, listening, muttering what sounded like prayers in their native tongue.

"Where is the last portal?" Killgan asked.

"It's outside Venatu. There's an ancient temple there that was built over that spot."

"They will kill many of their own people if they open that portal," Killgan said. "Monsters come out, devouring and destroying, burning everything around them in a fire as cold as ice."

Dryston shivered, remembering the horrifying creatures they'd seen in Evolis.

"We plan on invading the area and stopping it," Dryston said, hating the words even as he spoke them. He'd wanted to leave the humans alone for the rest of time, let the feud between Venatu and The Darkened City die off to nothing more than a vague memory. But they couldn't let this happen, they couldn't let this evil be unleashed on the world.

THEY STAYED that night in Lord Killgan's encampment. Onora cuddled next to him under the fur covers, pressing her face to his chest, but sleep found neither of them.

"Do you think Jackson is alive?" she whispered.

He stroked her hair. "I do. I think he's been smart enough to survive up to now, I'm sure he's still out there, protecting others."

"He's always been good at that."

"We'll find him," Dryston said. "After all this is over, we'll find him and everyone else with him."

Onora gave him a long look, as if she wanted to tell him something but could only convey it in her eyes, something deep and sad and final. He hated the look—he wanted to wipe it away and ease her fears, but he was battling his own.

"Promise me, when this is all over, you will find him," she said softly.

"We both will," he said.

"Promise me," she insisted.

"I promise."

He started to question where this talk was coming from, but she kissed him fiercely, the passion wiping away any thoughts of the next day or the future, pulling him into the now. For in that moment, he just wanted her. To be close to her. To hold her for as long as he was still able to.

## CHAPTER 50
# ONORA

Plains sprawled out for miles as they traveled, the sameness of it a weariness all in its own. Time seemed to stretch and warp, minutes feeling like hours, each step leading them to a future unknown. A danger unknown.

Onora felt it deep in her bones. Every second with Dryston felt too precious, too breakable. She committed them all to memory, absorbing every moment, every breath, as if it were her last.

only you have the power to defeat her.

The voice's words rattled in her brain all day. What would that entail? What would it mean to be the only one with the power to defeat Evoleen?

Onyx nudged her face, distracting her draining thoughts with a coo and a caress. She wrapped her arm around the gryphon, giving her neck scratches. Onyx leaned deeper into her, a rumbling purr coming from her chest as she did. This trip had been a bonding adventure with her, and she took turns flying, then circling back to walk with her amongst the others. There was no point in her moving too quickly.

For she had no idea what they would encounter when they came to the temple, and they very well could need the entire army.

Halst had brought several extra gryphons, ones that would obey her command, ready for any support they would need, and Onyx spent much of the day playing with them, rumbling in the grass, then flying up and twirling around one another in the air.

"You two are very close now," Dryston said, a soft smile on his face as he took in the way Onyx kept close.

"Are you jealous?" she teased.

"I would be, if I didn't like Onyx so much."

Onyx cooed, dipping behind Onora to come to Dryston and nudge him playfully. He laughed, pulling out a small treat and giving it to her. Dryston spoiled the gryphon rotten, but Onora loved it. He spoiled her too, and she'd grown more used to it. He had a need to provide for others, and she had to admit that his attention to what she liked and needed made her feel so safe with him, so calm.

Gods but she loved him.

It ached like a bruise, yet blissful as a cool summer breeze on her cheeks. All her old wounds had sealed up, healing over, only for this love to lay her bare, vulnerable, aching, giving it to him and begging him to be gentle.

And he was. Always. Bit by bit her trust came back to her. Inch by inch she found vulnerability with him easier. Others? Not so much. But with him, yes.

They passed over the Emerald Gorge by noon, the going slow across the bridges and the flyers all took to the air, keeping watch, exulting in the freedom of flight. Dryston teased and enticed Onyx to chase him, and Onora let out a yell of angry curses as Onyx lurched up, cawing as she flew, twirling to chase him.

He looked back, flashing a grin that suddenly turned to shock as his body lurched and he let out a grunt of pain.

"Drys!" she cried out, making Onyx fly closer.

She saw it then, the arrow in his shoulder. Cries greeted their ears from the ground. Bedlam broke out below. Elves had emerged from the forest, full of their glinting armor, long bows ready, scythes flashing as they slashed at their soldiers.

Dryston was already flying for the enemy, his hands poised and ready with shadowfyre. She flew over too, uncoiling her power and taking in a shaky breath. She didn't have great control yet and she still couldn't tap into the goddess's powers fully, but she hoped the ball of shadowfyre she was coiling up would work. Aiming to the farthest enemies from her allies, she let it go with a cry, and it barreled forward, narrowly missing Dryston and flashing on a hefty group in the back.

They screamed, the fires consuming them, and the others moved to evade, many falling to the swords of Killgan's warriors. Arms shaking, she held tightly on to the saddle horn, focusing to regain her power. That had taken a lot out of her. Smoky tendrils caressed her cheek, and she drew her bow, taking aim. She would have to go with her old training for now, though she'd only just started practicing aerial fighting.

She pulled her arm back, aiming, taking in a deep breath, when commotion in the other direction caught her attention. More came from behind the hills, a swarming mass of soldiers rushing them from behind. Onora focused there, unleashing her first arrow and hitting her target, then one right after the other.

More poured out of the forest, and the battlefield was a flurry of blood, shadows, and a variety of magic creating bursts of multicolored light. A blast hit the gorge and a wave sprayed up, taking warriors back with it, and Onora shifted Onyx, guiding her with her knees to loop around and go lower. It was more dangerous, but she needed to be closer, to help the people stuck on the ground.

She sent out arrows, more shadows, whatever she could muster in her to help those on the ground. But there were so many, so, so many. They would be overwhelmed. She leaned forward, patting Onyx on the neck.

"I need you to drop me in the middle," she said.

Onyx tilted her head, giving her a backward glance. It was a risk. One that might kill her. And perhaps it was foolhardy, but she needed to, she had to try.

*Will you help me?*

The goddess seemed to yawn, her power unfurling at the request.

*Maybe a little faster?*

A chuckle resounded in her mind.

Yes, dear, let's teach them a lesson.

Onyx dipped, understanding as she always did, and followed as Onora guided her to the middle of the enemies from the hills. They cried out as she came near, arrows whizzing past, when one sliced open her cheek.

She didn't have time to think about that. Pulling out her axes, she unbuckled herself from the saddle and when she was close enough, she jumped to the ground, rolling and somehow making it upright. She was surrounded, and she heard Dryston's cry of anger from somewhere, but she needed him to stay back, stay far away.

*Now!*

The ground beneath her turned first to frost, the crystals bursting from her feet outward, making the elves surrounding her back up, gasping. But they weren't quick enough, and it climbed up their feet and legs, claiming them, wrapping around them until their screams were covered up with ice.

Then darkness drifted around her, swirling and warping the world in her vision, and the warriors cried out. She was aware of them fleeing, feeling their footsteps reverberate in the earth and she somehow knew where each one was precisely. The darkness sought them, collapsing them in like a crumpled piece of paper, swallowing their cries into the void.

When it cleared, her breath puffed in the air and she looked around to see that they were all dead, save for a few fleeing far off on the plains, away from them. The warriors on the other side must have fled or been killed because all she saw were her allies staring at her in blank shock, then Dryston landing in front of her, sprinting toward her as the world went black again.

~

SHE WOKE in Dryston's arms. His hand stroked her hair and she nuzzled closer to him, enjoying the warmth of the furs.

"Where are we?" she asked.

"In the Harrow Woods," he said. "Only a little ways in. How are you feeling?"

"Good," she said, then sat up swiftly, checking him for his arrow wound.

He chuckled. "All healed."

She let out a sigh of relief. "No poison?"

"None that the orc healers couldn't fix."

"Did we lose very many?"

He shrugged, tucking a tendril of hair behind her ear. "Not as much as them."

"They were elves, Drys," she said, the information her mind hadn't been able to process before coming to her full force. "Wearing the armor of King Leeth's soldiers."

Sadness flashed in his eyes. "Yes. And it seems they were waiting for us—it was meant to be a trap."

She cupped his face, giving him a long look before she kissed him. "We know nothing yet."

He nodded, pulling her tighter against him. "We will take it one day at a time."

The flap to their tent opened and Enid poked her head in. "You're awake! Good, because Killgan wants to discuss strategy."

Onora scrambled to her feet, her body barking in pain as she did, and Dryston wrapped an arm around her waist to help steady her. They walked to Killgan's tent where the other leaders were all gathered around a table, lit by flickering lamplight.

"That was an interesting trick you did today," Killgan said, eyeing her appraisingly.

"I wish I'd done it sooner," she said.

"You saved many lives today—we're grateful," he said. "After the attack, we believe that the humans will be waiting for us. Enid, tell them what you saw."

"I went scouting with Kaemon earlier," Enid said, hand resting on the hilt of her sword. "I didn't go far enough to see everything, but there's enough fires and other movement in the fields between the woods and Venatu that it seems they are ready and waiting for something, at least. Either us, or they are preparing for the portal to open."

Onora drew in a deep breath. This was going from bad to worse.

Killgan gestured to the map on the table. "Avenay has been helping us chart where exactly the temple may be."

She leaned over, looking at it. The temple that Dryston's colony had been slaughtered at wouldn't be it, no, it would be one farther out. She'd spent little time in the woods outside Venatu, but enough strange folktales had been inspired by it that she had little doubt that it was where the temple was located.

"We need to focus on getting Onora to the temple safely," Avenay said, pointing to the woods. "It may take some time to locate it. There's a chance that it's shrouded, much like Evolis was. If this is the last one, then it is the most powerful source. I believe it is closer to the eastern edge of the woods, near Venatu. Older maps show a road leading to a spot there. We are four days away from the full moon. Based on the ritual in Evolis, and dates compared to the most recent attacks, we believe that is when they will be trying to perform the rite to bring Evoleen back."

"We will go to the woods, ready to engage and hold them off for you. But there very well may be many in the woods as well. We need all the flyers to go overhead and see if you can locate the temple that way first," Killgan said.

"This is dangerous," Onora said. "Can we not traverse those woods and avoid the human soldiers altogether?"

Killgan shook his head. "We would have to pass through the mountains, and these are too treacherous. The flyers could try that way first, but if you're attacked, we will be at least a day away from you."

"We can't risk that," Dryston said. "We proceed with the original plan."

Onora swallowed her protest. They were right. But it meant that many would die for this to happen. She had half a mind to leave in the night, go it alone with Onyx. But that would be foolishness. There was too much at stake now. Far too much.

## CHAPTER 51
# ONORA

Boot tracks littered their path the next day, many of them fresh and most likely from soldiers. They marched on through the woods, waiting for any sign of their enemies from before, but the forest was quiet, their travel easy. Three days through the Harrow Wood, and the easiness of it put them all on edge more than an attack would.

Onora's skin buzzed, her senses on high alert the whole time. She had the distinct feeling they were being watched, but other than some uncanny sense, she couldn't find proof of it. So when she heard the twig snap, she was the first to pull out her bow, nocking an arrow. As the rest followed suit, a host of arrow tips appeared out of the woods, sun glinting on their tips, coming from all directions.

She swallowed, waiting for the first arrow to fly, for the first hint that anyone would break the silent agreement they currently held.

"Who goes there?" Dryston called.

"I'd like to ask you the same question," a male voice cried out.

"I'm the Lord of Shadows," he responded.

"Oh, what a lucky day for me," the voice called back, humor lining his tone. "You're the most wanted male in all of Nemus."

"Lucky indeed," Dryston responded. "To have so many arrows pointed at you."

"Likewise, brother."

"Tell me your name."

The bushes rustled, then a male elf stepped out, long wavy hair falling over a dark green tunic. He held a bow in his hand, but it relaxed at his side and he looked them over carefully.

"Well, I'm going to safely assume you aren't here to rescue our prisoner—as he keeps threatening."

"Who is your prisoner?"

"King Leeth, of the elves."

Dryston's face hardened, and she could see his long-simmering rage coming to the surface, ready to boil over at the mention of the name.

The elf chuckled. "I see you share a similar regard for the old male." He gestured. "Follow me."

THEY WOVE through the woods on a trail that had been hidden by magic, the scene shifting and changing with a wave of his hand. Other elves lined the pathway here and there, keeping watch, but no longer threatening. Then they came to a settlement of treehouses, some carved in the bases, bridges connecting others. He brought them to a structure in the middle, the only one that wasn't a tree house and when they entered, they descended into a dungeon, cold and dark save for the flickering mage lights.

The stairs wound down and around until they came to the base, and in the back was a cell, cold and musty, holding King Leeth. He stood swiftly as the elf arrived, his eyes going wide in shock when he saw them.

Dryston crossed his arms. "Don't try to tell me that you've been here for the last so many months and that's why you ignored my missives."

Leeth pursed his lips. He'd always been gregarious, kind—affable. She'd been charmed by him on their first meeting, and she was not easily beguiled. But now, looking at him in this state, it was as if the mask slipped. A sneer graced his lips, his eyes narrowing on Dryston as a cold laugh echoed from him.

"You served your purpose, Lord of Shadows. I had no need of you anymore. Sorry I couldn't spare the time to tell you," he said.

Onora could see the hurt in Dryston's eyes, the anger. Leeth had been his first real ally; after years and years of trying, he'd finally thought he'd broken through and won over Leeth. Now it seems he was only using him. But for what?

"Why did you offer to help Kaemon?"

Leeth gathered his long robes, taking a seat on the stone bench and leaning against the wall, drawing in a deep sigh. "Because I needed you. I needed you and Enid. Imagine my luck when I'd been searching for a female demon to come on a quest. Imagine my luck when I thought I'd have to scheme and lie and manipulate and then, suddenly, one winds up on my front door, begging for my help, saying she'll do anything if I save her brother and his mate."

Onora's skin prickled. He'd been planning this for so long. "You wanted to revive Evoleen."

He gave her a dull look. "Well, of course. But we had to find Evolis first. And we had to open the first portal. Everything has fallen so nicely after that first hurdle. But really, it's always been the Erebus family that has made this possible."

Dryston shifted on his feet uncomfortably. "What do you mean by that?"

"The Cruel Lord was very misunderstood," Leeth said, examining his nails. "People thought he only wanted Nemus, that he only wanted to oppress and kill and wreak havoc here. On the contrary, he was a bit of a visionary. You see, he had the grimoire of Evonin and he'd learned, by some dark means, surely, that in it contained the spell to revive Evoleen. And he learned that there were portals that needed to be opened in order to do it.

"So he came here with force, taking over the land, enslaving and killing and pillaging, all in an attempt to find the portals. He was a fool, though. He placed temples on ley lines, assuming they were the portals. He never thought to follow the lines and find an even bigger source.

"Then your father kills him and takes over and tries to amend things, but when he comes to remove the temple off the ley line, your colony is slaughtered, as were many, many Hunters. And that sacrifice, coupled with the ritual, sent a shockwave through the portals.

"For the first time in centuries, our elves were able to sense Evolis and where it might be. We were able to sense Evoleen, and she spoke to many, beckoning them to find her.

"I've dedicated my life to reviving her. She first spoke to me a decade ago, and I've never forgotten her sweet voice." He stared into the distance, a religious fervor in his eyes. "It's all coming together now. Things are in motion you can't stop, no matter how hard you try, no matter what you do. She will be revived and she will bless her followers, destroying those who would challenge and imprison us."

Silence fell, an eerie feeling snaking through the dungeon.

"He's quite mad, as you can see," the elf said.

Leeth looked as if he were about to speak, but Dryston beat him to it. "I've seen quite enough."

The elf nodded. "Come with me. We'll get you provisions for your journey."

They followed the elf up the stairs and out into the open air. He greeted others along the way, many clapping him on the shoulder in a brotherly way.

"What is your name?" Dryston asked.

"Elgin," he said, and they both gasped. He raised his brows.

"You're Tannin's friend?" Onora said.

Elgin's face softened. "Yes, yes I am."

"He sent us to look for you."

"Many bad things have happened of late. I wanted to leave him with more information, but I couldn't spare any time. A great evil is upon us, and I had to speak to my friend in Orc Haven." Elgin frowned, squinting as he looked at Onora. "You wouldn't happen to be Onora?"

"How did you know?"

"I've been subjected to many poems describing your beauty."

She groaned, and he laughed.

Looking around at the encampment, she saw elves milling about, along with goblins, satyrs, and humans. She wondered where they had all come from. Had they seen an attack? Had they lost loved ones to that horror? A flash of a dusty blue cape grabbed her attention, and she caught her breath, breaking into a sprint, following it through the mass of people.

She was suddenly overcome with a sudden and wild hope. She weaved around others, bursting through the crowd. Humans stood in a circle, outfitted with a variety of weapons, listening to their leader talk to an elf in the center. They all wore dusty blue capes and the armor of Hunters.

She couldn't find the words, she couldn't form any thought as she stared in shock. The other humans noticed her first, some gasping, finally getting the attention of the man in the middle. He stopped talking and turned.

Jackson.

His jet-black hair was pulled back at the nape of his neck, those familiar half-moon eyes taking her in then blinking, slowly, very slowly registering what he saw.

Onora swallowed the sob that suddenly caught in her throat. Jackson, Jackson was here.

He ran forward, pulling her into a bone-crushing hug. She returned it, and they both laughed, the sound of his wet from tears, and she didn't want to let him go, couldn't stand it. But a hand rested on her shoulder and she looked to see Andrea, and she repeated the scene with her, then Jin and Avery.

"Where have you been? What has happened?" she asked Jackson.

He shook his head in sorrow. "They overhead me telling other Hunters that I felt there was a misunderstanding, that I didn't think

Dryston had done the attacks and that I didn't think you had done anything wrong. Instead of a reprimand, Brayden commanded my death. And that turned into Hunters defending me and others fighting them. There was a clear split, and we ran, picking up villagers and mercenaries along the way that saw the truth in what we were saying."

"I'm glad you're safe."

He pressed his forehead to hers. "I've been so worried about you. I barely dared hope I'd ever see you again. They have the king, Onora. He found out their lies and schemes and they've imprisoned him, saying they will only spare him if Evoleen grants it."

She could barely make sense of it all.

"What are you doing here?" he asked.

"There's so much to tell you."

THEY MADE camp there that night, Elgin enchanting the area to protect them from outsiders. They enjoyed a meal of venison and stew, sitting around the fire, catching up. They had learned that Jackson was leading the band of ex-Hunters, gathering more humans along the way, and had teamed up with Elgin's rebellion against Leeth. After hearing what Onora and Dryston had to say, what all they explained to them about what was happening, they decided to join them on the morrow to fight. Halst had introduced Onora's old squad to the spare gryphons, saying that if they would have them, then they were theirs.

Onora wasn't surprised when the gryphons took to all of them quickly, spending a little more time getting used to Avery and his gruffness. It felt nice that she would be fighting next to them again, able to have them have her back.

If she went with the others.

She took a large gulp of the wine and stared at the fire as Jackson joined her, having gotten another plate of food.

"You're lost in thought."

She looked around, ensuring Dryston was nowhere near. "Jackson, I might need your help."

"You have it."

She smiled, her heart warming as it always did at his eagerness to assist her. "The fighting will be terrible. I need to leave tonight and go to the temple by myself. I can take care of it, I know I can because of the goddess. But I need your help getting out discreetly."

"You're certain this is the wisest move?"

She nodded. "I feel the threat growing every day. If we wait too much longer, she will be revived fully and we won't be able to stop her. She will be too strong. I have to try."

"I'll help you."

She squeezed his hand as Dryston walked over, his gaze snagging on her in the way it always did, full of love and adoration, and a lump caught in her throat. She didn't want to keep this from him, didn't want to lie. But he would try to stop her. And she had to do this. To protect him and everyone else.

"Ready for bed?" he asked her.

She stood, taking his hand in hers and waving a small goodbye to Jackson as they went to their tent. They curled around each other under the covers, and she laid on his chest, breathing in the scent of him deeply, memorizing every note of it.

"What are you thinking about?" he asked softly. He knew, always knew, when her mind was tumbling.

"How much I love you."

He tilted her face up, his gaze piercing into her, and she could almost cry from the love there. "I love you so, so much, Onora."

There were so many words to say, so many things she wanted to express to him and didn't know how to. She could spend a lifetime trying to explain the depth of her feelings for him and she'd always fall short. So instead, she kissed him, long and hard and slowly. His tongue slipped into her mouth, and she let out a breathy moan. Their lips moved faster, followed by hands, slipping and desperate for more, more, more.

He removed her clothes, then his. She climbed on top of him, her body moving in tandem with his—with a desperate fervor that spoke of a bitter finality, of a sweet eternity contained to a singular moment. Something about it felt too final, and she almost stopped, almost telling him her plan, but instead she devoured his mouth, and he pulled her tighter to him, making love to him late into the night.

Because when dawn rose over the horizon, and they marched on the human lands as she flew to the temple, she had no idea if she would ever hold him again in this life.

## CHAPTER 52
# ONORA

She slipped out of the tent late that night, meeting Jackson by where the gryphons were tied up. Only, it wasn't just Jackson, but Avery, Jin, and Andrea, all suited and ready, their gryphons with tack already on them.

"We're going with you," Jin said.

"It's too dangerous," she replied, furrowing her brow.

"Sounds like my kind of mission." Avery grinned.

"You're not going alone." Andrea placed a firm hand on her shoulder, giving it a squeeze. "We're going to help you."

"To the end—whatever it may be," Jackson added.

A lump caught in her throat again at their words, at the calm that it gave her to know they were coming along. This was becoming an annoying recurrence for her.

"Very well then," she said. "Let's go."

"Not so fast," a voice said from behind, and she stiffened, recognizing it as Kalen's.

She turned, crossing her arms, not sure what to do. Would she have to tie him up to go? Would he yell and wake the others, who would then stop her?

"You're planning on going to the temple alone, aren't you?" he asked.

She tilted her chin up, defiant. "Yes. It's what's best. Going the other way will take too long. If we wait for the whole army to make it there, she will be unleashed."

Kalen stared at her for a long, scrutinizing moment, then he sighed. "Okay, but you're not going without me."

She blanched, shocked. "Kalen—"

He waved his hand. "I'll be damned if I let my Lady of Shadows go into battle alone. I'll be damned if I don't protect my best friend's mate. And I'll be damned if, as your commander, I don't go into battle with you."

Well damnit, there was that stupid lump again. But she only smiled and nodded.

They mounted their gryphons and flew off into the night, the cool air whipping against her cheeks, the moon high, stars blinking as they came to the mountains flying between the rocks and crags. The gryphons seemed to understand the gravity of the situation, focused, fast, and sure as they dipped between passes and over trees.

She kept an eye out on the ground for any signs of the temple. They flew for miles over the forests outside Venatu, coming close to the fields surrounding the city by morning, and she gripped her fists in fear. So many. So many soldiers encamped outside the city. This had to have been what Enid and Kaemon saw. Fires lit all throughout, tents and scouts and noises.

Their army was paltry in comparison. They had never stood a chance. Yet Enid hadn't told them that. She'd wanted to progress with the plan anyway, to get Onora to the temple.

This had been a suicide mission all along, and she felt even more sure that she was right in leaving when she did. If she could stop this before it started, if she could get it taken care of and send her people back, then no one would be harmed. She needed Kalen to make it out alive and get word back to Dryston to stand down.

They circled around the forest for an hour, looking at the spot on the map that Avenay had said was the most likely location, looking for a steeple, or stones glinting in the light, a clearing—anything at all that would show them a sign, to no avail. It had to be hidden—she was certain of it.

Then she saw it. A glinting light in the forest, a mirror at the helm of a building in a clearing, vines and ivy growing up around it. She signaled her crew, and they circled, flying down to land a bit away in case anyone was there.

They moved swiftly and stealthily through the forest, Onora leading as she looked for tracks or signs of anything sinister. Nothing save for that eerie quiet she'd experienced at the sacrifice sites. But this was even more profound. As if the earth itself had stopped, as if everything had halted its breath and motion to hide better from whatever evil lurked. So quiet that a snap of a twig could send a shockwave.

They came to the temple and hid in the trees, observing, watching. It was old, the gray stones worn with a weathered black, cracks here and there, ivy hanging brown and dead as it wrapped around it. As far as temples went, it was smaller, but she could see mirrors at different points, most likely to catch light and reflect it back, making it harder to tell exactly what it was. There were dark tracery windows, worn and smokey from age.

Evoleen's temple. She had this erected as the main pool for her. Where she drew power from the moon and stars. Digging into the void and pulling out their power like they were naught more than radishes. Shattering worlds.

Onora shuddered at the voice's words. Evoleen could shatter worlds? How would she have the power to stop her?

She slowly began to move forward when she saw movement, then others coming from the other side of the forest. She threw up her hand, halting those behind her, Jackson standing next to her. They exchanged a horrified look as elves in chains were led by soldiers. Following them was a woman in a regal robe, her hair spindly and gray, hanging beneath her heavy hood that hid her face. Carried on a plush bed was a being—terrible and beautiful, her skin gray, lips blue, eyes shuttered with purple veins pulsing and hair tangling with antlers over skin like bark.

Evoleen. She will be performing the rite when the sun is highest.

Noon. Onora had thought they had another day—the full moon was that night.

The moon temple was in evolis—the dark side. She is the light side, this is her temple and she will absorb from the sun.

Shit. That left them less time.

They waited until they all entered, then slowly left, searching the outside of the temple, taking their time gauging how to best go in. There were far too many to just rush in.

"Onora," a man said, and she swallowed.

Amherst.

She turned slowly, seeing him standing behind her with a few other Hunters, all with crossbows pointed at them.

This whole time she'd clung to the smallest hope she could—that Amherst hadn't been in on all of this. That his letter had been forged and other forces were at work. But seeing him here now, she knew that had been foolhardy.

"Why?" was all she asked.

Something like regret shifted in his eyes before they hardened. "I did love you like a daughter, Onora. You've been my pride. But you were getting in my way. I knew I had to sacrifice the few for the many."

"What in the darkest pit does that even mean?" Jackson spat, followed by a rumbling growl from Kalen.

Amherst sighed. "I'll explain. Perhaps you can forgive me in the next life. Perhaps you will see that what I'm doing is honorable.

"When Lord Dryston's family visited Venatu, when they were slaughtered, the shockwave of it woke Evoleen from slumbering in the pit. I heard her. She spoke to me and beckoned me to find her. I learned, years later, that King Leeth also heard her call, and we've been working for years to revive her.

"I always hoped you would help me, you would be the leader of her armies. As you grew in strength and power, you also grew in reputation. The Hunters loved and trusted you. So many of them would fall at your feet, obey your every command. Which I had hoped for.

"Then you became enamored with Lord Dryston. And I needed him as a cover. He was another sacrifice—all for the greater good. If we could pin the attacks on him, then we would not be stopped before we could finish. It would have worked so smoothly—if not for you.

"Your doubt, your unwillingness to condemn him outright sent ripples of dissent through my ranks. All I could do was paint you as an enthralled fool, a traitor who should be killed."

"A lot of good that did," Andrea said. "Half your Hunters abandoned you anyway."

Onora hadn't realized it had been that many. She was shocked, but also very, very proud of them.

Amherst sighed. "All because of Onora and Jackson. You both wield your influence so carelessly. You give no thought to the broader ramifications. Yet others would follow you to their deaths."

"I have thought of the ramifications," Onora said. "It's you who hasn't. Evoleen is a murderer. She can shatter worlds, devouring them. She will do that here."

"No!" Amherst's rebuke was sharp, and she jumped, hating that she still wanted his approval, still wanted this to be a bad dream she would wake from. "She will bring eternal life, everlasting peace. People will no longer be sick and hungry and die. People will live forever."

"Only the people that aren't sacrificed to keep her magic potent," Onora said. They'd learned that too well in Evolis. The long life, the well that healed any illness, had come from the sacrificial death of others. "Humans will go first, that's what she did in Evolis. We are nothing but animals to her, meant to feed her own murderous appetite."

The goddess inside her brushed against her senses—a comfort.

"You don't understand—" Amherst started but was interrupted when shadows twined around his neck, tugging, pulling, cutting off his words. The others did too, dropping their bows and grasping at their necks as if they could pull them off.

"I do, Amherst. I understand you would sacrifice not only the innocent, but those you love, and worst of all—your own integrity for the sham promise of a charlatan goddess."

He fired his arrow, the release quick and sure. It would have hit Onora, but Jackson tackled her, taking the hit in his leg. He grunted, and she reacted without a thought, twisting the shadows to snap their necks. They fell to the ground in a heap, and she shifted, laying Jackson on the ground and looking at his wound.

"Don't worry about me," he said. "We have to stop them from raising the goddess."

She shook her head, taking the arrow and yanking it out. He stifled his cry, and she placed her hands over his leg. She was using too much power, she knew this, but she had to heal him. She needed him to have the best chance of running if things went down. So she chanted in elvish, and he slowly healed.

Suddenly, the ground rumbled, rippling out through the forest, sending birds up and flying in the air. On instinct, as the voice helped her, she weaved a net of magic around her friends, reaching out into the forest for the gryphons as well, refusing to let their power be drained or hurt.

A blue light emitted from the tower, up to the heavens, blazing and glowing and horrible.

Fear prickled along her skin. They had opened the portal. Evoleen would be revived. Perhaps she already was.

Onora jumped to her feet and rushed into the temple.

# CHAPTER 53
# DRYSTON

Onora had fucking left.

"Calm down," Enid said as she and Kaemon circled him. He was busy strapping weapons to his body, ready to fly to the forest.

"She left long ago," Kaemon said. "She left for a reason. Because she thought it was too dangerous. The best thing we can do now is march with the soldiers and hope to give her support."

"She may very well be dead already!" he growled, and everyone in the encampment stopped packing to look at him as his voice echoed.

"We have to believe she's not. She has others with her."

Dryston swallowed, hating what that did to the pit of his stomach. "Why didn't she take me with her?"

Enid raised a bemused brow. "Really, Drys? Pray tell, what would you have done if she told you of her madcap plan?"

Dryston opened his mouth to respond, and then promptly shut it. He would have stopped her. He would have tied her up and thrown her over his shoulder and told her *no*.

"Exactly," Enid said. "Let's go and support her the best we can now."

~

Killgan had projected that travel would take a day to get them where the soldiers needed to be. But by some miracle, perhaps everyone pushed on by the need to get to Onora quickly, they accomplished it in a little over half a day. They were exhausted, every part of their beings aching, but ready for battle.

He flew overhead with the other demons, scouting. There were so many soldiers outside Venatu. He drew in a shaky breath, a feeling of fear coming over him that was uncommon. Most battles he'd been in, they had been smaller scale, the demons had plenty enough soldiers, or they were just skirmishes. There were so many. Far too many. They would be slaughtered.

"Well, we have to try, still," Kaemon said, seeing his expression. "We have to hope she can stop it all."

As he spoke, cries rose up from the people on the ground as the earth rumbled, and in the forest a blue light shot into the sky.

Shit.

That couldn't be good. But at least he knew where the temple was now.

Human warriors cried out in joy, many marching toward the forest.

"We have to hold them off," he said. If Onora had seen that, she would be heading to that exact spot. They needed to buy her time.

Killgan's men and the others seemed to have the same idea. They charged toward the ones at the front, and Dryston and the demons swarmed overhead.

Dryston cupped his hands, holding them out in front of him, letting a blast of shadowfyre leave his hand, hurling to the soldiers on the ground. Arrows whizzed past, and he rolled, tucking in his wings, ducking and twirling out of the way. He heard a grunt and knew another arrow had hit one of his warriors.

He didn't have time to see who it was as another volley of arrows flew at them. His wings curled around, and he ducked and dodged, but two struck him—one in a wing, the other his arms. He grunted, ignoring the lancing pain, and tried to stretch his wing out. He had little control over it with the arrow in it and he couldn't get it out himself. He'd have to land and fight on the ground before it gave out and he crashed to the earth. He tucked his wings in and dove.

He landed to the ground with a thud, immediately bringing his sword up to block a blow from a human. He thrust back and the man stumbled, crying out angrily, coming at him again, only for Dryston to dispatch him with a quick, short swipe from shoulder to hip.

He became lost in the battle, his blood pumping fiercely, blocking out the horror of it all, protecting the people fighting alongside him, using his shadows where he could.

Suddenly, he was surrounded, having been separated from the larger mass of warriors on his side and the few around him falling dead at his feet.

Well, shit. He was too far to run and join the fray there. He'd have to try his hardest and take them out. Or as many as he could before he died.

But something curious happened. It started with one man, his body lurching forward as shock rippled across his face, blood coming out of his chest as a phantom blade burst through. Then another, and another and another, making others cry out and retreat.

Then Enid appeared in front of him, dripping in sweat, covered in blood and mud.

"I'm always having to save your ass," she quipped, the humor, somehow, still in her eyes.

They both rejoined the fray, fighting frantically, astonished by the grit and skill of the humans they fought against, when, suddenly, the earth trembled again. A blast of magic hit, the humans crying out as the power coursed through them, being absorbed, then lightning arcing and splitting across the battlefield, hitting others indiscriminately. One sliced up Enid and she cried out, a searing burn slicing across her face.

Killgan blew the horn, a rallying cry, and his warriors cried out, the shouts resounding with the demons, humans, and elves joining in as they rushed forward, catching the other soldiers off guard, but not for long. The fight became more intense and Dryston sustained cuts and bruises and gashes that he would take stock of later—if he survived.

He clashed swords with a man, a helmet obscuring his face, and the man shoved back hard, the force of his hit making Dryston stumble back.

Fuck.

He was strong.

Lightning arced across their blades, leaping off one and onto the other.

"I'll finally be able to kill you," the man said.

Brayden.

Dryston readied his stance, both of them circling the other. "You can certainly try."

Brayden lunged at him, their swords clanging, the sound like thunder clapping. Dryston ducked, getting into his guard only for Brayden to leap back, swiping down again. He dodged, coming up behind him and swiping, Brayden moving swiftly out of the way.

They continued like this for what felt like an hour, neither able to best the other. Dryston used his shadows and Brayden absorbed them, throwing them back, only for them to twine and curl back into Dryston's. Magic wouldn't work effectively here—Brayden was too slippery.

He would have to be smart about this. Brayden wasn't a top Hunter for no reason. He knew what he was doing, even if he was a fool otherwise. Dryston threw blast after blast of shadows at Brayden, the man laughing derisively as none of them worked against him.

Their swords still clashed, but he kept it up, giving a noticeable pattern, letting Brayden fall into complacency. Then he threw another blast, followed immediately by another on the other side. As Brayden focused on absorbing those and blocking the hit of the sword he expected from Dryston, he didn't notice how Dryston stepped to the left, swiftly coming behind and running him through with the sword.

Brayden grunted in shock, wriggling for a moment before falling limply, and Dryston pulled his sword out. The man fell to the ground, looking up at Dryston in shock, eyes blinking. He leaned down, making sure Brayden could hear.

"That's for Onora."

Then he left him to die, going back into the battle.

He fought alongside Kaemon and Enid. The demons above still sent out shadowfyre, focusing on the archers, when a horrifying sound filled the air.

People screaming from inside the walls of Venatu. Screaming and screeching and growling. The ground rumbled and the walls of the city cracked and the human soldiers cried out, stepping away from the fight to see. People climbed on the balusters, one ringing the bell for the warriors to retreat, to return. They looked at the enemies in front of them, slowly taking steps back, Killgan blowing the horn for their warriors to hold off.

The front wall of the city cracked, crumbling open, a pile of stone and detritus. Like a flood, creatures of the void descended on the battlefield. Beings like dogs, warped and decayed, bone and sinew alongside flesh of bark, baying and barking, only wincing at arrows that hit them. They devoured the soldiers from behind and the humans cried out, for now there were enemies on all sides.

Dryston knew what was happening in the city. The same thing that had happened in Evolis. Void beings unleashed on the world, devouring anyone they came across. The soldiers could defend themselves, but what of the citizens inside?

The humans turned, rushing toward the creatures with cries to defend the city, hacking and slicing, their soldiers falling in the same numbers as the beasts.

Dryston looked at Killgan. "We have to protect the people in the city."

"It's not safe." Killgan shook his head.

"There will be children," Kaemon said. "And the elderly and infirm."

Killgan only frowned, looking forward at the mass of creatures wreaking havoc.

"They're not safe either, and they won't be able to protect themselves. And once they kill all these humans they will come for us—for your lands. You can refuse to join the fight right now, but it will come for you later."

Killgan said nothing, his warriors looking at him expectantly. "They killed our children, our elderly, our infirm."

"Not the people in the city," Enid said, readying her sword. "You can debate all you want. I'm helping."

She rushed forward, and Dryston whistled. The demons looked to him and followed where his hand pointed—toward Enid, toward the horde.

They flew forward, then Elgin and the elves joined, and the rebel humans as well, and finally, Killgan blew his horn three times—for them to advance and help the humans of Venatu.

They rushed to battle, fighting the beasts alongside the Hunters and soldiers of Venatu, no longer enemies, but reluctant allies, pressing on toward one common goal—protecting those who couldn't protect themselves. A Hunter on horseback, a commander who had been marshalling his men, rode between the lines, looking over at Dryston, Kaemon and Enid. "There are schools where the children will be, the eastern seaside. Can your flyers get to them?"

Dryston nodded, and Enid shot in the air with Kaemon to tell the others without needing his command. They flew fast, soaring over the sky to the edge of the city, and dipped down. He shot a blast of shadowfyre into the fray, killing many of them, but the horde kept coming. It felt endless, as if they were multiplying as each one was killed.

When, suddenly, blasts of flame and balls of light hit the creatures, making them hiss and hurl. The flapping of wings beat overhead, and Dryston looked up to see seraphs, a host of them descending on the horde and on the city. And amongst them, he saw one with wings of orange and red and yellow fire—Axlan.

Axlan saw the beasts and seemed to immediately understand what had happened; he rallied his soldiers, and they descended on the city, the screaming now turning to that of the creatures, making way for the rest of them outside the city to go in, hacking away, slashing and killing any of the monsters.

Dryston, Jorah, and Aife canvassed houses inside the city walls, looking for anyone hurt and marking them or helping them as they could, calling out for the healers to help. As they helped the city, he sent up a prayer to whatever god would listen to protect Onora.

## CHAPTER 54
# ONORA

Death coiled around her senses the moment her foot stepped over the threshold. A bone-deep cold blanketed her body, piercing past sinew and lancing her bones. She stumbled forward, her breath hitting the air in heavy puffs. Power radiated from the center of the temple where the body of Evoleen lay, hands over her chest, slow puffs of breath showing on the air in front of her.

Laying in a circle around her were the drained, contorted bodies of the elves in robes, their faces staring at the ceiling in horror, skin stretched over bones. The witch in the hood and a few soldiers remained, but many others lay at Onora's feet, spread throughout the temple. Pillars surrounded the atrium, providing dark, mostly covered, passageways.

She felt someone near her and looked up to see Kalen had followed her in, his hand steadying her elbow, protective and afraid.

She darted into one of the corridors, grabbing Kalen's wrist and slinking against the cool stone pillar, listening hard, trying to steady her breath to something quieter. She peeked around the corner and saw the witch bend down to Evoleen, pulling back her hood. Onora swallowed the gasp of horror that rose in throat as she clamped a hand over her mouth.

The witch was Hevena, the woman she had killed in Evolis. The witch that was loyal to Evoleen who had been fighting Dryston. But she was different, too. As she moved her image shifted and shimmered, like some sort of masking spell, one moment beautiful and young, the next a crone, half her face rotting and full of maggots. One moment her hair was lush and beautiful, the next it flickered thin, graying and frayed.

She sniffed, her nostrils flaring, and her head jerked up, hands coiled out in front of her as she looked around, sniffing the air. And That's when Onora saw it—her eyes, milky white, blind.

"I can smell your traitorous bodies," Hevena croaked out, her voice ancient and worn. "We hoped to have you here for this, what luck you've brought yourself."

Onora ducked back behind the pillar, heart racing. What did Hevena mean by that?

Her head darted to the doorway as steps clanged in the hollowness, echoing off the walls, and she could have cursed as her squad entered, following her and not knowing what awaited them. Evoleen sat up, blinking her eyes and flexing her fingers. She saw the intruders and pointed a long gnarled one at them.

"Bring them to me to feast on," she said, voice gravelly.

The soldiers rushed forward, swords brandished, and the clank of metal on metal filled the air. Onora wanted to join her friends, but she needed to sneak around to find some vulnerability. So she did, Kalen silent as a shadow as he followed, seeming to know intuitively what she was trying to accomplish.

She reached inside of her, finding those shadow powers, twining with the power of darkness from the goddess and sending it out, twining, twisting, probing. The portal opening had increased her power, she could feel it humming inside of her, wanting out. She tried to hone her senses on it like she'd seen Dryston do, and she gathered bits of information from it. A vague feeling of how many alive and dead were in the room, but nothing concrete.

The fight continued, and she peered around another pillar to look out. Her squad was winning, but they did outnumber the two remaining soldiers who looked roughed-up from the portal opening. Jackson finally ran through the last one, and he fell in a heap on the floor.

Hevena cried out angrily, raising her age-worn hand and sending out a blast of energy toward them. Onora stepped out, driven by instinct and held up her hand, wrapping it in a circle, and wind whipped up like a tornado, swallowing the energy before it could reach them, dissipating it into nothing. Hevena cried out again and turned as Onora sent another blast. Onora waved her hand to the side and the energy moved, hitting another pillar.

"I defeated you like a gnat last time, Hevena," she growled. "I'll turn your withered bones to dust this time."

"You fool! You could have unlimited power, you could rule the world—worlds! And you would fight and die to try and prevent the inevitable?" Hevena cried out.

Evoleen cackled, the sound like an ancient death knell, rippling through the room and slicing through Onora's skull—terrible and beautiful.

"She is like Evonin," Evoleen said. "Are you there, sister? Are you still poisoning your hosts' feeble minds?"

Evoleen promises the world life and power, only to destroy it with a flick of her wrists. This is not the first one. this will not be the last if you let her.

Onora heaved a sigh, raising her hand, flicking it to the side. In a moment, Hevena's neck snapped, and she fell to the ground in a heap. Evoleen narrowed her gaze on Onora before leaning over, grabbing Hevena by the neck, biting and sucking her dry.

Onora recoiled, her stomach roiling.

Jackson leapt forward, ready to kill Evoleen, but Onora threw her hand up, not sure how she did it or how she knew how, but a shield locked in place, preventing them from moving into the center.

"It's too dangerous. You all need to leave. Now."

"Not happening," Kalen said, gripping his sword tighter.

"Go, Kalen. Find Dryston and tell him that I lo—"

"Tell him yourself!" Kalen barked. "Like it or not, our magic is tied to each other. If we had the whole colony here, you'd be safer. My power amplifies yours, makes it stronger. Tell me to sit in the corner, but I'm here until the end, Onora. I'm not leaving."

She swallowed, nodding. She could see there was no arguing with him.

Let me free. I'll give it all back to you, but let me fight her.

Evonin hadn't let her down yet, but she still feared her—feared her power. She'd been double-crossed enough that she was afraid Evonin had been compliant and helpful only to get her here. Now that she had Evoleen, would Evonin still help her?

*Will you truly? You won't betray me or my loved ones?*

It felt as if something brushed up against her mind, and in a moment she saw it all, a history spanning ages and ages, going back to a cold darkness, two girls, twins, running on a ray of light against the blackness of the void, touching stars, curling up in fiery cores as if it were nothing. Of shared hopes and dreams as they grew in power and age and beauty—Gods they were beautiful, but not how Evoleen looked now. No, she was more an idea, a feeling, an image, not a corporeal body.

She fell for a mortal that Evonin warned her against, a mortal who made her give up her power, turned her into a beast that hungered for blood and destroyed so, so many. But a being full of power and charisma.

She killed mortal people, raising armies, taking over nations, ruling the world. So Evonin fell like a star from heaven, making a crater in the world, trying to save her sister. Then she fell in love with a demon. She found Evoleen in a city on a mountain, ruling them and creating witches, giving them power that no human had ever had before. She rivaled the strongest supernatural races of the world. She spoke of unending life, at the cost of the lives of others.

She tried to get Evonin to join her, saying they would rule together, taking as they pleased, and regaining their more powerful forms.

But Evoleen was too far gone, finding joy in creating horrifying beings as pets and warping people into creatures as depraved as her. So Evonin found Lemia and they sealed her away, both giving up their lives to do so, sealing off Evolis. Evonin's essence and the history were given to a witch who fled, passing it down for generations, fearing the day Evoleen was unsealed from her grave.

Onora removed the blocks in her mind, the ones she'd always carefully placed to keep out Evonin, and let her in. The feeling was cool—like a dip in water on a scorching day, relief and shock in equal measure.

Evonin requested control softly, carefully. Each new bit she took over she sent as a request until Onora's body was humming with power, cold darkness drifting around her like swirls of ink, shadows dancing with it like smoke, the room humming.

Evoleen snapped her head up, blood dripping from her face, color returning to her cheeks. She was even more beautiful and terrible than Onora had realized. A perfect face and a perfect form, her smile swore seduction and pleasure, her eyes drew her in like a siren's song. But Evonin's grief washed through her like a tidal wave, and she had to choke back tears.

The moments that passed next were like an entire lifetime captured in seconds. Evoleen rose and lunged at Onora, but she blocked, her instincts taking over as Evonin gathered power inside Onora.

Hold her off. I'm working on something to take her out.

So Onora did. She hacked at Evoleen, who slipped away from her slashes with a liquid grace, her cackling filling the air. Kalen shot shadows at her and she wrapped them up in her hand like a wet rag and threw it to the ground. He rushed forward, and Evoleen fixed her gaze on him as he slashed down, then to the side, nicking her. She hissed, thrusting with her hand, and an invisible force hit him, knocking him against the pillar, grunting.

Onora lunged again, hacking and slashing, unable to use her powers. The focus she needed to keep the barrier intact, even as her squad beat at it, begging to help, made it too hard. Evonin spooled up her remaining power, winding it tighter and tighter inside her. She felt odd, like her body was wrapped around and wrung out, but she pushed her discomfort aside and kept at it.

Evoleen was slowly gaining more power, more color returning with each movement, baring her blood-soaked teeth in a hiss as she lunged, knocking Onora to the ground. Her claws reached out to her face, and she turned, the slash making blood bubble out.

Evoleen's pupils blackened, consuming her whole eye as she became more frenzied, trying to lick it. Onora pushed against her, barely holding her off. She hit her with a knee in the ribs, and a crack echoed with Evoleen's cry as she threw her off. Kalen jumped up, slashing down on her back, blood soaking her gown.

Evoleen was undeterred, though, and she slashed up, making a gash across Kalen's middle. Shock rippled across his face as he fell to his knees, then his back, and Onora cried out in horror.

*Evonin, NOW!*

Only a bit more. Keep going, Onora.

She jumped to her feet, a new fury invigorating her as she ran, letting the barrier drop so she could use her shadow powers again, and she sent out a set of shadows that Evoleen laughed at as she dodged and then blocked away, missing the ones coming from behind that grabbed her arm, snapping it back and in two.

Evoleen's scream ripped into Onora like cuts across her skin, and she stumbled back from the force of it, fighting the fear that rose up in her, strangling her at the ancient horror in front of her.

Now.

Then she was floating—they all were. Darkness engulfed the room, and she felt like she was falling and flying and swimming all at once. Light rippled around them, arcing and spinning and twirling, some wrapping all around Kalen, and even more, brighter, burning to an intense blue and crackling around her. The light turned to a blazing fire that caught on her and lit her up like fire to a piece of paper. She shrieked, the sound swallowed up by the void of blackness around them as she was singed, her body withering and then turning to dust.

Eventually the world returned, and she was on her knees, bracing against the floor, breathing hard, completely drained. Evoleen was nowhere to be found, the other bodies naught but ashes.

Goodbye, moon child. Your mother would be proud, as am I.

*Where are you going?*

My consciousness is fading. I will pass on to the stars and become dust, but my power will live on in you and your descendants.

*Thank you.*

No, thank you, Onora.

The voice drifted like a dying echo down the hall and suddenly, the presence that had always been there was gone. She felt the loss of it like a family member and she grasped her chest, as if that could assuage the ache any.

She looked around. Kalen still lay on the cold ground. Her squad rushed up to her, but she crawled to him, checking his pulse. He was alive. Then she checked his wounds—healed. She sent up a prayer of thanks, realizing it was to Evonin and wondering if gods were ever reborn. If so, she hoped Evonin had a better existence the next time around.

She looked up to Jackson. "We need to find Dryston."

Bodies of humans, orcs, demons, and elves littered the field outside the forest. Beasts like they'd seen in Evolis were also everywhere, some still with their maws clamped around their victims. They searched the bodies as they made their way to the city, looking for anyone they knew and coming up short.

She didn't know if that was better or worse. What were the odds of anyone surviving this?

The destruction of Venatu was dizzying as they walked over the wreckage carefully, looking for survivors. They headed toward the guild, uncertain what had happened and where everyone was. Her heart ached with each step, with each new body she saw.

They came to the city center and there were tents set up, injured people being tended to, and Onora stopped, staring in wonder at what she saw. Humans, many of them Hunters, working with demons and seraphs, orcs and satyrs, elves and goblins. A demon passed a hot bowl of soup to a woman with the dusty blue cape of a Hunter and, while it was stilted—awkward even—it wasn't hostile.

Sun was setting over the ocean and she spied a familiar figure on the dock, looking out, with two other familiar demons standing next to him. She broke into a run, heart beating wild and fierce with hope and joy. Her feet made a racket on the wood, and they turned, relief washing over Dryston's face as he saw her. He ran to her, grabbing her into his arms, kissing her long and hard, his hands holding her tight against him. He pulled back and brushed a hair away from her face.

"Are you okay?" he breathed.

She nodded, tears forming in her eyes that she didn't bother to try and stop as they rolled down her face. "Yes. Yes, I am."

# EPILOGUE: ONORA

A warm wind hit Onora's face, and she threw her head back, closing her eyes. Onyx reached back, nudging her hand and she laughed as she stroked her neck, listening to her purr. Melina's gryphon swooped down next to her, the two nudging one another as the women laughed.

This had become a daily thing, going on flights with Halst, Enid often joining them as she did now, sometimes stopping to take a dip in the lake and eating a nice picnic lunch. They swooped around, and Onora attached the belt that kept her in the saddle down more tightly as she nudged Onyx into doing a flip, her thighs gripping tight, and she let her hands fall, the freedom of it sending a thrill through her.

They returned, putting the gryphons away before heading to Melina's house, where the males were cooking and the colony crowded around one another. Jackson joined them, lounging in the corner, talking to Kalen. He'd been making more frequent trips to The Darkened City, as the newly appointed chief of the Hunter's Guild.

Relations between humans and demons were still tenuous, but much better. King Leeth had been deposed for his role in the destruction, and a nearby relative had inherited the kingdom. She was ready to prove herself as a young elf and had eagerly entered the alliance with Dryston under new terms.

They sat at the table, and she took Emilia, who was the star of the night, as it was her one-year birthday. The colony had a stack of gifts in the corner for her.

She looked around the table, and she choked on the emotion in her throat. So many people to love, so many people to call her own. Even more still in Nemus. Her life, once isolated and dark, was vibrant—full of people and love and care.

She found that ruling with Dryston was easier than she'd imagined. The demons had heard of what she'd done from Kalen and bit by bit they all came around to appreciating her role in the realm. But she'd spent months listening and learning, visiting villages and clans. She traveled to the farthest reaches and learned their customs, and, when asked, taught them some of her own.

Dryston's hand rested on her knee, rubbing it softly as he looked at her with a love that blazed brighter than the sun and encased her deeper than the darkest void. He bent down and whispered, "Every day I think I can't love you any more, and every day I'm astonished by how much more I do."

"We're married now, Drys. You don't have to charm me like that anymore," she said, still blushing, still trying to accept these compliments and affections from him.

He tipped her face up with his fingers and kissed her forehead. "On the contrary, I need to do it even more. Get used to it, darling. You have a good long life of me saying mushy things to you."

"Good—because I love your mushiness almost as much as I love you," she said, and he grinned, the smile lighting her up on the inside and making her feel like she was melting, any and every defense she'd spent years building up becoming nothing in the face of that flame.

Her vow of all those years ago—of taking down the Lord of Shadows—had been said with violence. Yet it had somehow been love that had done it. Love that had also taken her down—all her defenses, all her anguish, all her angst.

Until all she was left with was this gentle, passionate, raging love for him. And for their people. All of them. Demons, humans, and everyone who they loved.

She leaned her head against him as Enid picked Emilia up, and his hand twined with hers. She searched her mind, looking for those old wounds that used to flare up and found only a few aching scars, only a few that needed more time to heal. She looked up at Dryston. With him by her side, she knew that they would, though. Perhaps it would take years, but they would.

A new day was dawning over the world, and she only felt a wild, wild hope for it all.

# GLOSSARY

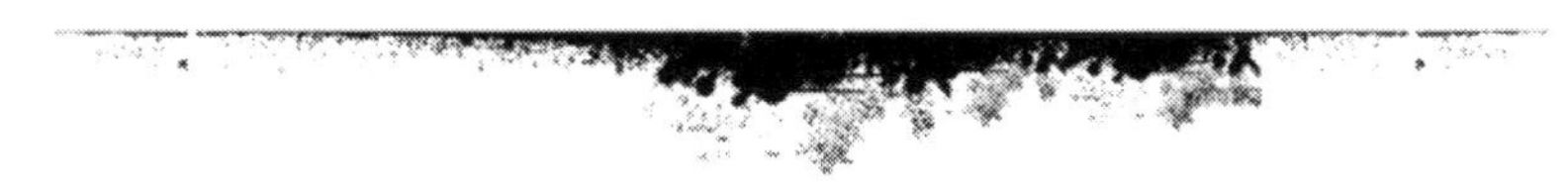

**Cirro (*si-roh*):** A fabled city said to reside in the clouds and hold a cure for any ailment

**Colony**: The name of a demon's extended family unit. This includes immediate family as well as extended, and even further out. This is several family units with magic that is tied into one another, amplifying their power.

**Conduit**: A type of magic that draws power from residual magic and manipulates it. This magic flows through the user and can be hard to control and contain (humans are the best conduits, and some of the only conduits in Iltain).

**Elf Glen:** Capitol City of the the Elven Realm of Nemus

**Entailish (*ehn-tay-lish*):** A dead language usually only used in elvish religious texts.

**Evolis (*ay-voh-lis*):** City of Cirro

**Evoleen (*ay-voh-leen*):** The Holy Mother, usually the elves use this to refer to her, but it is her name in Entailish

**Evonin (*ay-voh-neen*):** the name attached to an ancient grimoire that was, in

**Iltain (*ih-ltayn*):** the world that the story takes place in.

**Lemia (*Lay-mee-ah*):** a Folk Hero that many cultures claim as their own.

the past, a counterpart always kept with The Tales of Lemia. The Cruel Lord invaded Nemus, raided the elven temples and stole both books, giving The Tales of Lemia to the seraphs in a trade deal and taking the grimoire back to The Darkened City.

**Nemus** (*nee-muhs*): The continent where the Cruel Lord occupied and oppressed

**Medeis** (*meh-dees*): The larger continent near Nemus where demons, seraphs, and many other beings reside.

**Salian (*say-lee-ehn*):** the satyr language not oft used except in poetry, songs, and rituals. Satyrs all learn it but speak the common tongue.

**Silver Fern:** a prolific plant in Iltain with strong analgesic and healing properties

**Sink**: A type of magic that draws power from outside sources and manipulates it for spell work (elves are the most common sinks in Ilitain)

**Source**: A type of magic where the powers are inherent to the being, and can only be manipulated to a certain degree ( e.g. demons have shadow powers, but not light powers)

**Velin** (*vay-lin*): an herb that is harmful to beings with inherent magic. It causes their abilities to be greatly inhibited, causing their healing to slow down and their bodies to be weakened.

**Venatu:** Capital City of the Human Realm of Nemus

# AUTHOR'S NOTE

I want to say a sincere thank you for reading my book. I hope you enjoyed reading it and it brought some entertainment and joy to your life. There are three bonus chapters available for the previous book, from the point of view of Kaemon, Dryston, and Onora. If you would like to read those, you can sign up for my newsletter (which can be found on my website, https://authorwillowquinn.wordpress.com/). When you sign up for my newsletter, you will also receive a free novella following the romance of Aife and Jorah, taking place before The Demon of the Wood.

Reviews are the lifeblood of independent books, so if you enjoyed this, please consider leaving a review on Amazon or Goodreads.

If you would like updates on my work, you can subscribe to my newsletter (and you will receive free novellas and bonus chapters this way), or you can find me on Instagram @authorwillowquinn.

# ACKNOWLEDGEMENTS

It's a bittersweet moment to be finishing up the Fates & Fables series. I'm happy to move onto to other projects, (some in this world, some in others), but I'm sad to leave the Erebus family and their loved ones.

When I wrote The Demon of the Wood, I did it fast and hard and put it up on Amazon, expecting no one to read it. I thought it would be a good little practice round for me to see how indie publishing would go. I'd done my research and knew the odds of a debut book gaining much traction for an indie author.

I was blown away by how many people did read it, and how many people enjoyed my little story about Kaemon and Melina healing from their trauma and finding love.

From there, the world unfurled in my mind, stories coming to life and characters asking for their stories to be told.

Daughter of The Darkened City was a book full of growing pains and doubts and wondering if maybe I should quit. I loved Enid and Avenay but I wasn't sure I could do them justice. I wasn't sure I could do any of my stories or characters justice.

But I plowed ahead, because the muses had entrusted me with these stories and I couldn't stop writing, even when I had doubts if I should. I finished it and I have to say, that's maybe the book I'm most proud of because of that. Because of all the things I learned and all the ways I grew writing that book. The readers who stuck with me and encouraged me during that are the reason Daughter of The Darkened City was ever published.

A Storm of Shadows came to me quickly and easily, the tension between Dryston and Onora having haunted me since The Demon of the Wood. I hit a few hiccups and hurdles along the way, but otherwise this story came easily and fast and I'm thankful for that. I love their story, and I love the Erebus siblings and I'm so happy to give them a happy ending. And I'm happy to wrap up their stories for readers who've been along for the ride.

That's a long-winded way to say thank you to my readers. I know I thank you in every book, but just get used to it because I'm going to keep doing it.

Making a post saying you enjoyed my book or messaging me how excited you are to read it makes my day. It may not seem like a big deal, but it is to me.

Thank you for going on this journey with me. I hope to see you on the next one.

Made in the USA
Columbia, SC
11 April 2025